About

Sophia Williams lives ~~_____ ____ ____ ___ ____ family. She~~ has loved reading Regency romances for as long as she can remember and is delighted now to be writing them for Mills & Boon. When she isn't chasing her children around or writing (or pretending to write but actually Googling for hero inspiration and pictures of gorgeous Regency dresses), she enjoys reading, tennis and wine.

Regency Whispers

June 2024
The Wallflower Academy

July 2024
Scandalous Matches

August 2024
A Secret Past

September 2024
Inconvenient Temptation

January 2025
Forbidden Passion

February 2025
The Duke's Desire

Regency Whispers:

The Duke's Desire

SOPHIA WILLIAMS

MILLS & BOON

First Published in Great Britain 2025
By Mills & Boon, an imprint of HarperCollins*Publishers* Ltd
1 London Bridge Street, London, SE1 9GF

www.harpercollins.co.uk

HarperCollins*Publishers*
Macken House, 39/40 Mayor Street Upper,
Dublin 1, D01 C9W8, Ireland

ISBN: 978-0-263-39780-2

MIX
Paper | Supporting
responsible forestry
FSC™ C007454

HOW THE DUKE
MET HIS MATCH

To George

Chapter One

London, 1817

Alexander, Duke of Harwell, froze for a second as Lady Cowbridge, smiling broadly, ushered her daughter towards him. She couldn't have indicated her intent more clearly had she produced a bishop and had their wedding banns read.

This had to be about the tenth such approach made to him in the past hour. Enough was enough. Alex unfroze, inclined his head very slightly in the direction of the two ladies, and turned to march himself straight out of the ballroom's nearest doors.

Before he'd managed to cover the ten feet or so to the end of the room, yet another dowager placed herself in his path. This one was resplendent in a jade-green dress and was holding a bejewelled hand outstretched towards him. She gave the lavender-clad young lady she was accompanying a little push with her other hand, so that she stumbled almost right into Alex.

As he executed a swift sidestep to avoid a collision, Alex caught a glimpse of the younger lady's expression.

Her eyes were downcast, long dark lashes against her cheeks, and her brow was furrowed in a slight frown. By contrast, the older woman was looking straight at him with her wide smile increasing, as though she was about to address him.

Alex muttered, 'Excuse me,' and almost leaped out of the long, glass-panelled doors ahead of him into the garden.

He should have resisted his friends' entreaties to attend this ball. He didn't remember the season being quite as awful as this, though. Had the mothers and guardians of marriageable young ladies been as determined in their pursuit of him—like vultures circling their prey—the last time he was single? He didn't think so. But perhaps the full decade that had passed since then had dulled his memory. Or perhaps his elevation from viscount to duke had increased their determination.

Safely through the French doors, he was hit first by intense heat from the remarkable profusion of lanterns clustered around the door-frame, and then, as he moved a little to his left along a terrace that seemed to run all the way beside the house, by the freshness of the clear February night. And, God, that was good.

He closed his eyes and leaned his head back against the wall of the house, allowing himself a long moment to appreciate the peace, the coolness of the air on his cheeks after the claustrophobic warmth of the ballroom and the faint scent of the leaves from the trees in the mansion's small garden, infinitely more agreeable than the cloying perfume inside.

Amazing to think that he'd actually loved London life ten years ago.

Right now, all he wanted to do was to go home to

Somerset. In fact, maybe he'd bring forward his return to the country. He missed his land, the open space, the opportunity for long walks and hard riding. And his local friends and tenants. And, of course, he missed the boys, his sons. It didn't feel right to be away from them for any extended period since they'd lost their mother. Yes, maybe he'd return home tomorrow. Ask his man of business and his lawyers to attend him there.

His thoughts were interrupted within a couple of minutes by a couple crashing out through the doors and coming to a halt only a few feet from him. Instinctively, he moved further along the terrace into the shadows. He had no desire to stand right next to a lovemaking couple, and he wasn't ready to re-enter the ballroom. So shadows it was.

He hadn't moved far enough. The couple's voices carried very clearly to him across the still night.

'Let go of me,' the woman hissed.

Not a lovemaking couple, apparently.

Alex turned reluctantly to look at them, illuminated by the lanterns, as the woman seemed to struggle in her partner's hold. The man pulled her close to him with one arm and with his other hand gripped her face far more tightly than a lover would. The woman continued to struggle, and then suddenly went quite limp.

Alex took a couple of steps closer. He had no desire to get involved in any lovers' tiff, but what he'd seen so far indicated that this was something more sinister than that. He should check that the woman was all right. If he was sure then that all was well, he would apologise for interrupting them and leave them to it.

He opened his mouth to speak just as the woman, as suddenly as she'd gone limp, dipped her head and bit the man's arm, and simultaneously seemed to kick him on the shin from beneath her dress. The dress was a pale lavender, like the one that the green-clad lady's younger companion had been wearing. Perhaps the same woman.

The man jerked and let go of her, spitting the words, 'You vixen,' as she picked up her skirts and began to run towards the ballroom.

Alex was contemplating landing a punch to the man's face, to teach him a lesson in addition to the kick and the bite, when the man lunged forward and caught the young woman around the waist, pulling her back against him.

'You'll pay for that,' he growled as she tried to resist his pull, her arms flailing.

Alex sighed internally—he'd so much rather just go home and go to bed than get involved with this, but clearly he had no choice—and stepped forward.

'It appears that the lady doesn't wish to be mauled by you,' he said.

'Mind your own business.' The man's voice was slightly familiar, maybe someone Alex had known in town in his younger days.

Alex shook his head. 'Let go of her now,' he said, injecting as much steel into his voice as he could.

He could see the man properly now in the flickering light. Sir Peter Something. Always with a group of men scrabbling at the edge of polite society. He could see the woman's heart-shaped face too. She had clear, light brown skin and deep brown eyes, which were glistening right now. Definitely the young lady who'd been with the woman in green just inside the ballroom.

Sir Peter looked up at him and shrank away, as though scared, but pulled the lady with him. She did something with her leg and Sir Peter gave an unattractively high-pitched little howl and then shook her a little.

'Enough.' Alex took a step towards them and clamped his hand round Sir Peter's—puny—forearm, until he let go of the lady with another little mewl of pain. Truly pathetic. Alex moved between the two of them and held his arm out to the lady.

She looked at Sir Peter, and then at Alex, and then took the proffered arm. 'Thank you, sir.' Her voice was remarkably steady, given the situation.

They began to move together towards the steps, away from Sir Peter, the young lady gripping Alex's arm very tightly. Thank God he had been here. She'd done a good job of fighting Sir Peter off, but she'd have been no match for him in the end.

Alex was going to take her inside, return her to her chaperone, make sure that she was safe with her, and then leave.

'Do you—?' he began.

He was interrupted by a sudden commotion at the ballroom door above them and a man shouting, 'Miss Bolton, Sir Peter.'

As Alex looked towards the door Sir Peter launched himself at the lady—presumably Miss Bolton—and attempted to kiss her. Miss Bolton got one arm free and dealt him a forceful blow to the ear, which made Alex smile and Sir Peter howl yet again.

'You will not treat me so when we're married,' Sir Peter panted.

Really? Alex shook his head. Everyone was aware that rogues attempted to compromise young women into marriage fairly often, but Alex hadn't personally witnessed such an attempt before. The commotion at the door was increasing now, and the man who'd just spoken was shouting inside the room about what he'd just seen. Presumably a co-conspirator.

Alex felt his lip curl. He held his hand up and addressed the gathering crowd. 'I have been here the entire time and this man has in no way compromised this lady. Nothing untoward has happened between them.'

'Incorrect,' Sir Peter shouted, apparently a lot braver with a crowd supporting him. 'This young lady has given me her virtue. She is my fiancée.'

The woman in green who'd been with Miss Bolton inside the ballroom pushed her way through the throng and planted herself in front of them. 'Emma, is this true?'

'No, Aunt, of course not.' Miss Bolton's voice was shaking a little now.

'Look at her gown.' Sir Peter's voice was triumphant.

Alex's eyes followed where the man's spindly finger was pointing. The bodice of Miss Bolton's gown was torn, exposing most of her full breasts. It must have been ripped during their tussle. Miss Bolton looked down too, and pulled ineffectually at the fabric, while Alex began to work his arms out of his tightly fitting jacket.

'Miss Bolton and I will be married tomorrow,' Sir Peter announced. 'I have a special licence.'

'Emma, how could you?' her aunt moaned.

'I couldn't and I won't,' Miss Bolton stated.

'Yes, you will.' Her aunt spoke out of the corner of her mouth, as though that would prevent anyone from hearing her. 'You are ruined.' She indicated with her arm towards the crowd at the doors.

'No.' Miss Bolton visibly shuddered.

'Yes.' Sir Peter put his arm around her waist.

She tried to move away and he gripped her more tightly, pulling her further from Alex.

Oh, God. Alex had the strange sensation that he could see, almost feel, two avenues open to him. One, the easy one, where he walked away from this situation. These things were not unheard of in Society, and usually the young lady—the victim—in question wasn't lucky enough to have a saviour to hand. Had he not been here, Miss Bolton would now be affianced to Sir Peter and that would effectively be that.

Unfortunately, Alex *had* been here, and it seemed that he was going to take a second avenue, which he was pretty sure would be hell. It was as though he was observing the scene from a distance and could see catastrophe unfurling but could do nothing to avert it.

'We will be married by the end of the week,' Sir Peter said.

'No.' Alex stepped forward, holding his jacket. 'The young lady is *my* fiancée. Unhand her immediately.'

For God's sake. He was speaking like an actor in a cheap melodrama. And, a lot more importantly, he'd just announced that Miss Bolton was his *fiancée*.

Sir Peter didn't let go of Miss Bolton. Alex took another step closer and glared at him, and the man's grip on her slackened. Alex moved right next to them, clenching his fists, and Sir Peter shrank backwards. Nothing more pathetic than a cowardly bully.

Alex moved in front of Sir Peter and placed his jacket around Miss Bolton's shoulders, his hand brushing the bare skin of her upper arm briefly as he held the jacket so that she could put her arms into the sleeves. He fancied that he felt her shiver as he touched her, and thought he understood why; it felt oddly…what, intimate perhaps? When it absolutely shouldn't.

He shook his head slightly. His mind was going in all manner of strange directions.

She looked up at him, her eyes huge in her small face, and whispered, 'Thank you.'

'My pleasure.'

Which was about as far from the truth as you could get. He was struggling to process what had just happened, but he did know that it was bad, very bad. He'd just announced that they were *engaged*. He had just committed himself very publicly to *marrying* this lady. Marriage. He didn't want to remarry. For his sons' sake, for his own sake, for Diana's memory's sake. But he clearly wasn't likely to have any choice now. He couldn't honourably let Miss Bolton down.

God. He wanted to put his head in his hands and swear and swear.

He couldn't do that, of course. It would be rude to Miss Bolton; and many dozens of people were watching them, chattering about them. He wanted to shout about the hypocrisy of the *ton*: the way in which they regarded themselves as above ordinary people and yet fed almost feverishly on others' misery, mob-like.

The hum of the crowd's chatter began to increase, the air practically throbbing with it now. He and Miss Bolton both needed to leave.

He cleared his throat and held an arm out to her.

She stared at his arm for a long moment, and then took it with another whispered 'Thank you.'

He could feel her almost trembling, and reached his other hand over to press hers briefly for comfort. And strangely, for a moment, it felt as though the two of them were banded together against the rest of the world. Which was ridiculously fanciful and entirely untrue. They were complete strangers to each other, and, while it seemed unbelievable that they might indeed soon be banded together in name, they wouldn't be in practice. He would not be having any kind of real marriage with Miss Bolton—Emma—or any other woman. He just couldn't.

He closed his eyes briefly and then began to move towards the house.

And then the woman in green, Emma's aunt, trilled, 'Your Grace,' and sank into a deep curtsey before them.

It cost Alex a big effort not to roll his eyes above her head or snap at her. Now did not feel like the time for social niceties.

As Emma's aunt rose from her curtsey, a thought struck him and he looked down at Emma again, suspicious. Had this entire scene been enacted by her and her aunt to entrap him? Were they in cahoots with Sir Peter? He went very still for a moment, replaying the events of the last few minutes in his mind. No, highly unlikely.

He felt Emma shudder slightly again. No. Unless she was an outstanding actress, this absolutely couldn't be a scene of her making.

'Allow me to escort you home now?' he said to her.

'Thank you. I think that would be for the best. I must apologise. I am not normally so pathetic. I will recover my spirits directly. I must apologise also for your having been dragged into this situation.'

'Not at all,' Alex said with great insincerity.

God, he wished he'd left the house by the front doors after speaking to Lady Cowbridge. Or even just danced with Lady Cowbridge's daughter. Although, looking down at Emma's slim shoulders, dwarfed by his jacket, and her elegant neck beneath her dark brown, nearly black curls, he hated to imagine what might be happening to her at this moment if he hadn't been here. Nearly as much as he hated to imagine what was about to happen to both of them.

Barely credible, but he really had just announced to half the *ton* that they were betrothed. As in he really was going to have to marry her, because her aunt was right: she would be completely ruined if they didn't marry.

He shook his head for about the tenth time this evening. After his wife's death in childbirth he'd decided never to remarry. Even just the idea of allowing himself to love again and therefore lay himself open to the possibility of further loss was too painful to bear. And yet here he was.

Although, of course, this wouldn't be a love match. It would be one person helping out another, a marriage in name only. So he wouldn't, in fact, be betraying Diana's memory. He'd have to explain as soon as possible to Emma that this would not be a real marriage. He hoped very much that she wouldn't be too upset by that. If she was, it couldn't be helped, unfortunately.

Oh, God. What if she wanted children?

Why the *hell* had this had to happen?

He nearly groaned out loud, and then realised that Emma was speaking again.

'I wonder if I could possibly impose on you for a further few minutes of your time?'

It was an odd question to ask when they were about to be tethered for a lifetime, in name at least.

He was prevented from replying by Emma's aunt, wreathed in smiles, grasping their hands.

'Your Grace, Emma, I must congratulate you. Such wonderful news.' She half turned and waved to the hordes jostling behind her, almost as though she was seeking witnesses, just as Sir Peter had; and her rather odd turban—green, like her dress—slid to one side of her head.

She pushed the turban back into place, turned again to Alex and Emma, and said, 'I was well acquainted with your mother. I am Lady Morton.'

'How do you do?' Alex said, not bothering to try to smile.

Lady Morton really wasn't going to care whether or not he was happy; her ecstasy would do for all of them. He thought for a moment of his first betrothal—his and Diana's happiness, the sheer bubbling joy that had kept him permanently smiling and laughing for weeks afterwards—and wondered briefly if his head might explode.

Lady Morton began to talk volubly about weddings.

Alex just wanted to leave, get away from this nightmare.

Lady Morton's conversation turned to the miracle it was that her darling Emma had melted the heart of the Ice Duke. Really? The Ice Duke? That was what people called him? For God's sake.

He sensed Emma stiffen beside him and felt instant remorse. This situation was, of course, much worse for her than for him.

Her whole body seemed to heave and he looked at the top of her head more closely. Was she crying? He should get her out of here immediately, give them both a chance to begin to come to terms with what had happened.

'I'd like to escort my fiancée home now,' he told her

aunt, impressed that he'd managed not to choke on the word *fiancée*.

He'd walked the short distance here from his house, so he hoped Emma and her aunt had come in a carriage; it would be much better if they didn't have to walk back now. He should agree on a time to call on Emma tomorrow, so that he could explain that he could be married in name only.

'Of course.' The turban slipped again. 'Do you have a carriage? If not, please take ours. Dear Lady Cowbridge will take me home, I'm sure.'

Lady Cowbridge, who had beaten her way to the front of the scandal-drawn crowd swirling around them, looked as though she'd sucked a lemon. She gave one of the most insincere smiles Alex had ever seen and nodded her acquiescence.

Despite everything, Alex almost laughed out loud. From the looks of her, it would be some time before Lady Cowbridge would be forgiving Lady Morton for her ducal wedding triumph.

Emma squeezed the underside of his forearm surprisingly hard, and he looked down at her again. She must be desperate to leave.

'Good evening.' He nodded around the crowd and then began to walk forward with Emma through the hundreds of ball-goers, all of whom seemed to be attempting to get a close look at the two of them. They were obviously going to be the subject of much gossip for the next few days or weeks. Since there was going to be no way of avoiding the wedding, they should get it out of the way as soon as possible and escape to the country for a long time.

Being taller than most people, he had a very good

view of the fashionables swirling around them. Literally hundreds of people pushing. He caught a couple of snatches of waspish comments and felt Emma's shoulders tense. Glaring at anyone who dared to look directly at him, he tightened his hold on her and they picked up speed across the long room. Eventually, they reached a series of footmen and a butler in the large, marbled entrance hall.

The butler opened the front door to them as their hostess, Mrs Chardaine, pushed her way towards them and dropped into a deep curtsey, tittering as she did so.

'I shall be proud forever that you announced your love affair to the world at my house,' she said, fluttering her eyelashes at him. 'Such a great pleasure.'

'The pleasure is all ours.' Alex didn't smile.

'Thank you so much for a most delightful evening,' Emma said, not looking as if she was smiling very much either.

They finally made it out of the house, down the steps and into Lady Morton's carriage about five minutes later.

Emma sank onto the upholstered bench to the right of the carriage door and Alex seated himself opposite her. This was the first time he'd been able to take a good look at her. She was beautiful, but in a very different way from the current fashion for pale skin and blonde hair. Her skin was the warm light brown he'd noticed before, and her eyes and hair were very dark. She was perhaps a little older than he'd assumed she was, definitely in her twenties rather than in her late teens as most debutantes were. Maybe slightly older than he had been when he'd met and married Diana.

She started speaking almost before the footman had

finished closing the door behind them and Alex had sat down.

'Thank you so much for rescuing me. Obviously I won't hold you to your promise.' She was holding her shoulders square inside his jacket, which swamped her slender frame, and looking him straight in the eye, as though she meant what she said. 'I'll tell my aunt in the morning that it was all a ridiculous mistake.'

Alex felt his own shoulders actually physically relax for a moment at the relief of it, until a voice of reason from somewhere deep inside him shouted that telling everyone it was a mistake wasn't an option.

'You can't possibly do that,' he said. 'You'll be ruined.'

'No.' Her dark curls swung round her face as she shook her head with force. 'To speak distastefully frankly about money, I'm an heiress with a significant fortune. There will be men who are prepared to overlook what happened this evening. There is no need for you to marry me.'

'Yes, there is. You will be ruined otherwise,' he repeated.

'No, I won't. There are any number of impecunious aristocratic men who would be delighted to marry my dowry.' She cocked her head to one side and narrowed her eyes slightly. 'From the little I've seen of you, I would say that you have need of neither a wife nor a fortune?'

He looked at her for a long moment. He felt as though he should actually pretend that he did need one or the other or both.

He wasn't going to pretend.

'Correct,' he said.

'Then I cannot allow you to make this ridiculous sacrifice on my behalf.'

Alex raised his eyebrows. It was unusual for a young

lady to state that she would or would not allow a gentleman to behave in a certain way. Although nothing about this situation was usual.

'It isn't a sacrifice,' he said, the words sounding hollow. 'It would be my very great pleasure.' Oh, God, no. He didn't want to sound as though he wanted their marriage to be anything other than in name. 'That is, I...'

Emma snorted. In a small, very ladylike way, but it was definitely still a snort. 'Absolutely everything about your demeanour tells me that it would be a huge sacrifice and certainly not a pleasure. Clearly neither of us loves the other. I agree that some men, particularly those who have no need to marry for money, might be deterred by the events of this evening from wooing me, but I'm very sure that men like Sir Peter will still be happy to marry me.'

'Exactly. Sir Peter. A middle-aged roué, who would almost certainly treat you badly.' Alex thought for a moment with disgust of when Sir Peter had held Emma in his arms.

Emma opened her mouth and then closed it again, and then visibly drew a breath and said, 'Obviously, Sir Peter would not be my ideal husband. Indeed, I would rather work for my living than marry him, and will do so if necessary. However, I have it on great authority, that of my own aunt amongst others, that I "smell of the shop"—delightful phrase—and that that will already have deterred a number of suitors, but nonetheless my fortune has continued to attract a great deal of attention.'

'I'm sure that the attention is due to your beauty and your conversation,' Alex said with reflexive politeness.

Emma snorted again. 'Much like all the attention you received this evening was entirely due to your broad shoulders and wit rather than to the fact that you are a very rich widowed duke.'

Alex found himself giving a snort of his own—of laughter. 'Fair enough,' he said. 'Yes, I'm sure that you have received a lot of attention, for both good and bad reasons, but I'm not sure that any man with whom you might be able to live happily will now offer for you. You might not, in fact, have the opportunity to meet any more respectable and eligible men because if you don't marry me all fashionable doors might be closed to you. I think that you perhaps underestimate the snobbery of the *ton* and their delighted horror of scandal.'

'I think that you perhaps underestimate my father's fortune.'

Alex shook his head. 'I cannot see that you have any alternative but to marry me.'

'I'm grateful for your concern—indeed I'm very grateful to you for having rescued me from Sir Peter—but I do not feel that my future is any concern of yours.' She picked up her reticule as the coach slowed. 'Thank you again. If I might impose on you just a little longer, I'd be very grateful if I could keep your jacket until I reach my bedchamber. I will ask one of my aunt's footmen to return it to you tomorrow.' She bestowed a brittle little smile on him and moved forward as the carriage door began to open.

Alex frowned. Something was niggling in the back of his mind, something in addition to the big issue, which was that she was clearly doing the wrong thing.

He leaned forward himself and spoke to the coachman. 'My fiancée and I have not yet finished our conversation. Please drive on for another few minutes.'

'Actually, we *have* finished our conversation.' Emma's eyes were flashing as the coach drove off again. 'I would like to go inside now.'

She thumped on the silk-upholstered wall of the carriage with her fist.

'I'm sorry.' Alex banged on the wall with his cane and the coach came to a halt. 'That was very rude of me. I shouldn't have overridden your wishes like that. Could I ask one further question before you go inside?'

He'd worked out what had been niggling him.

Emma pressed her lips together for a moment, as though she was trying not to sigh, and then after a pause said, 'Yes, of course.'

'What did you mean when you said that you'd rather work for your living than marry me, and might do so?'

Chapter Two

Emma wanted to glare at the duke, get out of the carriage, go inside her aunt's house and up to her bedchamber, crawl under her covers to digest the fact that her prospects had changed so dramatically in such a short space of time, and then come up with a plan. But she owed the duke a huge debt. She was still shuddering every time she recalled that without his intervention she might now be betrothed to Sir Peter and she was truly grateful to him.

She widened her lips into the best approximation of a smile she could manage, and said, 'I meant that I don't *need* to marry because I am very well able to work instead.'

The duke's eyes were narrowed. 'But why should you need to work? What of your great fortune?'

Emma *really* didn't want to talk about this. But, again, she owed the duke a lot, so the very least she could do was be polite.

'My father left me his fortune as dowry on condition that I marry a man from an aristocratic family within two years of his death. If I don't, I inherit nothing. Ironically, I don't even know whether Sir Peter's birth would be acceptable under the terms of the will.'

The duke raised his eyebrows but said nothing.

For some reason, it suddenly mattered to her what he thought of her father.

'It sounds worse than it is,' she told him. 'I'm sure my father truly only wanted the best for me. It's often difficult to know what the best for someone is.'

That was what she'd told herself, anyway, when she'd been *incandescent* with fury when their family lawyer had explained the terms of her father's will to her.

'He was a textiles manufacturer from Lancashire and my mother was the daughter of an earl, whose father cut her off when she met and married my father. Being excluded from her own family's social circle made my mother miserable. My father hired governesses for me and sent me to an exclusive seminary in Bath, because he wanted me to be able to take what he thought of as my rightful place in society. He didn't want me to be as miserable as my mother.'

No need to mention that her mother had been *so* miserable that she'd left Emma's father and gone to live in Paris.

'Except he was very comfortable living with me, so he didn't actually want me to leave until he died.' *So* annoying that her voice *still* wobbled when she talked about losing him. 'So I'm a lot longer in the tooth than the average debutante. In fact, I really shouldn't be called a debutante. Anyway, thanks to his obsession with educating me like a lady, I'm *extremely* well-educated—much better than most ladies, in fact—and so I flatter myself that I would make an *excellent* governess.'

The duke looked at her for a long moment, his eyes

grave. 'I'm sorry to hear about the loss of your father. And to hear about the situation in which you find yourself with regard to marriage.' He paused and then continued. 'But, being brutally frank, I'm not convinced that many families would happily engage a governess who had just been ruined in front of half the *ton*.'

'I would very happily be a governess to a family living in the country.'

He shook his head. 'News travels.'

Hmm. Maybe he was right. Emma swallowed hard. She was *not* going to cry. This wasn't the worst thing that could happen to anyone. She was only twenty-five, which was still quite young if you weren't a debutante. She was healthy; she was resourceful. She would manage.

'In that case, I will approach the headmistress of my old seminary.'

'I imagine that news travels just as quickly to seminaries and the parents of prospective pupils.'

Yes, he was right. She hadn't been thinking clearly. It must be the shock of the events of the evening.

'Fine. There are other options. I could be a housekeeper.'

'Really?'

Honestly. So sceptical. Of *course* she could be a housekeeper.

'Yes.'

'I haven't been involved in hiring a housekeeper myself, but I wonder whether you would be expected to have some experience.'

'I do have experience. I looked after my father and our house for several years.'

'I'm not sure that would be sufficient.'

Emma pressed her fingers to her temples for a moment. 'I'm sure I could find *something.*'

'And I am genuinely not sure you could. Not something palatable, anyway.' He sat back and looked at her for a long moment, his brow slightly furrowed, while Emma fought tears again.

Why had she become separated from her aunt for that moment, so that Sir Peter had been able to get hold of her arm and pull her towards the garden? Things had been going perfectly well before this evening. She'd received several depressing proposals from men whom she'd been sure would be difficult husbands, but at least three pleasant, impecunious younger sons of two earls and a viscount to whom she thought she might be able to be reasonably happily married had looked as though they were on the brink of proposing to her.

She'd had high hopes that at least one of them would be so grateful to get his hands on her fortune that he'd agree to her retaining some independence and travelling after their marriage. And if none of them had proposed, she'd been prepared to walk away from her father's fortune and this world, to which she didn't really belong anyway, and work as a governess and hope to save enough to be able to travel when she was older.

It was difficult to comprehend that both options seemed to have been removed from her grasp in one fell swoop.

The duke smiled at her, and Emma suddenly wondered what it would be like to lean, both physically and metaphorically, against his broad shoulders.

'I really believe that your best option now is to marry me,' he said.

The kindness in his green eyes was almost too much

to bear. For a moment, she wavered. Of course, of the options available to her right now, marrying him would be by far the best one, if only she could allow herself to treat another person so shabbily. She couldn't, though, because he clearly had no actual desire to marry her. It was one thing accepting the loan of his jacket and his offer of temporary escape from the predicament in which she had landed; it would be another accepting his offer to spend the rest of his life married to a complete stranger just because he'd been in the wrong place at the wrong time.

A thought struck her. His affections might well be already engaged. 'Are you…?' How to word it? 'Is there not someone with whom you are already acquainted that you would rather marry?'

'No.' He spoke the word so baldly that Emma gasped.

'No,' he repeated in a milder tone, and shook his head. 'No one else.'

She closed her eyes for a second and then said, 'I'm truly grateful to you for all your help this evening, but I cannot accept your very kind offer.'

Ridiculous that it felt more difficult to turn down the clearly extremely reluctant duke than it had to turn down the eleven sincere offers of marriage she'd already refused.

Her aunt had been beside herself about some of those refusals. She might actually expire with anger when she discovered that Emma had refused the duke, and was very likely to refuse to have her to reside with her any longer. She really hoped that her aunt wouldn't ask her to leave immediately. She would need some time to organise employment, and it would be a lot more enjoyable doing that while living in a mansion in Berkeley

Square than in whatever cheap lodgings she would be able to find herself.

Things were going to be dreadful for a while. She'd better end the conversation immediately, or she might actually finish by accepting the duke's offer.

'Thank you. I should now bid you goodnight,' she said.

The duke made no move to open the door. Well, she would open it for herself.

She untwisted her fingers—she now realised she'd been clutching her reticule ridiculously tightly—and reached out for the door handle. It was utterly ludicrous that she actually felt a momentary twinge of sadness at the thought that she would never see the duke again. Maybe it was because he was one of the few people she'd met in London who'd been genuinely kind to her, with no apparent ulterior motive.

As she began to turn the handle, the rumble of his deep voice cut through her thoughts.

'I have a proposal for you. You're right that I have no desire to get married. But I do need a governess for my three young sons. We lost their mother four years ago.' He paused for a moment, as though collecting himself, and then continued, 'Marry me, in name only, and act as governess to my boys. I will settle your entire dowry on you. I think this is a bargain we could both benefit from. You won't be forced to marry a man who might treat you badly, and you'd be financially independent, while I will no longer have to fight off matchmaking ladies who'd like their daughter to be a duchess, and, more importantly, I'll have found a governess for my sons. I've interviewed an extraordinarily large number of unsuitable candidates and was beginning to despair.

Had I had the good fortune to interview you, I would have offered you the job.'

'Really?' Emma hesitated, and then released the door handle and perched back on her seat. 'In that case, could I not just be your governess?'

The duke shook his head. 'I had already thought of that. There would obviously be gossip if the woman who had been announced as my fiancée became my sons' unmarried governess. I do not wish there to be any gossip surrounding my household, for the boys' sake.'

Emma nodded slowly. He was probably right. Wasn't his offer madness, though? Surely he couldn't really be so desperate for a governess that he'd happily marry someone to whom he didn't wish to be married?

The duke cleared his throat and shifted his eyes away from hers before looking back. 'I should point out that in accepting this bargain you would be relinquishing the opportunity to achieve a love union or have children. I would not like any scandal to attach to us.'

Emma nearly gasped out loud again. He *really* didn't want to get married. Unless he just found her particularly unattractive, of course. What he was suggesting sounded like a remarkably unusual bargain. Unbelievable, in fact.

'I don't want a wife, but I really do want a governess,' he said, as though reading her mind.

He smiled at her, a slow, lopsided smile that got to her somewhere deep inside as it grew.

'And I think you'd be wonderful with my children. I have a beautiful dower house on my estate, which is in Somerset. You would be welcome to live in it if you'd prefer your own household.'

Emma shook her head. This was all too much to take in.

'I… Being honest, I really don't know,' she said.

Before her father's death, she hadn't really thought about marriage beyond an infatuation at the age of eighteen with one of the factory managers that had come to nothing after her father had heard of it. He had banned them from seeing each other, and the manager, to Emma's extreme disillusionment, had fallen in with her father's wishes, telling her that he had no option because he couldn't support a wife if he had no employment.

She'd then assumed that, as the possessor of a significant fortune, she would, unlike the vast majority of women, be able to live however she liked after the far distant event of her father's death. By then she'd reflected on how her parents' incompatibility had destroyed their relationship, despite or even because of their mutual love, and had come to the conclusion that the only reason for her to marry would be to have children. And that if she did decide she wanted to marry, it would be to someone whom she liked and with whom she felt she could live happily, rather than to someone with whom she was deeply in love, because, from what she'd seen, passionate love could easily turn to hatred.

Her decision had been made for her by the terms of her father's will, of course. Once she'd recovered from her fury, she'd decided that she would make the best of it; she would hope to find someone pleasant with whom she could rub along quite happily, and hopefully they would have children. Indeed, the majority of her fury had been because it was just so *rude* and overbearing of her father to have dictated to her in such a way.

She suspected that she'd already come to the conclusion before his death that she wanted to have children and therefore wanted to marry. And now, she realised, she really did very much want to have children of her own. Could she give up that opportunity? Or had it already been taken from her because the only proposals of marriage she might receive beyond this cold-blooded, marriage-in-name-only one from the duke would be from men like Sir Peter, and she couldn't bear to marry someone like that?

She'd have the duke's children to care for, of course. Although only as their governess, and if their marriage ended in separation she might not continue to see much of them.

'Perhaps I could call on you tomorrow and you could let me know then, if that will allow you sufficient time to come to a decision?' he suggested after a couple of moments.

'Yes, please.' She really did need some thinking time.

'Excellent.' And there was that smile again.

As he moved in front of her to open the door and descend the carriage steps, her eyes were drawn to the bunched muscles across his shoulders, clearly visible through his shirt.

It was unusual for an aristocrat to have such a developed physique. Perhaps he boxed. His arms looked very strong too. Very…solid.

'Miss Bolton?'

Oh. He was waiting to hand her down.

She clutched the jacket tightly as she stood up, to avoid giving him another view of her chest, and moved to tread down the steps. And, goodness, it was difficult balancing when your hands were full of jacket. Her foot missed the second step and she began to sail through the air, one hand still holding the jacket and the other scrabbling against the side of the carriage to save herself.

Within a very short space of time the duke had her,

his firm and also very muscly forearm barely moving as he supported almost her full weight, before righting her with ease and helping her down the remainder of the steps.

She took a final step onto the ground and said, 'I must thank you again.'

She was annoyed to hear a tremor in her voice. It must be all to do with shock and nothing to do with how embarrassingly aware she suddenly felt of the strength in his arm, of how the fabric of his shirt stretched deliciously across his chest, just in line with her eyes.

'Not at all,' he said.

'Mmm.' She looked up at him and saw him swallow. Which made her swallow too. He had a very firm neck, and his hair was just longer than was strictly fashionable, curling a little over his collar. And…she was staring. She was staring at him. He'd saved her from Sir Peter, he'd saved her from falling out of the carriage, and she was staring. And his forearm really was very strong. And she *really* had to stop staring.

And, goodness, she was still holding his arm.

She let go very suddenly, as though it were very hot.

'So, thank you. And goodnight.' Her fake breezy tone sounded utterly ridiculous. 'So, I'll go inside now. Thank you.'

Good heavens, what was happening to her? This was insane.

She took a deep breath and, still clutching the jacket across her chest, moved towards her aunt's house.

'Of course.' The duke moved with her. And now she had nothing to say to him. Nothing. She could comment on how beautiful the still night was. But it wasn't really, nights were usually much more beautiful in the countryside, and also it just felt too mundane and inane a topic following the magnitude of the conversation they'd had inside the carriage. Maybe she could comment on how wonderful the ball had been. No. It hadn't been wonderful; it had been awful.

She glanced up at the duke's face. He was staring straight ahead at the house, his profile stern, apparently not at all tempted to speak either.

They trod side by side across the pavement and up the wide steps to the imposing front door of her aunt's house in continued silence, and it was one of the most excruciating short walks of Emma's life.

When her aunt's butler, Finch, punctuated the awkward silence by opening the door wide for her and bowing her inside, she could have kissed him.

'Thank you so much, Finch,' she said, almost jumping over the threshold in her relief.

Then she stopped and turned round. Obviously, she ought to bid the duke a formal goodnight.

She held her hand out to him. 'Good evening, Your Grace.'

The duke remained motionless for a moment, and then took her hand in his much larger one. And, of course, his hand was firm and strong, like the rest of him. And, *really*, she was almost blushing now. For no good reason whatsoever.

'Good evening.' He inclined his head over her hand, and, finally more in control of herself, she wiggled her fingers. He let her hand go and turned and went back down the steps. And insanely—truly *insanely*—she felt almost bereft, as though she was suddenly adrift in a boat on a choppy lake, with her only oar gone.

She shook her head. Her thoughts were utterly nonsensical. She did feel, however, as though she could do worse than putting herself under the duke's protection. As long as he would truly allow her a high degree of independence.

Three minutes later, she'd exchanged a couple of words with Finch before whisking herself upstairs and into her bedchamber. She was desperate to get rid of Jenny, her maid, so that she could plonk herself down on her bed and just sob for a few minutes at the enormity of everything that had happened this evening. And then she would have to begin to work out whether she should—could—accept the duke's offer.

'You're wearing a gentleman's jacket, miss.' Jenny, who had been with her since they were both very young, more of a companion and close friend than a maid, sounded both scandalised and delighted, clearly expecting a comfortable gossip about the ball.

'My dress tore, and, um, one of the gentlemen there was kind enough to give me his jacket.'

'Indeed!' Jenny raised her eyebrows and waited.

Emma said nothing.

'Did you have a lovely evening, miss?' Jenny picked up Emma's hairbrush.

'I did, thank you.' Emma swallowed a big lump in her throat. 'But I have the headache now. Thank you so much for your help, but I think I'll prepare myself for bed this evening.'

'Lady Morton won't be pleased if you do that.' Jenny wasn't budging. 'She'll think it doesn't befit your station. She already thinks it doesn't befit your station to have *me* to help you.'

'Well, luckily Lady Morton isn't here to witness my

appallingly unladylike wish to nurse my headache alone. So we don't need to worry about her. Thank you again.' Emma held her hand out for the brush.

Jenny looked at her for a while and then gave it to her. 'Call me if you need anything. Shall I take the jacket?'

'Thank you, lovely Jenny, but I'll keep the jacket here until I'm in my nightclothes.'

Emma pulled it a little more tightly round herself. She really didn't want Jenny to see her dress torn as it was. And, to her shame, she *liked* the feel of the jacket about her shoulders and body. It felt…maybe comforting? And it smelled deliciously masculine.

Emma suddenly realised that Jenny would hear all about her engagement from the other servants and be hurt that her mistress, her *friend*, hadn't told her herself.

'I had a very stressful evening. I promise I'll tell you all about it tomorrow morning. Promise. But I just need to sleep now.'

Sleep. Ha. She was more likely to be awake all night, wondering what she should say to the duke tomorrow.

'Goodnight, then, miss. If you're sure.'

'I am. Thank you.'

Descending for breakfast had been a mistake, Emma thought six hours later, eating toast and fruit while her aunt talked at both high volume and high speed, with no apparent need for breath, about Emma's forthcoming wedding, wedding dress, wedding trousseau, wedding reception, wedding everything. And it seemed that she was very much looking forward to visiting 'my niece, the Duchess of Harwell'.

When Lady Morton began to talk, with an affected dab at her eye with a napkin, about how delightful it would be to be great-aunt to the duke and duchess's children, Emma felt genuine tears forming behind her own eyelids and decided that enough was enough.

She popped the rest of the apricot she'd been eating into her mouth and pushed her chair back. 'I might perhaps take a walk in the garden square,' she told her aunt.

'Make sure you take a parasol. The February sun can be surprisingly strong,' her aunt said. 'And do, of course, take Jenny or a footman. The future Duchess of Harwell must not be seen walking unaccompanied.'

Emma very much wanted to be alone with her thoughts. 'On reflection, I might instead retire to my chamber and write some letters.'

'As you wish, my dear. What time did you say the duke would be calling this morning?'

'Eleven o'clock.'

'Unfashionably early, but one must make allowances for a man deeply in love.'

Emma managed to smile, and to refrain from rolling her eyes, and left the room to return to her chamber.

Half an hour later, she was thoroughly sick of her circular thoughts.

The whole idea was preposterous. Although in many ways ideal.

She didn't want to marry for love and, if the duke was true to his word—which she sensed he would be—this arrangement would allow her as much independence as she could hope to gain so that she could travel. And being governess to the duke's boys would allow her many of the benefits of motherhood.

But was he just being chivalrous? He clearly didn't need or want a wife. Did he really need and want a governess? And would he really have chosen her for the post? Would she be taking advantage of his kind nature in accepting his offer?

Enough. She should go for a walk. Fresh air was a commodity sadly lacking in London upper-class life, and the stuffiness of the house was making her headache even worse.

If she took Jenny with her, she could take the opportunity to tell her that she was—for the moment—engaged. And if she went now, she'd have time to come back and spend half an hour adjusting her hair and her dress before receiving the duke.

An hour and a half later, Emma allowed Jenny to give a final twitch to the dress they'd decided she would wear to take the duke's call—a primrose-yellow sprig muslin that Jenny said showed Emma's lovely skin and dark curls off very well—and said, 'Thank you. I might just spend two or three minutes alone to compose myself.'

'Of course, miss.' Jenny blinked hard, sniffed loudly, and waved her hand in front of her eyes. 'I'm that pleased for you I'm going to cry.'

Jenny had charged headlong down the 'it's so exciting' path, and Emma just hadn't been able to find the words to say out loud that the duke only actually wanted her as a governess. She *had* told Jenny that she was sure that, should the marriage indeed take place, she and the duke would maintain quite independent lives, and that she hoped to travel to India in due course to visit her grandmother's birthplace, but that had just had the effect of increasing Jenny's enthusiasm rather than dampening it.

'We don't even know that the marriage will go ahead.' Emma didn't want Jenny or anyone else to get excited about something that might not happen. She'd realised that she herself *did* want it to go ahead, because of *course* it was her best alternative, but she just couldn't agree to the duke's proposition if he didn't seem sincere in wanting her as his governess.

'Of course it will, miss. Why wouldn't it? Oh, *miss*. You're going to be a *duchess*.'

Emma did her best to blink back her own tears and to smile through the immense headache that was now throbbing at her temples.

'Indeed,' she said.

Ten minutes later, Emma had regained her composure and was walking in her best seminary-learned stately and composed manner into her aunt's blue saloon.

And there was the duke, directly opposite the door, standing with his back to the marble fireplace, looking straight at her without even the hint of a smile on his very handsome face.

Emma checked over her shoulder and, yes, she really was the person at whom he was looking in such a forbidding manner. It was difficult to believe he was the same person who'd rescued her last night. Now she could understand why people called him the Ice Duke; it wasn't just because he appeared frozen to all the ladies who set their caps at him, it was because he was capable of looking like *this*.

Like a man who was very unhappy at the prospect of going through with the offer he'd made last night.

She was going to have to tell him that, on reflection, she didn't want to accept the offer. She couldn't ruin a stranger's life.

He shifted his position slightly and his broad shoulders seemed to expand even further, filling a good half of the gilded mirror above the mantelpiece. He really was very big. And almost raw in his stern masculinity. It seemed quite ridiculous that he was wearing such tailored clothing; it was like seeing a lion in a dress.

'Emma, my dear?'

Oh, her aunt had been speaking.

'I believe you have not heard a word I said. I will leave you and the duke alone for a few minutes. There can be no need for me to leave the door ajar, I believe, when I understand that you are to be married within the next few days.'

Few days! And the door not ajar! Was her aunt actively trying to ensure that they were even more compromised into marriage?

Well, yes, she probably was.

'Good morning.' The duke's voice was so deep. Emma rubbed her arms to try to dispel sudden goosebumps.

'Good morning.' She took a long breath, feeling suddenly distinctly light-headed and wobbly on her legs. And tearful. But she must *not* cry. It was entirely understandable and to be expected that the duke didn't want to go through with marriage to her, and she should accept it with good grace.

She gestured to the sofas behind her. 'Shall we sit down?' She walked towards the nearest sofa and arranged herself in the middle of it, so that the duke couldn't possibly imagine that she was inviting him to sit next to her.

'Thank you.' The duke sat himself stiffly down on a sofa at right angles to the one she was on.

He gave her a half-smile and cleared his throat.

Emma waited.

He didn't say anything.

And she couldn't find any words.

She should speak immediately. Release him from his obvious agony. It was the only honourable course of action open to her; she couldn't effectively force him to marry her. Maybe it would be better if she stood up again, to signal to him that he should leave.

She rose to her feet and said, 'Your Grace. I'm certain that you are regretting your very generous offer last night. I fully understand, and indeed have no wish to go through with the charade myself. I thank you again for your kindness and bid you goodbye.'

Chapter Three

She was all huge dark eyes and riotously curling hair and heaving chest. She was… She was beautiful.

And Alex did not wish to think about that. He'd come here this morning hating the fact that he'd found her attractive nearly as much as he hated the idea of marrying her. He'd been desperately hoping that she'd have decided overnight that she didn't want to go through with it. He'd been planning that, if she *did* repeat that she didn't want to marry him, he'd thank her and suggest that he settle a sum of money on her, to ensure her financial independence, and then walk away hugely relieved.

But now he was with her, and she was saying exactly what he'd wanted to hear, and he knew both that she wouldn't accept any financial settlement from him and that he couldn't stand by and watch the ruination of her life.

It beggared belief that she would genuinely choose near-certain poverty or marriage with someone like Sir Peter over the proposition he'd outlined last night. She was clearly just being stupidly kind in not wishing to hold him to a promise that she'd thought he hadn't wished to make. So he was going to have to persuade her that he genuinely wanted to marry her. Difficult, because he really didn't.

Ignoring convention, he remained seated.

'I do not regret my offer, and I don't regard it as generous,' he said slowly, searching for words that would convince her. 'I would very much like you to be governess to my children. Their names are Freddie, John and Harry, and they are nine, seven and four years old. They're lively, but never malicious. I should warn you that Freddie and John do like to play jokes involving planting large insects in the way of people they think will scream on sight of them, so you should make sure that you don't scream the first couple of times they do it and then they'll stop.'

He was rewarded with a small smile from Emma.

'Have you had other governesses?'

'Six. Or seven. I forget exactly. The boys got rid of all of them, about which I am now delighted, because I know you would be so much better than they were.'

She narrowed her eyes. 'Hmm. Why is that?'

'You fought Sir Peter. You didn't indulge in any kind of vapours. You're clearly very kind. You state your case clearly and succinctly.' Good Lord. If he carried on like this he'd be a fair way to convincing himself that he genuinely wanted her instructing his boys. 'I think you would be an excellent governess.'

He was fairly certain from the way she was half frowning that he'd given her food for thought.

'Also, it would be of great benefit to me to be married, so that matchmaking chaperones no longer hound me. I really would be deeply grateful if you would marry me.'

She looked at him and swallowed, but didn't speak.

'I feel as though I am fortunate that fate threw us together yesterday evening,' he said. 'Our marriage could be the perfect solution for both of us.'

He was pretty sure that it would be a reasonable solution to *her* problems, anyway, as long as she didn't mind too much not having children. He was also pretty sure that he was doing a good job of sounding sincere.

'Really?'

'Absolutely. Please marry me? According to what we agreed last night?'

'*Definitely* really?'

'Definitely really.' Alex dug deep inside himself and produced a smile.

'I…' She drew a deep breath and then said, 'Thank you, Your Grace. If you're certain that you will benefit from our arrangement, then I in my turn am deeply grateful to you and I accept your offer.'

Good. But also terrible.

Alex shoved away the many negative thoughts jostling for prominence in his mind and focused hard on the fact that he was doing the right thing.

'Thank you.' He stood up to join her; he felt as if he ought to, now that they'd come to an agreement.

'No, thank *you*.' She had her hands clasped together, fingers locked so hard that her knuckles were whitening. Alex stood a couple of feet away from her, wishing that he'd remained seated and very conscious of his own hands hanging loosely by his sides as he watched hers clasping even harder.

'So.' He cleared his throat yet again. 'Would you be happy for me to make all the arrangements for the wedding? And would you be happy to travel immediately afterwards to my estate in Somerset?'

Emma nodded. 'Yes.'

'That's wonderful.' He choked slightly on the word *wonderful.* 'Perhaps in a week from now?'

He was going to have to journey back to Somerset for a night or two, to explain to his sons that they'd be having a new governess and that she would be called the Duchess of Harwell. Thank God they were too young to understand about things like marriage and stepmothers.

'Perfect.' She smiled a tight little smile that didn't reach her eyes. The miserable smile pierced his own misery and on impulse he reached forward and took her clasped hands in his.

'We can make this work to both our advantages,' he said. 'We really can.'

'I hope so.' Her hands relaxed slightly, and she allowed him to hold them separately in his. Looking down at the top of her dark head, he felt a surge of sympathy for her.

'I'm so sorry this has happened to you,' he said.

She looked up at him, tilted her head slightly to one side, raised her eyebrows and said, 'Although to hear you speak it couldn't have worked out better for you, because you need me as a governess.'

Honestly. So cynical.

'I do need you as a governess.' He smiled blandly at her. He'd suddenly wanted to make that clear, because there was something about her dark liquid eyes, the way she was looking at him, that had him feeling things he hadn't felt for a long time. Physical things, though, not emotional. And, rationally, that didn't matter. Physical attraction he could deal with. What he couldn't deal with ever again, and wasn't going to, was falling in love with someone.

Images of Diana struggling and then fading after giving birth to Harry, her coffin at her funeral days later and his three motherless sons flashed into his mind. The loss of Diana... He never wanted to experience pain of that magnitude again.

The saloon door rattled and began to open and the darkness cleared from his head. Good Lord, he and Emma were still holding hands.

Emma snatched her hands from his, as though they'd been doing something they shouldn't, and took a couple of steps away from him, turning to face the door and smoothing her skirts with her hands as she did so.

'Your Grace, Emma.' Lady Morton swept into the room, beaming. 'Do forgive my interrupting you. I come bearing wonderful news. The Bishop of Locke is able to marry you on Wednesday.'

'But today is Saturday,' Emma said. 'That's only four days away.'

'Fortunately, Madame Gabillard is able to fit you in this afternoon, and will work tirelessly on Monday and Tuesday to prepare dresses for your honeymoon. I had thought of a wedding dress similar to Princess Charlotte's silver one last year, but we don't have time for that, so I think the cream gown with silver overlay—the one that you were planning to wear to the Castlereaghs' ball, dear. The wedding breakfast is easily arranged. My own household will be able to prepare it with only a little additional help, and we can host it either in our ballroom here or in the duke's. I've already spoken to Tubbs about flowers. We will send invitations directly. The Duke and Duchess of Harwell will be forgiven for inviting their guests at such short notice. The breakfast will be very well attended.'

Alex drew breath, not sure which of the woman's false assumptions to tackle first. 'That's very kind, but I am able to make my own wedding arrangements,' he told her. 'I have business to undertake before the wedding. We are planning to marry next week. And—'

'Your Grace.' Lady Morton sank into a deep curtsey. Too deep. She wobbled alarmingly and panted, 'Emma.'

Emma and Alex both hurried over to her and hauled her up with an arm each. Lady Morton righted herself, but didn't let go of their arms, so that the three of them were standing in an uncomfortably tight circle.

'Thank you. I do not wish there to be any scandal attached to my niece, Your Grace. As her guardian, I must request that you marry as soon as possible.'

'One week is hardly a long engagement, Aunt,' Emma said.

'I must insist.' Lady Morton's voice was suddenly steely, and so was her grip on their arms. Alex looked down. Red marks were actually appearing on Emma's skin.

'Your Grace? I presume that, like most young men who have just got engaged, you are eager to enter into marriage as soon as possible. Wednesday.'

'I… Yes, of course. However, I have important business to undertake first.'

'I'm sure that as your wife, Emma will not prevent you from undertaking any important business. Although I trust that it is not of a delicate nature.' She screwed up her face and waggled her eyebrows.

'Aunt!' gasped Emma.

'No,' Alex almost snapped. 'It is not of a delicate nature.'

Not the kind of 'delicate nature' Lady Morton was

obviously implying. He hoped that marriage to Emma wouldn't mean that he had to spend much time with her aunt. He looked at Emma, who was clearly trying not to laugh, and to his surprise found his own lips twitching a little.

Lady Morton was squaring her shoulders, blatantly prepared to fight for Wednesday. He supposed he could explain to his sons after the marriage that they had a new governess. And…stepmother. He felt his entire face tighten. The word 'stepmother' was all wrong. As though he was being disloyal to Diana.

'Wednesday?' Lady Morton still hadn't released her grip on their arms.

'I'd be delighted,' Alex said after a long pause.

'Wonderful.' Lady Morton let go of their arms and reached up to pat his cheek, while Emma, half laughing and half grimacing behind her, mouthed, *Are you sure?* at Alex.

He nodded at Emma and took a step backwards, away from the cheek patting.

'Thank you for making the arrangements with the bishop and the church. I will visit the bishop myself to finalise preparations. And thank you for the offer of planning a wedding breakfast. Emma and I have, however, decided to leave for Somerset immediately after the ceremony finishes, and will not therefore be holding a breakfast.'

He wasn't going to refer to her mention of a honeymoon.

'No.' Lady Morton shook her head decisively. 'There must be a breakfast. Many of my friends are extremely desirous of attending and wishing you well.'

'I'm so sorry, Aunt.' Emma looked as desperate as he

felt to avoid a breakfast. 'The duke and I have to leave immediately once our nuptials are completed. He has urgent business in Somerset.'

'Sounds like a complete faradiddle to me.' Lady Morton plumped down onto the sofa on which Emma had just been sitting. 'However, if I can't persuade you, I can't. We shall have the wedding breakfast without you. Should I have the bill sent directly to you?'

Good Lord. Outrageous. Alex couldn't help smiling again at her effrontery, though.

He glanced over at Emma, whose eyes were dancing.

'Absolutely,' he said. 'And now I must take my leave of you. I have much business to attend to before Wednesday.'

'Outmanoeuvred. I'm sorry,' Emma whispered as he bent his head to kiss her hand.

He smiled at her and bowed at her aunt.

As he left, he heard Lady Morton say, 'You need to marry him as soon as possible, Emma, so that he can't escape.'

'Aunt.'

Almost exactly four days later, Alex was standing at the front of St George's Church in Hanover Square with his younger brother, Max, and the Bishop of Locke, waiting for Emma and trying very hard not to remember that the last time he'd stood waiting in this exact spot in a church he'd been waiting for Diana.

'Nervous?' Max nudged him, grinning.

Alex summoned a smile from somewhere, and said, 'Ha, yes.'

He really wasn't enjoying deceiving Max, but he'd been so happy for him, and Alex had been so pressed for time, that in the end he'd just gone along with Max's pleasure that he'd finally met someone new. Max was bound to hear a fuller version of the gossip surrounding the betrothal soon, and then Alex would explain. When he'd come to terms with it himself.

Max nudged him again as the door at the back of the church opened and Emma entered on the arm of a thin, older man. Perhaps an uncle.

'She's beautiful,' Max said in Alex's ear.

Alex nodded. Objectively speaking, yes, she was. The simple pale blue dress that she was wearing set off her slim figure and dark beauty perfectly. Although hadn't her aunt mentioned silver? Maybe Emma had put her foot down. Her hair was done in ringlets, falling down her neck, and she had a hint of colour in her cheeks.

It wasn't her beauty that caused Alex's heart to clench, though, it was the fact that, in contrast to when he'd last seen her in her aunt's drawing room, trying not to laugh about her aunt's outrageous behaviour, now she could barely meet his eye.

And the fact that when you'd been through a *real* marriage once, one like this felt all wrong.

He turned to face the front, suddenly almost overcome with misery.

Max squeezed his arm and whispered, 'Diana would have wanted this, you know.'

No. She really wouldn't have wanted him to enter a loveless union.

'Thank you,' Alex croaked.

Damn Max for being at least partially intuitive, knowing he was thinking about his first marriage. And damn this whole hellish situation.

Emma took her place at his side and he painted a

smile on his face before looking down at her. She was staring straight ahead, almost unnaturally motionless. God, he was self-centred. This was no worse for him than it was for her. In fact, it might be a lot worse for her than it was for him. From what he'd seen of her, she didn't strike him as a woman who was particularly desperate to be a duchess, and that was essentially all he had to offer her.

'This won't take long,' he whispered.

'I know.' Her voice was a lot steadier than his. She still wasn't succeeding in meeting his eye, though.

The bishop hurried through the service at a remarkable pace. Alex couldn't work out whether he was just bored with repeating the same lines yet again, or whether Lady Morton had warned him that she thought there was a danger of the groom absconding.

And soon they were at the main part of the ceremony. The part from which there was no going back.

'With this ring, I thee wed.'

For the second time since he'd met Emma, Alex had the sensation that he was watching this experience from afar, as though it wasn't really him doing the actual getting married. Emma's hand was very cold, so cold that it was easy to slide the ring onto her finger, despite the fact that her hand was shaking somewhat.

They offered each other lips-pressed-together smiles and a few minutes later the service was over and it was time to walk down the aisle towards the outside world as man and wife. They looked at each other, and then Alex held his arm out because for the moment they clearly had to behave like a normal couple. After a moment's hesitation, Emma took his arm lightly and they began to process down the aisle.

Alex was acutely aware as they walked that Emma was holding herself stiffly away from him, nearly as stiffly as he in his turn was holding himself away from her.

And finally, after what had felt like an extraordinarily long walk—that aisle must be a lot longer than the average—they were outside the church.

'I shall miss you so much, my darling Emma.' Lady Morton hugged her niece, before almost shoving her into Alex's chaise.

'I'll miss you too, Aunt. Thank you for everything,' Emma said as Alex handed her up into his curricle.

Alex winced as Lady Morton squeezed his cheek and said, 'Enjoy yourselves tonight,' before he jumped up next to Emma. He would have laughed under any other circumstances.

The door closed behind them and here they were, together, alone, the two of them, complete strangers, newly married in name only, trapped together on a lengthy journey.

Thank the Lord Alex had his horse excuse ready.

'Beautiful weather today,' Emma said as she arranged herself in the corner of one of the seats.

Alex sat down on the other seat in the opposite corner.

'A lovely day for a journey,' she added.

'Indeed. But somewhat chilly. There are blankets here, and I've asked my housekeeper to prepare a foot warmer for you for the journey. She should have it ready when we get to the house.'

'Thank you. The current fashion for wedding garb is sadly lacking in consideration for a lady's comfort. But I'd assumed we were leaving London immediately?' Emma's luggage had already been collected by one of Alex's grooms from Lady Morton's house.

'We are.' Alex cleared his throat, suddenly feeling a little…not rude, maybe awkward. 'But I'm going to ride alongside the chaise. The only way to get my horse home.' Not precisely true. If he'd really wanted to travel inside the chaise he'd have trusted his head groom to ride Star, his horse. 'We're going back to the house so that I can ride from there.'

'Oh, I see. That makes great sense. And I'll be able to read my novel without having to make polite conversation with you.' She twinkled at Alex and surprised a laugh out of him.

A few seconds later, they drew up outside his house.

'We'll stop for luncheon and a break for the horses at around one o'clock,' he told her. 'If you can drag yourself away from your book, of course.'

She smiled at him and he nodded—a little awkwardly—and then opened the chaise door. Maybe he should travel inside the carriage with her. It would be more polite and his riding separately might give rise to gossip. No. He didn't want to spend too much time with her. He really didn't want to get close to a woman again.

Chapter Four

Emma found herself staring at the door that the duke had just closed behind him. It might be a metaphor for his clear signal that he planned to keep her closed out of his life as far as possible. That was completely understandable, of course, but, if she was honest, her spirits, which had not been high when she'd woken up this morning—her wedding day for goodness' sake—were now dragging even lower.

A journey spent in splendid isolation in this luxurious, velvet-upholstered carriage was going to feel very long, and a life spent in splendid isolation in the no doubt luxurious ducal castle would also feel very long.

Well, she would just have to make the best of it. She would have the duke's sons to care for, and he might accept her help in visiting tenants, and hopefully she would be able to make some local friends. And maybe, in time, despite his obvious reluctance, she and the duke might become good friends.

And now, at least she had time to read her book. She'd told the duke that she would be pleased to have some time to read—she'd even managed a little joke, of which she was very proud. She felt as though it was good to maintain one's dignity when one's husband had effectively told one that he didn't wish to share one's company at all. And she *was* pleased, actually, to have some peaceful reading time after the past few days packed morning to night with wedding preparations for a wedding neither of the two participants had wanted.

A few minutes later, she slapped the book closed, narrowly avoiding slamming her finger in it. It really was impossible to concentrate when out of the corner of her eye through the window she could see grooms, maids, all sorts of people bustling about, getting Alex's horses ready and finalising the packing of other carriages containing valises, trunks and servants.

It felt quite ridiculous, being incarcerated here by herself, so she was delighted when there was a knock on the door.

It was Jenny.

'The duke suggested that I travel with you, miss, oh, my goodness, *no*, Your *Grace*.' Jenny was practically bouncing on the spot, looking as though she was going to burst from excitement.

'Oh, *miss*.' Her eyes were saucer-like. 'Look at all the velvet. This is going to be *wonderful*. I'm so glad you're a duchess now.'

Hmm. It was kind of the duke to have thought of Emma's comfort, but maybe there was something to be said for isolation after all. Perhaps a journey alone would have been a good time for her to have begun to digest the fact that this morning she'd got married, when a week ago she hadn't even met the duke.

Jenny stopped bouncing and said, 'Would you *like* me to travel with you?'

Emma looked at her. She really didn't want to hurt

her feelings, and solitude *was* boring, and she could always pretend to bury herself in her book if she didn't want to talk. She was also likely to have a fair amount of time by herself over the coming weeks and months if the duke was intent on avoiding her, so she should probably take any company she could get.

'That would be lovely, Jenny.'

Jenny bounced herself into the chaise and took up residence on the opposite bench, while Emma tried not to find it annoying that so many people were pleased about her marriage.

'I've never been to Somerset before, miss.'

'Nor have I.'

'How long do you think it will take to get there?'

'I don't know.' Emma frowned, not pleased that she was so much at the mercy of the duke's whims. He had, of course, shown her nothing but kindness, but she would have liked to have had an idea of exactly where they were going and how long the journey would take.

She caught a glimpse of him out of the window, moving in their direction. He'd changed into riding wear, which showed off his strong physique marvellously well. Emma felt herself begin to smile in anticipation of him coming to speak to her again. She looked at the door, expecting him to knock, or open it. And…nothing.

And then the chaise jolted and began to move. Without another word from the duke.

Jenny actually clapped. 'Oh, miss, *Your Grace*, this is so exciting, isn't it?'

No, it really was not. More…profoundly depressing.

'Yes,' Emma said. 'I think I might read my book, if you don't mind.' She pulled it out of her reticule.

'Of course, *Your Grace*.'

This *Your Grace* thing was going to become annoying very quickly.

'You may continue to call me "miss" if you wish, Jenny.'

'Oh, no, miss, Your Grace, I couldn't do that.'

Emma smiled at her and shrugged internally. It probably wasn't going to be the worst thing about her new life.

The morning was long. Emma divided her time between trying to read but failing to turn more than a handful of pages—normally she was a voracious reader—and trying to look at the scenery and possibly catch a glimpse of Alex out of the window without catching Jenny's eye and having to talk. And, of course, just *sitting* the entire time. Frankly, doing absolutely nothing while feeling quite passionately irritable about life in general was exhausting.

When the chaise drew smoothly to a halt in a yard in front of an inn, Emma found herself almost beaming in delight. Luncheon. Something to *do*.

There was a knock at the door and it was pulled open.

'I hope you don't mind my intruding.' The duke's head and shoulders appeared inside the carriage and suddenly it felt significantly smaller. 'We stop here for luncheon.'

Emma regarded him, her head slightly on one side. Her husband. Her *husband*. How…odd.

As she had observed, his broad shoulders and sheer solidity showed off his riding wear to perfection, and the austere simplicity of his clothing was also perfect. It made one think very disparagingly of the frivolous frock coats worn by more foppish men.

Objectively speaking, he did look good.

Subjectively speaking, though, he was annoying.

He seemed to have literally no concept that she might not want to stop here, and that he should have asked her whether she would *like* to stop. Why should men make every single decision, from whether or not they should travel together, to when they should stop on the journey? Obviously she should be grateful to Alex—and she *was* grateful to him—but literally everything other than the fact that they'd got married in the first place seemed to be on his terms. Of course, it was the way of the world that men made all the decisions, but why should it be that way?

'Is this the only inn on our route? I'm not particularly hungry yet.' Emma realised immediately that she was starving. She also sensed Jenny twitching on the opposite side of the chaise; she was probably hungry too.

The duke looked at her. She really wished she could read the expression on his face.

'We need to change the horses here,' he said. 'The next good inn is twenty miles distant. If you'd prefer to wait until then to eat, we can, of course, do that.'

'Thank you.' Emma smiled at him while her stomach growled. Apparently she'd just bitten off her nose to spite her face.

The duke hesitated briefly and then said, 'Jenny, I wonder if I could have a moment alone with Her Grace?'

'Of course, my lord, Your Grace.' Jenny almost fell out of the chaise in her haste to comply, and was only saved from falling flat on her face by the duke catching her arm.

Emma's mind immediately went to when he'd caught *her*, the evening they'd met, and a shiver ran through her entire body.

Once he had Jenny solidly on her feet outside the chaise, the duke put his head through the door again and asked, 'Would you mind if I joined you inside the chaise for a moment?'

'Of course not.' Emma moved her skirts out of his way, taking her time to allow her suddenly uneven breathing to settle.

Being alone in here together seemed very…intimate. Especially since Jenny would probably be watching them from a discreet distance—or possibly not so discreet. It felt much more intimate than it had the evening after the ball, because she'd been far too stressed then to think about the intimacy. Since they were now man and wife, they might be expected to be in any number of intimate situations, of course.

A lot of women would be sad in her position— desperately sad—about the fact that they wouldn't be engaging with their husband in the most intimate situation of all. But, other than the fact that it meant that she wouldn't be having children of her own, Emma was fortunate in being perfectly happy about that. *Perfectly* happy. Really. She had no particular desire to engage with the duke in that kind of thing at all. Really.

The duke pulled the door closed behind him and took the seat opposite her, where Jenny had been sitting. Emma swallowed. Each time she'd seen him, she'd been struck by how *large* he was. Right now, it seemed as though he was filling the entire chaise, which previously had seemed extremely roomy for two people.

He cleared his throat. 'I've been thinking. Obviously, for our own reasons, neither of us wishes there to be any gossip about our relationship.'

Emma inclined her head, her throat suddenly tight with an emotion she couldn't name.

'During our journey, therefore, I think that we should eat our meals together—in a private room, if possible, as that will be expected of us—and sleep in adjoining bedchambers.'

He was clearly right. And frankly, after the boredom of the journey so far, Emma realised she would welcome conversation with him over their meals. And they ought to get to know each other a little better, given that they were, effectively, co-conspirators.

There was no reason whatsoever for her to feel a little hot at the thought that they would have adjoining bedchambers for a night. Or two nights?

She really wanted to know how long the journey was going to be. During luncheon would be an ideal time to question him. There were a lot of things she'd like to know about her future life.

'I agree,' she said.

'Still not hungry?' he asked.

Emma wondered if he'd actually heard her stomach rumble.

'I have just this moment become a little hungry. Perhaps it would make sense to luncheon here after all.'

Enough was enough when it came to her asserting her right to eat when she wanted to.

The duke bowed his head.

Emma was fairly sure he was hiding a smile as he did so, which should have been annoying, but made her smile too.

The ducal crest and servants had worked a lot more magic than the mere greasing of palms that Emma's father had been able to do when he had travelled as a plain mister, however rich. The landlord of the inn and his staff were all bowing so low Emma was surprised they didn't lose their balance.

'Our best private dining room is at your disposal, Your Grace.' Had the landlord bowed any more deeply his ample stomach would have been dusting the ground, and had his smile been any broader his face might have split.

'Thank you very much.' Emma and the duke spoke as one, and then glanced at each other as one, which shouldn't have pleased Emma as much as it did. Given that her life had just taken a huge turn for the unknown, though, there was something nice about feeling that the two of them might occasionally be… She didn't know quite what. Maybe a team?

The two of them made *very* small talk—exclaiming over the delightful cottage garden they could see from the window of the dining room and commenting on the carved panelling in the room—until the table had been laden with more food than two adults with even gargantuan appetites could possibly eat and the landlord had bowed himself out of the room a final time.

'Can I help you to some of these sweetmeats?' The duke looked as though he was going to continue with the small talk.

'Yes, please,' said Emma, not even looking at the dish. While she had him with her, she had questions for him that were a lot more important than sweetmeats. She passed him her plate and said, 'Could I possibly ask you a few questions?'

'Of course.' He inclined his head.

'Firstly, could I ask what my duties as governess will be?'

'Duties?' The duke spooned three choice sweetmeats onto her plate and looked around the table at the other food, as though she hadn't just asked a very important question. 'No duties. As I said before, I'd be extremely grateful for your help with the boys, but I can't possibly ask you to take on formal duties. If you're happy to be involved in their care, or indeed take charge of it, I'd be delighted, but, equally, if you don't feel that you wish to be involved, I will look for another governess. If you do wish to be involved, then of course we can discuss matters of import, for example the hiring of tutors and a broad timetable. Buttered cauliflower?'

'No cauliflower, thank you.' Emma was fast losing her appetite, not something that happened to her very often. 'Was your professed need for a governess perhaps an invention?'

He placed three cauliflower florets very carefully on his own plate before looking up at her. 'It wasn't an invention. I do need a governess for my boys. I find, however, that I cannot possibly instruct *you*. You're—' he waved a fork at her '—you. *You*. The Duchess of Harwell. *You*.'

'I'm only the Duchess of Harwell because you were forced to marry me, and the only reason I agreed to your sacrifice was that you told me that you needed my help.'

Emma cut one of the sweetmeats in two, hard, her cutlery clattering against the plate, and sniffed as quietly as she could. Tears and anger were battling inside her, and she didn't wish to give in to either of them.

'I would like to help with the boys. If you would like me to.'

She'd believed they'd had a bargain, but it seemed that he'd completely hoodwinked her. He'd clearly just told her that he needed her help to prevail upon her to accept his offer. Out of kindness, of course. And she'd allowed herself to believe he needed her help because she'd *wanted* to believe it, because it was her best option. Really, she'd hoodwinked her*self.* Also, she couldn't *make* him allow her to help with his children—and indeed she didn't want to press her services where they weren't wished for—but if she couldn't help with them, what was she going to do with herself all day, every day?

'Yes, of course, and thank you. But not as an employee or a servant or social inferior of mine in any way. I didn't mean that I can't instruct you because you're a duchess now; I meant I can't instruct you because you're *you*, Emma, the person you are. I plan to settle your dowry on you so that you can live in any manner or style you like. As I mentioned before, there's a dower house on the estate to which you may wish to remove in due course. You would be very welcome to have it refurbished to your own specification.' He smiled at her, apparently unaware that she was now… Well, she didn't know what she was, but it wasn't good. She was either furious, or desperately miserable, or both.

'We had a bargain and I intend to stick to my side of it,' she told him. 'I would very much like to help with the children. Perhaps I could also help you in visiting tenants who might be in need?'

'Certainly. Thank you.' The duke busied himself with the food on his plate while Emma blinked back another few tears. She was, of course, being ridiculous. There was no reason for her to feel tearful; this was hardly the worst thing that had ever happened to anyone. Many of the debutantes she'd met in London would be ecstatic to be in her position now, setting aside the fact that they wouldn't be having children of their own. Really, she was very lucky.

She loaded a second mouthful onto her fork.

'These sweetmeats are quite delicious,' Emma said eventually, into the fairly long silence during which they'd both…chewed their food.

Oh, the romance of this wedding day. She didn't want a passionate love match, but this… This wasn't how she would ever have imagined her marriage to be.

'Yes, they are.' The duke's conversation was as scintillating as hers.

There was more chewing from both of them, and then he said, 'You said you had more than one question for me?'

Oh, yes. *Would you mind if I travelled to India to explore my grandmother's birthplace if I'm not going to have anything else productive to do with my time?*

No. Maybe not a conversation to have until she'd gauged how conservative he was.

'Yes. I wondered how long our journey to Somerset will be?'

'Assuming that no unforeseen incidents occur, I hope to arrive tomorrow evening. One night at an inn, therefore.'

'Wonderful.'

And then they lapsed into near silence for the remainder of the meal, any conversation revolving entirely around the food—which was nice, but not outstandingly so, although any deficiencies in quality were made up for in extreme quantity.

After what felt like a long silence-filled time later, which turned out to have been perhaps twenty minutes, the duke said, 'If you don't mind, I feel that it might be better for us to be on our way sooner rather than later, so that we arrive at our staging inn this evening well before nightfall.'

Emma gave him a big smile in relief that the meal was at an end and in response to the fact that he'd asked, rather than told, her about their departure.

'Of course.'

An extraordinary number of people seemed to have gathered in the inn's entrance hall to witness their departure. During the extreme bowing and curtseying that ensued, a woman stepped forward and introduced herself as the landlord's wife.

'I'm so sorry that I wasn't here before, Your Grace,' she addressed Emma. 'I was shopping in the town. Praise be that I got home in time to see you.' Goodness. The allure of a duchess.

'Indeed.' Emma smiled at her.

'I wondered—' the woman must have thighs of steel; her curtsey was remarkably low and yet still steady '—whether Your Grace would like to see my kittens?'

'Kittens?' Was that a euphemism for something? Or a country word?

'Baby cats, Your Grace.'

Emma laughed. 'I'm so sorry. You must think me quite odd. I hadn't realised what you meant. I'd love to see your kittens.'

'And then we must be on our way,' the duke said.

Emma turned to look at him, one eyebrow raised. He might be reneging on the governess part of their bargain; he was *not*, if she could help it, going to renege on giving her autonomy.

'If you don't mind,' he clarified after a pause.

Emma smiled. 'I'm sure we can spare a few minutes,' she said, 'and then I think we'll need to leave.'

'Oh, my goodness. They're adorable,' she breathed a couple of minutes later as the landlady opened a stable door for her. 'How old are they?'

'Two months, Your Grace.' The landlady dropped into yet another curtsey. Emma really wished she could ask her to stop curtseying, but she was fairly sure the woman would be offended. It seemed as though she was going to have to get used to being curtseyed to.

She bent down and then knelt on the straw next to where the kittens were lapping from a bowl.

'Your dress, Your Grace. If I might be so bold.'

'I'm sure it won't be damaged. This straw looks very clean.'

And it was her wedding dress, but her wedding had been a complete fake and she knew that she would never wear the dress again, because today was not a day that she was going to want to remember.

'May I?' She indicated one of the kittens, which had finished drinking.

'Please do.'

Emma reached forward and picked the kitten up, stroking its silky fur. The tiny creature mewled and arched into her.

'It's beautiful,' she said.

Today was a very lonely day, and it seemed that her life might be quite isolated from now on. Her new husband clearly had no interest in any kind of friendship with her, and she could already see that the vast majority of people she met were going to be very interested in her, but not actually in *her*, just in her persona as a duchess. Even Jenny, whom she'd known for over a decade now, was trying to treat her differently now she was a duchess.

It felt wonderful for another living creature to wish to cuddle into her, as the kitten was doing, for no reason other than that they were fellow creatures.

She picked up a piece of straw and tickled the kitten with it, and soon they were playing together. For a few moments she forgot that she'd got married and just enjoyed the kitten.

And then a large shadow appeared above her and she heard the duke say, 'I'd like to leave now, if you're ready.'

No, she wasn't ready, but she might never be ready, and of course it would be better to arrive at the next inn before nightfall.

'Of course.' She carefully picked up the kitten and with great reluctance placed it back with its mother. Now she needed to stand up. She looked around. There was nothing to hold on to. She was going to have to scramble to her feet by pushing herself up from the ground, which she wouldn't mind at all without an audience, but as it was…

The duke stepped forward and held his hand out to her. Yes, that was clearly her best option. A bit of an analogy for her marriage to him, really.

'Thank you.' She took his hand and found herself almost flying to her feet.

The duke loosened his fingers on her hand, as though he was going to let go, and then re-tightened his grip and drew her arm through his. Of course: he'd done it to avoid gossip, which they'd agreed they both wanted to do, so she smiled up at him in her best wifely manner, actually a very easy thing to do, because he did have a lovely face when he wasn't doing his stern Ice Duke thing.

He was looking at her, and smiling back at her, and Emma felt her entire body bask in the smile even though she knew it was fake.

'Your Grace?' The landlady was scrape-the-ground curtseying again. 'If I might make so bold? Would Your Grace like to take the kitten? It will be very difficult for us to find homes for them all.'

Emma realised immediately that she'd *love* to take the kitten. She looked back up at the duke, who rolled his eyes slightly.

'Is it practical to transport a kitten from here to Somerset in the chaise?' he asked.

'Oh, yes, Your Grace. We can provide a box and bedding and food and milk.' The landlady was nodding emphatically.

'I'd love to,' Emma said, ignoring her new husband's raised eyebrows. 'I wonder... Would it be lonely without a sibling?'

'Probably,' the duke said, rolling his eyes more, but smiling. He turned to the landlady. 'You must allow me to pay you for the kittens.'

'Oh, Your Grace. I couldn't.' She already had her hand held firmly out. 'Thank you.'

In the end they took three kittens, and Emma's mood had lightened considerably at the prospect of something to do and the company the cats would provide.

'People are certainly very interested in the movements of the Duke and Duchess of Harwell,' Emma murmured as she and the duke stood in the courtyard while the landlady gathered together necessities for the kittens.

More people than she'd imagined the inn even held had assembled to see them off.

'They are.' He didn't smile. 'I appreciate the many advantages of my station, but it would take a better man than I to enjoy that side of my life.'

Emma felt strangely comforted from knowing that he didn't love this weird adulation either.

'It's better at home in the country, though. People get used to your title and possessions, and to some extent start treating you as the person you are, especially the household retainers who've been with our family for many years, and some of my tenants, not to mention friends.' He looked down at her. 'Are you sure you're happy to travel in the chaise with the kittens? It could be very difficult. And possibly smelly.'

Emma laughed. 'I'm very happy to,' she told him.

'Have you spent much time with cats?' he asked.

'No.' She could see his lips twitching. 'What?'

'Nothing,' he said, smiling blandly.

A few minutes later, as she sat in the chaise and watched him ride off, she realised that she was almost looking forward to seeing him later, when they stopped for the evening.

Chapter Five

As Alex strode away from the chaise in the direction of his horse, he could have sworn he heard a little squeak, possibly of pain, from Miss Bolton—Emma, the new duchess, how to think of her?—in the interior of the chaise. Maybe one of the kittens had scratched her.

He wondered how long it would be before she'd be seriously regretting her impulse purchase. He was fairly sure that unless the cats were lulled to sleep by the movement of the vehicle they'd play merry hell with her. So much so that he was almost tempted to travel in there with her, just to enjoy the spectacle.

Not that tempted, though. He really didn't want to get too close to her, and he always enjoyed riding.

Mid-afternoon, he saw ahead of him, on a long, straight stretch of road, a broken-down stagecoach, half tilted into a ditch, with passengers struggling to disembark and trunks and bags strewn across the road. Reining in his horse, he stopped and dismounted, looping the reins around a tree and securing them before heading over towards the coach to help passengers out.

A few minutes later, working in his shirtsleeves, he heard another carriage come to a halt and realised that it was his own. Shortly after that, Emma was standing next to him on the dusty road, asking what she could do to help.

'You would be best placed by returning to the chaise and continuing your journey,' he told her. 'This is no place for a gentlewoman.'

There were some extremely angry people using some extremely fruity language not far from them, and Alex had already had to wade in to prevent an argument coming to serious blows.

'I am an adult, not a baby, nor a Bath miss. Some of these people are clearly in distress. Why would I not help?'

Alex tried very hard not to sigh out loud, and was pretty sure that he'd succeeded.

'Obviously you *can* help,' he said, 'but a duchess is always a target for thieves and vagabonds, and the stagecoach is not a particularly—' he sought for a polite word '—*exclusive* mode of travel. It is entirely possible that one of the passengers might seek to relieve you of some of your jewellery, for example.'

'Then I will shoot them.' She said it so calmly that he really couldn't tell whether or not she was joking. It *sounded* like a joke. Because obviously she *wasn't* going to shoot anyone. Except… He'd already noticed that when she was joking there was a little quirk to her lips. And the quirk was not there.

'Just through the fleshy part of their arm or leg, obviously. I wouldn't want to kill them.' She patted her reticule. She really didn't seem to be joking. Did she have a pistol in there?

'My father, while not a duke, was an extremely wealthy man, and he wished to ensure that his only daughter was protected.'

This time Alex did not succeed in not sighing out loud. 'I'm not sure that a shooting, even just through the fleshy part of someone's limb, would help any of us. And there would, of course, be the risk that your aim faltered and greater injury occurred.'

'It would not falter. I was taught very well and I have an excellent aim.'

'Real-life situations are not the same as practice ones, though,' he pointed out.

Why was he even engaging with her?

'True,' she said. From over her shoulder.

Because, totally ignoring Alex's wishes, she was on her way to speak to some female passengers, who were sitting by the side of the road.

He'd already noticed during their stop at the staging inn, when she'd blatantly pretended that she wasn't hungry just to make a point, that she was clearly not planning to allow him to tell her what to do in any way. Which, of course, was completely understandable, and he didn't *want* to tell her what to do. Most of the time, anyway. Right now, he would very much have appreciated her doing what he'd asked.

He nodded at two of his grooms, both of whom immediately moved towards Emma. Their mere presence would protect her, and he, of course, would be constantly looking over his shoulder to check that she was all right.

To give her her due, she really did help very enthusiastically, and her presence did, to some extent, quieten people down, partly because so many of them were watching her open-mouthed. His grooms did a very good job of intimidating the livelier of the little crowd, and it was not long before Emma had managed to calm a woman who'd been having full-blown hysterics.

Soon Emma was sitting in a little group of other women, talking away about their children, from what Alex could hear, and very quickly it was as though they were fast friends. He'd better just hope they didn't have any kittens or other animals to sell her.

When the stagecoach was eventually righted, and its broken wheel shaft mended—Alex hadn't felt he could leave before that—he joined Emma in bidding farewell to all her new friends.

'I'll try that new recipe, Your Grace,' said an older woman dressed in a voluminous grey dress and wearing a large, bright yellow hat.

'You'll be delighted with the results, I'm sure,' Emma told her.

Alex nodded at all the women and then said, 'I believe that the stagecoach is ready to depart, and we should be on our way too.'

'She's a lovely duchess,' the lady in the yellow hat told him.

Alex nodded. It did look as though she was going to be. And, to be fair to Emma, she *had* helped, and there had been no unpleasantness nor any problems. Perhaps she genuinely would be able to look after herself with a pistol as well. It certainly seemed as though she was a woman who should not be underestimated.

He nodded and smiled at the woman. 'I agree.' He held his arm out to Emma and she took it, and they made their way back to the chaise, where her maid had been patiently waiting with the kittens.

'You should take a short walk to stretch your legs, Jenny, before we set off again,' Emma told her.

'Thank you, Your Grace, if you're sure.' Her maid smiled broadly at her, and Alex reflected that there was a fighting chance that even his famously prickly housekeeper might like Emma.

Once Jenny was out of earshot, Alex leaned in so that no one else could possibly hear, and said, 'You should keep that pistol very much out of sight. And be careful.'

As he leaned, he caught Emma's scent, which reminded him of summer, and something sweet, and made him just want to keep on standing close to her.

That didn't feel right, so he took a step backwards, which gave him an excellent view of the little flash of anger in her eyes as she said, 'Should I *really*? Thank you so much for your sage advice. I was planning to wave it around and, indeed, hand it to any aspiring highwayman on a platter to help him with his job.'

Alex laughed. 'Fair enough. I'm sorry. Perhaps I sounded a little patronising there?'

Emma raised an eyebrow.

'*Very* patronising,' he said. 'My apologies.'

'Thank you.' She nodded at him and entered the chaise, immediately bending down to speak to the kittens, sounding a lot happier to be talking to them than to him.

'I'd planned to stop near Andover, at a good staging inn that I know. Would you be happy to spend the night there?' he called into the chaise in the interests of harmony; in an ideal world he and Emma would be on good although distant terms.

She turned to look at him, cuddling a kitten, and bestowed a wide smile upon him, which transformed her face from very pretty to…extremely beautiful. Objectively speaking.

'I'd be happy to, thank you.' And then she turned back to the kitten.

'Excellent, then. So…have a good journey,' he said to her back.

'Thank you. And you,' she said over her shoulder, one eye still on the kittens.

Excellent, then.

Alex arrived at the inn at which they were spending the night a little before Emma. He took his horse round to the stables, and then returned to the yard in front of the inn to wait for her, so that they could enter the building together.

When the chaise drew up, he moved forward to open the door, interested to see how Emma and Jenny had fared with the kittens.

'Pleasant journey, I trust?' He held out his arm to Emma so that she could descend the steps.

'Delightful,' she said, smoothing her somewhat dishevelled hair as she reached the ground.

'Did you get a lot of reading done?'

'We were both somewhat occupied with the kittens,' she said, with as much dignity a woman with straw in her bodice and scratches on her arms could produce. Alex laughed out loud as Emma continued, 'I shall enjoy reading my book this evening instead.'

'Not planning to share your bedchamber with the kittens, then?'

'Jenny has very kindly volunteered to find a place for the kittens to stay overnight, perhaps in the stables. They are *truly* delightful.'

'But?'

'Very lively and not yet trained. Although *certainly* delightful.'

As Alex laughed again, he was interrupted by his head groom, who had a question about one of the horses.

'Forgive me,' he said to Emma, handing her over the threshold into the inn. 'I'll return to you very soon.'

When he got back, Emma had her back to the main door into the inn's reception area and was engaged in conversation with a little group of other travellers, who all appeared from their attire to be members of the *ton*. He could see from the way she was holding herself that she wasn't enjoying the conversation.

When she'd been chatting to the stagecoach travellers, he couldn't have said precisely how, but she'd looked relaxed. Now, her shoulders were just a little frozen, and her head was angled to one side in a slightly unnatural-looking manner.

'Indeed, you played your hand remarkably well,' one of the other ladies in the little group said, accompanying her words with a titter.

Alex thought he recognised her as one of the many women who'd been thrown, or had thrown herself, in his direction during the course of the last few weeks.

'Did you have any accomplice beyond your aunt?' she continued.

'Perhaps Sir Peter was the accomplice,' mused another of the ladies in the group.

This one bore a strong resemblance to the first one—in both looks and apparent nastiness—and accompanied her words with a gloved finger to her chin and an artful tilt of her head, as though she was thinking.

Emma visibly stood a little taller, as though she was

bracing herself, and her voice was a little higher than usual when she said, 'I'm afraid—'

Alex strode forward before she could continue—because really there was nothing she could conceivably say in response that would improve the situation—and slid his arm around her waist, sure that the only effective way of shutting down this gossipy cattiness was to demonstrate, if he could, that their union was at least some way towards a love match.

As he pulled her in, tight against his side, she gasped and looked up at him. From nowhere, he was struck by the thought that she fitted very well against him, as though their two bodies might have been made for each other. As might many people's, though, actually. That was just human biology.

The two women and their companions—an older woman whom he recognised as Lady Castledene, presumably their mother, and two men, perhaps brothers—were all looking at him and Emma appraisingly.

Alex really did not appreciate the way they were doing so. If they wanted something to appraise, he was going to *give* them something to appraise.

He dropped a kiss on Emma's forehead, catching that delicious scent again, and squeezed her waist a little more tightly. Her curves really did mould very well against his side.

'Your Grace.' Lady Castledene had produced a sycophantic smile and was curtseying very deeply. 'I do hope that you find yourself…well.'

She rolled her eyes, just very slightly, in Emma's direction as she spoke. Emma stiffened and Alex glared. How *dare* this woman imply…well, the truth. Yes, obviously it was the truth, of course he wouldn't have married Emma or anyone by choice. But how *dare* she be so rude to Emma? And in front of him. Emma was a good person, and Alex was going to do everything he could to prevent her becoming a social pariah.

He wanted to be extremely rude to Lady Castledene and her party, but that probably wouldn't be the right approach, given that they probably didn't realise he'd overheard the last part of their conversation before he'd joined them.

'Yes, very well, thank you,' he said, continuing to grip Emma's waist very tightly. 'I count myself a very fortunate man and am greatly looking forward to taking my wife home to begin our honeymoon.'

He pressed his lips again to Emma's hair, which felt odd, given that they really were not man and wife in the conventional sense, but was no great hardship, because that scent was just…*tantalising*. It drew you in.

He looked Lady Castledene in her narrowed eye and smiled. It really shouldn't be too hard to convince people that he was happy to be married to Emma. By anyone's standards she was a beautiful woman, and she was known to be an heiress, and the *ton* was a hugely shallow environment. They—*he*—just needed to brazen things out.

'Indeed.' Lady Castledene produced a smile of her own, very tight-lipped, and added, 'We must wish you well, Your Grace.'

She'd actually managed to turn her body so that it was as though she was speaking only to Alex and not to Emma.

'Thank you.' Alex bowed his head, shifted himself and Emma a little, so that they were both facing the group, and said, 'We're both very grateful for your good wishes.'

'We enjoyed your wedding breakfast, but were concerned that something might be amiss when we saw that you weren't able to attend yourselves.' Lady Castledene gave him a smug *How will you trump that?* smile.

'We wished to return home to the children as soon as possible. The only thing that's amiss is that the journey is long, so we haven't yet been able to be alone to begin our honeymoon,' Alex said.

Thank God they wouldn't know that he'd chosen to travel separately from Emma today. In hindsight, that had been a mistake from a gossip perspective.

'If you'll excuse us?' He removed his arm from Emma's waist and took her hand, linking his fingers through hers, and tugged her gently towards a doorway through which he could see his man, Graham, indicating, presumably, the private dining room that had been arranged for them.

He kissed the top of her head again as they went through the door, as Graham made a discreet exit.

Alex waited until the door was firmly closed before releasing Emma's hand and walking round to the other side of the table that had been laid for them to pull her chair out for her.

'Thank you,' she said as she sat down. 'And I must thank you also for rescuing me. Again.'

Alex shook his head. 'I'm only sorry that you had to experience that.'

'It wasn't a great surprise,' Emma said, taking a small bread roll from the basket he was holding out for her. 'I've met those women before on several occasions, and they had a lot to say about my father's origins.'

'I'm sorry.'

'Really, there's nothing to be sorry about. There are nice people and not-so-nice people everywhere, and I don't think I'm the only woman not to have loved her Season. There might be a particularly large amount of venom amongst the *ton*, but I always feel that one of the reasons so many of them engage in such awfulness is that they just don't have enough to *do*. I can't imagine a lot of people thriving in that environment.'

'I think you're right.' Alex broke off a piece of his own bread roll. 'Although, in fairness, I did have a lot of fun during the Season when I was young.' He paused for a moment as he was hit by a memory of meeting Diana, then collected himself and continued. 'But men have boxing and horses and financial affairs with which to busy themselves, in addition to all the social events.'

'Indeed. Whereas for women there's only gossip, shopping and visits to the dressmakers. And perhaps it isn't so enjoyable for slightly older men?'

'I certainly didn't enjoy *this* Season,' Alex agreed.

'Partly because you were being hounded by fortune-hunters such as myself?' Emma said.

'Exactly.' He smiled at her. 'That plan you hatched with Sir Peter and your aunt was *fiendish* in its ingenuity.'

'I know. We are geniuses.' Emma paused. 'Joking aside, I'm going to apologise and thank you one more time.'

Alex shook his head. 'Don't. We both know that neither of us would have chosen this, but I'd like to think we can make things work adequately for both of us.'

He was beginning to think that he was going to be able to cope reasonably happily with Emma being in his life. It was a positive sign that they could already laugh together about how they'd been compromised into this situation. He wasn't sure it was going to be so good for her, though. She obviously didn't have a single friend in Somerset and, going by the way she kept chatting to people, she was sociable and would be lonely if she was ostracised by the neighbours.

'I wonder whether, with your permission, it might be sensible to demonstrate our mutual affection a little more in front of those people.' Good Lord. He'd just had the thought that it might be a good idea to *kiss* her in front of them.

'They are some of the most gossipy of all the gossips,' Emma said. 'Maybe we ought to. If you think it wise?'

'Probably.'

Good Lord again. He didn't even *mind* the thought of kissing her, since there was going to be a good reason for it. If it happened. It might not happen. They might not see them again.

Maybe they should change the subject.

'What do you know of Somerset?' he asked.

Dinner was pleasant. Emma was very interested in the history and geography of the south-west of the country, and had interesting knowledge to impart on Lancashire and the rest of the north-west, an area that Alex had never visited.

They whiled away the time with amiable conversation, which at times even led to proper laughter on both sides.

'So, the pistol?' he found himself asking some time later. 'Your father deemed it important to educate you at a seminary for young ladies...and also to teach you to shoot?'

'Yes, indeed, and to fence. And to assist him in the

running of the factories. I learned about the machinery, the different fabrics, and the economics behind the business. My father taught me as he would have taught a son. He was very forward-thinking.'

'Indeed.'

Not so forward-thinking that he hadn't tried to force his daughter into marriage with an aristocrat, whether she wanted it or not.

'Other than in regard to his ideas on marriage, of course,' she said, as though reading his thoughts. She paused, and then asked a little hesitantly, 'And you...? Were you very young when you got married?'

'Yes,' he said. 'Twenty-three.'

Emma smiled at him and tilted her head a little to the side, as though expecting or hoping for elaboration. He wasn't going to elaborate. He couldn't talk about Diana this evening. He might become uncomfortably emotional.

He reached for the pitcher between them and said, 'Would you like more wine? I find this a very tolerable red. If you enjoy wine, you will be pleased to hear that we maintain a large cellar at the castle.'

He began an anecdote about smugglers on the Somerset coast, and before long had Emma laughing and the conversation moved far away from any further questions about his late wife.

'Would you like another drink?' he asked Emma some time later, when they'd agreed that the inn's cook was very good but that they could neither of them eat any more.

'No, thank you. I think...' She looked at him, as though trying to gauge what he'd like her to say. 'I think

I might perhaps go to bed now. Unless you'd like to stay downstairs a little longer?'

'Now is perfect for me.'

But he was thinking of the oddness of their going upstairs together, and from her suddenly more reserved demeanour it looked as though Emma was too.

They moved towards the door together—very politely, barely speaking—and Alex opened it for Emma to pass through.

As luck would have it—as though the woman had been listening out for them—the door opposite them opened precisely as they were leaving the room, and one of Lady Castledene's daughters came out.

'Good evening,' she said.

'Shall we?' Alex said into Emma's ear.

'Yes,' she whispered.

He reached his arms around her waist from behind and turned her towards him in what he hoped was a convincing show of husbandly ardour. Then he leaned down to kiss her on the lips, one eye on the woman opposite, whom he was pleased to see was now outright staring at them.

He lingered in the kiss for a moment, wanting to ensure that he looked suitably enthusiastic, and moved his hands to cup Emma's face, because that was what you did when you were kissing someone passionately.

The kiss was as chaste as a kiss on the lips could be, and purely for show. And then...

And then he became aware of the softness of Emma's lips, smelled that frankly almost intoxicating scent again, and felt his entire body begin to respond to her nearness, to the sensation of her lips under his, his hands on her face. He found himself moving his hands into her

thick hair, holding her tight against him, enjoying—
really enjoying—the way she was beginning to open
her mouth to him.

Their tongues met, and explored, and almost danced
together, and then he lost awareness of their surroundings, deepening the kiss ever more, conscious only now
of Emma, and the way it felt as though his entire body
were aflame.

She tasted wonderful. Sweet, tempting, in a different
way from Diana.

Diana.

He didn't want to enjoy kissing a woman he *knew*.
And he didn't just *know* Emma, she was his *wife*. He
didn't want to become close to her and then lose her.
One terrible grief in a lifetime was enough.

He could feel himself freezing, his hands, body,
mouth now unnaturally still. Emma was clearly sens-
ing his stillness too; she herself had stilled and with-
drawn slightly.

He opened his eyes, which he must have closed somewhere along the way, and, yes, that damned woman was
still standing opposite them, still staring.

Well, they'd been at it long enough now, he judged,
for it not to look odd if they stopped.

He drew back slowly, keeping an arm around Emma,
and coughed.

'Good evening,' he said to the lady.

She might still gossip about Emma having compromised him, but she would be less able to describe him
as an unwilling participant in their marriage now.

She flushed a deep red and whisked herself back inside the room out of which she'd come. Which was ideal,
because it made Emma look up at him with pure glee

on her face, which made him laugh, which made what could have been a very awkward post-fake kiss moment much less awkward.

He held out his arm to her again and they headed over to the inn's staircase.

'Your Graces.' The landlord had emerged from nowhere—he must have been waiting for them so perhaps he'd witnessed their kiss too—and was bowing. 'Allow me to escort you to your chambers.'

And up the stairs the three of them went.

Alex's man was waiting outside his room and Jenny was outside Emma's, a little further along the corridor.

'Thank you so much,' Emma said to Jenny. 'But I think I can prepare myself for bed this evening.'

'Oh, no, Your Grace, I need to help you.' Jenny swivelled her eyes in the direction of Emma's door, clearly keen to be involved in her wedding night preparations.

Alex had to try hard not to wince.

'Really, Jenny, there is no need. Thank you, and I'll see you in the morning.' Emma's voice was impressively steely; if she used that voice on Alex's sons they might even do as they were told.

As Jenny left them, followed by Alex's man and the landlord, Alex opened the door to his chamber and held it so that Emma could go in ahead of him.

She walked straight into the middle of the room and then turned to face him as he closed and locked the door.

'I think we should lock your door too,' he said, very quietly, in case any of the apparently many interested parties were listening on the other side of the door.

He looked at the bed. He was going to have to remember to make it look as though they'd both been in it for at least a portion of the night.

Emma was looking at the bed too. 'I'll take great care to make my bed in the morning so that no one can tell that I slept in it,' she said. 'Fortunately I don't toss and turn at night.'

Alex really didn't want to think about Emma in bed, in her nightdress. Perhaps her maid had put a wedding night gown out for her. Well, of course she would have done.

He swallowed. This was not going the way he'd planned; he didn't want to be having thoughts of this nature about Emma. Time to bid her goodnight and force his thoughts in a more sensible direction.

Chapter Six

'Excellent,' the duke said.

'So, goodnight, then,' said Emma, trying hard not to stare at his face, his chest, his…everything.

For the last few minutes, since their amazing kiss downstairs, she'd been struggling not to think all manner of things she shouldn't.

Why had he seemed so lost in the kiss and then suddenly frozen?

What might have happened next if they'd been alone in a room together?

How would she have felt if it had continued?

Would it ever happen again?

She hoped not, obviously. Really, she did. Although it *had* been very nice.

The duke swallowed again and Emma realised that she was staring at his strong neck, the movement of his Adam's apple, his jawline, those firm lips that had only a few minutes ago been against hers…

'Goodnight,' he said. 'Sleep well.'

His eyes slid to the wide bed to the side of them as he spoke, and Emma's followed his, and now she was swallowing, too, as her mind went in all sorts of directions about what a normal wedding night with him might have entailed.

'Thank you. And you too,' she said, and stepped forward, fast, to get herself into her own bedroom and stop having these ridiculous thoughts.

She put her hand on the door handle and turned. Nothing. She jiggled a bit. It was locked.

'Um. Your Grace. Alexander.' How should she address him? She turned to face the duke, to discover that he was already searching for a key, along the mantelpiece and then on the shelves in the corner of the room at the end of the wall the door was in.

'Call me Alex.' He opened two drawers in a little table in the corner and closed them again. 'It must be here somewhere,' he said.

Emma squared her shoulders; it was hard not to feel put out that he sounded *quite* so desperate to get rid of her. Although he was probably tired after his long ride today. And perhaps he wanted to be alone—as she did, she reminded herself—to digest the fact that for better or worse they, two complete strangers, were now legally bound together.

As the duke—Alex—reached for a high shelf, she saw the muscles in his shoulders flex, and shivered, remembering how he'd looked earlier today when, in his shirtsleeves, he'd been working with the coachman and coach hands to right the stagecoach.

And she'd been pressed right up against all that muscle and hardness earlier, when they kissed.

For the first and last time, obviously.

'I can't find a key anywhere.' Alex turned round, put his hands on his lean hips and scoured the room with his eyes. 'This is ridiculous. It must be an oversight.'

'Perhaps we should go and ask for it.'

'I doubt people would expect us to have noticed yet.'

Emma nodded. It was true. They would be expected to be otherwise engaged. Kissing and…more. You couldn't grow up in the country, even with a father as protective as hers had been, without gaining a certain amount of knowledge of the way intimacies worked. And you really couldn't spend several hours in a chaise with Jenny on your wedding day without gaining further knowledge on the subject.

Five minutes' more fruitless searching convinced them both that there was no key to be found.

'Right,' said Alex, hands on hips again, 'we need a plan. You can sleep on the bed and I'll sleep in this chair.'

Emma slightly wanted to cry at the ridiculousness of their supposed wedding night and she *really* wanted to use the chamber pot, and she didn't want to do either of those things in front of Alex.

'I know what we could do,' she said, finally summoning up some clear thought. 'If you went round to my chamber via the corridor, perhaps with your boots off, that would look, um, intimate, husbandly, and you could perhaps, if you don't encounter anyone, just stay in there while I stay here?'

'You're right. Panic was clearly addling our brains.' Alex took his boots off, and then also his jacket, while Emma focused on a picture on the wall, again not wishing to look as though she was staring at him, particularly because she actually *did* want to stare.

'Yes, I think the best thing would be if I stay in there and then return in the morning. Perhaps we can swap then, to get dressed. Right. I'm off.' He did an exaggerated tiptoe towards the door, which made her laugh through the misery that had suddenly threatened to engulf her.

'You look as though you're an actor in a farce,' she hissed as he poked his head out of the door and looked left and right.

'This *is* a farce,' he whispered, and then made a dash for it, closing the door behind him, while Emma tried not to reflect on the fact that many a true word was spoken in jest.

Alex had just referred to their situation as a farce and…that did not feel good. Even though it was true.

She looked at the closed door for a moment and then shook her head. There was no point standing here feeling maudlin about her new life situation. Things could be worse.

She looked over at the bed. Things could be better, actually. Practically speaking, she didn't have a nightgown, or her hairbrushes, or *anything*. She'd very much like her book, at the very least, because she didn't feel as though she was going to sleep easily tonight.

She walked over to the bed and thumped down in the middle of it, then sniffed and wiped under her eyes with her forefingers as a couple of tears trickled out. She shouldn't be feeling this miserable. Tonight wasn't going to be wonderful, but once they arrived in Somerset things would be much better.

She flung herself backwards and wriggled herself into the very comfortable bed. She needed to cheer up immediately. This really wasn't the worst it could have been; it was in fact far better than it might have been. Of *course* she could be happy in a marriage with Alex without intimacy. It would just be like living with a friend. She might, for example, have been dealing with Sir Peter's husbandly advances right now. Or already on her way to living in penury. And this bed was *so* comfortable.

Hearing a clatter at the connecting door, she raised herself on one elbow. And then Alex walked through the door, saying, 'Surprise. The key was in the other side.'

'Oh. *Oh*. I can't believe we didn't think of that.'

'That's panic for you.'

'Well, thank goodness.' Emma gave up on trying to sit up from where she was—the bed was so soft that she'd sunk too far down to be able to get herself straight up—and turned onto her side, trying to ignore the fact that this was remarkably undignified.

As she turned, Alex's legs and—she gulped—more appeared in front of her, and he put his hand out.

'Thank you,' she said.

He hauled a little too hard and she almost flew off the bed, landing against his hard chest. He let go of her immediately and took a step backwards, clearly extremely eager not to touch her at all if he didn't have to.

'I think I misjudged your weight.' He smiled the slightly twisted smile she was already coming to recognise as very particular to him.

'Yes.' And suddenly she was so tired of this day. 'Goodnight, then.'

'Goodnight.'

Once she was in her own room, she locked both the door to the corridor and the connecting door and then lay down on the bed, the events of the day jostling in her brain.

The 'I now pronounce thee man and wife' moment featured heavily, and so did the acquisition of the kittens, of course, as did the true nastiness of Lady Castledene and her party. But the thing that she couldn't stop thinking about the most was the kiss. Or The Kiss, as she was fairly sure she'd think of it in her mind for evermore.

She'd kissed a few men before, including a couple of the men who'd proposed to her—while she'd decided that she didn't need or indeed *want* to be in love with the person she married, she'd thought it would be better to *like* them, both emotionally and physically, so she hadn't been averse to a little experimentation—and none of those kisses had been anything compared to the one she'd shared with Alex.

And it hadn't even been a proper one; it had only been for show.

It might be the last time she ever kissed a man.

After several hours tossing and turning—she was going to have a *lot* of work to do before she left the room in the morning to make her bed look un-slept-in—Emma was finally in a very deep sleep when she was woken by what she realised was a persistent tapping on the connecting door.

She dragged herself out of bed and walked over and opened it, putting only her head round the edge, so that Alex wouldn't see her in the embarrassing wedding-night nightgown her aunt had had made for her and Jenny had put out for her to wear last night.

She'd worried a lot during the night that she'd been too enthusiastic when Alex had kissed her, and she really didn't want to look as though she was throwing herself at him when he clearly had no interest in her.

'I'd very much like to leave as soon as possible,' Alex told her. 'If that's all right?'

'Of course. I'll be ready as soon as I can.'

Maybe she should make the bed very carefully and

then call for Jenny, she thought as she closed the door. Or maybe that would be too risky. Maybe Jenny would be able to tell, somehow, that they hadn't...

Yes, she should probably dress herself.

Living a life of deception was going to be ridiculously complicated. She and Alex should probably find a way of her removing to his dower house as soon as possible.

Fifteen minutes later, she was extremely hot from trying to do up all her buttons. She was never going to manage to look suitably duchess-like without help from *someone*. The question was: should that someone be Jenny...or Alex?

She walked back to the bed that she'd spent ages smoothing down earlier, and then looked around the room. Going by what Jenny frequently had to say, about all sorts of people from all walks of life, she had a very strong nose for lying and also for anything to do with marital or extramarital relations. She'd probably have a strong nose for a lack of marital relations too.

Sighing, Emma walked over to the connecting door and knocked, before opening it slightly. Alex was sitting on the chair in the room, putting his boots on.

'Good morning. I wonder if you could help me finish dressing? I thought that might be best, just for today.'

'Of course.' Alex stood up, one boot on and one boot off. 'As you will see from my footwear, I also decided that today it would be best to dress myself, and am also struggling.'

Emma laughed. 'I imagine that your man and Jenny would both be delighted to know that they're genuinely indispensable. I'm sure you'll be able to do my buttons up, but I wouldn't let you loose on my hair, and I have literally no idea how anyone gets someone's foot inside boots that fit as tightly as those.'

'I know. Graham is a true genius.' Alex moved towards her. 'Where are these buttons?'

Emma felt suddenly breathless, as though her dress was too tight, which was ridiculous, given that it wasn't even fully done up yet.

'Just at the top, at the back.'

She turned round for him and lifted her hair out of the way. How was it that she was fully dressed and was indeed asking him to dress her *more*, and yet felt almost naked at this moment?

She sensed Alex move closer to her and lift his hands towards her neck. She could barely breathe. He took the fabric very gently and tugged at it a little. The room was completely silent other than the sounds of their breathing—such as it was in Emma's case—and the very faint rustle of the silk as Alex tried to do up the buttons.

'This is a lot more difficult than you would think.' Alex's breath skimmed across her skin as he spoke. Clearly, he had his head bent close to her so that he could see what he was doing, and Emma was sure that the tiny hairs on the back of her neck had risen.

'Jenny's obviously a genius too.' Emma cleared her throat to get rid of the croak that her voice suddenly contained.

'Would you mind if I…?' Alex's voice was croaky too now. 'If I moved your hair a little further?'

'Of course not.'

Emma was braced for the contact, but she still almost jumped a mile when Alex's fingers brushed the skin at the base of her neck as he carefully lifted her hair. She was remembering now how he'd thrust his fingers into her hair during their kiss last night.

'Nearly done,' he grunted.

Emma was struggling not to close her eyes and just melt into the feeling of his fingers against her when suddenly she felt actual pain. *'Ow,'* she squeaked.

'Don't move.'

He tugged some strands of hair very gently, and, *oh*, his fingers against her scalp and her neck felt good.

'You have some hair caught in a button. I am *really* not good at this.'

'Mmm,' Emma said.

He was wrong. He *was* good. *So* good. His fingers were gently moving more of her hair now, and she just wanted to lean into his hand. If she just took a step she'd be leaning against his very solid chest, too, and…

And… What was she *thinking*? He was literally doing her buttons up for her, very incompetently; and this wasn't a matter of *intimacy*, it was just a matter of expediency.

His fingers were still working at her neck and it was utter torture. In a very blissful way.

'This time I really have finished.' His voice sounded heavier than usual. He stepped backwards and Emma turned round, suddenly incredibly self-conscious for no good reason at all.

'Thank you so much.'

The hairs at the nape of her neck were going to be standing on end for hours to come at the memory of how he'd touched her there, she was sure. She was struggling to remember what time of day it was, even. *Breakfast.* It was breakfast time.

'Should we perhaps go below stairs for breakfast now?' she suggested.

'We should. As soon as I've wrestled myself into my other boot.'

'I'd like to offer to help, but I've no idea what I could do.'

'I'll be fine.' Alex sat down again and inserted his foot into the boot. 'I'm a grown man. Of course I can dress myself. How hard can it be?'

Very hard, it seemed.

Emma gave up on politeness quite quickly and laughed and laughed, which was an excellent way of recovering from his doing up her buttons.

Finally properly booted, Alex stood up and shook his head at her. 'I'm not sure people are going to expect the Duchess of Harwell to behave with such a lack of decorum.'

'I'm not sure people would expect the Duke of Harwell to be so incredibly incompetent at putting his own foot into a boot.'

They smiled at each other and then Alex said, 'Right. Breakfast.'

'Your Graces.' The landlord was bowing almost as low as had the man at the inn where they'd stopped yesterday at midday. 'I must apologise. I didn't realise you would be descending so early in the day for breakfast. Allow me just a minute or two to make a private room available.'

'Do you mean that you're going to ask someone to leave a private room?' Emma asked.

'Yes, Your Grace. I'll make sure that they're quick.'

'No, please don't.' Emma was horrified: this felt awful. It was a good reminder that she was going to have to be on her guard constantly to ensure that other people weren't frequently inconvenienced just because she was a duchess. 'We can very well eat in the public room.'

'But Your *Grace*. You're…' The landlord gave a hand wave in her direction that clearly meant *You're a duchess*. 'You're newly married.'

'Even so, we cannot be the cause of the ruination of others' breakfasts.'

'And we will have many other breakfasts together, just the two of us, once we reach our own home,' Alex said, so soulfully that Emma nearly laughed. 'My wife and I are indeed very well able to sit in the public room. I see that there is a table free there.'

He held out his arm to Emma and turned towards the table.

'Very good, Your Grace, if you're sure.'

Settled at the table in the public room, Alex broke his fast with ale and steak, while Emma chose a selection of fruits and some toast. They filled the first few minutes of their meal with low-voiced small-talk, about the journey to come and the Somerset climate, until very suddenly Alex leaned in and said, 'The Castledene party—and they are staring.'

Emma's hands were empty, and he reached across and took them in his and drew them towards him.

Emma said, *'Oh,'* and then tried to change it into something that sounded more amorous than surprised. *'Ooh.'* No, that just sounded odd.

'Ooh?' Alex whispered, still holding on to her hands.

'I was trying to sound amorous.'

When he was looking at her in that half-laughing way, it wasn't actually very difficult to imagine feeling amorous. In a purely physical way, obviously.

Alex squeezed her hands, then let go of them and picked up his cutlery again. 'They definitely noticed.'

'You look very smug.'

'We're excellent actors.'

'Oh, yes, we are.' Emma batted her eyelids at him and pouted, and he grinned at her. This acting thing really wasn't that difficult with someone who was as easy to be with as Alex. She'd found it a lot more difficult to pretend that she enjoyed the company of most of the men her aunt had been so desperate for her to get to know earlier in the Season.

She heard a loud throat-clearing behind her, and glanced over her shoulder as one of the Miss Castledenes stared at her for just a second too long—clearly on purpose—and then dropped her eyes without smiling.

She turned back to Alex and almost gasped at the way his eyes had become like flints and his lips had tightened to a thin line. His Ice Duke demeanour again. She hoped that he'd never look at *her* like that.

'Bordering on the cut direct,' he said. 'I will *not* have you treated like that.' He put his cutlery down, took her hands in his again, and said in a low voice, 'We should have thought of this before, but I suppose we've been caught up in too much of a whirlwind. We should concoct a story about how we first met.' He smiled at her. 'We were, of course, secretly courting before the ball at the beginning of the week.'

'Oh, yes. And we kept our mutual affection secret because we sensed that it was something perfect and we didn't want to risk it being spoilt by too much attention.'

'Yes, our love was pure and strong, but also delicate and fragile.'

'Alex, you should try your hand at poetry. I think you would be competition for Byron himself.'

Alex laughed and then, making his eyes very wide, said, 'I'm not a natural poet. It is you and you alone who brings this out in me. It has been so since the first moment we laid eyes on each other.'

'Across a crowded ballroom?'

'Certainly not. Nothing so mundane. We were...' He stopped and frowned, and then said, 'Um, what *were* we doing? We didn't meet at a ball or any other kind of party, did we? Because people would have seen us. And obviously talked.'

'Don't you remember?' Emma said, struck by a brainwave. 'You were my knight in shining armour. I was riding early one morning with my maid when my horse ran away with me and I was saved by you on your horse. As we were riding alone, neither of us knew who the other was, and neither of us wanted to reveal our true identities, but we both knew that Cupid's arrow had immediately struck and that we should keep our pure, strong but delicate and fragile love to ourselves for the time being, especially as neither of us was sure that Society would approve the other as an appropriate match for us. We then met surreptitiously in a variety of secret locations. We were on the brink of announcing our love to the world when Sir Peter forced our hand by attempting to compromise me. We are now, of course, deeply grateful to him, as we might otherwise have ended up waiting longer to marry.'

'I like that,' said Alex, nodding approvingly. 'Have you perhaps invented a big lie before? You're very good at it.'

'Never.' Emma shook her head. 'But I agree that I do seem to have a great talent for it. I'm pleased to have discovered it.'

'Yes, I'm sure it will stand you in excellent stead on any number of future occasions.' Alex squeezed her hands again and then let go. 'I'm still hungry. I can't keep holding your hands because then I can't eat.'

'Is not love alone enough to sustain you?'

'Love and just a little more of this steak, purely because it really is delicious and I don't want to offend the landlord. And I have a long way to ride today.' He took a mouthful, and then said, 'Actually, I ought to ride in the carriage, I think, if you don't mind. Just for the first part of the journey.'

'Yes, you're probably right.' Emma eyed Miss Castledene, who was now staring at them from across the room. 'I almost want to *slap* that woman.'

Alex nodded. 'Indeed. So, we're agreed about me coming in the chaise with you for the start of the journey? I wonder if it might be better for Jenny to travel in one of the other carriages at that point.'

'Definitely.' If Jenny was with them they'd have to play-act all morning. 'But we can still have the kittens with us.'

'Really?'

'Really. They're adorable.'

And they would also be something to concentrate on instead of Alex, because this was suddenly feeling too much again. It was confusing. Currently, they were trying to demonstrate to everyone that they were a normal married couple to avoid gossip. How and when were they going to stop that?

She wanted to ask Alex, but she wasn't sure how to

broach it. Maybe it would be easier once they were in Somerset. They would settle down, the staff would learn that they weren't a particularly amorous couple, and everything would become easier. *Hopefully.*

A few minutes later, Alex had finished demolishing his steak and was sailing past the Castledene group with Emma on his arm.

'I shall look forward to calling on you in London, Your Grace,' said the younger Miss Castledene to Emma, who nearly gasped out loud at her effrontery.

How could anyone go from that level of rudeness to pretending to be friends with someone mere minutes later? Lady Castledene and her older daughter were both nodding vigorously.

'I shall look forward to receiving you,' Emma said, and almost achieved a real smile. Really, her acting skills were superb, if she said so herself.

'I think it worked,' Alex said as they got into the chaise.

'Really?' Emma wasn't so sure.

'Well, of course. People will hate you for a while, because you snaffled a duke, and there are never that many of us available on the marriage mart at any given time. But once they've come to terms with the fact that you are the new duchess, and as long as no gossip attaches to you and you are seen to be regarded highly by me, they will all endeavour to be your friend and invite you to everything.'

'How delightful,' Emma said. 'I look forward to a lifetime of fake friendships.'

'Indeed.' Alex smiled at her and Emma smiled back—

a real smile—and then they both fell silent, and she remembered that they were near strangers, bound together only by their farcical marriage.

Chapter Seven

Alex would never under normal circumstances choose to travel in an enclosed space with three cats, but it was actually a relief when his groom deposited Emma's kittens with them.

His plan to remain aloof from her had very much not gone to plan during their stay at the inn, and he was keen to withdraw a little, but he didn't want to be rude, and it wouldn't be particularly pleasant for either of them to travel entirely in silence—unless Emma was actually engrossed in her book for hours on end—so the kittens would be a welcome diversion.

He settled back into his corner of the chaise, unable to help smiling as Emma immediately started cooing over the kittens and tickling and playing with them.

He really did need to remember to maintain a distance between the two of them. He'd enjoyed their kiss far too much—indeed, he might easily have gone a lot further had they been alone—and during breakfast he'd found himself furious on Emma's behalf that the Castledenes were being so insolent to her.

Apparently, he'd already started to care a little for her.

As a friend, he supposed. You didn't enjoy kissing your friends, though. Well, maybe you did when the friend was such an attractive woman. It had probably been just a natural physical reaction.

It was fortunate that they'd be arriving in Somerset by the end of the day. He'd switch to his horse again well before that, too.

He'd better remember to agree with Emma in advance of the horse change where they were going to stop for their luncheon; there was no point annoying her in that regard again.

'You're beautiful,' Emma told the kittens, for about the twentieth time.

Alex laughed. 'You're spoiling them.'

'I'm not. I'm just stating facts.' She kissed one of the kittens on the nose and it purred contentedly. She and the kittens did make a lovely picture together as she played with them, her thick, silky, dark brown hair falling over her face and their tiny black bodies.

'Are you enjoying travelling with them?' he asked as she got one of the kittens into the box they'd brought for it in the nick of time.

'Of course,' she said.

When the kitten had finished its business, she picked it up and deposited it with its siblings in their bed, shut the basket, then leaned back against the bench and closed her eyes for a moment, the picture of exhaustion.

'You know, I would never have guessed that you hadn't been familiar with cats before.'

Emma ignored him. 'We might need to stop and change their straw.'

Alex sniffed. 'Sooner rather than later, do you think?'

'Probably.'

'I knew you'd soon think better of having them as travel companions.'

'No, they're delightful. I think they could do with a sleep, though. They're very young.'

'Of course.'

She narrowed her eyes at him. 'Are you laughing at me?'

'Yes, I think I am.'

'Hmm. Well, if you don't mind, I think I'm going to read my book now.' She made a great show of pulling it out of her reticule, before shooting him a cheeky little grin, at which Alex could do nothing other than smile.

He couldn't help noticing that she didn't turn a lot of pages while she was supposedly reading. But he shouldn't talk to her. He was supposed to be remaining aloof. It really was very boring, though, just sitting doing nothing. This was why he'd always rather ride.

'What are you reading?' he asked eventually.

'A book called *Emma* by the author of *Pride and Prejudice.*'

'Oh, yes.'

Diana had read and enjoyed that. He took a deep, slow breath to dispel the unwelcome dark thoughts that often still washed over him when he was reminded of his loss, and then raised his head to find that Emma was looking at him.

'Are you all right?' she asked.

No. Not really.

It was odd when your new wife—Emma *was* actually his wife—reminded you of your late one. Especially when you'd had no wish to marry the new wife.

'Just a…difficult memory. My late wife enjoyed those books.'

He frowned. He hardly ever mentioned Diana, and certainly not to near strangers, but, oddly, he could almost imagine talking more to Emma about Diana, telling her what an avid reader she had been, and even how much he missed her. It was as though over breakfast they'd breached the barrier between mere acquaintance and the beginnings of a friendship, which was not what he'd been planning.

'I'm so sorry; it must be very difficult. You must miss her hugely.'

Alex swallowed hard and nodded. 'Yes. Thank you.'

They both lapsed into silence, and it was a relief when they arrived at the next inn. Firstly, because the cats' straw really did need to be changed, for the comfort of their travelling companions, and secondly, because it gave Alex the opportunity to switch to horseback. It was unsettling, talking so much to Emma.

'So we'll meet in about an hour and a half for luncheon,' he confirmed with her before they set off again.

The inn at which they'd agreed to stop was a small one, which Alex hadn't used before, his favoured one being closed for refurbishment following water damage, and it didn't contain a private room. It also didn't contain any guests whom either of them knew personally, so they were able to sit down in the public room without incident.

'May I ask a few more questions about life in Somerset?' Emma said.

'Of course.'

'I presume that your household is a large one?' she asked, once the landlady had placed a steaming rabbit stew in front of them and apologised for a second time that she didn't have any more elegant fare for them, and Emma had reassured her for a second time that there was nothing that she wanted more at this moment than rabbit stew.

'Yes, I suppose so. Yes, it is.' Alex hoped Emma wasn't going to try to work the conversation round to Diana again. He took her plate and picked up a ladle. 'Are you hungry?'

Emma looked into the tureen, where there were a few lumps of something that was presumably rabbit in a thin broth with blobs of grease floating on the top.

'Just a little,' she said. 'It looks delicious, but I ate very well at breakfast.'

Alex nodded, also strongly tempted to rely on his breakfast to see him through until dinnertime.

'So, your household?' Emma prompted, staring at the three twisted pieces of meat and the oily liquid he'd placed in her bowl.

'You'll meet my—*our*—housekeeper, Mrs Drabble, when we arrive.' Alex was surprised to note that he didn't particularly mind the thought of sharing his staff with Emma. 'She's a wonderful housekeeper, but notoriously difficult. If you ask…' His words petered out as he thought that the best person for Emma to have asked about Mrs Drabble would have been Diana.

'Your late wife?' Emma supplied after a pause. 'I'm so sorry.'

'Thank you.' Alex turned his attention to his stew to hide his emotion, and unwisely took a large mouthful.

He was still chewing some time later, grateful that Emma hadn't said anything further about Diana, when she leaned forward and said in a low voice, 'Will I also meet your chef?'

'Emma. What are you implying…?' That this food was the most inedible he could remember tasting in years? There were many advantages to being a duke, and one of those was that he was nearly always served well-cooked meals made from high quality ingredients.

She twinkled at him, and he laughed around the piece of gristle he was *still* chewing.

When he'd eventually swallowed it, he pointed his knife at her plate accusingly. 'Have you had any?'

'Yes.' Emma nodded. 'You gave me a large portion, which I've very much enjoyed, but having had an equally large breakfast, I find myself unable to finish these last three morsels.'

'You're already utilising your newfound talent for invention,' Alex said. 'I'm impressed.'

'Thank you.' She beamed at him and he laughed again.

They passed the rest of the mealtime in inconsequential chatter, before setting off in good time to arrive in Somerset before dark, Emma in the chaise and Alex riding at a safe distance from her far too beguiling presence, but close enough to keep an eye on her entourage.

Once they were within striking distance of the castle, and Alex was sure that he was no longer required for Emma's protection, he rode ahead in order to arrive well before the carriages. He wanted both to welcome Emma—while this situation hadn't been his choice, it hadn't been hers either, and it was clearly the least he could do—and, more importantly, greet his sons and explain to them that there was a new member of the household.

'Papa,' hollered Freddie, the oldest, tearing across

the great hall towards him, followed by his two younger siblings.

Alex swept the three of them into a huge bear hug and just stood there, holding them tightly for a while. He hated the fact that he'd had to be away from them, and he hated the fact that he was about to foist upon them a new— God, *what*? Stepmother? Governess? Temporary house guest before she moved to the dower house?

He couldn't believe that only a few hours ago he'd been sitting merrily eating with her and laughing about rabbit stew. He should have been thinking about the impact her arrival might have on his sons. And last night… he'd only been thinking about Emma.

All wrong.

'Did you bring us presents?' asked Harry, the youngest.

Alex laughed. 'Excuse me, young man. You should be pleased to see me, not wondering if I have presents for you.'

'I am pleased to see you, but did you bring me a present?' Harry said.

'I might have a little something in one of the coaches when they arrive.' *Oh, yes, and also a new duchess.* 'Boys, there's something I need to tell you.'

'Is it a bad present?'

'No. The presents are *splendid*.'

They were. He didn't like the idea of spoiling them any more than the sons of dukes were by the very nature of their birth going to be spoilt, but on this occasion he'd taken some time the day before his and Emma's departure from London to buy a life-sized rocking horse, which he had to acknowledge was entirely a guilty purchase.

'I need to let you know that I have…'

He looked at them. Freddie and Harry favoured him, but John, his middle son, was completely Diana. Their mother. Whom he could not and did not want ever to replace. He couldn't describe Emma as their stepmother, or his wife. He just couldn't. He had to, though, because she *was* his new wife. Legally.

'I have married someone. Her name is Emma and she's very nice. I think you're going to like her. She's going to spend a lot of time with you, a bit like a governess would. So you won't need another governess. For now, anyway.'

John and Harry both nodded, but Freddie said, 'That's strange. Will she be called the Duchess of Harwell? Like Mama and Grandmama?'

'Er, yes, she will. She is…' Alex cast around in his mind for some words—good words—to make this sound better. 'It's just a name,' he said eventually. 'The Duchess of Harwell. Like there are three grooms called Mikey.' The boys had always loved that coincidence. 'Now there's another Duchess of Harwell. Because I, er, married her. So I'm the duke and she is the duchess.'

Excellent avoidance of the words *wife* and *stepmother*.

John and Harry nodded again, but Freddie shook his head. 'That does *not* make sense,' he said.

Correct. It did not.

They were interrupted by the sound of carriages outside.

'And here's the carriage with your present in it,' Alex said.

And here was Emma too. God, he was a coward.

In his defence, this was not an easy situation, and it was not one he'd wanted or planned *and* he'd only had a few days' preparation for it. However, Freddie's furrowed brow and look of suspicion were causing his stomach to twist uncomfortably.

He'd had the whole journey to prepare for this. He should have practised how he was going to tell them.

He realised as he went outside with the boys that, despite the advanced hour of the day, Mrs Drabble had what looked like the entire household lined up to welcome Emma—or to gawp at her and take an immediate dislike to her.

If he'd had any space left in his heart to pity anyone beyond his sons, he'd have been feeling very sorry for Emma right now.

Alex looked at his boys and then he looked at the chaise. He didn't want to betray or upset the boys by appearing to be too close to Emma. But he also didn't want to let them down by setting them a bad example.

He pressed his fingers to the bridge of his nose for a moment—he was beginning a thumping headache—and then moved forward to open the chaise door and hold his arm out to Emma.

'Thank you.' She leant on him only very lightly, and then almost immediately let go, and walked over to his butler, Lancing, and Mrs Drabble, at the head of the line of servants, directing a bright smile at them and holding her hand out.

As Mrs Drabble bobbed the tiniest of curtseys without meeting Emma's eye, Alex realised that he was almost holding his breath.

'I'm so pleased to meet you,' Emma said. 'I'm afraid that, although I ran my father's household, I have no experience in running a household of this exact nature and will need to rely heavily on your expertise.'

Having known Mrs Drabble for over twenty years,

Alex knew a chink in her armour when he saw one, and she definitely twitched—in a good way—before returning to her *'It'll take more than that to win me over thank you very much'* stance.

'Indeed, Your Grace,' she said, moving her eyes to Emma's face for the merest of moments before resuming her stare over her left shoulder.

'That was a long journey,' Emma said, for all the world as though Mrs Drabble wasn't being stunningly unfriendly. 'I wonder whether, after I've been introduced to the household, you would be able to show me to my chamber so that I might freshen up before dinner?'

'Of course, Your Grace.' There was that little twitch from Mrs Drabble again.

There was a scuffle from behind Alex, and he looked round to see John with Harry in a headlock.

'Boys,' he said in his deepest, sternest voice.

John let go, and Harry aimed a kick at him as he did so. Freddie was standing a couple of feet away from his brothers, glaring in the direction of Emma. Alex swivelled his eyes between them all and sighed internally. In time, Emma might perhaps be able to perform the miracle of winning Mrs Drabble over, but would she be able to win the boys over?

That would probably be a miracle too far for anyone.

'I should introduce you to my boys,' he said to Emma, who whipped straight round, almost overbalancing.

'I'm so sorry,' she said, moving towards them, her arms outstretched. 'I didn't see you there in the dusk.'

John and Harry immediately stood behind Freddie and looked at him, as though to see how he was going to react. And Freddie… Well, it was almost like looking in a mirror. Alex had glimpsed himself from time to time in lavishly mirrored ballrooms when faced with someone to whom he really didn't want to talk, and knew that he did the same straightening of the shoulders and complete lack of facial expression.

'How do you do?' Freddie barely moved a muscle as he spoke, but then held his right hand forward.

Emma diverted her outstretched arms—clearly intended for a hug—into shaking hands with Freddie. As they shook, the merest hint of distaste—a tiny curl of the lip and very slightly raised eyebrow—crossed Freddie's face, before he withdrew his hand just a fraction too quickly.

If he hadn't been torn between deep misery on behalf of his sons, mortification at Freddie's rudeness and sympathy for Emma, Alex would almost have been impressed. As it was, he felt as though he ought to try to improve the situation.

He took a step forward and put his arm around Freddie's shoulders, just as Emma said, 'I can't imagine that you want to waste any time talking to me when your father is just home after his stay in London. You must have so much to tell him. Why don't the four of you spend some time together while Mrs Drabble begins the mammoth task of introducing me to the house?'

She looked at all of them with a very bright and, to Alex's eyes, very forced smile, and then continued, 'In fact, I am very tired after such a long journey. I wonder if my dinner might be brought to me in my chamber just for this evening, after you've shown me around a little, Mrs Drabble? If that wouldn't inconvenience anyone too much?'

Freddie's shoulders relaxed very slightly, Mrs Drabble's

mouth twitched at the corners, as though she was on the brink of smiling, and Alex almost wanted to hug Emma.

He barely saw her again for the rest of the evening, other than a couple of glimpses of her rounding corners with Mrs Drabble and occasional snatches of her voice in conversation, and spent an enjoyable time immersing himself in the world of his children again, eating supper with them in their nursery.

Freddie didn't mention Emma at all, and neither did John or Harry. Instead, they filled him in on the dam they'd been building in a little river to the west of the estate, and the fish that they'd seen in the river, and the big fight that John and Harry had had, during which John had made Harry's nose bleed and after which Mrs Drabble had given Harry an extra custard tart to make him feel better.

It was the best evening Alex had had since before he'd left for London. In fact, now that he was back here, it was almost possible to believe that the entire marriage was a nightmare that had never really happened, until— weary after last night in the inn tossing and turning thinking about Emma, their situation and their kiss— he took himself off to bed and looked at the connecting door between his and Emma's suites and began to think, really hard, about the fact that she was just on the other side of the shared sitting room that that door led to. Probably in her nightgown.

God.

After another less than optimal night's sleep— hopefully he'd get used to Emma's presence in the house quickly—Alex was up early to break his fast before Emma could feasibly be expected to be awake, let alone ready to descend for her own breakfast. He'd see the boys and then take himself off on business around the estate. There was always more business in which he could involve himself, so it wouldn't be difficult for him to be so busy with his work and the boys that he would have little time to spend with Emma.

By the evening, his mood had calmed. Once they'd got used to the situation they would easily be able to achieve an amicably distant marriage; many aristocratic couples managed it. They could establish a routine similar to the one they'd had today, and then Emma would move to the dower house, and all would be well. She would essentially be just another pleasant person whom he knew and saw for short periods reasonably regularly. He was surrounded by people all the time, after all.

Before going to see the boys while their nurse began their evening routine, he sat down at his desk to write a quick note to let Emma know that he would unfortunately not be able to dine with her this evening. He'd contemplated sending her a message via Lancing, but that had seemed a little rude.

Oddly, it was difficult to find exactly the right words.

He screwed up the fourth piece of paper he'd started and dipped his quill into the ink for perhaps a tenth time. What was wrong with him? All he needed to say was that he was paying a long overdue visit to a neighbouring friend. There was nothing wrong with that. They'd agreed that they would lead separate lives. He hoped she wouldn't be lonely, though.

He looked at the stack of invitations to one side of the desk. Perhaps they should accept a few of those, sooner rather than later, and attend them as a couple, so that Emma had the opportunity to make friends in the neighbourhood.

It wouldn't be a problem attending dinners and dances together; it would be very different from spending time together at home.

Back to his message to Emma. What should he say?

Eventually he finished the two-sentence note—time spent on it approximately two minutes per uninspired word—and rang for Lancing to pass it to Emma, telling him that he was unavoidably required to go out this evening.

Lancing looked at him for maybe half a second longer than would have been usual and then said, 'As you wish, Your Grace.'

He was without question criticising Alex for not staying at home with his—no, Alex couldn't even *think* the word 'wife' without qualification—with Emma. This was the problem with devoted lifelong retainers. Obviously they were wonderful most of the time, but sometimes, when you just needed a bit of privacy and no criticism for your actions, you could do without them. Much like certain members of your extended family, really.

'Thank you,' he said firmly, and Lancing gave him another slightly too long look before leaving with the note.

The boys were eating their dinner when Alex reached the nursery. Emma was sitting at the table with them, helping Harry cut up his food, while Freddie and John both sat somewhat unnaturally far from her.

'Good evening,' she said to Alex, standing up. 'I hope you've had a good day. I will leave you to spend some time with the boys and bid you goodnight.'

'Goodnight,' said Alex, feeling guilty that he was effectively abandoning her to an evening of solitude.

Once she'd left the room, the boys, as always, had a lot to say—or shout—about what they'd been doing today. And Alex, as always, wondered if he should be making a better job of fatherhood.

Perhaps Emma would be able to instil a little more discipline into them, while not squashing their personalities. It was a difficult balance, and one that he didn't feel he'd achieved very well, because his main aim since they'd lost Diana the day Harry was born had been to make them feel loved, with no great regard for anything else.

'Emma took us for a walk,' Harry told him.

'She knows a lot about frogs,' John said. 'And she wanted to know about our studies and what we like doing best.'

Freddie didn't say anything for a while on the subject of Emma until, when pressed by John, he conceded that she wasn't the worst governess they'd ever had and did know a lot about animals.

'But she won't stay. They never do.'

Alex hadn't understood until he had his children quite how much being a parent could break your heart. Telling his children that they'd lost their mother and seeing the anguish of the older two had magnified his own grief immeasurably. Right now, he just wanted to hug all three of them. He also wanted to reassure them and tell them that Emma *would* stay, because she was different from the many governesses who'd left because they... Well, he hadn't *married* them. Difficult to put that into words, though, without discussing things best left undiscussed.

'You know you're the best three sons in the world?' he said instead.

'So can we have extra pudding?' John asked.

* * *

Two hours later, Alex, seated in front of a fire in the library at the great baronial hall of his friend and neighbour Gideon, Viscount Dearly, reflected again that it was good to see Gideon. They'd known each other since they were in leading strings, as their estates backed onto each other and their fathers had been friends, and then they'd been to both Eton and Oxford together; and they shared the same sporting interests and genuinely liked each other. It was a real relief after all the fakeness and plotting and, frankly, nastiness of a London Season, followed by his surprise marriage, to be home relaxing with his closest friend.

Until, inevitably—as he should have realised it would—the conversation turned to the rumour Gideon had heard about Alex's marriage.

'It's actually *true*?' Gideon said.

His incredulity wasn't surprising. Under normal circumstances there would have been no possibility of Alex's marrying without Gideon being involved.

Alex nodded. He didn't have any words. He couldn't say *Yes* without qualifying it with *unfortunately*, but that felt incredibly rude and something else—disloyal, perhaps, to Emma.

'Congratulations?' Gideon raised an eyebrow.

Alex didn't twitch. 'Thank you.'

'Please don't feel that you have to say anything, but if you do wish to talk, you know I'm the soul of discretion.'

That was true. Gideon was an excellent person in whom to confide. He was not only very discreet, but also very understanding and supportive. Perhaps that was why Alex had decided to come here this evening, he thought. Had he subconsciously wanted to talk about it?

'You got married only a couple of days ago and yet you're here with me this evening. Rumour has it that the young lady's aunt forced you into the marriage?'

Alex looked at Gideon's wide, so familiar, and currently very concerned face. And then he thought of Emma's face, and the way she looked when she was laughing, or smiling, or had concern in her eyes. Funny how you could quickly get to know someone quite well. And, God, what was he thinking? He really did *not* know her well. He couldn't betray her, though, even to his oldest and dearest friend.

'No, her aunt didn't force me into it,' he stated. 'I…'

Gideon said nothing; he just poured them both more brandy.

Alex really did want to talk about it, he realised, but he didn't want to say anything bad about Emma.

'Basically, I saw Sir Peter Fortescue trying to compromise her into marriage. He managed to tear the bodice of her dress and summon a huge crowd of people to witness the whole thing. She would have been ruined if she hadn't finished the evening betrothed, and I couldn't abandon her to that fate. So I asked her to marry me.'

'I see.' Gideon nodded. 'And that was that?'

'It actually wasn't. She tried very hard to refuse me. She's an extremely honourable woman. One of the few young ladies I've met who wasn't desperate to become a duchess, and she didn't want to see me trapped into a marriage she knew I didn't want. I had to convince her that I needed her as governess to the boys.'

'And do you think you could be happy with her?'

'No.' The answer shot straight out of Alex's mouth. 'I will never be happy with another woman. I don't want to be.'

'Because?' Gideon stared. 'Oh. You're scared of losing someone again.'

Alex nodded, not surprised by how perceptive he was.

'I'm sorry. That's a very difficult situation.'

Alex nodded again. And then he said, 'A game of piquet?'

Because now he'd told Gideon everything—pretty much everything anyway—and why was he thinking about their kiss at the inn again—there was nothing more to say.

Difficult situation summed it up well.

Chapter Eight

Having visited the kittens in the stables, and then eaten a lonely dinner, Emma plonked herself down in the chair at the writing table in the very lovely boudoir that Mrs Drabble had informed her was now hers. She pulled open the drawers to each side. They were filled with paper, envelopes, quills, ink, everything a duchess might need for her correspondence.

Had they belonged to the last duchess?

What had Diana been like?

Emma was never going to be able to compete with her in anyone's affections. She didn't *want* to compete with Diana, and she didn't *want* a marriage filled with grand passion, but she *did* want to be held in at least a modicum of affection by someone in her new life, or she'd have a very lonely existence.

She took out a piece of paper. Sitting by herself doing nothing wasn't going to do her any good, and writing to someone would engage her mind. Perhaps she'd write to her great friend Lily, whom she'd met at her Bath seminary and with whom she'd maintained a regular correspondence ever since, through Lily's marriage to a very respectable squire who resided in the county of

Hampshire and her subsequent speedy production of three little girls.

Perhaps she could go and visit Lily. Hampshire was nearer to Somerset than London, and a duchess could certainly travel without her duke as long as she took a maid and a footman.

A few minutes later she put her quill down. She didn't have the words now to describe to Lily her meeting with the duke and subsequent marriage to him. She *should* write to her soon, in case Lily heard about the wedding and was hurt that Emma hadn't told her herself, but it wouldn't make any difference if she left it until tomorrow.

She would do some embroidery. She'd brought with her the slippers on which she'd been working at her aunt's. Maybe she should get those out.

She hated needlework. She'd been embroidering these slippers since the beginning of the Season and had accomplished very little. There were advantages to being a duchess, and one of them had to be not doing embroidery very often.

She would read instead. Maybe she'd go and sit in the shared sitting room between her bedchamber and the duke's and read there before getting into bed. It would be too depressing to sit in her own chamber for the entire evening. She'd better allow Jenny to help her into another one of the bridal nightgowns she had, and then tell her she wouldn't have any further need of her services tonight.

Jenny insisted on brushing out Emma's hair and arranging her near-transparent nightgown just so, for Emma's imagined night-time encounter with the duke. When she'd finally finished, Emma locked her bedroom door, hauled a robe around herself and went into the sitting room, locking the door from there to the corridor outside too. She really didn't want to see Jenny again this evening. It was too wearing—and if she was honest, also depressing—parrying all her comments about what Emma and the duke would be getting up to tonight.

She tried very, very hard and eventually managed to concentrate a little on her book, to the extent that she even turned some pages and became quite interested in what might happen between the book's heroine, Emma, and her neighbour Mr Knightley. Normally, she absolutely adored this author's writing, but she wasn't in the mood for reading this evening.

She could just go to bed. She wasn't at all tired, though. Maybe she should start again from the beginning of the book and concentrate better this time.

She was still awake, curled up in the corner of the sofa, when sounds from the duke's chamber alerted her to the fact that he must have returned home and retired for the evening. She'd better go and get into bed immediately; it would be mortifying if he came in here and found her, as though she'd been waiting for him, when he so clearly didn't want to see her this evening.

Perhaps he didn't want to see her any evening. That was a lowering thought, although it was of course exactly what they'd agreed.

In her haste to jump up, she caught her foot in the end of her robe and tripped and fell onto the floor. As she picked herself up, the connecting door into Alex's chamber opened and he appeared in the doorway.

'It's you,' he said. 'I just wanted to see what all that clattering was.' He moved forward and unnecessarily held out his hand to her.

'Thank you,' Emma said, not taking the hand. She

didn't want to look as though she was desperate for physical contact with him. 'I tripped. I was reading in here.' She held her book up as though it was evidence. 'And now I'm going to bed. Goodnight.' She put her hand on the sofa to lever herself up.

Alex took a step backwards and said, 'I trust that you are unhurt?'

'Yes, indeed I am.'

Now that she was back on her feet, trying not to wince at where she'd landed heavily on the side of her bottom—she'd have a big bruise there in the morning—she could see that he was struggling to keep his eyes on her face. They kept straying down to her décolletage. She looked down and realised why. Her *robe de chambre* was open and the frothy lace at her bosom had fallen down, so that her nightgown was far too low, only very barely skimming her nipples, and, in fact, it was so close to see-through that she might almost be naked.

Her entire body suddenly felt warm, and all she could think about was the way his eyes were on her and the look of appreciation in them. The room was cooling now, and the air on her skin, together with his gaze, almost made her feel as though he was touching her.

He swallowed and she took a deep breath. Suddenly, she realised that she was standing still, half-naked, being gazed at by a man who, while he *was* her husband, had explicitly stated that he did not wish to engage in husbandly activities with her.

She whipped the robe around herself, making sure that it covered her up to her neck, and said, 'So, goodnight.'

If there was one tiny note of satisfaction in the incident, it was that Alex's voice was definitely hoarse when he replied, 'Goodnight.'

* * *

Emma struggled to get to sleep because it was very difficult not to think far too much about both her boring evening—the first of many to come, presumably—and Alex's eyes on her body in her nightgown.

She was still eating a relatively late breakfast when Lancing informed her that His Grace would be grateful if she would go and see him in his study when she was ready.

'Thank you so much for coming,' he said when she entered the room.

It suddenly felt very similar to the occasions during her teenage years on which she'd been required to go and see the head of her seminary, when she'd behaved in a manner 'unbecoming to a young lady of quality', in the head's words, for misdemeanours ranging from running in the garden to giggling with Lily during lessons to exchanging notes with the very attractive piano master.

Emma was not going to enter into a head-of-seminary-versus-naughty-schoolgirl relationship with Alex, so instead of standing in front of his desk, which was what he seemed to be expecting, she took a seat in a comfortable armchair to one side of the desk, so that he was forced to turn to look at her.

'Not at all,' she said when she was comfortable in the chair. 'Did you have something you wished to discuss with me?'

'Yes. I wanted you to know that I've asked my man of business to settle on you formally the fortune and other assets comprising your dowry, so that whatever might happen to me you will be financially independent for life.'

'Thank you.' Emma realised that she wasn't at all surprised; Alex had already demonstrated himself to be both kind and a man of his word.

'Also, I thought you might like an introduction to the estate. If you would like, I could drive you around it this afternoon.'

Emma genuinely couldn't imagine anything she'd rather do today. She needed to get to know her surroundings, and during their journey from London Alex had proved to be a very pleasant companion. He would, of course, be the ultimate expert on his own land, and she certainly didn't wish to spend any more time than she needed to alone.

'I'd like that very much,' she told him.

'Excellent.'

And then he didn't say anything else, which gave her the impression that, much as when her seminary headmistress had finished telling her off each time, she was being dismissed.

She didn't want to be dismissed. Obviously, Alex had been extremely kind to marry her, and this situation was not of his choosing, and she had gained a lot from it while he had gained nothing, but they were still going to have to find a way of dealing with each other with which they could both be reasonably happy. And Emma could not be remotely happy if Alex treated her as though he was in charge.

'Would two o'clock be acceptable for us to set off?' she asked.

'Yes, I...suppose so.' He seemed like an inherently kind and decent man who had, however, fallen into the way of being a duke and got used to things being on his terms, including what time they might set off anywhere.

She beamed at him. 'Perfect. Well, if you'll excuse me, I need to go and see the boys now.'

Emma was ready, in one of her smart new pelisses, a dark green velvet one, covering a pale grey walking dress in worked muslin, also new, in good time for their drive, and arrived in the castle's great hall at the same moment as Alex, who was wearing a greatcoat, which showed his shoulders to excellent advantage and made him look very, well, big.

'Good afternoon,' she said, trying to ignore the shiver that just seeing him seemed to have caused.

That kiss had a lot to answer for.

'Good afternoon.' He did have a very nice voice. Deep and kind of...*throbby*. In a very alluring way.

For goodness' sake. She was losing her wits.

'I have had my curricle brought round to the front,' Alex said, indicating the door ahead of them.

'Thank you,' Emma said, and they walked out of the castle together, for all the world like a normal couple.

'I'll take you out in a gig another day, so that we can go cross-country, but today I'd like to give a recently acquired pair an outing,' he said, holding his arm out for her as they descended the wide steps down from the castle's main entrance.

'How exciting to see a new pair being put through their paces,' she said, wondering if there was any chance that he'd allow her to drive for any part of this afternoon.

Alex handed her up into the curricle and gave her a blanket for her to wrap around her legs, before leaping up himself and taking the reins.

He was a good driver, Emma noted as they set off. Fully in control, but not forcing his horses in any way.

He was also a man who knew and loved his land, it seemed.

'There's been a settlement here since the turn of the twelfth century,' he told her as they skirted the nearest village after he'd—very proudly—pointed out the school he'd had built and told her that the village girls as well as boys were educated there.

'We're heading up towards some of my farming tenants now. The earliest farmers here were Normans. The land's particularly good for sheep and wheat, but we farm as great a variety of crops as we're able, for the nutrition of the soil and the health of the crops.'

He definitely had his tenants' interests very much at heart. The properties that she saw were all well-maintained, and Alex had a lot to tell her about the hospital that he'd had built over the past few years. He was also very enthusiastic about agriculture.

'I presume that there must have been a revolution in farming techniques with the invention of so much new machinery in recent years?' Emma asked.

'Yes, very much so. My own father, as a landowner, was resistant to it, as are some of the farmers. Others worry that the introduction of mechanised labour will result in the unemployment of workers. But my view is that it's very much a good thing—and indeed we've seen that workers' activities are now merely diverted to other uses relating to crop rotation and field enclosures, for example, which expands our economy rather than causing unemployment.'

Emma nodded. 'It's similar in the textiles industry. My father was a very early adopter of new machinery and practices, and we intend to continue that in the factories. We have adopted additional security in case the Luddites' attacks spread to our region.'

'*You* intend to continue that? *You* have adopted additional security measures?' Alex asked, without looking at her, concentrating on negotiating a tight bend in the lane.

'The manager of the factories—my cousin—asked me to continue advising him by correspondence. He and I worked closely together before my father's death. I would like to visit the factories and the villages where the workers are housed from time to time. My father was quite devoted to his employees and ensured the safest possible working conditions and good pay for them, and my cousin and I intend to continue similarly. I am very grateful to you for settling my father's assets on me so that I might continue to be involved in a more formal manner.'

'It sounds as though you and I might both benefit from an exchange of information in our different ventures.' Alex turned his head briefly to smile at her before refocusing on his driving.

'Yes, I think we might.'

Emma had to admit to herself that she was impressed at Alex's ready acceptance of her intention to continue her involvement in the running of the factories. A lot of men would have been horrified by her links to trade, and by the fact that she, a woman, thought she had anything of an intellectual or managerial nature to offer.

Maybe he would be open-minded enough to allow her to drive him.

'I was thinking of buying myself a carriage,' she said. 'Perhaps a phaeton.'

'Indeed?'

'Yes. I drove a lot in Lancashire and missed doing so while in London. I love driving.' She paused for a moment and then said, 'Today is a very good day for driving.'

Alex slowed his horses and looked at her. 'Are you suggesting that you'd like to drive now?'

'Yes.' Emma smiled at him.

He didn't look as though he was keen to hand the reins over. 'This pair are particularly lively,' he said. 'And strong. And this is a curricle.'

'And I am a good driver,' Emma said.

'Although unpractised in recent months. Have you driven a curricle before?'

'Yes, I drove my father's curricle, on his instruction, and while I *am* unpractised in recent months, I was so practised before—over many years—that I don't think the lack of recent practice will have made any discernible difference to my skill.'

'Really?'

'Yes.'

Alex turned to study her again for a moment. He didn't say anything for a few seconds, and they both sat and looked ahead at the horses and the lane in front of them.

Then he said, 'I'll take you to a quiet, straight length of road and you can drive. I must warn you again, though, that these horses are wonderful, and very well-matched, but require an experienced and strong driver.'

'Thank you—and thank you for the warning. However, I think we and the horses will survive my driving very happily.'

When they got to a part of the road that Alex told her he judged to be a suitably easy place to drive, he handed her the reins.

Emma found herself smiling just at the feel of them

in her hand again. She moved her fingers very lightly, to get the measure of the horses, how they would respond. They did indeed feel very lively, and very well-matched. She would of course have expected nothing less of Alex's horses.

Once she was sure that she was ready, she set off. Soon she increased their pace, conscious the entire time of Alex hovering very close to her, clearly not at all confident that she could handle his team.

'You drive well,' Alex said after a few minutes.

'Why, thank you,' Emma said, slowing very slightly for a corner. 'You will note, however, that while I do think that you drive very well, I did not comment on your driving as I did not wish to patronise you.'

'You will perhaps have noted that most men of the *ton* do drive but the majority of women do not.'

'Well, I told you that I am a good driver.'

'And you are.' He nodded. 'Very good, in fact,' he added as Emma negotiated a sharp double bend in the road at speed.

'You are a very good driver too.'

'Er, thank you. I feel I should perhaps apologise for prejudging your driving.'

'Not at all.' Emma accompanied her words with her best sarcastic eye-roll, all the while focusing on the horses and the road, and Alex laughed.

They had come to another more open, straight section of road, and Emma increased their speed again.

'I might have been a little patronising before,' said Alex, 'but now I'm not being patronising. I'd say this to anyone—man or woman—you're driving so well that I'm literally relaxing in my seat. That is not something that happens when anyone else drives me. In fact, it's very rare that anyone *would* drive me. Not even my best friends, all of whom are good drivers. And, as I say—and as you are obviously aware—these horses require an experienced handler. I care very much about my horses, and I would not like anyone to job their mouths. Before you drove, I obviously had no idea whether or not you were any good, other than your clear belief that you were.'

Emma laughed. 'I'll take that as a compliment. Thank you for trusting me enough to allow me to drive them in the first place.'

'If I'm honest, I was prepared to take the reins if necessary.'

'Oh, really? I didn't notice you hovering and breathing down my neck at *all*.'

Alex laughed again, Emma gave him a sideways smile, and then he said nothing about re-taking the reins himself, and she drove all the way back.

Jim, the head groom, came running out as they came into sight. 'Are you injured, Your Grace?' he shouted.

'I'm very well, thank you, Jim,' Alex called. 'He's never seen anyone drive me before,' he told Emma, 'so he naturally assumed that a disaster had befallen me.'

'It seems I must thank you again.'

'Not at all. I was merely trying to compliment you again without patronising you. And, yes, I do think you should buy your own carriage. And horses. Should you like to arrange the purchases yourself, or would you like to discuss them with me? Or you will be very welcome to drive any from our stables here.'

'That's very kind.' Emma hadn't felt this contented for months. 'I believe that I should draw on your local expertise.'

'At your service.' Alex gave a mini salute and she laughed. 'Do you also ride?' he asked.

'I do ride, but only very averagely,' Emma said, rising with reluctance to alight from the curricle.

'You know, I begin to think that little about you is average.' Alex held his arm out for her and she took it lightly.

'I'm going to take that as another compliment,' Emma said.

'It is.' Alex smiled at her and she felt even more contented than she'd felt a couple of minutes ago, if that were possible. 'Now, I hope you don't mind, but I have some more papers to look through before I go to see the boys. I thought I might eat with them in the nursery this evening.'

Oh. A very clear message that for the second evening running he wasn't going to eat with Emma.

And just like that, her mood deflated.

She had her pride, though. 'Perfect,' she said. 'I'm very tired and thought I might take my supper in my chamber again.'

'Ideal. I will see you tomorrow, then.'

'Indeed.'

And so, after what had felt like a wonderful afternoon, she walked inside to begin another miserable evening.

Chapter Nine

Alex felt extremely guilty watching Emma go. He shouldn't abandon her like this.

On impulse, he called out to her. 'Emma. Why don't you join the boys and me in the nursery for supper? If you like?'

She stopped, and even from a distance he could see that her shoulders grew a little rigid, and then she turned round to face him.

He moved closer to her so that he'd be able to hear her response, as she said, 'Thank you, but I do not wish to intrude on your time with your boys.'

Alex opened his mouth to tell her that it wouldn't be an intrusion. Except that wasn't true and he couldn't say the words because he was obviously going to put the boys' happiness above Emma's, and he was fairly sure that they benefited from time alone with their only parent.

He could see her features settling into what looked to him to be a careful mask, to hide any emotion she might be feeling. He recognised it because he often wore such a mask himself. And he realised that he couldn't do this to her. On the occasions he'd seen her with others she'd

seemed very friendly. He couldn't consign her to loneliness every single evening.

When he'd asked her if she'd like to go for the drive
today it had been because he'd felt—had known—that
he had a responsibility to ensure her happiness as far
as he could, without engaging too closely with her. The
drive had been perfectly enjoyable; it wouldn't be a terrible hardship to eat dinner with her two or three times
a week.

'I realise that I am not yet particularly hungry,' he
said. 'I don't think I will eat with the boys, therefore, but
will instead take dinner in the dining room later on, after
I've spent some time with them in the nursery. Would
you care to join me?'

Emma was standing very still, clearly reflecting. After
a few seconds, she said, 'I'd enjoy that, thank you.'

'Excellent. I'll see you then.'

She came down for dinner wearing a pale pink dress
that he didn't think he'd seen before, and against which
her dark hair and light brown skin looked very beautiful.

'I believe that Martin—I presume you've been introduced to our chef—has produced some particularly
delicious dishes for this evening,' he said.

It felt important to keep the conversation on mundane matters, because he'd been enjoying her company
far too much and had struggled greatly to banish from
his mind the image of how she'd looked last night in
her nightgown. He needed to regain some self-control.

'I look forward to tasting them.'

As they finished bowls of velvety chestnut soup, Emma
said, 'The boys are wonderful, a credit to you.'

'Thank you.' Alex smiled at her and then, almost to his own surprise, added, 'Much credit must go to their mother, for her influence in the early years with the older two.'

Where had that come from? He didn't usually choose to mention Diana.

Emma nodded. 'Tell me about her? If you'd like to?'

Alex knew that he didn't have to reply—knew that although she would be interested in his answer she would understand if he chose not to say anything—but, actually, found that he did wish to tell her.

'She loved our children. She loved dancing. She loved to laugh. She loved playing backgammon. She hated apples, of all things. And she was beautiful. And funny.' He felt a little choke in his throat and clenched his jaw.

'She sounds wonderful. I'm so sorry for your loss.'

'Thank you.'

Oddly, Alex felt as though some of the emotion washing over him was due to the sincerity in Emma's regard, not just his bereavement.

He really should try not to become too close to her.

He did his best to keep the conversation on food, a potted history of his family and questions about Lancashire for the remainder of the meal, and, other than a couple of occasions on which Emma caused him to laugh out loud, it wasn't particularly different from making mild conversation with a pleasant acquaintance. He could certainly do this, remain emotionally and physically aloof from her while being polite and not ignoring her. He hoped that they could rub along very happily together like this.

After Emma rose from the dinner table, Alex had half a glass of port in boring isolation, and then went to join her in the drawing room, just to bid her goodnight out of politeness.

She was sitting next to the fire, her dark head bent over some embroidery. It was a slightly incongruous picture, in that it was difficult to imagine someone as energetic and vibrant as he'd learnt that Emma was spending hours with a needle.

'What are you making?' he asked politely.

'Gentleman's slippers,' she said, holding up the one she was working on. 'They were initially intended as a gift for my uncle, but since they aren't going to be worthy of parcelling up and sending by post I think they might have to be for you.'

'That is very kind,' Alex said, stunned.

So far in their acquaintance she'd demonstrated herself to be very competent at a wide range of things, everything he'd seen her do, in fact. Until now. She was *not* a gifted embroideress.

'They are…' Good God. Would he have to *wear* them? 'They are, sadly, relatively small.' Thank heavens. 'Sadly, I have very large feet.'

'Oh, don't worry.' Emma bestowed a sunny smile upon him. 'I'm sure that with my needle skills I'll be able very easily to alter them to fit you. I could perhaps sew an extra piece on the end.'

She *had* to be joking. She looked deadly serious, though.

'Thank you,' he said while she continued to sew, very slowly and, to Alex's eye, very unevenly.

'Perhaps a brocade strip,' she said, eyeing his feet.

'Wonderful.' Alex shifted slightly in his seat. How was it possible that, while sitting opposite a woman mangling a pair of slippers that she was threatening to make him wear, all he could think about was the fact that she was looking at his feet, and how she might look at the rest of him? Really, how was that possible?

She raised her eyes to his and smiled at him. 'You're genuinely scared, aren't you?'

'I'm not scared,' he said.

She leaned towards him and he leaned forward too, in a reflex action.

'I'm not going to make you wear them,' she said.

'I knew that,' he told her.

Emma laughed, a lot, and then Alex laughed a lot too.

'I might have been worried for a minute,' he admitted eventually, which made her smile in a very victorious manner, and that made Alex smile too.

And now neither of them was speaking, nor smiling. They were just looking at each other. Alex could see the rise and fall of Emma's chest, a tiny pulse beating at the base of her delicate neck. She moistened her lips, the lips that he'd kissed two nights ago in the inn.

No.

His mind was going to places it really shouldn't, and if he wasn't careful he might act on his thoughts.

'I think that, if you don't mind,' he said, 'I will retire now.'

It should be up to Emma to decide first to retire, but two people who'd just become legally married shouldn't have to stand entirely on ceremony with each other.

'Indeed,' she said immediately, 'I too am tired.'

They didn't speak at all as they went upstairs together. When they reached the corridor outside their rooms, Alex indicated their shared sitting room with a small nod of his head, and Emma nodded in response.

He opened the door and held it so that she could pass

inside the room, before closing it behind them. Emma had come to a halt a few feet away from the door and was standing looking at him, her hands clasped in front of her, her chest rising and falling more rapidly than usual.

Alex wanted to go straight to bed. He didn't want to be seduced into doing something ill-advised, or even just to be thinking ill-advised thoughts, like how much, all of a sudden, he wanted to kiss her plump lips, pull her against him, make her moan with desire for him, begin to sate his own physical desire for her.

He didn't want to think about that at all.

Emma bit her lip, and then lifted a hand and pushed back a ringlet that had escaped the ribbon holding back the rest of her curls. The ringlet fell forward again. As though propelled by an unseen force, Alex stepped towards her and, very gently, tucked it back into the ribbon, his hand brushing the softness of her cheek as he did so.

He wasn't gentle enough; apparently the hairstyle was quite fragile. His fingers had dislodged the ribbon and now her hair tumbled around her shoulders.

And it was as though his fingers had a mind of their own. He *should* have taken a step backwards and bidden Emma goodnight, but instead he found himself running his hands through her curls, then tugging her hair very gently and cupping the back of her head. And then, as though some invisible cord was pulling him, he was reaching down to brush her lips with his.

Emma sighed against his lips, and the small sound was the undoing of him. He kissed her again, lightly, and then deepened the kiss, parting her lips with his tongue. Emma sighed again, then ran her hands up his chest and around his neck. She was soft, pliant, warm, eager, *perfect*, against him.

He wanted more of her, he wanted to lift her, carry her into his room, place her on his bed…

The marital bed.

He didn't want a real marriage with her. What if she got pregnant? Died in childbirth as Diana had? He didn't want to do that to another woman. And, for himself, he didn't want to grieve again.

As images of the aftermath of Diana's death crowded into his mind, he let go of Emma.

He heard her say, 'Oh,' and dragged himself back to the present.

'I…' He looked at her, beautiful, with her tumbled hair and swollen lips and still half-closed eyes. He wanted to say something nice to her, not hurt her feelings in any way. But he didn't have the right words.

She opened her eyes slowly and smiled uncertainly at him. He found himself shaking his head very slightly. Her smile dropped and she pressed her lips together. She looked…shocked. And—from the way she was now wrapping her arms around herself—maybe as though she had realised that he was shutting her out and was trying to protect herself.

God. He really didn't want to hurt her. But, however much he wanted to say something, he just couldn't talk now.

'I'm sorry. Goodnight.' He took the few steps necessary to enter his chamber and closed the door firmly behind himself without looking back.

That should not happen again.

He made sure that he breakfasted early in the morning, having noticed that Emma was not a particularly early riser. There was no point in laying himself open to disturbing thoughts—any kind of temptation—when he didn't have to. Sharing his meal with a newspaper rather than Emma was a much better way of spending his time.

He went up to the nursery after he'd finished eating. A few minutes after he'd sat down with the boys, Emma came into the room.

'Good morning,' she said.

All three of the boys' heads shot round and they all chorused, 'Good morning,' very over-eagerly.

Alex frowned.

'I hope that none of you are scared of spiders,' Emma addressed the boys.

Harry immediately giggled, and Freddie kicked him under the table. Alex opened his mouth to reprimand him, but Emma was still talking.

'If so, you'd better be very careful because there were a lot in my bedchamber last night.'

Harry giggled again.

Alex glared at him The boys were clearly involved in this, but maybe he should speak to them when Emma wasn't there.

'I'm so sorry,' he said. 'I'll call Mrs Drabble immediately.'

'There's no need,' Emma told him. 'I got rid of them all myself out of the window. Fortunately, I'm not at all scared by spiders. Indeed, I like them, and count myself quite an expert on the different varieties we have in England.' She sat down next to John and put a monogrammed handkerchief down on the table in front of him. 'I believe that this is yours.'

John's eyes widened and he said, 'Oh.'

'I must tell you,' Emma said, 'that it would be polite to thank me for the safe return of your property. Something else I must tell you is that I now have a spy watching my door. One further thing: if any other small creatures should find their way into my chamber, assisted by anyone, I might lose my temper. And I am *fearsome* when I'm angry.'

She smiled sunnily at the boys, and as one they all shrank backwards.

Alex nodded, impressed. *Masterful*, he mouthed at her. She turned her still-sunny smile on him and he couldn't help laughing.

'I'm going to leave you all to it now,' he said, 'and I shall look forward to hearing whether or not any of you make Emma angry.'

As he closed the nursery door, he decided that he would have a polite dinner with Emma this evening, but other than that would not see her today.

Later, as he was eating a quick luncheon in the library, Lancing brought him a note from his aunt—his late father's older sister—informing him that she would be visiting that afternoon as she was desirous of meeting the new duchess, of whose existence, she wrote, she would have liked to have been notified by Alex.

Alex in turn sent word to Emma, and then, reckoning that he had two clear hours, took himself off to the stables to discuss possible horse purchases for Emma with Jim.

Almost exactly two hours later, Alex and Emma were waiting together in the grand saloon next to the castle's great hall when they heard the unmistakable noise and bustle of an arrival.

Lancing flung open the doors and announced, 'The Countess of Denby.'

Alex watched Emma as his aunt walked slowly into the room, wanting to see her reaction. His aunt was an elderly woman and, having embraced and apparently loved the elaborate fashion of the later eighteenth century, had made no concession to the less ostentatious modes of dress favoured by women for the past thirty years.

It wasn't every day that you saw a lady dressed for a country afternoon call in the enormous panniered skirts and huge wigs that had characterised pre-French Revolution fashion, but Emma barely twitched at the spectacle before her and walked forward and took his aunt's outstretched hands.

Alex was impressed; most people reacted more overtly to his aunt on first meeting her.

'Good afternoon, young lady.' His aunt had no regard for convention, and in Alex's experience it was highly unlikely that she would treat Emma as anything other than a much younger lady to whom she would offer a great deal of probably unwanted and possibly incorrect advice.

'Good afternoon.' Emma smiled at her.

'I need tea.' Alex's aunt strode forward, her immense skirts rustling around her, and arranged herself on a sofa in the middle of the room. 'Sit near to me, girl. Alexander, where's that butler of yours? Tea!'

'Of course, my lady.' Lancing had materialised out of nowhere.

Alex was sure that his household, led by Lancing, would magic up all manner of sandwiches and cakes very quickly.

'So what's this I hear about you compromising my nephew into marriage?' his aunt asked Emma, who frowned only a very tiny bit before producing what might almost have passed for a serene smile.

'It's nonsense,' Alex said. 'Emma and I met in Hyde Park and fell almost immediately in love, but kept our relationship secret for a while.'

'Sounds like a complete faradiddle to me,' his aunt boomed, adjusting her ear trumpet. 'But so does the compromise story.' She poked Emma with the black fan she'd been holding. 'I like the look of you. I don't see you behaving badly.'

'Thank you,' Emma said.

'What?' Alex's aunt turned the ear trumpet again.

'I said thank you,' Emma said loudly.

'You have a very quiet voice. Now, tell me about your family. I knew your mother. Bad business when she ran off with your father.'

Emma replied slowly, and loudly, repeating herself when asked, answering an extraordinary number of questions, smiling throughout, even in the face of some quite remarkable incivility.

'So your grandmother was Indian? Your beauty is very unusual. Quite out of the common way. I like it, though.' Alex's aunt smiled at Emma, as though bestowing upon her an enormous favour rather than enormous rudeness.

Emma said, 'I'm honoured,' sounding as though she was trying not to laugh, which was a relief, because a lot of people would just have been offended.

Alex stood up, though. Enough was enough.

'Would you care to take a turn about the gardens, Aunt? And see the boys? Your great-nephews would be delighted to see you.'

'How old are they now?' his aunt asked, not moving from her sofa.

'Nine, seven and four.'

'No,' she said. 'Too young. I don't like young children. Perhaps the oldest. Frederick. Perhaps not, though. I've been feeling rather bilious recently.'

'The garden, then?' Alex persisted.

'No. Too cold. I have my own gardens, you know. One garden is much like another. Sit down, young man.'

'Of course,' Alex said.

He glanced at Emma out of the corner of his eye. She was definitely struggling not to laugh now, which made him smile. A good thing, he realised, because normally an hour into a visit from his aunt he'd be feeling irritated, at best.

'I'm tired,' his aunt said abruptly. 'I think I'll have to spend the night here with you.'

Alex's eyes swivelled straight to Emma's. She was looking as horrified as he felt. Neither of them spoke for a moment, and then Emma, projecting her voice magnificently, said, 'Oh, how wonderful. You'll be able to see the boys properly. We always eat dinner with them in the evenings.'

'They should be in the nursery.'

'I'm afraid that Alex is a very modern parent, and I, of course, follow his…lead. We cannot consign them to the nursery.'

'Help me up,' Alex's aunt said to him. 'I must leave before it gets dark.'

'Masterful again,' Alex whispered to Emma over her head.

'Masterful what?' his aunt asked.

Alex stared at her. Was she in fact not really deaf? Or had he just been unlucky?

'It's been so wonderful to meet you,' Emma said, diverting his aunt's attention in—yes—a masterful manner.

She offered her arm to the older woman, and they passed out of the room together.

'I can only apologise,' Alex said to a laughing Emma, when his aunt's eighteenth-century landau had passed out of sight.

'Not at all. I'd like to think that if I become old and infirm I shall take advantage of it in exactly the same way. I'm sure she has a kind heart.'

'I think it might be your own kind heart imagining the same in her.' Alex smiled at Emma and tried to imagine her old, infirm and rude. She'd still be beautiful if she became old and, please Lord, she would indeed attain old age, unlike Diana. God. He forced his thoughts away from Diana's early death and tried to recapture his previous train of thought. Infirm, that was it. Well, that wasn't a particularly pleasant thought either: he'd hate to think of Emma becoming infirm. He turned his mind to rudeness: it was impossible to imagine Emma becoming rude.

'Perhaps we should indeed both eat with the boys this evening?' Emma suggested. 'So that we didn't take their names in vain.'

Alex nodded, relieved to have his thoughts diverted from hoping that nothing would befall Emma and that she would indeed become an old woman in due course. 'I think you're right.'

He began to regret agreeing to her suggestion within minutes of the meal starting. John and Harry seemed to have thawed dramatically towards Emma, but Freddie, well, Freddie was behaving as though he'd inherited his social skills from his great-aunt.

'I don't want to sit next to Emma,' he began.

'I'm very happy to sit here.' Emma sat down between John and Harry.

'Did you enjoy your walk with Nurse this afternoon?' Emma asked.

'Better than walking with you,' Freddie muttered.

Alex opened his mouth to tell him to apologise immediately, but Emma hurriedly began to talk to John and Harry about frogs and tadpoles. She lifted her eyebrows and indicated Freddie with her eyes, all the while smiling and continuing to talk to the other two, and eventually Alex deduced that she thought he should talk to Freddie.

When they'd finished eating, Emma pushed her chair backwards and said, 'I'm quite exhausted by my busy day today. I'm going to retire to bed now.'

Perfect. If they retired to their chambers at different times, there should be no danger that Alex would succumb to temptation and kiss her again.

'I'll see you in the morning, boys. Alex, I wonder if I could speak to you for a moment outside before you read together?'

'Of course.' Alex stood up and followed her outside. Perhaps she was going to tell him that she couldn't bear to look after the boys any more. He really hoped that wasn't it. 'I'm so sorry about Freddie's rudeness. I'm going to have a very firm word with him now.'

'Without wishing to dictate to you about your children, I'd like to say that I really don't think you should tell him off,' Emma said. 'I think something's happened. I think you ought to ask him what's wrong. When he's on his own.'

Not at all what he'd been expecting her to say. Alex reflected for a moment; maybe she was right.

Half an hour later, as John and Harry were engrossed in a game of sticks, Freddie suddenly blurted out, before Alex had had the opportunity to ask him anything, 'So, are we going to get another baby in our family?'

Well. It seemed as though Emma was right; Freddie didn't sound happy.

'No,' Alex said cautiously. 'Did someone tell you that we would?'

'Mikey said.'

Damn. If Freddie was going to visit the stables, why couldn't the grooms just have done their usual swearing and letting Freddie throw fallen orchard apples and ruin the head gardener's prized ornamental lawn?

'No. We are not,' he said firmly.

'But Mikey said when people get married, like you and Emma, they usually have babies.'

Alex frowned, realising all of a sudden just how carefully he was going to have to tread in setting an example for his children. He wanted them to experience strong, loving marriages as adults, the kind he'd had with Diana and his parents had had. So it wouldn't be good if they witnessed him and Emma in a soulless marriage. But he couldn't allow himself to develop feelings for her, both for his own sake, in case something happened to her, and for the boys, because he couldn't have them thinking that their mother had been replaced.

Should Emma perhaps move to the dower house sooner rather than later so that any gossip could happen and be overcome? And so that the boys would understand that this was a different type of marriage from the one he'd had with Diana? Or should he work hard to get over the ridiculous physical attraction he knew he felt towards Emma? Get used to the fact that they had adjacent bedchambers and be friends with her while she remained in the house?

Whichever, they should begin to attend social events together, so that he could signal to people that, whatever their living arrangements might eventually be, he expected her to be treated as his duchess socially, and so that she could make some friends with whom she could remain friendly in the event that she did move to the dower house.

He had an idea. They should go to a ball, or a dance, and he would dance with her. That would serve a dual purpose. It would send a strong signal—the entire neighbourhood was aware that he wasn't a keen dancer, and indeed had almost never danced with any woman other than Diana—and Emma would meet some of the other ladies who lived locally.

In the meantime, he needed to address this issue, and now John and Harry were listening too.

'Not everyone has babies,' he told the boys. 'Instead of having babies, Emma and I will…dance.'

What? What was he talking about? And why had he just imagined holding her in his arms on a dance floor and liked what he'd imagined?

'Emma likes dancing,' John said.

'How do you know?' Alex asked, surprised.

'She told us in the apple orchard yesterday. And then we danced, and we laughed and laughed,' John said.

'I like Emma,' Harry said.

Damn, this was complicated.

The next day, thinking while he breakfasted alone that he would ask Emma over dinner that evening if she'd like to go with him to some local dinners and dances, Alex realised that they were already falling into a pattern of not really seeing each other during the day, but having dinner together in the evening. If he was honest, the companionship was pleasant. If he could just get over his physical attraction to her—which he was sure he would in time—they could rub along more than happily, from his side, anyway.

'I'd love to,' Emma said, when he broached the subject that evening as they both tasted a particularly good turbot and gooseberry dish.

'Excellent. We have an invitation to a dinner dance tomorrow evening, with some neighbours who live about ten miles away. I think several amongst my acquaintance will be there and think you might enjoy it.'

'That sounds wonderful.'

Chapter Ten

'The Duke and Duchess of Harwell,' said a footman, flinging open double doors as though he was auditioning for a role in the royal household rather than announcing guests at a country squire's evening dance.

Emma smoothed the skirts of her gauze overdress for the third time since they'd left their carriage.

'You look immaculate,' Alex told her, and put his arm out for her to take. 'Beautiful, in fact. Nothing to worry about.'

Emma tried not to grimace at him. She'd never felt like this in London, but in London she hadn't really cared. Now, though, she felt as though this mattered, since she was likely to be seeing these people regularly, and she'd like to have some local friends.

They took a step forward together, and Alex said a re-signed, 'And *smile*,' into her ear, while doing a big, obviously fake, smile of his own, which *did* make her smile as they entered the drawing room, interested eyes watching them from all angles.

He stayed with her and introduced her to almost everyone in the room, for all the world like an adoring new husband. Quite a contrast to how he was at home. There, while he was unfailingly polite—and indeed thoughtful in a number of his suggestions to make her life more comfortable, including taking dinner with her, showing her around the estate in his curricle and accepting the invitation to this dance to enable her to meet their neighbours—he clearly didn't want to spend a lot of time with her.

Which, of course, she was completely happy with. Neither of them had wished to marry the other, and they'd been clear that their marriage would be a bargain that did not include close friendship or anything more intimate. And Alex's behaviour since the second of their two kisses had made it very obvious that he didn't wish anything intimate to happen between them again.

If she was honest, Emma was still struggling not to be upset—deeply hurt, in fact—that Alex clearly regretted their quite earth-shattering second kiss, and was finding it difficult not to be spine-tinglingly aware of him whenever he was anywhere near her. But she must not complain, not even just internally. Alex had been completely open with her from the beginning and this was the bargain they'd made.

'And this is my oldest friend, Gideon,' Alex said, as a large man with red hair and a smile almost as wide as his very broad shoulders shook Alex's hand vigorously.

'Delighted to meet you.' Gideon bowed and then said, 'May I have the pleasure of a dance with you? Only so that I can tell you scurrilous stories about Alex, of course.'

Emma laughed, immediately liking him. 'I'd be delighted.'

'If we're allowed to dance with the duchess, I'd like

the honour of staking my claim now,' another man said, and within a minute or two they were surrounded by several men, all wishing to stake dancing claims.

To Emma's surprise, Alex didn't relinquish her hand, but remained at her side throughout the clamour that ensued, and then raised his voice just slightly, so that the other men fell silent, and said, 'My wife isn't available for the first dance; that pleasure is mine.'

Emma nearly squeaked out loud at the thought of dancing with Alex. Firstly, it was deeply unfashionable for a married couple to dance, even at a private party like this, so it would be a strong signal to the assembled guests that Alex was a devoted husband. And secondly, if she was honest, she'd already imagined dancing with him last night, when she'd been struggling again to get to sleep, thinking about their kisses and him in his bed two doors away from her. But she hadn't expected *actually* to dance with him.

She realised now that when she'd imagined dancing with him she hadn't done him justice. Resplendent in simply cut, sombre-hued and yet glorious evening wear, he eclipsed every other man here tonight. He could be the worst dancer in London, and yet it must feel like an honour to be on his arm, because he *looked* like the best dancer a man could be.

'If the duke and duchess are to dance together, then the first dance must be a waltz,' announced Lady Felicity, the squire's wife. 'Followed by a series of quadrilles and a *danse espagnole*. You will find us bold in this county, Your Grace.'

'Indeed,' said Emma, torn between a giggle exacerbated by the loud grumbles from several disgruntled misses who would now not be able to join the first dance of the evening, as they didn't yet have permission to waltz, and thinking, *Oh, my goodness, I'm going to waltz with Alex.*

The string ensemble at the end of the room struck up and all the women who were dancing stepped into their partners' holds.

Emma had waltzed many times before—her aunt had ensured that she got the permission of the Almack's hostesses early in the Season—and her emotions had ranged from annoyance, or even disgust that she had to dance with a particularly unpalatable partner, through mild irritation, or pity that a perfectly pleasant man was an incompetent dancer, to enjoyment of a partner who had the winning combination of good conversation and competent dancing skills.

She had never once felt any kind of a stomach-flutter or *tingle*. Now, though… Now it was as though all her senses were coming alive for the first time.

As Alex held her right hand lightly in his left, with his other hand skimming the small of her back, it was as though every nerve in her body was attuned to where his body was and where they might touch as the dance progressed. She could smell his deeply masculine scent, sense the rise and fall of his chest almost brushing her own chest, feel the warmth and hardness of his body so close to hers… On the face of it, he was far too tall for her, but somehow it felt—from her perspective, anyway—as though they were the perfect match physically.

They were completely silent as they moved, but the silence wasn't awkward; it was as though their movements were doing the talking. The way they were dancing felt both deliberate and yet entirely natural, as though they couldn't help themselves giving in to the music.

It was wonderful.

Emma loved it when they moved slowly together in the slow parts of the dance, and she loved it when they danced in perfect time with each other in the faster parts.

She only realised the music had stopped because of the sudden movement and chatter around her of others stopping their dance and then leaving or joining the dance floor.

She looked up at Alex. He was still holding her hand and her waist, and was gazing down at her with partly closed, glazed eyes.

He began a slow smile, which Emma felt right to her centre, and suddenly she was feeling hot and as though her insides were liquid and as though she could barely stay standing without the support of Alex's arms.

'I…' he began. And then suddenly Gideon was next to them, and Alex stopped talking. Emma *really* wanted to know what he'd been about to say. Probably nothing… but maybe something.

'And the next dance is mine, I believe,' said Gideon with another of the broad smiles Emma was already beginning to expect from him on the strength of less than one hour's acquaintance.

'Um.' Alex pulled his eyes from Emma's and turned them to Gideon with what looked like a big effort. After a long moment, he said, 'Of course.'

'Thank you for the dance,' Emma said, and then thought how utterly ridiculous that sounded, given that he was her husband. Legally, anyway.

'I enjoyed it,' Alex said, very simply, and Emma's cheeks warmed as Gideon led her away.

* * *

Gideon was a very good conversationalist, with all sorts of harmless gossip and useful, often funny information to impart. He was a perfectly good dancer into the bargain, and yet Emma found herself a little distracted throughout their quadrille.

At one point, during another dance, she realised that she was looking away from her temporary partner, Sir Robert—the squire, and their host for the evening—in an attempt to see where Alex was.

She snapped her head back and beamed at the squire, and said, 'Oh, *indeed*,' in response to his comment on the beauty of an apple orchard in full bloom.

She did love dancing, and she did enjoy the fourth and fifth dances, with the squire's younger son and the single and very charming Viscount Bagley respectively, but it was as though they were just rehearsals for the sixth dance, which—almost scandalously, really, given that they were a married couple—she'd agreed would be with Alex.

And when he made his way to her side the second the dance finished, she felt her whole body lightening and a big beam beginning on her face. Alex was smiling too, seemingly oblivious to the people around them. If she hadn't known better, she'd have thought he was genuinely very pleased to see her. He was clearly a very good actor.

Someone was clearing his throat next to Emma and she gave a start, then realised to her horror that it was her last partner, Viscount Bagley. This was awful. She was behaving like an infatuated debutante, ignoring everyone around her other than the subject of her dreams. What was *wrong* with her this evening? It had to be the shock of their very sudden marriage catching up with her.

The one saving grace was that the viscount was so charming, good-looking and reputedly rich that he must be fawned over by the majority of his dance partners, and his feelings would surely be robust enough to cope with Emma's distraction.

'Thank you,' she said to the viscount, who was now bowing deeply over her hand.

'I very much enjoyed our dance,' he said, still holding on to her hand.

Alex cleared *his* throat, and Emma and the viscount both looked up. Alex's face held a remarkably forbidding expression all of a sudden, and the viscount dropped Emma's hand very quickly. Then, quite ridiculously, Alex immediately took it.

Emma really wanted to tell him that he was over-acting, looking not so much like a fondly loving husband as a jealously obsessive one. If she was honest, though, she was thoroughly enjoying the over-acting. In fact, she was thoroughly enjoying the entire evening.

Still holding her hand, Alex moved with Emma towards the middle of the dance floor to join the next quadrille set.

'Your husband is clearly besotted,' their hostess trilled, dragging Gideon past them. 'I can't remember the last time he danced. Probably not since the last time he danced with Diana.'

She bestowed a huge smile upon the two of them and Emma decided that she had very large teeth and she didn't like her. Really, who would bring up someone's late wife at a moment like this?

'Ignore her,' said Gideon to Emma, just before the

squire's wife dragged him off. 'She had high aspirations for her sister to marry Alex. It's jealousy.'

It might be jealousy, but it wasn't particularly nice to know that, in addition to everything else he'd been forced to do on her behalf, Alex was now being forced to dance when he clearly didn't want to.

She looked up at him and said in a low voice, 'Please don't feel that you have to dance with me.'

'I enjoyed our first dance and I'm looking forward to this one.'

'Really?'

'Really.' He spoke into her ear, so that only Emma could hear him. 'Lady Felicity said that entirely to make you feel uncomfortable. It seems a lot of people are a little jealous of a new duchess. I've been enjoying dancing with you. But even if I didn't, it wouldn't hurt me, would it? So, you shouldn't feel guilty. And I did enjoy it. And apparently I'm talking in circles.'

He smiled at her, and she laughed and said, 'Thank you. And it is true. Dancing twice in an evening is not the biggest hardship for even the most hardened of anti-dancers.'

Certainly it was nothing in comparison to getting married when you didn't want to.

A couple of seconds later, she was whisked into the start of a very energetic country dance. And, *oh*, the gorgeous anticipation of knowing, as she was twirled around by a succession of partners, that she would end up holding Alex's hand again. They smiled, they laughed, they danced in perfect time together, and for the duration of the dance it was bliss.

'I really did enjoy that.' Alex was still laughing slightly, as they all had been, at the antics of a couple of the other men, which had annoyed Lady Felicity considerably, going by her pursed lips and wagging finger.

'A final quadrille set,' announced Lady Felicity, 'and then we go next door for supper. I've planned the night along London lines, Your Grace—' she nodded at Emma '—so that you will feel at home.'

'Thank you so much,' said Emma.

'I'll be back to escort you.' Alex smiled at her as she accepted the arm of her next partner, a very pleasant-seeming man named Mr Scott, and moved away from her to join the squire and another man in the corner of the room.

Emma spent the entirety of the next dance wondering whether Alex would stay with her throughout supper and feeling annoyed that she couldn't stop thinking about him.

When the dance ended, Alex was nowhere to be seen.

'Allow me to escort you?' Mr Scott asked.

'I…' Emma couldn't believe how disappointed she felt. She should really stop this. She and Alex had a non-romantic arrangement and this evening he was doing her a huge favour and she should remember that. 'Thank you.'

'Emma. Scott.' Suddenly, Alex was bowing in front of them, and equally suddenly Emma felt as though the evening had brightened. This truly was ridiculous. She almost wanted *not* to go with Alex, just because she shouldn't be feeling like this. Also, though, she really wanted to go with him.

He held his arm out to her and she took it, and within a short space of time they were seated at a small table in the room next door with two other couples.

'I'm going to perform the introductions again,' Alex

said. 'You met so many people earlier that I'm sure you won't have retained all their names.'

'I'm Letitia,' said the lady nearest to Emma. 'I'm Gideon's sister.'

Emma could see the resemblance—the same hair colour and the same ready smile—and liked her as much and as quickly as she'd taken a liking to Gideon.

'And I'm Maria.' The other lady leaned round her husband and grinned at Emma.

'Or Lady Merrick. As you can see, she's a complete hoyden,' Letitia said, smiling at her friend. 'Well, we both are, but it's all right because we're both respectably married. Like you. So, tell me, have you fallen foul of Lady Felicity yet? She was *desperate* to get her sister married off to the duke, which was never going to happen, because she's one of the rudest people anyone's ever met, and Alex is *not* rude, although he does live up to his Ice Duke name when he's annoyed.'

'I'm not rude? Did I hear you say that?' Alex was grinning at all three of them, looking about as far from icy as the sun.

Supper time flew by, and by the end of it Emma genuinely felt as though she had new friends in Letitia and Maria. Which, of course, she realised, had been Alex's design in escorting her into supper and ensuring that they sat in that group. Again, she couldn't fault his kindness.

'Don't dance every dance if you haven't already committed to doing so,' Letitia said to her as Lady Felicity urged them to return to the other room to continue with the dancing. 'Sit at the side with us and have a good gossip. It's one of the advantages of being sensible married women.'

'Sensible!' scoffed her husband, smiling at her good-naturedly.

Never mind the music, Emma wanted to dance at the thought that she had these lovely new friends.

Letitia and Maria were as good as their word in terms of gossiping by the side of the dance floor, and within fifteen minutes Emma had heard excellent stories about almost everyone in the room.

She was enjoying herself so much that when Alex approached her to ask her to dance Lady Felicity's much-trumpeted *danse espagnole* with him, she was almost annoyed. Not entirely, though: the idea of a third dance with Alex was extremely enticing.

'Three dances in one evening?' Lady Felicity remarked very loudly as they passed her. 'I declare you have your husband quite under your thumb, Your Grace.'

'Not at all.' Alex had a touch of the Ice Duke in his tone all of a sudden. 'My wife was enjoying a comfortable cose with her friends, but I begged her to dance with me again.'

'That was satisfyingly fierce of you,' Emma said as they took their places.

'She was very rude.'

'True. Thank you for introducing me to your friends. They're lovely.'

'I thought you'd like them.' He produced an exaggerated look of smugness, which made Emma laugh. And they laughed together through most of the dance, which Emma thoroughly enjoyed.

'I did not realise that it was now acceptable for married couples to dance thrice together in one evening,' the vicar's wife, Mrs Hardy, said very loudly to her husband, just as the dance finished.

Apparently complaints about marital triple dancing were the order of the evening.

'Ignore her,' Letitia said, materialising at Emma's elbow as Alex moved away. 'She had designs on Alex herself a few years ago, and is still put out that he did not succumb to her lures.'

Goodness. No wonder he'd felt hounded by matchmakers.

'And as for a married couple not dancing three times together when we all know what they do in the privacy of their own bedchamber...'

'Letitia!' Emma was trying to laugh, but all of a sudden she felt completely deflated. How would this relationship of hers and Alex's develop? Would they be pretending like this for ever? When she was forty and childless, and had never had intimate relations with a man, would she still be pretending? Suddenly, she just wanted to leave, go home—if the castle could be called her home—and go to bed. Clearly alone.

As if by magic—or maybe just through excellent observation or a coincidental sudden desire to go home himself—Alex reappeared in front of her.

'Are you ready to leave, Emma?'

'Yes, indeed. I find myself very tired this evening. I think perhaps all the country air has exhausted me.'

'That or the fact that it's three o'clock in the morning,' Alex said.

They said their goodnights and thank-yous, and then Alex led the way out to their carriage, holding Emma's arm in what felt like an extremely *polite* way. Especially when she could make out Letitia and her husband getting into their own carriage ahead of them, definitely being a lot more tactile in a much less polite but much more romantic and lovely way that demonstrated an easy and close affection.

Emma swallowed a sigh and sat down on the forward-facing seat of the carriage, slightly to one side in case Alex might be tempted to sit next to her. He sat down opposite her, right in the middle of the seat. Of course.

'Did you enjoy the evening?' he asked as they set off.

'Yes, thank you, very much.' Most of it, anyway, apart from the references to Diana and the reminder just now that he and Emma would never be more than friends. 'Did you?'

'I did, thank you. Despite the scandal I have caused by dancing with you three times.' He smiled at Emma. 'You seemed to get on very well with Letitia and Maria.'

'Yes, I did. I plan to call on them this week.'

'Very good.'

Clearly, he'd been feeling guilty about leaving her to her own devices during the day, and had hoped to provide her with some friends by introducing her to their neighbours, which was very kind of him.

A few minutes later, they were still chatting about the evening and some of the neighbours—Alex had a very good story involving the vicar, a croquet mallet and some cheese, which made Emma almost snort with laughter in a very unladylike fashion—when the carriage drew to a sudden halt.

Emma flew forward from her seat and put her hands out to save herself. They met a solid wall of chest, and she was saved from being flung any further by Alex's hands gripping her arms.

'Ermph,' she said into his chest.

'Are you all right?'

Was she? Yes, except she felt slightly as though she'd lost her wits. All she could think of was the muscly hardness of his chest and the way she was pressed up against him, almost sitting on his lap.

'Yes, thank you,' she managed to say.

'Good.'

Alex let go of her arms and put his hands on her waist and moved her very gently to the side while Emma fought with herself not to give in to the temptation of sinking right into him as he held her for this moment in time.

'I should check that all is well,' he said after a second.

'Of course!' Emma moved away fast. He'd clearly been experiencing *no* temptation, and just as clearly was *not* still thinking about where their bodies had just touched and feeling almost singed by the contact.

The coachman appeared at the door of the carriage just as Alex opened it. 'A deer in the road, Your Grace.'

'Did you hit it?'

'No, Your Grace, we stopped in time.'

'Excellent. Thank you.'

Emma moved back to her side of the carriage as the door closed and then they sat in silence for a few seconds until, slightly desperate to break the tension that seemed to have sprung up between them, she said, 'Do you have many deer on your land?'

And they passed the rest of the journey determinedly talking about livestock.

When the chaise drew up at the castle's main entrance, Alex descended first and then helped Emma down. He thanked the coachman and then led Emma towards the front door, still with her hand tucked through his arm.

'The stars are amazing.' Emma pointed upwards with her free hand. 'That was something I missed in London. Every night in the countryside I think how magical they are. Look. Argo Navis is so clear tonight.'

'I'm impressed. I don't think I could have named that one.'

'I've always loved the constellations. Which is a good thing, given that I'm educating your boys.'

'Very true.' Alex nodded, and then smiled at her. They'd reached the steps up to the wide front doors. 'I hope Lancing has gone to bed,' he said in a low voice. 'I always tell him and Graham not to wait up for me on occasions like this, but I appear to have little authority in my own home, because they often completely ignore me.'

Emma laughed. If there was one person who, apparently effortlessly, seemed to have a lot of authority, it was Alex. And not just because he was a duke, but because he was *him*.

Her arm was still in his as they went into the empty hall together.

'I see Lancing has abided by your wishes,' Emma whispered.

'Indeed. He's left a candle for us here, look.'

One candle. For them to share. Emma suddenly felt very tired. This pretence was…hard. Although clearly she shouldn't complain, even inside her head, because if Alex hadn't married her who knew what she might be doing now? Almost certainly something worse than pretending to be sharing a bedchamber with a very attractive man.

Alex picked the candle up, and Emma realised that she was still holding his arm.

'Are you ready to go upstairs?' he asked, and she nodded, not sure whether or not to pull her hand away.

In the end she didn't, and they began to move towards the staircase together.

The darkness licking around them, the shapes of furniture and paintings distorted by the candle's flickering light... All of it would have felt eerily intimidating without Alex's solid presence beside her. Emma found herself wanting to continue to hold his arm, just to reassure herself that he was there apart from anything else. She'd always hated the darkness. And, yes, of course it was just *nice* being arm in arm with him.

'We should probably enter our sitting room together, rather than going into our bedchambers separately from the corridor.' Alex's whisper brushed her ear, and she shivered. 'Walls have ears. Well, eyes.'

'You're right,' she whispered back, hoping that her voice wouldn't vibrate as much as her body seemed to be doing.

They carried on up the stairs in silence, arm in arm, Emma almost breathless from her awareness of Alex next to her.

When they finally reached the top of the stairs, rounded the ornate newel post at the top of the banisters, walked along the corridor and arrived in front of their sitting room door, it was almost a relief to be able to let go of him.

Emma removed her arm from Alex's and took the candle from him so that he could open the door quietly, to avoid waking the rest of the household, and in they went.

'So neither Jenny nor Graham waited up for us,' Alex said, once he'd closed the door.

'No.' Emma cleared her throat to get rid of the croak that had come from nowhere. 'No.'

She and Jenny had fallen into a routine where Jenny helped her get ready for bed—usually into a frothy confection of a nightgown with which Jenny presumably imagined Emma would impress Alex—and then left Emma for the night. Emma was sick and tired of all the night-time pretence, and thoroughly relieved that Jenny wouldn't be there tonight.

'So.' Alex cleared his own throat. 'Goodnight, then.'

'Goodnight.'

Neither of them moved.

Then Alex said, 'I should, that is to say, would you like me to light your candle with this one? Or perhaps you'd like to light it yourself?'

'Of course. Thank you.' Emma took the candle from him. Their fingers brushed as she did so and she nearly dropped it.

'Can you manage?'

'Yes! I don't know what happened there. Very clumsy of me. I'll bring it back directly, so that you may use it in your own chamber.'

It took her three attempts and a further near-drop of the candle before she had her own properly lit. Alex was having the most extraordinary effect on her this evening.

'Done,' she said as she returned to the sitting room.

Alex was at the window, looking out into the moonlit garden.

'It's beautiful in the moonlight, isn't it?' she said.

'It's beautiful at any time. Although I don't really feel

as though it's my land, rather that I am a custodian of it for future generations, and I feel very fortunate.' He turned and walked towards her to take the candle. 'We really should bid each other goodnight now that you have your candle lit; it's very late. Almost time for an early breakfast, in fact.'

'Yes.'

Again, neither of them moved.

Alex looked dark, brooding, very serious in the candlelight.

'You…' Emma began, and then stopped, not sure what she had been trying to say. 'Thank you for this evening. I very much appreciate your kindness in introducing me to your friends and in demonstrating to everyone that we—'

'You have nothing to thank me for.' His voice was rough.

'No.' She wasn't really sure what she was saying because all her focus was on his face lit by the candle between them, the shadow of his beard growth, the *size* of him standing there in front of her.

Alex took the candle and placed it on a chest to one side. 'We don't want to get burnt.'

'No,' Emma said again.

She might not get burnt by the candle, but she felt as though she was being burnt by *something*. She could feel heat in all sorts of places.

Alex took a step closer to her, and she moved closer too, taking a deep, shuddering breath as they drew together. Memories, images from when they kissed at the inn, were playing in her mind now.

'I enjoyed our dances,' he whispered.

'Me too.' Emma was whispering as well.

Alex was so close now she could barely breathe from anticipation.

He lifted one hand and very gently traced a finger down her cheek. 'You look beautiful in that dress.'

Emma couldn't speak. All she could do was smile and tilt her head up towards his. He was going to kiss her again, and it was going to be the perfect end to a wonderful evening.

Chapter Eleven

Alex allowed his fingers to wander down the smooth skin of Emma's cheek and to trace the shape of her lips. So soft, so beautiful. The tip of her tongue peeped out and she moistened her lips, and he felt a shudder throughout his entire body. He found himself moistening his own lips in response, and leaning his head nearer to hers.

Their mouths were less than an inch apart now, and they were edging ever closer to each other, heads tilted one way and then the other, mirroring each other like two pieces of a puzzle that were about to fall into place.

He could feel the anticipation building inside him. He knew from their first two kisses how Emma's lips tasted, how well she fitted against him, and he was desperate for more.

Their lips were so close now that he could feel her breath against his mouth. She murmured something unintelligible and suddenly he pulled her against him into a hard kiss. She gave a deep shudder and returned the kiss, threading one arm around his neck, pressing her other hand tight against his chest.

Holding her against him with one arm and continuing

their kiss, ever deeper, he ran one hand from her hip to her waist, and then up to the swell of her breast, feeling her shiver as he touched her. He nipped her lower lip with his teeth and then allowed his thumb to skim her hardened nipple through the fabric of her dress and felt her shudder again against him.

Damn, he wanted her. He wanted to taste all of her, feel her softness against his hardness, explore her body, work out what made her come alive, make her shudder and shiver again, be entwined with her, enter her, be as one with her.

As one with her.

Like man and wife.

Like he had been with Diana.

He stilled. He couldn't do it.

It wasn't even the thought of betraying Diana, because it wasn't a betrayal, was it? She was gone and she'd have wanted him to be happy.

He dropped both his hands and lifted his head.

He knew what it was. It was the fact that he *did* want to be happy. And the thought of allowing himself to care that much again for a woman, even a fraction of that amount, was too frightening. If he allowed himself to love Emma and anything happened to her, he'd be plunged into the depths of despair again, and he didn't want that, couldn't cope with it. He just wanted contentment, a happy, serene life without the possibility of any further grief.

He definitely wasn't doing this.

He took a step backwards and said, 'It's late. We should probably go to bed.'

Emma was just standing there, unmoving, staring at him with a dazed look on her face, as though she couldn't understand what was happening.

He shook his head. 'I...' He should apologise, somehow. 'I'm not... I can't...' He drew a breath and then said, 'I'm sorry. This isn't right for me.'

It was as though his words snapped Emma out of the near-trance she'd been in. 'Of course. Goodnight. Thank you for a lovely evening.'

And then she gathered her skirts and whisked herself through the door into her bedchamber.

Alex stared for a couple of seconds at the closed door before turning to go into his own chamber.

He'd absolutely done the right thing. It was right for both of them. So he should be feeling pleased, positive.

He didn't feel happy at all.

He was sure he would tomorrow, though.

Alex awoke later that morning not feeling remotely refreshed. Despite the late hour, he'd been unable to sleep, and had tossed and turned for what had felt like most of the remainder of the night, replaying the evening in his mind. He'd danced with Emma in order to demonstrate to his friends and neighbours that she was very much his wife, whatever rumours they might have heard to the contrary, for the same reason that he'd kissed her at the inn, and both times it had turned into something unexpected and quite unwelcome.

There was an obvious solution: avoid her as far as was polite when there were no onlookers to be impressed, and avoid actual physical contact when there *were* onlookers. In due course he'd have his physical impulses under control—he hoped really quite soon—and then Emma would be an accepted presence in his life, and they could continue as friends living under the same roof.

So he hauled himself out of bed and down for a quick

breakfast and out for the day before a polite dinner with Emma in the evening.

It worked. It definitely worked.

After their polite and pleasant dinner, they retired upstairs together, entering their bedchambers via their shared sitting room, as was now becoming their custom, and Alex found the strength of mind to go straight into his bedchamber without allowing himself to linger, or dwell on just how much he'd like to...

No, he shouldn't even allow himself to think that behind closed doors. That way lay insanity. It was fortunate that he was so tired after only a couple of hours' sleep last night that he actually nodded off quite quickly, thinking about how he and Emma had joked together over dinner, and her infectious laugh. But it was perfectly normal to go to sleep thinking about your evening...

The next afternoon, having received an invitation from Gideon's sister Letitia, Alex decided to visit the nursery, firstly to spend a little extra time with the boys, and secondly to ask Emma if she'd like to attend an impromptu dinner at Letitia's house the next evening.

Emma was in full flow when he let himself into the room, and the boys were rapt, which was the first time he'd ever seen them like that with a governess.

They were so rapt that they didn't appear even to notice his arrival.

Emma was doing an excellent imitation of a tiger, insofar as it was immediately recognisable, if not accurate, complete with a description of where tigers liked to roam, hunt and sleep.

'Do tigers eat people?' asked John.

'Not very often,' Emma said.

'Do they eat fish?' Harry asked.

Emma's answer morphed into a discussion about the apparently very many rivers in India.

'Papa!' Harry suddenly interrupted Emma, having finally noticed his father.

'Shh.' Alex put his finger to his lips. 'Emma's talking.'

'What's the longest river in India?' Freddie asked, the most animated Alex had seen him about anything other than the stables and horseplay for a long time.

'Have you heard of any of the rivers?' Emma asked. 'What do you think it is?'

'Something beginning with G?' Freddie said.

'That's right,' said Alex.

Simultaneously, Emma said, 'That's what a lot of people think, but in fact it isn't.'

Alex raised an eyebrow and Emma smiled at him and said, 'I believe that the Ganges is the third longest river in India and the longest is the Indus.'

He smiled back at her, impressed.

'Your knowledge of geography is certainly better than I could ever have hoped for in my boys'…' His boys' *what*? He couldn't call her a governess in front of them. She was, after all, legally at least, their stepmother. 'In any instructor of my boys. Or indeed anyone I know, frankly.'

'My grandmother was Indian, and during my childhood she told me a lot of stories about her own childhood. I've been fascinated by the country ever since and have read as much as I can on the subject.'

'Did she live in England?' Freddie asked.

'Yes, in Lancashire with my grandfather.'

'How did she come to live here?' Freddie's questions were almost too much, but Alex decided not to reprimand him.

He was still very young, and also Alex was very interested himself in Emma's answers but didn't want to discuss his own affairs, particularly Diana, and so he couldn't reasonably ask Emma too much about her background.

'My grandfather owned a textile business and travelled to India to find new fabrics. He was asked to dinner by my grandmother's father, who wished to sell him silks from his land. He was a maharajah, and my grandmother was a princess. She met my grandfather and they fell in love, and she embarked on the long journey across the Near East by land and then over the Mediterranean Ocean and all the way to the North of England with him.'

'That's a really long journey,' John said.

'It is.' Emma smiled, and something about her—something wistful in her eyes—told Alex that her interest in India was more than academic.

'Do you perhaps wish to travel there yourself one day? If you don't mind my asking?' he said.

Emma hesitated, and then said, 'Yes.'

Alex nodded, surprised by how unsurprised he was. Women rarely undertook such journeys, but the more he learned of her, the more he realised that Emma was a rare woman. A woman who was very different from him.

'Have you travelled?' she asked.

'I was fortunate enough to do a Grand Tour. Europe. I very much enjoyed it and saw some wonderful sights.'

'But?' She had one eyebrow fractionally raised.

'I like my corner of Somerset,' he told her. 'I enjoy being here, doing my best to be an attentive landlord.'

He counted the schools and the hospital he'd built in recent years as far greater achievements than swanning around the continent as the idle, rich young man he'd been at that stage of his life. And of course his sons were here. His *life* was here.

Emma nodded almost imperceptibly. 'I can see that.'

Their eyes met. She looked as though she was weighing up what she saw before her, much as he was. She nodded again, and he did too. He had the feeling that her urge to travel was as great as his to remain at home.

They were indeed very different.

Emma hesitated for a moment, and then said, 'I would very much like to travel extensively.'

He realised that she'd probably been waiting for the right moment to tell him that. Well, he certainly wouldn't stop her. Indeed, perhaps it would be for the best for both of them that she travel, as long as scandal did not attach to anything she did. When she returned home, any residual attraction between them would hopefully have been erased by time spent apart.

And if the thought of Emma travelling simultaneously scared him and made him realise that he would miss her company, all the better that she go.

'That will be your prerogative,' he told her.

She didn't smile, but just said, 'Thank you.'

Alex felt as though he'd taken a test, but he couldn't tell whether he'd passed or failed. He did know that following their conversation he felt a little miserable.

Emma opted to take her dinner in her chambers that evening, citing a headache, and again, Alex wasn't sure why. He also wasn't sure whether or not he was pleased.

The next morning, the routine into which they seemed already to have fallen since the addition of Emma to the household was disturbed, as they all woke up to a beautiful thick blanket of snow covering everything within sight. The boys were desperate to get outside, and the adults in the household were split between those who agreed with them and those who didn't want to get cold and wet.

The small child in Alex adored the snow, but as Parsons, his man of business, kept telling him, he had a huge amount of bookwork to do.

'Perhaps I might have finished by late morning,' he said, wondering if to Parsons' ears he sounded like a child, pleading to be allowed out to play.

'I hope so, Your Grace,' Parsons said, his creased face impassive.

Alex was still toiling away—how was it possible that these numbers totalled a different amount every time he looked at them—when sounds of shrieking and laughter reached him from the sparkling white lawn outside his study window.

Emma had the boys thoroughly muffled up, and he could see from her gestures and the scarf and twigs she was holding that she was encouraging them to build a snowman. The boys were half engaged in rolling an enormous ball for the snowman's body, half engaged in throwing smaller snowballs at each other.

Alex was struggling even more now to make sense of the figures in front of him.

He'd had enough. He'd done a lot of work this morning; he definitely deserved a break.

If he could get the numbers on the page at which he was currently looking to add up, he'd go outside for a few minutes to show the boys how good snowballs were *really* made.

Five minutes later, he'd come to the conclusion that

the numbers were never going to add up, and that it would be madness not to take advantage of the snow, because who knew when winter playtime conditions would be as good as this again?

Approximately sixty seconds after that he was pulling on a greatcoat and loose walking boots, winding a scarf around his neck and striding outside.

It looked as though he was the first person to emerge that day from the side door by which he'd left the castle. As his feet sank into the pristine snow and he breathed clean, frosty air into his lungs, he took in the beauty of the scene surrounding him. If he were the kind of man who painted, he'd love to attempt a landscape of this. It was…

Thump.

Something heavy and wet had hit him squarely in the face.

'Eurmph,' he spluttered, tasting snow.

'Ha-ha-ha,' shouted Freddie from the shelter of a group of trees in a copse to Alex's left, and then another snowball hit Alex on the shoulder.

'War,' Alex shouted, bending down to roll a snowball of his own.

He was bombarded by surprisingly accurate shots until he got himself hidden behind a large oak tree and poked his head round it to see Emma directing the boys in making the snowballs while she held one with her arm back, very much primed to throw, and looked around for her target, presumably *him*.

Well.

Alex bent very carefully and quietly and set about rolling the perfect snowball. Times four. They needed to be big, but not so big that they wouldn't fly perfectly through the air, and also wet, to ensure maximum dis-comfort when they landed one after the other on Emma and the boys.

Work finished, and his ammunition lined up at his feet, he stood up with a small grunt of satisfaction to check where his prey now were. As he straightened, he realised that they'd gone very silent. He couldn't hear anything at all other than a couple of cracks of twigs and…

Thump, thump, thump, thump.

When he'd cleared the snow from his face and could see again, he realised that the four of them, in addition to pelting him with one large snowball each, had jumped on his ones and destroyed them. They'd well and truly trounced him.

For the moment.

He smiled at them all lined up in front of him, laugh-ing. 'Very good. You got me there.'

'You shouted, "War," but we won,' crowed John.

'You certainly did,' Alex said.

And then he leapt forward and swept the boys into his arms and ran with them towards the snowman's body, before dumping all three of them into it.

'Outrageous,' said Emma, standing at a safe distance. 'You've ruined our morning's hard work.' She was def-initely smirking. 'And now the boys will be soaked to the skin and will need to go inside to get changed and have warm baths.'

'Have you ever heard the word "hypocrite"?' Alex asked, advancing towards her.

'No!' she said, and then picked up her skirts and ran towards the castle, shouting, 'Boys, inside now.'

Two things surprised Alex: firstly, she was fast, and

secondly, the boys actually obeyed her and sprinted inside after her.

She was an impressive woman, he reflected as he climbed the stairs in order to dry himself off.

She wasn't just an impressive woman, he thought a couple of hours later, as he looked out of the window. She was a determined one.

He wouldn't have noticed if he hadn't happened to glance out at that precise moment, but she and the boys were definitely trying to keep out of sight. They had skirted the edge of the castle, carrying what looked like some of *his* clothes, and now seemed to be occupied in rolling another big snowball. A couple more inches of snow had fallen since they'd gone out this morning, so the conditions were ideal for snowman-building again, and they were clearly planning to build a large one and dress him in Alex's clothes.

Maybe he'd wait until they'd finished and then go outside and land just one perfectly formed snowball on Emma. And then admire the snowman. And then come back inside and finish looking through these blasted books.

Twenty minutes later, he'd achieved strictly nothing further and was feeling as though he was missing out on a lot of fun with the children. He should go outside and find them. And, good Lord, how could he not have had the idea sooner? They had sledges somewhere; he should ask someone to get them out.

He asked Lancing about the sledges, shrugged himself back into his coat and boots, and went outside, following the sounds of laughter and good-natured shouting to a sheltered area.

'My word,' he said, coming to a stop in front of the snowman to which they were putting the finishing touches of what looked like one of his favourite hats, his best gloves and a scarf to which he was—had been—quite partial. They'd already finished its quite hideous-looking face. 'It looks...'

'Surprisingly lifelike?' Emma supplied. 'Like an uncannily good likeness of you, perhaps?'

'Yes, that's right.' He nodded. 'It was on the tip of my tongue to say that looking at it is like looking in a mirror.'

'Why don't you stand next to it so that we can admire our handiwork?' Emma suggested.

'Yes, Papa,' the boys clamoured.

And so he stood next to the gargoyle-like snowman, while the boys told him that it looked *exactly* like him, and Emma congratulated them on how clever they were and laughed at Alex.

He couldn't remember a time when he'd enjoyed himself so much in such a simple way.

He was going to get his revenge on Emma, though.

His opportunity came later, when they'd finished their sledging as dusk fell. The boys' nurse came to take them inside for their second warm bath of the day, leaving Alex and Emma to make their way inside after them.

'The boys have had so much fun today,' Emma said.

'I must thank you,' Alex said. 'I'm not sure how you've done it, but you've worked wonders with them. They actually seem to obey you, and they are learning from you *and* enjoying themselves.'

Emma shook her head. 'You have nothing to thank me for. Without your generosity I could very well be in dire straits now. And the boys are truly lovely. It's a pleasure spending time with them, and I love seeing them happy and enjoying themselves. And who wouldn't enjoy the feeling of victory that for the time being they seem to have called a truce on the introduction of small creatures to my chamber? In fact, I should thank *you* for the opportunity to feel victorious.'

'Very true. Perhaps we should make a mutual agreement to stop thanking each other?' Alex said.

Emma laughed. 'Perhaps.'

'I do have one last little thank-you for you, though.' Moving as fast as he could, for the element of surprise, Alex scooped a large handful of snow from the top of a wall and planted it down the back of Emma's neck.

'You *wretch*!' she shrieked. 'That's so *cold*!'

'I learned all about cold snow earlier today,' Alex said, standing a few feet away from her, ready to dart out of snowballing distance should she decide to retaliate.

She looked at him for a long moment and then smiled. 'I think we're even now.'

She held out her hand and he took it, smiling a gracious smile that said, *I think we all know that I beat you*.

She took his hand in a tighter grip than he'd been expecting, though, and suddenly pulled him very hard. She took a swift sidestep at the same time, and then let go so that he fell into a snowdrift against the wall.

'You look *hilarious*,' she said as he sat up, very much covered in snow.

Alex nodded and smiled, and then very suddenly lunged forward and pulled her down into the snowdrift too, and gave her a little roll for good measure.

'Oh, my goodness,' she gasped. 'Stop! It's so cold.'

'I'm not sure that you should mete out punishments

that you wouldn't be prepared to accept yourself for the same crime,' Alex said with a very serious air.

Emma laughed, and he did too.

And then she stopped laughing. And so did Alex.

Because it suddenly felt as though something had changed; the air between them was practically crackling with tension.

They were lying on their sides next to each other in the soft snow, their faces and bodies only inches apart. Alex still had his upper arm around Emma's waist from when he'd rolled her in the snow.

For fun. It had been for fun.

It didn't feel like fun now. It felt like... It felt like temptation.

It was snowing again, very lightly. He could see snowflakes on Emma's beautiful long, dark eyelashes. Her brown eyes looked deep and mysterious in the twilight, and her lips were slightly parted. He could see the rise and fall of her chest, her full breasts straining against the fabric of her pelisse.

He didn't have the strength to resist the temptation this time.

Very slowly and carefully, he raised himself on his elbow, and then bent his head towards hers.

They didn't sink into a deep kiss immediately. Alex brushed Emma's lips with his own with the lightest of touches, and then drew back slightly. She looked at him for a long moment, a small smile on her lips, before reaching up to him. And then they were almost dancing around the edges of the kiss, nipping at each other's lips, moving away and then back again, like opposing magnets irresistibly drawn together.

Suddenly, it was as though something just snapped

and it happened. His mouth was on hers, or maybe hers was on his, even though he was above her. Their tongues met and he felt his entire body respond to the sensation, as though he'd been waiting just for this for a very long time. He ran his hand down her side, in and out of the dip of her waist, and felt her tremble as he touched her.

'Are you all right?' he whispered.

'Yes,' she said on a sigh.

Alex moved his hand to cup her beautiful face, which he was beginning to know so well, and then slid his hand round to her neck, tugging at her hair, drawing her even closer to him.

As he held her close with one arm, he moved his other hand to cup her breast, and even through several layers of clothing he felt her respond. She arched her back so that she was pressed against him, and pushed her hands into his hair.

This felt like the natural culmination of everything that had come before, the physical temptation, the time they'd spent getting to know each other, talking, laughing together. Now his entire being, from his soul to his body, wanted to get to know more of Emma.

He was dimly aware that this was not wise, but with Emma in his arms like this, he was unable to do anything other than focus on the here and now. And, damn, she was tempting.

He kissed down her neck and undid the hook and top buttons of her pelisse with almost shaking hands, so that he could kiss and lick the hollow at the base of her neck. He undid more buttons and licked and kissed all the way down to the neckline of her dress. When he slid one hand inside and pulled the dress lower, bending his head further to take her nipple in his mouth, she moaned and arched even more. *Damn*, he wanted her, wanted her more than he could have thought possible.

He very vaguely knew that this wasn't the best idea, but he couldn't remember why. All he could think about was the taste of Emma, her seductive scent, the curve of her lips, the way her breast fitted perfectly in his hand, the smoothness of her skin, the eagerness of her kisses, the way his own body was responding to her and the promise of more.

Chapter Twelve

It was as though every nerve-ending in Emma's body was on fire. Her stomach was dipping, warmth pooling low inside her, as Alex worked magic with his mouth and his fingers on her breasts. Her hands were clutching at his hair and his upper arms—feeling the strength of his muscles there—almost scratching him with her nails in her desire to keep him there next to her.

He continued caressing, licking, sucking, and then he kissed his way back up her chest and neck and took her mouth again, his hands continuing to tease her breasts. When he moved his fingers a little away and traced around them, all she wanted was for him to move them back to her nipples. And when they were there, she could hardly bear the pleasure, and yet she knew that she wanted more, for him to touch her more, in other places.

It was mind-blowing, intoxicating. She couldn't breathe, she couldn't think, all she could do was kiss him back, mould her body to his, loving the weight of him on her and the feel of him pressing against her.

She pulled at his neckcloth and his shirt, wanting to touch his skin as he was touching hers. Wresting his shirt from his breeches, she ran her hands up his muscled torso, shivering as she did so. The hardness and latent strength in his body exactly matched his personality: he was the very embodiment of masculinity.

He pulled slightly away, smiling down at her, and his deep green eyes locked on hers for a long moment before they moved to look at her lips, and then her exposed breasts. The admiration in his eyes was so potent it was making her shiver.

He leaned down again to take her nipple in his mouth again, and then he reached beneath her dress.

'Is this all right?' he asked as he stroked her inner thigh, high up, towards the place where she felt the heaviness between her legs.

'Mmm.' She couldn't speak. All she could focus on were the sensations he was producing and where she was exploring him in her turn with her hands and lips.

And then he began to touch and caress her most intimate parts, and as sensation built she gave a deep, juddering sigh. She knew that she was moist there, and it was as though the rest of her entire body had turned to liquid too. She reached for the front opening in his breeches, fumbling, and he eased himself away to enable her to touch him better, producing a deep, 'Yes,' as she found him.

And then something large and wet landed on her face and she nearly choked.

What was that?

'Snow,' Alex said. 'The tree.'

He brushed snow away from her breasts, the touch of his fingers as they skimmed her skin making her jump.

'The branch couldn't bear the weight.' He smiled at her and leaned down towards her again, and then another large pile of snow fell on them.

He sighed and drew back. 'Maybe we should move.'

Emma nodded, hugely disappointed.

Alex sat up, and pulled her up too.

Immediately, the moment in which they'd been was entirely broken. They were now sitting next to each other in damp clothes, chests exposed, Emma's dress lifted, Alex's breeches open. And now she thought about it she was freezing cold.

Beyond their legal marriage, they weren't truly man and wife, nor in any way romantically involved with each other, so they couldn't just move to somewhere more sheltered in the garden or to a bedchamber, and continue what they'd been doing, because…

Well, they just couldn't. Because clearly neither of them had intended this to happen, and without the impetus of hot-blooded desire, or temptation, or whatever it had been, they obviously weren't going to resume.

They certainly weren't going to, anyway, if Alex didn't suggest it, because Emma was not going to lay herself open to the possibility of his refusing her.

Without looking at him she pulled her dress up and down, so that she was covered, and then drew her pelisse around herself. When she was more properly attired, she glanced at Alex and saw that he'd been busy tucking his shirt in.

The misery and disappointment that struck her in that moment showed her that she'd been hoping that he might somehow find the words—*want* to find the words—to suggest they go somewhere else together, maybe one of their bedchambers, and continue this…whatever it had been.

But of course he'd never been going to do that, and

in the interests of dignity, she certainly wasn't going to demonstrate to him that she was disappointed.

Using the tree trunk as leverage, she began to haul herself to her feet, and immediately slipped on the ground beneath. The snow there had been compressed to near-ice by the weight of their bodies a few minutes ago.

Alex shot an arm out to prevent her falling flat on her face, and had her standing solidly on her own two feet on some fresh snow within seconds, all without making any kind of eye contact.

As soon as it was clear that she wasn't going to fall over again, he let go of her as though she was scalding hot, and said, 'It's getting dark and you should get into some warmer clothes before you catch a cold.'

'You should change too,' Emma told him.

Alex nodded and they set off together in the direction of the house. They walked in complete silence, not a comfortable one, both of them looking straight ahead, and then Emma went directly upstairs while Alex made what she was sure was an excuse about needing to speak to Lancing before he changed.

Jenny was waiting for her when she got to her bedchamber. 'Oh, miss,' she said, 'you're soaked to the skin. You'll catch a chill.'

Emma felt heavy tears behind her eyelids and a very strong desire to be alone for a few minutes.

'Thank you, Jenny. I'm sure I'll be fine. I'm very healthy. And I think I'll dry myself. Thank you so much.' She took the towels from Jenny, who was frowning.

'But, miss, sorry, Your Grace, you're very, very wet.'

'And very, very capable of drying myself,' Emma said, immediately feeling guilty for her impatience. 'I'm sorry, Jenny, I'm just tired. I am so grateful for all that you do for me, but on this occasion I really can dry myself and dress myself for dinner and I will do so. Thank you.'

Jenny left the room, still protesting slightly, half under her breath. Once she'd gone, Emma sank down onto a wooden chair and put her head in her hands. She needed to be very careful. She wasn't completely sure what she was feeling now, but she did know that she had very much enjoyed Alex's company, and the way he'd made her feel just now...

Well, there were no words to describe it. It had been amazing, wonderful, glorious, and she'd wanted so much to continue, to discover how good it might have been if they'd done what she knew people did. Perhaps this was the beginning of love? Yes, she was probably falling in love with her husband. Who had made it very clear that he didn't want to love her, or perhaps just couldn't. He was almost certainly still grieving for his wife, the mother of his children, still in love with her memory.

And they wanted very different things—for example she wanted to travel and he wanted to spend his entire life here in Somerset—and she'd seen first-hand how unhappy her parents' marriage had been, despite their love for each other, because they'd been from different backgrounds and had had different wishes and needs. Indeed, it was almost as though their love had driven them apart, because they'd had such different goals that their relationship, with strong love on one side and different ambitions on the other, had become so unbalanced. She'd seen how their love had turned to near-hatred and it had been awful.

This wasn't good. Sitting alone with her depressing thoughts wasn't going to help her situation in the slightest. And she was unpleasantly damp and cold.

Shivering, she peeled her wet clothes off with difficulty, and then picked up a towel and began to rub herself dry very vigorously.

She didn't know what she ought to do next in regard to Alex, but she did know that she needed to be very conscious of her emotions and keep them under tight control.

Fortunately, it seemed that Alex felt exactly the same way and was going to take things a step further and avoid her, who knew for how long?

He made his excuses about dinner—apparently he had *huge* amounts of work to get through this evening, even though surely a duke had all manner of people to whom he might delegate—and didn't appear at all the next day, even when she sledged with the children and made another snowman with them, and allowed them to scream and shout as much as they liked, just to see if it would inspire him to come outside.

Alex had a note sent to her just as she took the children inside as dusk fell, which definitely indicated that he'd known exactly when they'd finished playing outside.

In it he 'suggested'—his word, which, despite everything she was feeling did make Emma smile, because he'd definitely noticed and responded to the fact that she did not enjoy being told what to do—that they leave at half past six for their evening with Letitia. Apparently, he'd received word that they were continuing with the dinner, as there had been no further snow during the day and the roads were all passable.

'Goodnight,' she bade the children, wondering whether she should tell Alex that she was too tired to go to the dinner this evening.

She'd woken this morning with a headache, due to her lack of sleep during a night the majority of which she'd spent turning over and over in her mind the events of the previous afternoon. Her hours outside in the cold air with the children today had cleared her head, but her headache was returning now, and the last thing she wanted was to spend an evening in Alex's company, knowing what they'd been doing yesterday, but having to behave like relative strangers.

But of course she should go. She'd very much liked Letitia when she met her at the squire's dance, and she had a life to make for herself here in Somerset. If she wasn't going to have Alex's company—which, of course, he had never promised her, so she couldn't complain— she'd be much happier if she had local friends.

She checked the clock above the boys' heads. She would need to hurry to be ready on time.

She was not ready on time.

After spending far too long choosing which dress to wear, and then having Jenny do her hair in three different hairstyles—when you'd been as intimate with a man as you'd ever been, and then he'd spent the next day doing his best to avoid you, for the sake of pride you had to look as good as you could when you next saw him— she hurried downstairs at a quarter to seven.

Alex came out of the library just as she reached the bottom of the stairs, clearly having been listening out for her.

'Good evening,' he said. 'You look lovely.'

'Thank you,' Emma said, suddenly breathless.

Just *seeing* his mouth, which looked so stern and thin in repose, but which when he smiled suddenly seemed so generous, was having a really quite unnerving effect on her. She couldn't help remembering what he'd done with it yesterday.

'Shall we go?'

'Go?' What was he talking about?

'Go outside to the chaise?'

Of course. She was losing her wits.

'Yes, wonderful,' she said.

No, not wonderful. It wasn't wonderful to go out to the carriage. It was just, well, nothing, really.

'Excellent.'

He held his arm out to her and she stared at it for a moment before recollecting where she was and what they were doing and taking it, very gingerly, because right now she felt as though touching him at all might make her feel far too much, and she really didn't want to get flustered again just before dinner. Or at all, in fact, if it wasn't going to lead to anything positive.

They walked out to the chaise, neither of them speaking, and then sat down on opposite benches. The carriage began to move, and still neither of them said anything. Emma concentrated on her gloves, and then on the blackness outside the window.

'I hear from the boys that you made another snowman and that they very much enjoyed more sledging today,' Alex said after some time.

'Yes, it was great fun,' Emma said. 'The boys are lovely. They're a credit to you.'

Alex smiled and inclined his head, and then he looked down at his knees, and then at the wall of the chaise to the right of Emma and above her head. And then in the direction of the window.

Emma, her throat holding a large lump all of a sudden, cast around for something unexceptionable to talk about that might lessen the distance between them.

No, she couldn't think of anything that wouldn't sound like an utterly pathetic and desperate attempt to create conversation out of nothing.

So there was no further conversation between them for the remainder of the journey, which in reality was perhaps half an hour but felt far longer than that.

It was a great relief when they finally arrived and could descend from the chaise.

'I'm so glad that you were able to come.' Letitia had dispensed with formality and was hugging Alex and Emma in turn. 'I hate it when we have snow and the roads are closed and we can't see anyone for ages.'

'And have to suffer only our own company and that of our neighbours to whose houses we can walk in under ten minutes, even in the deepest of snow. It's a hard life.' Arthur accompanied his words with a fond smile at his wife. Emma tried very hard not to think about the fact that Alex was never going to look at *her* like that, in either public or private.

'Honestly.' Letitia pouted at her husband, and he laughed out loud and put his arm around her waist. 'We should go inside before the newlyweds catch their deaths of cold.' She put her free arm through Emma's and said, 'I trust your husband kept you warm in the carriage?'

'Oh, yes,' murmured Emma.

Pretending really wasn't very enjoyable. If you liked the person to whom you were pretending, you felt very guilty. She almost wanted to confide in Letitia this minute the truth of her reality, so that they could begin the friendship she hoped they were going to have with honesty and openness.

'Your house looks so beautiful in the snow. Almost ethereal.'

'Your very abrupt subject-change tells me that your husband kept you *so* warm you really don't want to discuss it in polite company,' Letitia said, laughing. 'Don't worry, I'm not going to torment you any longer. Come and warm yourselves in front of the fire.'

They found four other couples in the drawing room, and were soon absorbed into the group, chatting about inconsequential matters of yet great weight, such as the ribbons newly stocked by the haberdasher in Yarford, the nearest town.

'When the snow has gone we must take a trip there together,' Letitia told Emma.

'I should very much like that.'

It was wonderful that it seemed that Letitia was as desirous as she of forming a mutual friendship. Emma did not need the companionship of Alex who, forbiddingly handsome, was currently standing talking to the other men, having positioned himself about as far from Emma as was physically possible without actually leaving the room. She was already making lovely new friends. There were plenty of women who would be ecstatic to be in her position, and she should make the most of the many positives.

She threw herself with great determination into the conversation and really did enjoy much of it, despite Alex's unnerving presence.

She was still enjoying herself when Letitia said, 'My butler has now caught my eye approximately fifty times, and is starting to look quite put out, so I must ask you all to make your way with me to the dining room, so that the food isn't quite ruined by our chattering for too long.'

She moved unceremoniously towards the door of the room, not waiting for her husband to escort her.

'I'm afraid that I'm being quite fashionable and have seated couples far apart from each other.'

Perfect. Emma's eyes flew to Alex's face in reaction to Letitia's words, and his eyes found hers at exactly the same moment. They stared at each other unsmilingly for a second or two, before both shifting their gazes away.

Emma took a deep breath. Things would settle between her and Alex; it wouldn't always be this difficult. She took another breath and fixed a smile to her face before moving into the dining room.

Emma found her name card between those of Arthur and Gideon, both of whom she liked tremendously and with whom she knew she would very much enjoy conversation. The seating plan would have been perfect for her if she hadn't been almost exactly opposite Alex across the wide table; it was going to be difficult to avoid looking at him and getting distracted by his handsome face, sombre this evening in repose, the sound of his deep voice and the way his strong hands held his cutlery.

She noticed with a flash of irritation how very much he seemed to be enjoying his animated conversation with Letitia and their friend Maria. However, both her table neighbours proved themselves to be more than adequate conversationalists, as she had known they would, and Emma found herself thoroughly enjoying herself as long as she didn't look at Alex, and focused very hard on not thinking about him either.

Some time later, they were all exclaiming at Letitia and Arthur's cook's truly wonderful swan-shaped ice cream, and Letitia was recommending that Emma request her housekeeper to purchase or have made any number of ice cream moulds in the shape of perhaps a peacock and a hare at the very least.

Emma nodded. She was definitely going to do so, although she would choose her own designs, perhaps in the shape of one of her kittens, or a pineapple from the castle garden's exotic fruit greenhouse.

Her thoughts were interrupted by Mrs Hardy, the vicar's wife, leaning across Gideon and saying, in a particularly piercing voice, into a lull in the conversation, as the company all enjoyed the creaminess of the ice cream, 'I think we still don't have the full story of how you and the duke first met, Your Grace.'

Emma tilted her head very slightly to the left and regarded Mrs Hardy and her astonishingly smug smile. Clearly, Mrs Hardy believed that she *did* have the full story, and clearly Mrs Hardy was feeling particularly malicious.

'I…' she began, not certain where she was going with her sentence, but very sure that she'd like to make Mrs Hardy feel less smug.

'Her Grace is hesitating—' Alex's voice rang out a little loudly, and every head at the table, including Emma's, shot round to face him '—because we didn't tell anyone initially. Strong, pure emotion feels like a private matter.'

'Oh, but you're amongst friends now,' cooed Mrs Hardy.

Emma found herself gripping her spoon very tightly in lieu of, frankly, *slapping* the woman, who was smiling even more smugly than before, as though she knew that she'd caught Emma and Alex out and was ecstatic to have done so.

'You're right.' Emma turned to Alex and produced a coo of her own. 'Should you tell the story or should I?'

'Why don't you?' If Alex didn't exactly coo back at her, he did manage a fond smile.

'Well. It all began one morning in Hyde Park…'

With a few embellishments on the original—including details about their clothing, their extremely heightened emotions and the weather—Emma reproduced the story they'd concocted in the inn about Alex's horseback rescue and their subsequent secret courtship.

'Even the weather was quite propitious,' she said soulfully as she drew her monologue to a close. 'The sun was warm, but not too warm, and there was exactly the right amount of breeze. It was as though the elements understood that we were at the beginning of something delicate and special and important, and that they needed to nurture it.'

'How very beautiful,' Letitia said, grinning at Emma.

From the way her eyes were dancing, it seemed clear that she'd heard something approaching the real story too, which did make it seem odd that she seemed so certain that Alex and Emma were now a real married couple.

She turned to Alex and said mischievously, 'We'd all love to hear the story from your perspective, Alex.'

Alex coughed. 'I have nothing to add. It was indeed, as Emma says, a…beautiful beginning to what I'm delighted to say is a beautiful…' He tailed off.

'Relationship,' Emma supplied. 'I feel extremely lucky.'

'I'm sure you do.' Mrs Hardy had spoken beneath her breath, but she'd definitely said it.

'The luck,' said Alex, glaring at Mrs Hardy, 'is all mine.'

'I don't know when I've more enjoyed hearing someone's love story,' Letitia said, 'but perhaps we ladies should remove to the drawing room now, to allow the gentlemen their port. Mrs Hardy, I do wonder whether you might be wise to depart quite soon. I hear that there's been a particularly severe snowstorm, very much centred on the road between here and the vicarage, and Mr Hardy would, I'm sure, be distraught not to be able to return to his parishioners. I'll ask Harris to call your carriage. It's been wonderful to see you; thank you so much for coming.'

Once Letitia had completed her skilful dispatch of the Hardys, Emma thoroughly enjoyed herself, drinking tea with Letitia, Maria and the fourth lady still present, Lady Clinthill.

Until Letitia leaned towards her and said, 'I wish to apologise for what Mrs Hardy said. I don't like to see people being rude under my roof. Arthur and I had barely met when we got married—our marriage was arranged very much between our parents—and we're now deeply in love. Obviously that means that I am beholden to my mother forever, about which she reminds me far too often, but aside from that it's wonderful, and it serves as an example of how people can meet in somewhat ridiculous-sounding situations and yet develop very strong feelings for each other. I'm so pleased that the two of you were thrown together in the way in which you were.'

'I… Yes.' Emma just wanted to *squirm*.

'I'm so sorry. I didn't mean to make you uncomfortable. The two of you look perfect together, and are so clearly in love, that I'm sure you'll be able to overcome any obstacles that might arise from two relative strangers marrying. I just wanted to say that others have been in the same position and overcome those issues and become stronger.'

'Thank you.' Emma could feel tears pricking at her eyelids. She wasn't sure whether it was due to the fact that she and Alex were clearly *not* in love, and were never going to be, or to how lovely it was that Letitia was being so kind, if slightly scarily outspoken on fairly regular occasion.

Their conversation was curtailed by the men coming into the room. Emma wasn't sure whether or not she was pleased; she felt that she'd have liked to have had the opportunity to glean some details about the early days of Letitia and Arthur's marriage.

Pleased with her own cunning, she had seated herself on a chair rather than a sofa, so that no comment would be occasioned if—when—Alex chose not to sit next to her. He was the second of the men to come into the room, and after hesitating for a moment, sat himself down on a chair reasonably close to Emma, but not within knee-touching distance, perfectly unexceptionable for a husband.

For no reason at all, things were feeling a lot more complicated now that Alex was here.

Maybe she should confide the truth in Letitia and begin to forge a spinster-within-a-marriage existence for herself sooner rather than later.

'You didn't take long to join us.' Letitia smiled up at her husband. 'Did you miss us?'

'Apparently so.' Arthur plonked a kiss on her cheek and sat down beside her on the loveseat upon which Letitia seemed to have chosen to sit precisely for the purpose of cosying up to her husband. Emma felt another pang that she would never share such an easy familiarity and blatant affection with Alex.

'I think we should play whist,' Letitia said, interrupting Emma's thoughts. 'Eight's the perfect number for it. We can have four sets of two and rotate. How shall we decide on partners? Having been fashionably apart at dinner, should we perhaps unfashionably partner our spouses?'

Everyone except Alex and Emma immediately exclaimed how lovely that would be. The two of them exchanged a quick glance and then both joined in with the exclamations, both perhaps a little too loudly.

Within less than five minutes, Emma was seated at a card table with Alex as her partner. He took the cards to shuffle them and suddenly Emma was fixated on his hands. They were strong, capable and lightly tanned, even though spring had barely begun, so he clearly spent a lot of time outside. And yesterday, in the late afternoon, those hands had been touching her, and just the memory of that was causing her to feel extremely hot again.

'Emma, are you all right?' Letitia asked. 'You look a little flushed. Would you like some ratafia?'

'Yes, please,' Emma said as Alex looked up from the cards.

'Are you sure you're perfectly well?' he asked her in a low voice.

The irony of him asking her if she was all right because everyone thought that she might be ill because she'd just been slightly overcome at the thought of what they'd been doing yesterday. And, oh, for goodness' sake, now she was thinking about his shoulders and his chest and how he'd touched *her* chest.

'Yes, thank you. I'm very well.' Emma buried her face in the glass of ratafia Arthur had just passed to her, took a long draught and nearly choked.

'Are you sure?' Alex asked.

'Yes, thank you, very sure. I hope you're going to prove to be a good player,' she told him, aiming for a playful just-married-and-still-coquettish-with-her-husband tone. 'We've never played cards together before,' she explained to the others.

'I will endeavour to satisfy you,' Alex replied with a little smile, which, had she not known that he was acting just as much as she was, would have caused Emma's heart to leap a little and her insides to flutter again.

He *did* satisfy her. Whist partnership-wise, anyway. He was intuitive, he was able to keep his face entirely expressionless so as not to give away any clues to the contents of his hand, and he adapted his game to hers very well. Emma liked to think that she adapted hers to his as well, and indeed that she had all the same attributes as a player.

Certainly, they beat everyone else quite resoundingly, and one of the most satisfying characteristics in Alex as a partner turned out to be that he was quite as competitive as she was.

'Perhaps just one more round?' he suggested, after the first one for a while that he and Emma hadn't won. *We can't finish on a loss*, he mouthed at her.

Emma was very tired, having slept very badly the night before, but was in complete agreement.

As soon as they'd won the next round, Alex said,

'I'm so sorry to break up the party, and indeed I'd very much like to continue showing the rest of you how it's done, but I think Emma's tired, and I see that it's very late indeed, and we don't wish to outstay our welcome.'

'I hope it hasn't snowed much more,' Emma said.

'You're always welcome here, as I hope you know,' Letitia said, 'and indeed you must also know you will be more than welcome to stay here overnight with us if the snow has made the roads impassable.'

'It has indeed snowed further while you've been here,' Arthur reported from behind the room's heavy curtains. 'I think you might all be forced to stay overnight.'

'That's perfect. I couldn't have planned it better. We will absolutely love to have you,' Letitia said, beaming. 'I will ask Harris to prepare a bedchamber for each couple. An impromptu house party! I already have plans for tomorrow.'

Emma felt that she and Alex had grown adept at reading each other's glances through their card games this evening, but it didn't take a lot of skill to read the horror in Alex's eyes at this moment, mirrored, she was sure, by her own. Well, perhaps not horror in her eyes; perhaps shock. The two of them sharing a bedchamber? Good heavens.

'I feel that we should investigate further,' she said. 'I think Alex and I would both like to return home to the boys tonight if possible.'

'I agree.' He nodded. 'Especially after my recent absence in London.'

'I'm not sure you're going to be able to do so,' Arthur said, still peering out of the window. He let go of the curtains and said, 'Let me go and see.'

'I'll accompany you,' Alex said.

As they left the room, Emma couldn't work out whether she'd rather they could or couldn't get home that night. A traitorous part of her felt that it might be very nice, albeit a little embarrassing, to be forced to share a chamber with Alex.

Chapter Thirteen

How was it possible that so much snow had fallen in one evening? Ridiculous.

As he and Arthur trod a path around the house, Alex stamped his boots viciously. He was absolutely not going to share a room with Emma tonight. It had been bad enough talking to her at dinner and playing cards with her this evening. He'd enjoyed her company far too much. He hoped he had enough willpower to resist her obvious attractions if they shared a room, but based on yesterday's idiocy he wasn't so sure that he did.

He wasn't going to share a room with her. So at least one of them was going to have to go home and, looking at the depth of the snow in Letitia and Arthur's drive, they weren't going to be able to take the chaise.

Fortunately, there was a full moon, and horses dealt very well with fresh snow; they only had difficulty when there was a frozen crust on top of the snow, which could lacerate their legs. Alex would ride carefully home in the moonlight and Emma could return in the chaise when the snow would allow her. She might have to stay here for several days, which, frankly, would be ideal in terms of allowing them both to cool off after yesterday's insanity.

Back in the house, Alex told the assembled company of his plans and Letitia swept everyone except Emma into the drawing room, saying, 'We must allow the two of you a moment to bid each other adieu for however long it might be.'

'Goodbye, then,' Emma said, her hands gripping each other tightly in front of her. 'Be careful as you ride.'

'Thank you. I will.' It was ridiculous that Alex now felt a wrench at leaving her. In case someone was watching, and because it felt rude not to, he took a step towards her and kissed her cheek, her scent flooding his senses as he did so. 'Goodnight. Sleep well.'

'Goodnight.'

Alex didn't enjoy his journey home. He alternated between walking Star and riding slowly, but that wasn't the problem. The problem was his mood. He felt bereft, as though home would be odd without Emma there. And he felt guilty, as though he'd engineered leaving her behind, and worried in case she was upset.

It was going to be a good thing, though, having time apart.

It was still snowing when he awoke after a short night's sleep. The snow continued until midday, and it was clear that carriages wouldn't be able to travel that day.

By the time Alex took his luncheon with the boys, he still wasn't sure how he felt about Emma's being stranded with Letitia and Arthur.

Extremely heavy snow came with consequences for agriculture, for people living in poverty, for those who needed to travel and for many more, especially this winter after last year's lack of summer. For Alex, it had also had the unexpected consequence of giving him a reprieve from being under the same roof as Emma, having to fight the attraction he felt for her, never sure whether he ought to spend time with her out of courtesy—and enjoyment, if he was honest—or avoid her because he enjoyed her company too much.

Was he pleased to have that reprieve, though?

If he'd been asked a few days ago how he would feel about this situation, he would have stated without hesitation that it would have been very welcome. And it was still welcome, in theory, but in practice he wasn't so sure.

He hoped that she was all right.

'When will Emma be back?' asked John for about the fifth time.

'I want her,' said Harry.

Freddie looked at Alex, and then he looked at his younger brothers. 'We can manage very well without her,' he said.

Alex paused, his fork halfway to his mouth. If he wasn't mistaken, Freddie had calculated that Alex would be pleased that she wasn't there, and had decided to come down on the side of his father rather than his brothers. This was terrible; Alex was setting a very poor example.

'I very much look forward to her returning,' he said. 'And while we can indeed manage without her, I know that we all miss her. I hope that she'll be able to return tomorrow.'

And then he busied himself helping Harry with his food, until he was sure that Freddie wasn't studying his face any more and the conversation had turned to a dead squirrel that the boys had seen being eaten by crows.

The next morning was Sunday and, following no further snow and a rise in temperatures, the roads were passable, albeit somewhat slushy, and Alex attended church with the children. He always chose the village church rather than the chapel on his estate; the chapel was heavy with memories of Diana's funeral, and in addition he wanted the boys' upbringing to be as informal as possible, given that they were the sons of a duke.

'Your Grace,' trilled Mrs Hardy as they left the church. 'Is Her Grace indisposed?'

'She was detained at Letitia and Arthur's by the snow, but we look forward to her return today.' Alex carried on walking.

Mrs Hardy was not a tall woman, but such was her determination to continue the conversation that she managed to lengthen her stride to keep pace with him.

'Perhaps a welcome break from the cosh of wedlock for you?' She accompanied her words with a little titter, while Alex tightened his lips. 'But travelling on a Sunday... I don't believe I can condone Her Grace's intention.'

'My wife's regard for her husband and sons must transcend any small feeling of guilt over undertaking a short journey, which, after all, is not that much further than some people must make between home and church,' Alex said, stony faced.

Mrs Hardy made a sound a little like 'Pfft,' and flounced away, which made Alex smile. He wished Emma had been there to see the flouncing.

Emma was alighting from the chaise as they arrived back at the house.

'Emma!' Harry hurtled towards her, followed by John.

Freddie looked at Alex, who had to struggle not to shake his head at the situation. He actually *was* pleased to see Emma. He did not wish to be pleased to see her, and he did not wish to act on that feeling, but he did need to set a good example of a respectful, if not passionate, union to his boys, particularly Freddie, it seemed.

Living a lie was hard.

He smiled at the boys and then walked forward to greet Emma. He placed his hands on her upper arms and a decorous kiss on each of her cheeks.

'As you see, we're all delighted to see you returned,' he told her.

'Oh,' she squeaked, her cheeks looking a little warm, before she recovered herself and said, 'I'm delighted to see you all.'

As they all went inside the house together, Alex couldn't help thinking that from the outside they must look like the perfect family picture.

He didn't know how he felt about Emma, so it was fortunate that they had the boys to distract them over the luncheon they ate together. Afterwards, in the absence of the excuse of work on the Sabbath, he took Freddie out for a long walk during the afternoon, arriving back only at dusk.

He joined Emma for dinner that evening in the grand dining room. She was dressed in a light green dress, against which her almost black hair looked stunning. The dress was low cut, and Alex caught himself gazing at the neckline for just a little too long, and remembering their interlude in the snow the other day.

He forced his gaze upwards, but that was no better. Emma's lips were slightly parted and she was looking at him as intently as he was looking at her. It was as though there was some kind of indefinable tension between them. Indefinable, but very thick, so thick that he could almost have cut it with the knife in front of him.

'It started snowing again just as we returned to the house after our walk,' he said.

There was a good reason that English people talked about the weather so often: it was the safest of subjects and there was so much of it.

'Quite heavily, in fact,' he continued as they took their seats at the table. 'I wouldn't be surprised if we were snowed in again. Freddie had a lot to tell me about snowflakes and their different constructions, and the fact that geographers believe that no two are the same.'

Good grief, he'd resorted to reciting snowflake facts.

Emma frowned, ignoring his inanities. 'That can't be good for the crops and livestock. The drifts had only barely begun to melt.'

'Indeed.' A week ago, Alex would have been surprised that her mind had gone straight to agriculture, but now he knew her better. 'I will visit my farming tenants tomorrow to discuss what can be done to help, on foot if necessary.'

'And your other tenants? Are they able to cope in this weather?'

'I trust so. They are well-housed, and I ensure that their rent is set at very reasonable levels.'

'I would like to visit the more vulnerable amongst them, if I may. Perhaps the elderly, or any families with numerous offspring who might be struggling.'

'Of course. When the weather is improved.'

'I am also able to visit on foot.'

'It's a long way.' Alex speared some peppered broccoli.

Emma nodded and didn't say anything else, instead focusing on cutting her veal escalope into dainty pieces. Clearly, she was going to ignore him.

'If you *do* go,' he said, 'I would prefer you to take your maid, or a footman, or perhaps both.'

Emma inclined her head and placed a piece of veal in her mouth. Watching her delicate chewing, Alex completely lost his train of thought. She raised her eyebrows at him slightly as she took her next mouthful, and indeed he knew he was staring. Or gazing. Both were a little embarrassing for a grown man at his own supper table. Surely he could find some non-contentious conversation about something beyond snowflakes?

'How did you spend your second evening at Letitia and Arthur's?' he asked. He'd asked whether she'd enjoyed her stay when they sat down for luncheon, but the boys had taken over the conversation from that point on, and they hadn't had the opportunity to go back to it. 'I hope you enjoyed your stay.'

'Thank you; I did enjoy it. We played whist again yesterday evening. I was partnered with Gideon.'

'Oh, dear.' Alex had lost count of the number of times he'd trounced Gideon at the card table. Gideon was not a gifted player, and cheerfully acknowledged that fact.

Emma laughed. 'Indeed. I missed your partnership sorely.'

And then she stopped laughing, and so did he, and he realised that they were gazing at each other's mouths and eyes again. There was something about the word 'partnership'.

'I understand that it often snows very heavily in Lancashire?' Alex said, swallowing.

Snow was apparently the safest topic of conversation this evening, and they stuck to weather-related topics for the entirety of the rest of their dinner, which did less to take Alex's mind off Emma's smile and beautiful eyes than he would have liked.

* * *

They awoke in the morning to the deepest March snow in living memory, according to Lancing, who had a longer memory than most. It had already stopped snowing, though, and while travel by carriage or horse would be difficult, as any flattened snow was icing over, it was possible to walk as men had been out clearing the roads.

Alex spent an hour after breakfast discussing his farmers' needs with Parsons, and then directed footmen and grooms to divert their energies from their usual work to helping on the land where needed, and then set out on foot to check on the inhabitants of a cluster of cottages east of the castle, which were occupied by some elderly people and one couple who had three young children and were expecting a fourth imminently.

He took one of the grooms named Mikey with him. Once they'd checked on those tenants Mikey could send for any necessary assistance, and Alex would walk on to the nearest farm.

The first cottage at which he arrived was that belonging to the young couple. He knocked on the door and it was opened by...*Emma*. Holding a toddler on her hip.

'Emma?'

'Alex?' She opened the door wider to allow him entry.

'I didn't expect to see you here.'

'I thought you knew that I was planning to come?'

'I...' He looked at her. 'Your skirts, though. In the snow.'

'My pelisse is thick, and I'm wearing stout boots and where my skirts got a little wet they're now dry from the fire. The roads are entirely passable as you know.'

'Where's Jenny? Where's *everyone*?' It seemed to be

just Emma, the toddler and two slightly older children in the little cottage.

'Jenny is less hardy than I, and I knew she wouldn't want to come, so I came alone. Thomas is out checking on his livestock and Eliza is very tired, as she's eight months pregnant, so I suggested that she have a sleep while I look after the children for an hour or two.'

'Your walk here might have been dangerous, though.'

'It wasn't that far, and also…'

He looked at her. 'Don't tell me. You brought your pistol.'

Good God.

Emma laughed. 'The expression on your face is very amusing.'

'I'm glad to hear it.'

'Alex?'

'Yes?'

'I wonder whether you would look after the children while I tidy a little for Eliza?' Emma gestured around the room and Alex nodded. It could certainly do with being a little tidier.

And so the Duke of Harwell looked after three—fairly grubby—small children, while the Duchess of Harwell tidied and scrubbed.

Mikey did some outside work, directed by Emma, until Alex asked him to go and check on other tenants.

When Eliza awoke from her sleep, she almost cried in gratitude. Emma hugged her, and then the two of them hugged all the children to them, and Alex couldn't help smiling at the sight.

'We should leave,' he said eventually. 'I'm afraid I have other appointments.'

'Of course.' Emma disengaged herself and picked up

her coat from the back of a kitchen chair. 'I'll call on you again very soon, Eliza.'

'Are you going on somewhere else?' she asked Alex when they got outside.

'No, obviously not.' He gestured at the ominous clouds above them. 'I predict further snowfall today. I'm going to escort you home.'

Emma opened her mouth and Alex shook his head.

'Irrespective of your pistol, and your coat and stout boots and your desire not to be told what to do—which I do fully understand and respect—I am going to escort you home.'

'I was going to say thank you,' Emma said, raising one eyebrow.

Oh.

'Well, great,' Alex said, smiling in appreciation of her ability to take the wind out of his sails frequently. 'Let's go.'

Emma set off at a significantly brisker pace than he was expecting, which was a good thing, because it started snowing lightly within minutes of their leaving the cottage. When he worried that she was only walking at that speed because she thought she ought to keep up with him, she increased her pace even further, which made him laugh.

'This is so beautiful.' She didn't sound at all out of breath. She put her arms out and tipped her face up to the sky as she continued to walk.

'Tempted to throw any snowballs now that you're one to one with your snowball foe with no shelter nearby and might come off worse?'

Emma looked round at him, blinked snowflakes from her lashes and narrowed her eyes. 'Is that a challenge?'

'Maybe. Maybe not. Just something to think about.'

'Going by your threats, I see that your defeat still rankles.'

'Defeat is a strong word.'

Defeat was completely the wrong word for what had happened. They'd made each other soaking wet, and then they'd…

Why? Why had he brought that up now? Now all he could think about was what they'd done in the snow.

Emma was capable of thinking of other things, apparently. She'd stopped walking and put her hands on her hips.

'I see what you're doing. You're attempting to plant seeds of worry in my mind. There could be a snowball around any corner. And just as my morale is low, which might affect my strategic planning, you will attack.' She started walking again, fast, and said over her shoulder, 'Just be aware that you might have longer and better throwing arms than me, but I'm sure I'm significantly more cunning.'

Alex laughed out loud and took the three strides necessary to catch her up.

He didn't practise any snowball warfare during their walk, not keen to be tempted into any further intimacy in the snow. Instead, he showed Emma various points of interest, from a very ancient oak tree, reputed to date back to the sixteenth century and to have witnessed a visit from Good Queen Bess herself, to a copse in which he and his brother played as children.

As they reached the top of a hill, from which it was possible to see for many miles—all the way to the sea on a cloudless day—the snow suddenly changed to a heavy, driving force. Within minutes, from having been almost able to make out the horizon through light snow, they could see barely a few feet in front of them.

'Oh, my goodness,' a white-covered Emma said.

Alex took two steps towards her, reached for her hand and linked his fingers firmly through hers. 'We must hold hands so that we don't lose each other.'

The swirling snow was incredibly disorientating. Alex knew his land like the back of his hand, and still he was in great danger of losing his bearings unless he concentrated hard. The snow was very wet and very cold, and they would do well not to stay in it for too long. He was beginning to feel chilled to the bone, despite his greatcoat and winter boots, and Emma's clothing was less robust than his. She also had a much smaller frame than he, so she would be freezing very quickly.

They began to walk slowly forward, Alex feeling the way slightly ahead of Emma, using his feet. Within only a few steps Emma tripped. He caught her and pulled her to a halt next to him.

'Are you all right? You haven't twisted your ankle or anything?'

'Yes, thank you.' She was gripping his hand and arm as tightly as he was holding hers now.

'I think we need to take shelter nearby until this is over,' he said. 'I think it would be very difficult to get all the way back. I can't believe it will last more than an hour or two, and there's a barn about a hundred feet to our left.'

It was perhaps two miles to the house, and that was a very long way in a blizzard, especially for someone in female attire.

Arm in arm now, they inched towards where Alex

thought the barn was, guided only by his memory of how the hill's contours went.

'I think I might have misremembered,' he said eventually, after they'd been trudging into driving snow for what seemed like an extraordinarily long time. 'I'm so sorry. Hopefully we will at least find a wall soon, behind which we can shelter.' The snow was biting, literally painful against one's face, and he sensed Emma wince every so often. If they found a wall, he would do his best to shelter her from the storm. 'We can't walk too far, though.'

There was a river running through his land not far from here, and there were several dips in the terrain that were negligible to people who could see them, but which in this weather could cause one or both of them to break a leg or worse.

'Wall!' said Emma about ten seconds later.

'I beg your pardon?'

'Wall. I just hit a wall with my hand.'

Alex turned carefully, with his own free hand outstretched, and felt around. Yes, they'd found a wall.

'Thank God,' he said. 'I'm sure this is the wall of a building. It must be the barn.'

Emma made to let go of his hand, but he tightened his grip on hers.

'I really don't think we should let go of each other at this point,' he said. 'Let's not fail now, when we're so close to shelter.'

'Yes, you're right.' Emma moved back towards him and said, 'Let's go to our right along the wall, not letting go of it, until we come to a door or opening.'

'Good idea.'

They found the opening on the third side, and walked

through the edge of the blizzard inside, towards the back of the barn, which was fully covered and dry and half full of hay.

'That is *such* a relief.' Emma took her hand out of his. 'I can't remember ever feeling so truly ecstatic to find a pile of dead grass.' She reached up to her head and pulled at her bonnet, which had begun the day a fairly rigid, pointed shape, but which was now entirely sodden and drooping. 'My fingers are barely working from the cold.'

Eventually, she had the bonnet off and shook out her hair. 'May I sit on this hay?'

'Certainly.' Alex climbed over towards the back of the barn and held his arm out for her to take. 'If you come here you'll find that it's much warmer, or at least less freezing.'

Emma took his arm for support and climbed over, and then let go and sat down. Alex joined her, although sitting a cautious few feet away from her.

'We were lucky that we were so close to the barn when that started,' she said. 'And that you know your land so well. Or perhaps you have some kind of super-natural ability to see through incredibly heavy snow.'

Alex laughed. 'Yes, I am possessed of a special winter vision belonging only to Somerset natives. No, I've spent many, many days on this land, and I do know it well, even more so now, from a different angle, since I inherited the running and husbandry of it.'

'Well, thank goodness. I'm sure we would have been all right had we stayed out there, albeit extremely cold and wet, but I have to say I vastly prefer being inside, even in a barn. Indeed, at this moment the barn feels positively like a princess's palace.'

'It does. And I'm sure it's very good for us to be re-

minded not to take our creature comforts for granted.'
Alex paused, hearing a slightly odd sound, and studied
Emma. 'Is that sound your teeth chattering?'

'N-n-no…' It wasn't just her teeth that were chattering; her whole body was beginning to judder.

'You're freezing.'

'Please don't worry; this hay will serve very well
to warm me.' Emma pulled some hay against herself,
turning herself into a ridiculously sorry sight as some
stuck to her damp clothes while other wisps floated away
from her.

Alex stood up and took his coat off to wrap her in it.
But, no, that would be no good; it was very wet on the
outside and the damp had penetrated right through it in
parts. His jacket was also wet, and not thick enough to
provide much warmth.

Emma was shivering more and more now, her whole
body jerking. Alex knew that he needed to do something
fast, and could think of only one solution.

'I think you need to take your wet coat off, and then
I'm going to sit very close to you to warm you.'

'Really?'

'Yes.'

She pulled ineffectually at the buttons of her coat,
her fingers clearly too cold to work properly at all now.
Alex moved over to sit beside her and began to undo
the buttons, working as fast as he could, scared by how
very much she was shivering. He had the coat off very
quickly, and laid it out on the hay behind them in the
hope that it might dry a little, before wrapping both his
arms around her. Her dress was a little damp, unsurprisingly.

'I don't see how we can get entirely dry, short of divesting ourselves entirely of our clothes.' He wondered immediately why he'd said that, struggling to force his mind away from the thought of Emma divested of her clothes. 'But I think that if we huddle together like this our body warmth will heat the wetness, which should hopefully warm you up.'

'Thank you.' She could hardly get the words out round her chattering teeth.

Alex was getting even more scared. He could feel Emma's slender shoulders shivering in huge jerks. There was still too much of her exposed to the cold air.

'Come here.' He lifted her onto his lap and wrapped himself around her as much as he could.

'Thank you,' she said again, her voice now muffled against his chest.

They sat like that for a while—Alex couldn't tell how long—until Emma wriggled a little and said, 'I'm starting to feel a reasonably normal temperature again. Thank you so much.'

'Good,' said Alex, not releasing his grip on her. 'Let's not count our chickens too early, though. We must get you as hot as possible before I let go of you. Even when the snow's subsided enough for us to make our way back we're going to get very wet again, and you're going to have to put your wet coat back on.'

'How's it looking now?' Emma raised her head and peered over his shoulder.

'Still remarkably fierce. If we weren't wet and on foot and stranded in a barn a good couple of miles from the house, I'd be lost in happy awe of the elements.'

'It is beautiful,' agreed Emma, wriggling some more, presumably to get a better view out of the barn entrance.

Now that he was a little less worried about her, Alex

was a lot more aware of the fact that she was sitting on his lap, in his arms, and that she was wiggling her gorgeously rounded bottom against him. He really hoped she couldn't feel the effect she was having on him.

She suddenly stopped moving and… Yes, she probably had realised.

There wasn't a lot that embarrassed Alex, but this, yes, this was embarrassing. And there was nothing he could do to extricate himself from the embarrassment because he had to keep holding Emma the way he was, so that she wouldn't get cold again. So he was just going to chat to her about something mundane, and then he'd stop being so aware of her, his body would get itself under control and all would be well.

'I wonder what we'll have for luncheon when we return to the house,' he said.

Food was certainly a mundane topic.

'Something warm and hearty. Perhaps a beef stew. Followed, perhaps, by something deliciously sweet.' Emma shifted again on his lap and Alex almost groaned out loud.

'What's your favourite dessert?' he persisted.

They just needed to talk about food for longer. That way he could absolutely stop his mind and body from being so focused on what Emma was doing with her body.

'I'm not sure. I think…' Emma paused. Alex couldn't see her face, but he knew what she looked like when she was thinking. She'd have her nose ever so slightly wrinkled, and if she was about to say something sarcastic or cheeky, her eyes would be dancing.

'On a day like this, something very rich. A smooth chocolate mousse, perhaps.'

Now Alex was imagining her putting a spoon into a mousse and then into her mouth, her tongue peeking out. And now of course he was imagining kissing her again. God.

'What would you like?' she asked.

'What?'

'What would you like to eat?'

'To eat? Of course.' Alex could barely remember what food was at this point. It felt as though he had one physical need only, and it wasn't food.

Emma twisted her head to look up at him and smiled. It was the smile that undid him. If she hadn't done it maybe he could have resisted, but the smile was both sweet and slightly mocking, as though she knew what he was thinking.

He found himself adjusting her so that he could reach her face better—and, *damn*, it felt good as she moved in his lap—and then, very slowly, he lowered his head to hers. She moved to meet him and suddenly the slowness was gone and they were kissing, hard, urgently, passionately.

Far in the depths of his brain Alex knew that this was a terrible idea, but apparently he was completely powerless to resist.

Chapter Fourteen

Emma was almost panting as she kissed Alex back as hard as he was kissing her.

From the moment her teeth had stopped chattering so hard it had felt as though she might bite right through her tongue, and she'd had the ability to think about where she was, she'd loved being enveloped in Alex's arms. And from the moment she'd warmed up and moved on his lap and felt the evidence of his desire for her, she'd wanted this.

She had her hands in his thick hair, his arms were round her waist and her shoulders, and his body was still wrapped right around hers. It was truly wonderful, but she wanted *more*.

It wasn't just the physical sensation that she wanted, although she was quite desperate for that. It was also that she wanted some kind of affirmation of how their relationship had developed, in her eyes anyway. They made each other laugh, they seemed to be able to talk about all manner of topics, and Alex was a very kind, decent person whom she *liked*.

She hoped he liked her too.

She didn't just like him. She loved him.

And at this moment, she was in his arms, and she wanted to give him everything she had and receive everything he could give her.

She wriggled against him again and he groaned, deep in his throat, a sound that made her breath catch. She moved one of her hands from the back of his head and ran it up his hard chest. Then she took her other hand and pulled at the fastenings of his shirt, wanting to feel his skin as she had the other day.

She moved further against him and he groaned again, and then he plunged his hands into her hair and pulled very gently, so that her head went back a little. He kissed down her neck, licking, nibbling, nipping, caressing her shoulders with one hand and still holding her waist with the other. His kisses were moving ever lower, but slowly, and Emma felt as though her entire body was becoming taut in anticipation.

And then suddenly he lifted her, so that she was lying on her back, nestled away from any draughts, on a big bundle of hay, with him above her. With one hand he was caressing her breast and the other fumbled with ribbons and buttons, trying to remove her dress. Emma found herself pulling his shirt out of his breeches as urgently as he was trying to undress her.

Alex paused for a moment and found her eyes with his. He raised his eyebrows slightly, as though seeking her consent to continue.

'Yes, please,' she said. And if she sounded as though she was begging, she didn't care.

She smiled at him, a heartfelt invitation, and he smiled back. Then he lowered his lips to hers again, this time kissing her gently, slowly, deeply, all the while exploring with his hands.

Emma's breasts felt as though they were on fire now, and the sensation was spreading to her most intimate parts, so that she was almost *aching* for him in a way that she couldn't even describe.

He drew back for a moment, and just looked at her. 'You're beautiful,' he said.

Emma looked down at herself and gasped. Somehow she was almost entirely naked. Then she looked at him, and gasped again, because he was almost entirely naked too, and he was…magnificent.

And then she lost the ability to think because Alex began to kiss her everywhere, while his fingers touched her between her thighs gently, then more insistently, until she was arching and turning and her body was almost *singing* with sensation.

Then his body was above hers, so close, and he was looking at her again with that raised eyebrow, as though confirming again that she was happy. She nodded, realising through the haze of sensation that there was nothing with which she wouldn't trust him. Kissing her and murmuring her name the whole time, he pushed slowly inside her.

When, after the first shock, she was comfortable—comfortable to perfection—he began to thrust and thrust, and if she'd thought that her body was singing with sensation before, it was positively crying out now.

She opened her eyes for a moment and looked at his face—the face she knew now that she loved, at which she could never tire of looking—and she smiled at him and whispered, 'Alex.'

And then he began to thrust harder and harder, and she was lost, one hand in his hair, the other almost scratching his back, almost screaming with the desire for more and more of him.

Suddenly, she felt the most glorious sensation, her whole body flooded with it, and this time she really did scream, while Alex grunted, 'Yes, Emma, yes.'

And then he gathered her to him as they both lay panting.

Emma looked up at his strong jaw, his kind eyes, his mouth that could set in a forbidding line when he was angry and yet curve in such a sweet way at other times, and knew that she would never be the same again.

She didn't know how he felt about her, but she knew that she'd fallen in love with him, and that it wasn't going to be the kind of love you recovered from quickly. Or maybe ever.

She gasped again—she'd been doing a lot of gasping today—as he eased himself out of her and said, his voice hoarse, 'That was… That was not what I was expecting to do today.'

'Nor I,' Emma said after a moment, her heart cracking, because it was extremely clear that he hadn't been lying there thinking that he'd fallen in love with her.

If you'd just realised that you'd fallen in love with someone the first words that came out of your mouth would not be that you hadn't expected to do that today.

Maybe he could come to love her in time, though? Or at least enjoy her company and making love to her enough to want to live with her as man and wife, properly?

Would he want to make love to her again? Regularly? And would that be enough for her? Would she be able to hide from him how she felt?

If she couldn't hide it from him things could get very embarrassing on both sides.

She could hide it, should hide it, if it meant they could be together. Or should she? Would she in time begin to resent him? Would her love drive a wedge between them, as her parents' love had driven a wedge between them when it had become apparent that they wanted and needed different things in life?

'So.' Alex released her gently and Emma looked down at their nakedness. Alex did too. He was stirring again as they looked at each other. She felt her breath catch in her throat as she felt her own body responding to his obvious desire, and then he cleared his throat and moved a little further away from her.

'The blizzard has stopped,' he said. 'We should return while it's safe to do so, and before anyone becomes worried about us.'

Emma took a deep breath to cover her disappointment, and when she was sure that her voice would sound close to normal said, 'We should, indeed.'

She rolled to one side, away from him, looking for her clothes to cover herself. It turned out that nakedness during lovemaking was wonderful, and natural, but nakedness when the man who had just made love to you just wanted to go home felt embarrassing. And cold when you were in an open barn on a snowy day.

Alex passed her her dress and she said, 'Thank you.'

They dressed with their backs to each other. Emma couldn't remember feeling this miserable for a long time. Ironic that she'd thought—known—she could trust him with anything. She realised now that she could trust him with absolutely everything except her heart.

The good thing about getting dressed in wet clothes surrounded by hay was that it was quite difficult, and it gave Emma time to think a little more and pull herself together. The bad thing about how difficult it was was that she couldn't entirely manage by herself.

She turned to Alex. 'I'm so sorry, but I wonder if you might help with my fastenings?'

'Of course.'

As he carefully pulled her hair aside, his fingers brushed her neck, and Emma almost leapt a mile. She was really going to have to work hard to get herself under control.

'I think you should wear my coat,' Alex told her. 'It's thicker, and it didn't get so wet on the inside.' He held it up against her and said, 'Oh.'

It was many inches too long.

'It might keep me warmer, but I might fall and break a leg instead,' Emma said.

'Indeed. Each to their own coat it is, then.'

They said very little further as they made their way out of the barn, Alex helping Emma clamber over the bales of hay, and their conversation during the walk back was restricted to the most basic of issues, such as Alex's request that Emma hold his arm and hand again, in case the ground was slippery or there was a further sudden snowstorm.

Emma couldn't quite comprehend how the linking of their arms now felt so entirely functional, when their arms had been wrapped around each other so passionately so very recently.

Well, it was a strong sign of how Alex felt, and since she was going to be seeing him every day still, she would have to hide her emotions for both their sakes.

She was sure he was still grieving for his wife.

She remembered their conversation over dinner a

week or two ago, when he'd described Diana in such a tender way. Of *course* he was still grieving for her.

She felt sorry, deeply sorry, for him. She knew that if something awful happened to him now she'd be devastated, and she'd only known and loved him for a few weeks. If something bad happened to him in a few years' time she would find it horrendous.

So, having loved Diana for several years, as he obviously had, and having three children with her, he must have been utterly grief-stricken when he'd lost her. Awful. She hated to think of Alex in pain.

If she was honest, though—and this probably made her a truly terrible person—she couldn't help feeling a tiny bit (very) sorry for her own loss too, because when she thought about it like this it was quite clear that Alex was still deeply in love with the memory of his wife and that Emma would never be able to compete with that.

There was nothing she could say to him now.

They walked on in silence all the way back to the castle.

Perhaps it was a good thing that Alex was still in love with Diana and that Emma couldn't compete with that love. The two of them clearly wanted very different things, just as her parents had, and she didn't want to follow in their footsteps and have her love turn to near-hatred because they were so incompatible.

As they approached the main entrance to the castle, she took a quick glance up at his profile. He didn't twitch. She felt as though she'd lost him today, somewhere in the moments after they'd made love.

'Your Grace,' cried Jenny, hurrying out to meet them. 'Come inside directly. You'll catch your death with that wet coat on.'

Emma realised that she was indeed very cold.

'Thank you, Jenny.' She turned round to bid Alex farewell and discovered that he'd already gone.

'You need to have a bath immediately.'

Jenny and Mrs Drabble both busied themselves calling for so much hot water that the entire household could have had hot baths if the footmen had obeyed them.

'Thank you so much. But I'm very well able to bathe myself,' Emma told Jenny when the bath was ready.

She didn't want to undress in front of Jenny; what if there had been some physical change in her today that Jenny could discern?

'You're shivering. I don't want to leave you, Your Grace.'

'Thank you, Jenny, but I assure you that I will be warm again as soon as I get into the bath.'

Jenny grumbled for so long that Emma feared the bath water might already be cold. When she eventually gave in and left, Emma locked the door behind her and undressed herself before climbing into the bath. She looked down at herself. There did not, in fact, seem to be any noticeable physical change.

She had certainly changed emotionally, though; she was certain now that she'd fallen deeply and irrevocably in love with Alex.

Now she was shivering again.

She rubbed her arms hard to warm herself up. Her body, anyway. It felt as though her heart might never be warm again.

Chapter Fifteen

Alex spent only the time it took to get changed into dry clothes and visit the kitchen for a flying luncheon—to his chef's expressed horror, but not very well-hidden delight—before readying himself to set off again on foot to visit other tenants. He needed to check that the more vulnerable amongst them were all right, and he also needed not to be alone with his thoughts.

Those thoughts had intruded as he'd changed and eaten and parried comments from his chef, and they continued to intrude as he shrugged on a dry greatcoat.

This morning was the first time he'd been intimate with a woman since he'd lost Diana. He couldn't… He didn't… He wasn't sure how he felt, other than that the experience had been truly spectacular from a physical perspective and utterly terrifying from an emotional perspective.

Physically, he just wanted to do it again.

Emotionally, well, emotionally, what did he want?

He wanted to know that Emma would always be happy. He wanted—that was to say, he was *tempted*—to look after her, cosset her…

Damn it, he wanted to… He almost wanted to love her.

No. He did *not* want to love her.

The image of her smile as they'd lain together on the straw came into his head. Hell and damnation. What if she decided to go out again this afternoon and some accident befell her?

He called Lancing, and every footman he could see, as well as Mrs Drabble and Jenny, to instruct them that they must not allow Emma to leave the house in the snow by herself again.

At the last minute, just before he left, he realised his own hypocrisy. Even if he didn't have a responsibility to himself, he did to many other people, not least his motherless children. He asked his head groom, Jim, whom he knew was very fit and, crucially, also a man of few words, to walk with him.

They set off on a long and silent march into biting wind, enlivened by the occasional sideways flurry of skin-prickling frozen snow, which suited his mood very well.

Visibility this afternoon was dramatically better than it had been this morning, and he could now see the barn from some distance. Thank God they'd found it when they had. And thank God he'd been with Emma. If she'd been alone she might have been killed in that blizzard.

She was so brave. And so stupid. And so adorable. Not to mention beautiful.

He forced his mind away from the memory of her naked beneath him, and then from another, of how, in the aftermath of their lovemaking, her smile had changed from one of physical bliss to uncertainty, when she'd clearly seen that he wasn't going to repeat the experience.

That change in her smile had nearly caused him to gather her up in his arms, rain kisses on her and tell her... Tell her that he felt... Damn. He couldn't. He couldn't love her. He could not allow himself to do so. It would be very easy to do so. But difficult too. Because what if something bad happened to her?

She was extremely competent, but there were things that very few people could survive, like, for example, a fully clothed fall into a near-frozen river in a blizzard. He couldn't bear the thought that she could have died today.

He stepped up his pace and Jim grunted, 'You're in a hurry today, Your Grace.'

Alex found a small smile for him. 'You not up to it, Jim?'

'I'm up to it, Your Grace. Just a little surprised.'

Alex nodded. He was surprised too. This morning had taught him something that he hadn't known. He hadn't believed that he could ever love another woman again after Diana. Now he knew that while he would always carry his grief for Diana with him, he was capable of loving again.

What he was *not* capable of, though, was coping with being in love. Because if Emma *had* died this morning, or even just been injured, it would have devastated him, and he'd only known her for a few weeks. If he allowed himself to make their marriage real it would destroy him if anything happened to her. And the way the boys were going, loving her as they already did, it would destroy them too. He just couldn't do it.

Emma had friends now. She was established socially, he hoped. They should probably move on to the next phase of their marriage. She could move to the dower house and begin to live independently. He would make clear to his friends and acquaintances that she should be respected as a member of their circle. Perhaps he would confide in Letitia as he already had in Gideon.

'Your Grace!'

'Jim?'

'You didn't tell me we'd be running.'

'Not running, Jim, just walking fast.'

Alex increased his pace even more, so that they were working too hard for speech or, importantly, further thought. Thinking was not pleasant today.

Some time later, as they skirted the edge of a small wood at the base of a hill, a bough broke under the weight of the snow it had been holding and fell just in front of them, scattering snow as it went.

The sensation of wet snow on his skin made him think of snowballs with Emma, rolling in the snow with Emma, making love to Emma a few yards away from a blizzard. Which was ridiculous, because he was thirty-three years old and he had encountered a lot of snow with a lot of different people; but it seemed that he couldn't get Emma out of his thoughts this afternoon.

He flexed his shoulders as some of the snow went down his neck and imagined her laughing at him. Damn, he'd miss her if he didn't see her any more. Perhaps he shouldn't make too hasty a decision; perhaps he should think more about their situation first.

They arrived shortly after that at the home of Caleb Wilson, one of Alex's tenant farmers. Caleb was an elderly man who had broken his leg badly a few weeks ago, tumbling from a shire horse that a man of his age really should not have been riding.

As Alex ducked his head to go through the doorway into the cottage's main room, having asked Jim if he would go and check on Caleb's livestock, he saw Caleb huddled in a chair close to a dying fire. There was a large pile of logs on the other side of the fire, but it looked as though Caleb wasn't mobile enough to be able to reach them.

Alex had made sure that all his less well-off tenants had a ready supply of firewood over the winter, so it had to be a mobility issue rather than a financial one. That or Caleb enjoyed freezing in his own home. Other than next to the fire, the room was barely any warmer than the temperature outside.

His heart going out to Caleb, but knowing from experience how proud he was, Alex clapped his hands together, and said, 'It's a cold day out there, Caleb. I'm chilled to the bone. Would you mind if I built your fire up? I'm not sure I'll be able to get through the rest of the day happily otherwise.'

'You're a good lad, Your Grace. Thank you.' Caleb produced a toothless grin for him, and Alex's heart twisted again. Sometimes his responsibility for all these good, decent people weighed on him particularly heavily.

'I hope you don't mind if I join you by the fire?' Alex drew up a stool and sat down next to the old man. 'How's your leg healing?'

Caleb had a lot to say, giving the impression of a man somewhat desperate for company. He would normally be busy all day, and would see his neighbours regularly too, but now with his broken leg he was at the mercy of how much time they could spare to visit him, and in conditions like this they wouldn't have a lot of time.

'Tess, my daughter-in-law, she's been in,' he said. 'She's a good woman, but she's busy with those bairns of hers.' He paused and stretched out a hand to Alex, who took it. 'You'll understand this, Your Grace. I always miss my Jeanie—' his wife had died about five years ago '—but it's at times like this, when I have thinking time, that I miss her even more.'

Alex was not in the habit of talking about his feelings but, looking at Caleb's lined face, into his faded blue eyes, he knew that at this moment he needed to make the effort for Caleb's sake. It didn't come naturally, though. And while he had experienced the terrible loss of his wife, at a horrifyingly early age, he'd never, due to his different station in life, found himself sitting all alone in the near-freezing, near-dark for hours on end.

'Yes. I was reflecting earlier today that too much thinking time is dangerous,' he said, feeling for words that would demonstrate to Caleb that he understood.

'It is. We need to move on with the future. You have your children and I have mine, and I have my grandchildren. We need to think about them, not the past. We're both lucky. Not everyone has children.'

Alex didn't want to think about the fact that he'd effectively prevented Emma from having children of her own. Unless, of course, she'd become with child as a result of their lovemaking this morning. How would he feel if she had? Pleased for her that she'd have a baby but utterly terrified that she'd die in childbirth, as Diana had.

He returned the squeeze of the hand that Caleb gave him and said, 'We might be lucky with our children, but the loss of one's life companion is very hard.'

'It is that.' They sat in silence for a moment, with Alex feeling quite useless, and then Caleb said, 'Thank you, Your Grace. Much appreciated.'

Maybe all Caleb needed from Alex was what he could

give him: his company, and the feeling that they were in the same boat.

He looked up as he heard a muffled sniff from Caleb, and reached over and squeezed his shoulder.

'Thank you again,' Caleb said after a few moments. 'I'm getting emotional in my old age. I just miss her.'

Alex clasped Caleb's hand and looked into the fire. Currently, he was dealing with life better than Caleb was. He'd reached a point where, while still grieving for Diana, he had been able to develop feelings for another woman and enjoy making love to her. He didn't want to regress, be like this again. He didn't want to be a lonely old man, missing his wife so deeply. He wanted to be happy, but not so happy that the loss of that happiness would cause a repeat of his devastation over Diana's death.

'I need to cheer myself up,' Caleb said. 'We have to let go, don't we, when we've lost someone?'

Alex nodded. 'Yes. We do.'

He wasn't talking about Diana, though. It was Emma whom he needed to let go of now. He hoped she wouldn't be hurt, but he had, after all, told her right from the beginning that he couldn't offer her anything more than his name and his protection.

If he and Jim had walked fast on the way there, now, on their way back to the castle, they'd almost give a horse a run for its money.

'May I ask if everything's all right, Your Grace?' Jim panted at one point.

'Certainly.' Alex didn't look at him; he just kept on marching, too fast for further thought.

He and Jim were very hot when they arrived back.

'Thank you for your company,' he said to Jim. 'Apologies if I walked a little fast.'

'I enjoyed it, Your Grace,' Jim said. 'Even if my feet didn't,' he added under his breath, as he headed off towards the stables with a slight limp.

Alex smiled at his departing back. Thank God he had staff who didn't stand on ceremony with him. If he didn't, he could end up as lonely as Caleb. He would make sure that he or someone else from his household visited Caleb regularly until his leg was mended.

Striding into the house, he was stopped by Lancing, who told him that Mrs Hardy had called for tea and had expressed a particular desire to see Alex, should he return before she left. She was currently in the green saloon with the duchess.

'Of course.' Alex could barely imagine a person to whom he'd less like to speak today, and was strongly tempted to turn tail, but he couldn't leave Emma to Mrs Hardy's mercies.

He entered the saloon just in time to hear Mrs Hardy, seated with her back to him, say to a rigid-looking Emma, 'And I must repeat: if you would like any advice on comportment, you know you only have to ask and I shall be very happy to guide you. I am, of course, the granddaughter of an earl. In my capacity as vicar's wife I am here to assist those less fortunate than myself, such as you with your background.'

Emma's eyes had widened as Mrs Hardy spoke. Now she said, one eye on Alex, 'I count myself incredibly fortunate to have you available to assist me should I require such help. Thank you.'

Alex knew that she was being sarcastic, and he knew that she would be able to laugh about Mrs Hardy's ridiculous rudeness, but he was nonetheless filled with real rage at how the woman had spoken to Emma, not least because he was scared that others would hear her express such thoughts and imitate her.

'You are indeed kind to make such an offer, Mrs Hardy,' he said, injecting ice into his voice.

Mrs Hardy turned her head very fast and then rose to her feet, wreathed in smiles, before curtseying. 'Your Grace,' she said, holding her hands out to him.

Alex ignored the hands. 'While you are kind, Emma has no need of your advice. Firstly, she is herself the granddaughter of an earl, through her mother, and also of a princess, through her father. I am certain that she is too well-bred to have discussed her breeding with you, so you were perhaps not aware of that.'

He could see Mrs Hardy's smile fall at his implied criticism and Emma, beyond her, smiling at him, her eyes beginning to dance.

'Secondly, of course, true breeding comes from within, and certainly from my perspective I have nothing but admiration for Emma's character and comportment, and I am sure that the vast majority of her acquaintance feel the same way. Good afternoon.' He moved back to the door and held it wide open and bowed to Mrs Hardy.

'I see that you are in a bad humour this afternoon, Your Grace,' she said, glaring. 'No doubt it is the weather. Much can be excused of a duke, fortunately.'

When she'd huffed herself out of the room, Alex closed the door behind her very firmly and sat down on a sofa opposite Emma.

'Thank you,' she said. 'That was spectacular.'

'I cannot regret my rudeness. The way she spoke to you was completely unacceptable.'

'She was so rude that I just wanted to laugh. But I was very glad that you were there to witness it, to share in my enjoyment.'

Alex laughed. '"Enjoyment" is a charitable word.'

There was a short silence between them.

They needed to talk.

He put his hands on his knees, and then lifted them to adjust his jacket. Perhaps he should have changed before they started this conversation. No, formal clothing would not have helped. He placed his hands back on his knees and crossed his legs, and then uncrossed them.

How to begin?

'How has your afternoon been?' Emma asked into the uncomfortable silence. 'I believe you went to visit other tenants?'

'Yes.'

Describing to Emma his visit to Caleb was a relief: it felt like a partial unburdening, or at least a sharing, of the responsibility Alex felt.

'So he's going to feel his loneliness greatly while he remains incapacitated with his broken leg?' Emma said when Alex had concluded the story of his visit.

He nodded.

'We should arrange for him to have regular visitors. Certainly, I shall visit him, perhaps with one or more of the children, by carriage if you think it appropriate?'

'Yes, I do, and indeed I trust you quite implicitly in your judgement in regard to the children.'

Emma's cheeks flushed. 'Thank you. That's quite the most lovely compliment anyone has paid me for a long time.'

This wasn't really how Alex had envisaged his conversation with Emma going, although he was very grateful to know that she would visit Caleb.

'We need to talk,' he said, more shortly than he'd intended.

'I am at your disposal,' Emma said, her smile gone.

Alex took a deep breath. And then said nothing for a while.

Emma straightened her shoulders and took a deep breath of her own.

'I feel,' Alex began eventually, 'that perhaps now might be a good time for you to move to the dower house.' He looked at her. 'If you would like to.'

No. He couldn't. He could not actually ask her to move out of his—now their—house. How could he have said that? Appalling.

'I'm sorry; that was unconscionable. Please don't move there, unless you'd like to. You might wish to do so. You might not. I'd like to make it very clear that I am, in fact, in no way asking you to move there. I thought that perhaps you would be more comfortable there. But of course you might feel that you would be more comfortable here.'

He stopped talking, aware that he was sounding like the imbecile he apparently was.

For a long moment, Emma just looked at him. Then she leaned forward a little, and said, 'I feel that now is a time for honesty.'

Oh, God.

'And, honestly, you were babbling.'

Alex pressed his lips together and nodded. After Mrs Hardy's departure, he'd sat down, planning to tell Emma that what had happened between them earlier today couldn't be repeated, and that he thought it would be best if she moved to the dower house. Or he thought that was what he'd been planning to say. Now he could barely even recollect what his thoughts had been.

Whatever the case, something had happened in the space of perhaps a minute, and now he didn't know what he wanted. He did know that he'd made an incredible mull of attempting to explain in a dignified fashion that he could offer Emma no further intimacy. All the dignity was on Emma's side.

'My observation,' she continued, 'is that you wanted to tell me that you regret what happened between us today and would prefer not to repeat it. You therefore thought that you wanted me to remove immediately to the dower house, but, on saying the words aloud, you realised that you were telling me that I had to leave your house, and since you are a kind person, you don't feel that you can, in fact, do that.'

'I…' Alex shook his head. And then nodded. Yes. She was probably right. She *was* right. But…

'I have something to say.' Emma was sitting very upright now. She looked very stern and very beautiful, and if he were a different man with a different life he would want nothing more than to take her in his arms and make slow, reverent love to her for the rest of the day. For the rest of time.

But there was no such thing as the rest of time, as both he and Caleb knew.

'Go ahead,' he said.

'It seems to me that you are still grieving the loss of your wife and still in love with her. I cannot compete with that, and I do not wish to compete with that. I agree that what happened this morning was a mistake. I am happy to remove to the dower house if that is what you deem best for both of us, and of course for the boys, but I am also perfectly content to remain in the main house, to live amicable but separate lives. Like you, I would not like to repeat this morning's mistake.'

Alex thought he saw her eyes glistening before she lowered her lids and studied her hands with seeming great interest. He wanted so much to correct her misapprehension that he couldn't love again. But if he told her he loved her he would be doing both himself and her a great disservice.

'Perfect,' he said.

He didn't even know what he was agreeing to.

Chapter Sixteen

The snow disappeared almost overnight. The temperature rose too, and when Emma and the boys went outside in the late morning to begin a walk, Emma realised immediately that they would need to change their thick coats for lighter ones or be uncomfortably warm in the bright sunshine.

'It feels as though we dreamt the snow,' Freddie observed as they sat down on sun-dried grass, next to the lake at the far end of the lawns directly in front of the castle. 'It's so hot. But there was a blizzard this time yesterday.'

'I agree,' Emma said.

She did agree. At approximately this time yesterday, she and Alex had taken refuge in the barn and made love. Today, only four-and-twenty hours later, it was as though their lovemaking had never occurred. Well, not entirely; it wasn't something she would ever forget. But their relationship had in no way developed as a result of it. Well, it *had* developed, but backwards rather than forwards.

As Freddie had said, it now felt almost as though the whole thing had been a dream.

'Emma!' Harry had his face very close to hers and she jumped as he shouted. 'You weren't listening.'

'I'm so sorry,' she said. 'I was a little distracted thinking about the snow.'

And your father. And the miracles he was working this time yesterday on my body.

She shivered. No. She should try hard not to think about that again, and she should try *really* hard not to think about it in front of the boys.

She forced her mind away from Alex and said to Harry, 'Tell me again what you said and I promise you that I will listen very carefully.'

And she did concentrate very well on his surprisingly detailed monologue about dragonflies. She simply needed to apply herself carefully and she would soon be able to stop thinking about Alex in a romantic way. Hopefully.

By the afternoon, the last vestiges of the snow had melted away under a March sun as unseasonably strong as the snow had been, in direct contrast to the frost that seemed to be settling more and more around Emma's heart as the day wore on. An entire day spent with three lively young boys left little time for reflection, and yet, bit by bit, the full reality of what had happened yesterday, and her own and Alex's reactions to it, were permeating her brain.

Later, she couldn't help revisiting in her mind yet again the situation between her and Alex as she finished reading an excerpt from *Gulliver's Travels* to the boys in the nursery.

It had been as though an invisible force had drawn the two of them together. From her side at least it had been based on both a strong physical attraction and a thorough enjoyment—even love—of his company. Their lovemaking had been wonderful and, while Emma had no previous experience to draw on, she was certain that Alex had simulated nothing and had been equally as passionate as she in that moment.

However, where she had then known for certain that she was in love with him—a feeling that was increasingly settling inside her—he had clearly realised that she could never compare to his Diana. He had therefore done his best to inform her that they should henceforth lead separate lives. It was the only time she'd experienced him being inarticulate.

She sniffed.

'Emma, are you crying?' Harry pointed his chubby finger at her face.

Emma shook her head, wiped her fingers under both her eyes and said, 'I think the wind must have blown down the chimney and sent a little smoke from the fire in my direction.'

'Oh.' Harry climbed onto her lap and hugged her. Emma wrapped her arms around him and buried her face in his hair for a moment. Children's affection was so much more straightforward than that between adults.

Alex came in shortly afterwards to see the boys.

'Excuse me,' Emma said, directing a bland smile at them all. 'I must go and change before dinner.'

'And get the smoke out of your eyes where it made you cry,' Harry shouted.

'I think we might all be able to hear you without you shouting so loudly,' Alex admonished gently, avoiding looking directly at Emma.

Did she want to move to the dower house, she wondered as she closed the nursery door behind her.

She didn't want to live by herself. After her father had died, an elderly aunt had come to join her for her mourning period, and the two of them had lived together with her father's servants in splendid and very lonely isolation. Emma had no desire to live like that ever again.

She would also miss the boys, and she hoped she wasn't flattering herself in believing that they would miss her too; and they certainly should not be made to suffer. But she was sure they could be very happy with a new governess, and Alex clearly wanted her to go. And of course she didn't want to make him miserable by inflicting her presence on him.

Dinner was a miserable affair, involving many plates of delectable food for which Emma had absolutely no appetite, and stilted conversation with Alex. The highlight of their interaction was when a conversation about the next day's weather involved a small, unintentional pun involving crows on Alex's part, which they both realised at the same time and which caused them both to smile a little.

Other than that, Alex was very much living up to his Ice Duke sobriquet. Emma didn't feel as though she had the energy to coax him out of it, and she had far too much pride to try. If making love to her once had caused him to be like this, then that was the way it was. She could only be grateful that she'd had the strength to tell him that their lovemaking had been a mistake from her perspective too. If she was going to have to carry on seeing him regularly—and while that would be difficult, it wouldn't be as bad as not seeing him at all—she needed to keep her pride and dignity intact.

* * *

After a miserable night, Emma was delighted at breakfast the next morning to receive a note from Letitia, asking her if she would like to visit the shops in Yarford with her that afternoon. She had her response written and dispatched within minutes of receiving the note.

A few hours later, she and Letitia met outside the draper's on Yarford's high street.

'I hear that they've just taken delivery of the most divine silks, medium-weight, from India, perfect for spring robes.'

Letitia pulled her into the shop.

'Where precisely in India do these come from?' asked Emma as the shopkeeper showed them different fabrics.

'I believe them to be from the Bengal and Gujarat regions,' he said.

After some detailed discussion on the different fabrics, Emma directed Letitia to some plain silks from Bengal and some more elaborate ones with flower designs from Gujarat, which she thought would be ideal for the dresses Letitia had in mind.

'I'm impressed. You're very knowledgeable about both silks and India,' Letitia told her.

'My grandmother was an Indian princess, and my grandfather met her travelling in India to buy silks and calicos for his textiles business, which my father inherited from him.'

'I see, and that's where your famous wealth came from? That's fascinating. Would you care to walk through the town with me for a while? I have so many questions to ask you.'

Emma hadn't realised until now quite how restricted she'd felt in polite company, having had it drummed into her by her aunt that she must not under any circumstances discuss *trade*. She'd spoken to Alex about her background, but very quickly after their marriage he had ceased to feel like *company* and had felt more like, well, family, she supposed.

'I do declare that I'd like to set up a factory myself,' Letitia enthused. 'Think how much pin money we could claim for ourselves. And, on a serious note, it's wonderful that you ensure such good working conditions and pay for the factory workers. It's so interesting to learn all these facts. There's so much wonderful history involved.'

Emma smiled at Letitia. Their conversation reminded her of ones she'd had with Alex, which just showed that she could be perfectly happy spending time with her friends rather than with him. Really, she could be perfectly happy maintaining only a distant relationship with him. She did not need him.

'The weather is so beautifully clement that I wonder whether we should continue our promenade for longer?' Letitia suggested.

'Certainly. I would like that.'

As they strolled, Emma asked Letitia to tell her more about the plans for her husband's land. She'd already learned that the fashionable, frivolous exterior Letitia presented to the world hid a shrewd brain and a strong interest in agricultural advances.

Letitia's shrewdness wasn't confined to agriculture.

'I do enjoy discussing all these things with Arthur,' she said as she concluded her thoughts on field enclosures and the introduction of different crops such as clover to increase soil productivity. 'Of course, whenever we disagree, we discover subsequently that he was wrong and I right. How are you and Alex settling down into married life?'

Emma blinked. Letitia was clever. Emma had not expected her to manoeuvre the conversation so easily in this direction.

'We…' She really wasn't sure what she wanted to say.

'It must be difficult, being married to a widower?' Letitia asked, considerably more tentatively than usual. Emma nodded. Suddenly, she wanted to hear anything that Letitia might know that she didn't. 'I know that he loved Diana very much. Still loves her very much. It must have been incredibly hard for him when she died.'

'Yes, he did and yes, it was.' Letitia paused, and Emma waited. 'Rumour did reach us, even here in the depths of Somerset, that you and Alex didn't have an entirely conventional beginning to your marriage. Although, what is convention in the ridiculous circles in which we move?'

'Indeed,' said Emma. She wanted to say, *Tell me everything you know about Alex and Diana, now.*

'We, Alex's friends here, all care very much about him. Well, not everyone cares about him. Mrs Hardy, for example, before her marriage cared a great deal about his title and wealth and nothing for his happiness, and is quite green with envy that you have succeeded where she did not. However, those of us who are his true friends do wish him every happiness, so we were, of course, a little concerned for him at first, on hearing about his very sudden wedding. But when we met you we were just delighted. I am selfishly delighted, because I like you so much as a friend for myself, and I'm also delighted for Alex, because the two of you seem so, well, so in love. Which is, of course, deeply unfashionable amongst the *ton*, but I'm unfashionable like that and so is Arthur, and so were Alex and Diana. And you and Alex seem so particularly well-suited.'

'Thank you,' said Emma faintly.

'The way he looks at you when you aren't looking at him is too adorable. And you do it to him too. The clearest sign that two people love each other.'

'Oh.' Emma would love to think that Letitia was right. And perhaps Alex *would* have loved her if he hadn't met Diana first. But he *had* met Diana first and that was that, and of course Emma couldn't begrudge him his marriage to her. He had the boys as a result of it, and they were wonderful.

'It is difficult, though—' Letitia flicked an imaginary something off her shoulder, as though she was trying to appear nonchalant, which gave Emma the very strong impression that she'd been planning whatever she was about to say for a while '—in the early days of a marriage, when you are not particularly well acquainted with each other, however easily you have tumbled into love. There must of necessity be a period of adjustment on both sides, which might feel quite difficult at times.'

'You're a wonderful friend to Alex,' Emma said, suddenly wanting to confide in Letitia. 'I do love him, and I do think that he might have loved me if he hadn't met Diana first. But he did. I'd like to tell you something in confidence.'

'Of course.' Letitia took Emma's hand.

'Alex and I do not have a real marriage.'

An image of Alex kissing her on the hay pushed its way to the front of Emma's mind, and she pushed it away again, hard.

'We made a bargain. He is wonderful, and kind, and

did not wish to see me ruined, so he offered me his name when someone else tried to compromise me, as perhaps you heard, but he made it very clear that he was unable to offer more than that. He suggested that if I would like to I could act as informal governess to his boys, and that is working very well. But we do not have a real marriage.'

'And yet,' murmured Letitia, 'when he looks at you he really does look like a man in love.'

Emma shook her head. 'He is a very good actor. As indeed am I. I am feeling a little despondent about our situation, but I think I've hidden my despondency very well from him. From everyone except you now.'

'Oh, Emma. It has been very little time. Love can grow. Perhaps he does not yet realise that he loves you.'

Emma shook her head. 'We have…explored our situation very thoroughly, and we have established together that we will not have an intimate marriage.'

'I'm so sorry.' Letitia squeezed her hand hard.

'Thank you, but I must not be an object of compassion. But for an accident of fate, Alex might not have been there that evening, and then we would never have met, and I would instead be either married to someone quite dreadful or working as a governess or indeed much worse. I count myself fortunate indeed and must never complain.'

'Emma, you have every right to complain, at least to yourself and to your closest friends, if the man you love does not love you. Although I believe that he does.'

Emma shook her head. 'All I need is some time to recover myself.'

An idea was dawning. She couldn't pretend to herself any more that it was going to be easy to see Alex every day in the near future.

'I think that I should perhaps make the journey to Lancashire to visit my family's factories and my cousins. And then perhaps I will journey to France.'

It would be practice for the much longer journey to India that she hoped to undertake in due course. She could visit Paris and the half-siblings she had never met, her mother's younger children. But even Letitia might not be open-minded enough not to be shocked if she described *that* scandal to her, so she wouldn't elaborate on that for now.

'Not alone, I trust?'

'Not alone, no. I will be accompanied by my maid, and perhaps two or three male servants for safety. And I will visit relatives, so that no scandal can possibly attach to my travels.'

'Or you could stay here a little longer first, so that you and Alex can get to know each other better?' Letitia suggested.

Emma shook her head. 'I don't think so.'

She and Alex had already got to know each other quite a lot better than she was going to admit to anyone. She needed some time away from him, to come to terms with her love for him coupled with his inability to love her. Travel would be the ideal distraction, and until then she would make herself very busy in preparing for her journey, together with visiting Alex's more vulnerable tenants and caring for the children.

The next few days passed in a blur for Emma.

During the daytimes she was very busy with the children, and with setting in train preparations for her journey. She also visited tenants, including Caleb Wilson and Eliza and her new baby.

Holding the baby caused Emma's stomach to twist horribly. She would have loved so much to have had the opportunity to bear and hold a baby of her own one day, but unless she was very lucky and last week's lovemaking led to pregnancy, she would never be in that position.

On the first two evenings, she and Alex dined together and made horribly desultory conversation, so on the third evening Emma sent word to him that she had the headache and thought it better to dine alone in her sitting room, and she did the same the next day.

And each night she struggled to sleep, due to the thoughts going round and round in her head, so before long she had extreme tiredness to add to her general misery.

Her misery increased when her monthly courses came and she had to accept that she wouldn't be having a baby.

She knew now, she thought one afternoon, as she walked back from visiting Caleb, that of course a journey to Lancashire wouldn't cure her of her love for Alex.

Somewhere along the way, she'd realised that the fact that her parents' love story had ended badly wasn't relevant to her own love story, or lack thereof. If Alex could love her, she knew that she would abandon her travel plans and stay in Somerset for ever with him rather than lose him.

She couldn't continue like this, and she would find it very difficult to be happy living in loneliness in the dower house, catching sight of him every so often.

What she should do was return to Lancashire and set up home there with Jenny, and make herself busy with local matters and visiting and hosting her friends.

Decision made, she felt her shoulders already less rigid and her step lighter. Perhaps she would allow herself one final dinner with Alex tonight. Not just dinner, if she was honest with herself. It would be one final attempt at trying to tempt him into falling in love with her.

If she didn't succeed tonight, well, she would have lost nothing, and tomorrow evening she would retire very early in preparation for leaving at dawn the morning after. She would tell no one in advance other than Jenny, so that Alex wouldn't make any kind of quixotic attempt at preventing her from going or accompanying her.

She dressed for dinner with care, choosing a new gown of lilac silk overlaid with delicately embroidered net. The dress suited her, she thought, regarding herself critically in the mirror, and, if there was a hint of grey shadow under her eyes from tiredness, Alex would, she hoped, be distracted by the very flattering neckline of the dress.

It was perfect: it looked nice without being too overtly dressy, the ideal dress for a duchess trying for one final time to…yes, seduce her own husband.

At the very least, she decided, as Jenny brushed her hair into an elaborate chignon, she would tell him tonight that she cared greatly about him, so that, even if her seduction of him didn't work, he would have that memory of her. Even if he couldn't love her, she didn't want him to think that she couldn't love him.

Her heart was thudding in her throat as she descended the grand staircase for dinner.

'His Grace is still above stairs,' Lancing informed her as she waited nervously by the great fireplace in the drawing room opposite the dining room.

'I will await him in the dining room,' she said.

It was irregular, but surely she could do as she wished

in what was—for now—her home, and standing there alone was not enjoyable.

Shortly after she sat down, Lancing brought her a note, her name written on the envelope in Alex's distinctive hand.

Emma stared at it for a moment, before opening it slowly, quite sure that she wasn't going to want to read the contents.

Alex had written that he expected she would be eating in her own sitting room again this evening, but just in case, he wanted to let her know that he had supped early, in his study, and was now setting off to visit Gideon for a quiet evening of cards.

'Thank you, Lancing,' Emma managed to say around the enormous lump that had appeared in her throat.

And then, for Alex's sake more than her own, to avoid more gossip amongst the servants than there had to be, she sat in solitary state and ate her dinner. Which she supposed, thinking about it—and there wasn't a lot else to do than think while she ploughed miserably through several dishes—was exactly fitting for her last full evening under the same roof as Alex.

Chapter Seventeen

The next morning, back from a furiously fast crack-of-dawn gallop across his land, which had afforded him only short-lived respite from thinking about Emma, Alex shoved open a side door to the castle and crashed straight into Emma and Harry.

His superior size and speed knocked them both off balance, and he shot his arms out to hold on to them both, so that for a moment the three of them were effectively locked in a three-way hug, tangled up with his riding crop.

'Papa, you were *running*,' Harry said, throwing his arms round Alex's legs to join in with the hug.

'I imagine that he was in a hurry.' Emma was very much *not* joining in with the hug. Her arms and hands were very firmly clamped to her sides and from where he still had an arm around her shoulders, Alex could feel that her entire upper body had tensed.

'Yes, I was. Very silly of me. I apologise.' Alex let go of Emma fast and swooped Harry up into his arms. 'Where are you off to?'

'Emma has been telling us about Maggan and sailing. We're going to the lake to imagine it's the ocean and think about sailing round it.'

'Maggan?' Alex queried.

'Magellan. I'm killing two birds with one stone—history and geography—and talking about his circumnavigation of the globe.'

'The first ever circumnavigation?' Alex thought he remembered learning about Magellan.

'Yes, we believe so, although of course we don't *know* that the Vikings did not sail all the way around the world.'

'I want to be a Viking,' Harry shouted.

Emma laughed, not catching Alex's eye, and said, 'We should go and find your brothers.' As Alex put Harry down, she glanced at him. 'Their nurse is with the boys. I did not send them to the lake alone.'

Alex shook his head. 'I had not even questioned it in my mind. I have full confidence in your care of them.'

Emma's eyes met his for a long moment and then she said, 'Thank you.'

Alex couldn't take his eyes from hers. One would never tire of looking into their rich brown depths. 'No. Thank *you*. The peace of mind is wonderful.'

It was the only thing that made up for the torture of her still being here in the castle. To be fair, it was a big thing. And the fact that she was so good with the boys did make it very difficult to countenance the idea of her entire removal from their lives. They would still be able to see her every day if she were living in the dower house, but he would not be so conscious of her presence.

'We must go and join the others,' Emma said again, pulling her eyes from his.

'Yes. Of course.' Alex put his son down and Harry immediately put his hand into Emma's.

Alex couldn't help remaining in the doorway for a few moments to watch the two of them as they walked across the lawn. He was indeed lucky that Emma was educating his boys, and with such enthusiasm. He wouldn't mind listening to her lesson on Magellan himself.

After a good hour of dull correspondence at his desk in the library, during which Emma intruded into his thoughts more than he would have liked, he stood up and walked over to where his father—a keen historian— had kept his world history books. Sure enough, after a few minutes of searching, he found an entire book that seemed to be devoted to the life and travels of Magellan.

The book was written in Spanish. Or maybe Portuguese; Alex was not particularly familiar with any of the Iberian languages. It might still be of interest to Emma and the boys, though. It included a number of interesting maps and, knowing Emma, she might well turn out to be proficient in whichever language this was.

It wouldn't be hugely respectful to the memory of his father, or indeed to anyone who might aspire to own such a fine volume, to take it outside on what was now a drizzly morning and possibly ruin it, so he would wait until Emma and the boys came inside before either taking it up to the nursery to show it to them or inviting them into the library to look at it.

Just before luncheon, his correspondence completed for the time being—praise be—he decided to go up to the nursery to show the boys the book.

When he got there the door was slightly ajar and Emma was sitting in an armchair, in full flow, still on the subject of Magellan. The boys were rapt in front of her. Even Freddie's habitual air of nine-year-old cynicism had disappeared.

'Yes, we do remember him today as a very brave man and a hero,' she said, apparently in response to a question from one of the boys. 'While he did die during the voyage—which was very sad—he died doing something he loved, and I'm sure that he would never have regretted his choice to make the journey. It's important to stay as safe as one can, of course, but if one doesn't take any risks at all, one risks never being truly happy.'

Alex stilled. She might have been talking about him. Perhaps she *was* talking about him. No, of course she wasn't; he was being vain. Perhaps she was talking about herself. Or perhaps, and more likely, she was answering a final question about Magellan and attempting to instil some wisdom into the boys.

Her words had resonated strongly with him, though, as she spoke. Would he be better off taking the risk of allowing himself to love again, or just not loving again? With greater risk came the possibility of greater reward, as well as greater misery. How brave was he? Brave enough to allow himself to love Emma and live a rich life full of joy—for now, anyway—or not? Was it better to live a duller, less happy life, but one which would not then be marred by loss?

He was beginning to think that Emma was right, that one should be brave.

He stepped into the room and cleared his throat. 'I found a book in the library that might be of interest to all of you,' he told them, holding it out.

'This is beautiful,' breathed Emma.

'Do you know what language it's written in?' Alex asked.

'Catalan,' she said, not looking up from the book. 'It's surprisingly easy to read if you speak French, much easier than Castilian Spanish, in fact.'

Alex nodded, pleased that he'd been right. Of course she knew.

He continued to be preoccupied with his thoughts as he ate a solitary luncheon. When he had finished, he stood up, knowing what he wanted to do this afternoon.

He sent word to the stables to ask for Star to be saddled for him, and then made his way there. He felt as though he was in too much of a rush to walk.

Twenty minutes later, he dismounted outside Caleb Wilson's cottage.

Caleb was limping around the corner of the building with the aid of a stick. 'Good afternoon, Your Grace. Good of you to come to visit.'

'My pleasure, and I'm delighted to see you on your feet again.'

'It certainly makes life more interesting.' Caleb nodded his head in the direction of his chicken house. 'I'm about to collect some eggs. Just trying to work out how to do it with my stick.'

'Perhaps you'd like some help?' Alex looped Star's reins around a tree.

'I would that.'

'You know,' said Alex a few minutes later, 'I haven't collected eggs since I was very young. There's something very enjoyable about it. I think my boys would very much like to visit you and meet your chickens.'

'They came yesterday, Your Grace. Did Her Grace

not tell you? We had a marvellous time. We agreed to the visit in advance, just to make sure that I wouldn't be out gallivanting when they arrived.'

Caleb roared with laughter at his own joke and Alex smiled, enjoying Caleb's humour and completely unsurprised that Emma had been to visit without trumpeting it, and that she'd brought the boys too.

Eggs—including some beautiful pale blue ones—collected, Alex accompanied Caleb inside his cottage, warm from the now very well-made fire in the corner.

'I have a question for you, Caleb,' he said, accepting a glass of ale. 'I want advice, I suppose.'

'Go on, Your Grace.'

'I wanted to ask…' He stopped and shook his head. 'No, I realise now that it's a stupid question, and one to which I already know the answer.'

Caleb looked at him steadily, but didn't speak.

'I was going to ask whether you had any regrets about marrying Jeanie because you've been so sad since you lost her. But of course you don't.'

'No, I don't. Do you regret loving and marrying Diana, Your Grace?'

'No. I don't.'

'But you're scared of loving again and losing again.' Caleb's words were a statement, not a question.

Alex nodded. 'I think I'm beginning to be less scared, though. Who knows what the future holds?'

'I count myself fortunate, young man, that I've had the happiness I have. I wouldn't have had that happiness without Jeanie, so I could never regret anything. I do miss her, as you know, and I always will, but she lives on in my memories of all our wonderful years together and in the lives of her children and grandchildren.'

'You're very wise, Caleb.'

'Of course I am, Your Grace. I learnt most of what I know about life from Jeanie, and she was a very wise woman. Your new duchess is another wise woman.'

Alex nodded again. 'She is indeed.'

'Seems to me that you might have something to tell her?'

'Yes, I think I do.' He was going to need to be careful with his words, though, not rush straight into conversation and say something stupid. He would spend the evening planning what to say and then he'd ask Emma tomorrow if they could talk.

He'd allowed her to believe that he was unable to love her because he was still grieving for Diana. He needed to explain how wrong he'd been and hope that she felt the same way about him as he felt about her, and that she would believe that he wouldn't be so stupid again.

Alex slept better than he had for a long time that night and woke later than usual. He partook of a leisurely breakfast before going in search of Emma and the boys, none of whom he had seen yet today.

He found the boys in the nursery with their nurse, but there was no sign of Emma.

'I wonder if you know where Emma is?' he said.

'She's going on a journey,' Harry told him very seriously.

'A journey?' Alex replied, not really paying a lot of attention.

He'd spend a few minutes with the boys now, and then ask Lancing if he knew where Emma was. He realised that he didn't know her daily routine; he'd been too busy recently trying to distance himself from her.

'She's gone to see the factories,' John said.

'In Lancashire,' Freddie clarified. 'She said we can visit her there one day when we're old enough, but she needs to discuss it with you first.'

'I'm afraid I don't understand,' Alex said, frowning.

'Emma has gone on a journey to visit the factories in Lancashire,' Freddie repeated slowly, as though to a person with limited comprehension. 'She's gone for a very long time, but we will see her again, because we can visit her there and she can come and visit us here too.'

Damn. *Damn.*

Alex stood up. 'I have to go.'

He went straight to the library for some solitude in which to think. Why had she not told him she was going? She'd told the boys. She'd said they could visit her. But she couldn't have left for good? No, surely not. They must have misunderstood what she'd said. They'd definitely misunderstood; they were only young. She wouldn't have just gone. He was quite certain of that.

A trickle of fear was making its way down his spine, though.

He found himself pacing back and forth beneath the long shelves, his mind going in circles. The library was on two floors, the upper floor accessed by narrow wooden staircases at each end of the room. He walked up one flight of stairs and along the gallery, not pausing to look at any of the books, and then down the flight at the other end.

This was silly, he realised on his second turn past the long windows in the middle of the room. He should ask Lancing now what he knew of Emma's plans. He would word his question so that he didn't sound as though he had absolutely no idea whether or not his own wife had left for Lancashire.

He turned towards his desk to ring for Lancing and saw an envelope propped up against the inkwell, with the word 'Alex' written on it. He recognised the script as Emma's, from letters she had left out to be franked.

The trickle of fear that he'd been feeling turned into a veritable deluge of panic as he pulled a single sheet of paper out of the envelope.

Dear Alex,

I had planned to tell you this in person, but in the end did not find an opportunity to do so.

I wanted to let you know that I have decided to travel back to Lancashire and make my home there.

I have made arrangements with Nurse to continue the boys' studies according to the notes that I have left, and hope that you will soon find a replacement governess.

I have come to love the boys very much and did not wish to leave them. I hope that they will not miss me—but am not sure that growing up with the example of our distant marriage will be good for them.

I—like you, I imagine—would hope that they will grow up to marry for companionship and intimacy, or not at all, should that be their choice.

I have told them that I am leaving, and that I hope you will allow them to visit me in Lancashire, where the landscapes are quite different from those in Somerset but equally beautiful.

I have left the kittens in the stables so that the

*boys are able to continue to play with them. They
have grown quite attached to them, and I did not
want to add to any loss they might feel on my departure.*

*I must thank you again for your great kind-
ness in marrying me and saving me from what
would, as you rightly said, have certainly been
an unpalatable alternative. I will remain forever
in your debt.*
Yours,
Emma

Momentarily stunned, Alex re-read the letter.

She'd left. Left *him*.

Or had she in fact been driven away by his effective
rejection of her after they'd made love? Would he ever
know now?

What if something bad happened to her on the journey? What if she was set upon by highwaymen? A
duchess travelling with only a small entourage must inevitably attract a great deal of attention. She would no
doubt have her pistol, which he was sure wouldn't help
her in the slightest in such an eventuality.

What if the carriage developed a fault, or one of the
horses were injured, or startled, or any one of a number
of things, and Emma were injured herself?

What if something truly terrible happened to her and
she never knew that he loved her?

He put the letter back in the envelope and then took
it out again.

What if, in fact, she didn't love him?

He read the letter for a third time. What would she
have written if she *did* love him? If she *didn't*? And what

if there was nothing that he would be able to say to convince her to return?

He needed to stop imagining catastrophes and he needed to know.

He stood up, almost knocking his heavy oak chair over in his haste. He was at the library door in a few strides and at the stables only a couple of minutes after that, instructing Jim to prepare Star.

He needed to leave immediately.

The hard ride helped calm the very worst of his fears. By the time he was passing by Bristol he was able to believe it was highly unlikely that any accident would befall Emma. It was also unlikely that he would fail to catch her up or indeed ride straight past her while she stopped for a rest, because, even journeying with just one carriage, a travelling duchess would always occasion comment.

Alex stopped regularly to ask if she had been seen, and ascertained that she was heading directly north. She'd set off very early this morning, and had two or three hours' advantage over him, but the chaise had been built for Alex's mother in her later years and had been designed for luxurious comfort rather than speed.

Perhaps Alex would ask Emma if she would like a new travelling carriage, one designed to her own specification and needs. One built for more regular travel, if that was what she'd like.

When he thought about it, she'd fitted herself into the extremely small space he'd made for her in his life and tried very hard to make the best of it, while he had made little effort to accommodate her.

He spurred Star to go faster, desperate to catch Emma.

As the morning ended, he began to wonder where she would take her luncheon. There was no sign of her at the first two staging inns at which he enquired, and as he left the second one he wondered whether somehow he'd missed her. It was busy and the people at this inn hadn't been able to say either way whether she'd passed by on the road outside.

And then, at the third inn, he found her. Accompanied by Jenny, she was leaving the inn as he arrived in a flurry of dust in the courtyard.

He dismounted, handed Star's reins to an ostler, and strode forward.

'Emma.'

'Oh!' She hadn't been looking in his direction when he arrived and clearly hadn't realised that it was him.

'Alex. Is something wrong? Has something happened to one of the boys? No, you'd be with them if something had.'

'Nothing has happened.' Other than that he'd come to his senses. Hopefully not too late. 'I came to speak to you.' He looked around. 'I wondered if we could talk somewhere, alone.'

Chapter Eighteen

Emma stared at Alex, standing in front of her, sternly handsome in his riding garb. What was he doing here? Was it a coincidence that he was here? Had he been planning to journey north anyway? Surely not. It seemed a lot more likely that he'd actually ridden all the way here to speak to her. About what, though? Did he think that she ought not to move to Lancashire? Was he worried about the scandal that might ensue?

He was looking at her, bright-eyed, his eyebrows slightly raised, as though he was waiting for the answer to a question.

'Would you be happy for us to talk in private?' he said.

Oh, yes, he *had* been waiting for the answer to a question.

Emma didn't want to speak to him. Even just seeing him here in front of her hurt. But she'd left him with no notice and she owed him a lot.

She drew a deep breath and said, 'Yes.'

'Thank you,' he said, smiling faintly.

He held out his arm to her and after a moment's hesitation she took it, trying not to react to the feel of the corded muscle in his forearm.

'Perhaps inside? In a private room.'

'Of course.'

Her voice sounded a lot steadier than she felt on the inside. She had no idea how she was going to respond to whatever he had to say. If he wanted her to return and live in the dower house, she didn't know whether she could bear to go. He must have something of note to say, though; it was hard to believe that he would have ridden *ventre à terre* such a long way just to say goodbye in person.

The landlord, who'd been very kind to Emma and Jenny, was now bowing deeply in front of the two of them.

'We'd like to be shown to a private parlour, please,' Alex said.

'Of course, Your Grace. Allow me just a few moments to make one ready.'

Shortly afterwards, there was a small commotion. It seemed that several young men dressed in aspiring Corinthian style had been asked to leave the room they were in.

'Alex, we can't—' Emma began.

'We can,' he said. 'Good afternoon, Giles.' He nodded at one of the men. 'Younger brother of a friend of mine,' he told Emma. 'They're young and fit and can very happily go somewhere else. It cannot be possible that what they have to say is as important as what I have to say.'

'Oh.' Emma was beginning to feel so overcome that it was a good job that she had Alex's strong arm for support.

'The room is ready, Your Grace,' the landlord announced a very short time later, having had what must have been almost every member of staff in the entire inn flying around with cloths and brooms, while Alex and Emma stood in uncomfortable silence in the inn's entrance hall.

'Thank you.' Alex pressed several coins into his hand and held the door wide for Emma to enter the room.

She walked in ahead of him and over to the window, which looked out onto an inner courtyard, which was populated by chickens and goats. She clutched the windowsill for support for a moment, feeling momentarily lightheaded.

She heard the door click closed and felt goosebumps from head to toe. This was it. The moment. Alex was about to say whatever it was he wanted to say to her. This could be the last conversation they ever had.

Would she have the strength to tell him now in person that she loved him? Just so that he knew? She'd wanted to tell him before she left, but hadn't found the words to include the sentiment in her letter.

He joined her at the window, standing at her side, perhaps two feet away from her, and then…said nothing.

Emma waited.

Alex cleared his throat twice, but still…nothing.

'This is a very pretty view, isn't it?' Emma said eventually, unable to take any more of the silence, but not wanting to say anything that would precipitate the conversation she knew she didn't want to have. She pointed out of the window. 'I particularly like those black chickens.'

'Delightful,' Alex said. 'Emma…'

She sensed him turn to face her.

'Emma,' he repeated.

'Yes?' She turned her head in his direction, but couldn't bear to look at him properly.

'Emma.'

She looked at his face and her breath caught in her throat. He was gazing at her with a very tender look in his eyes and smiling a crooked little half-smile that caused her...

That caused her to *hope*.

And that hope made her stomach clench uncomfortably and her heart beat faster.

'Thank you for agreeing to speak to me,' he said. 'I followed you here because I want to tell you something.'

'Yes?' Emma found herself clutching the windowsill again.

'What I want to say is...'

What was *wrong* with him? Whatever it was, she just wanted him to get on with it now.

'*Yes?*'

'Um.' And he stopped again.

For goodness' sake.

Emma was on the brink of screaming, *Tell me*, when Alex very suddenly went down on one knee in front of her. She gasped and put her hands to her mouth.

Alex reached up and took her hands while Emma tried to squash the enormous hope now blossoming inside her, just in case, somehow, she was misreading the signs.

Alex cleared his throat. 'This is the way it should have been,' he said, holding her hands tightly. 'What you deserve, and what I would have done if I had already known you and learned not to be scared.'

'Scared?' Emma was so stunned by seeing Alex on his knee before her that she felt as though she'd entirely lost her wits.

'When I met you, I was scared of grieving again the way I grieved after Diana died. I didn't know whether or not I could ever fall in love again, but I did know that I was determined not to, because I didn't want to lay myself open to the pain of loss again, and love does often give rise to grief.'

Emma nodded, unable to speak but still hoping.

'Since we stumbled into each other's lives I've learned two big things.' He drew her towards him. 'Firstly, I learnt that I was able to fall in love again, because I fell in love with you. I know that I allowed you to believe that I was still in love with Diana, and I suppose I am, or at least with her memory, but I'm also deeply in love with you. I was scared to allow myself to become close to you. But I'd already fallen in love with you, and I realised that without you in my life I wouldn't be happy. I overheard you talking to the boys about Magellan and bravery. *I* need to be brave. I want a full, happy life, with you, not an emotionally safe but empty one without you.'

Emma was beginning to smile.

'What I'm trying to say, in a very verbose way, is that I love you. I love you so much, Emma. I love your smile. I love your passion for knowledge. I love the way you tilt your head to one side when you're considering how to reply to me when I've annoyed you. I love your kindness. And in addition to that, I would like to be married to you, properly. If we weren't already married, I would be proposing to you now.'

'Oh,' said Emma.

She could hardly breathe and she could barely process Alex's words. This was everything she could have hoped for and indeed so much more. She sniffed, but a tear still plopped out and landed on their hands. She sniffed again and more tears fell.

Alex folded his lips together and swallowed, and then said, 'Emma?'

'Tears of happiness,' she said.

'Are you sure?'

'Yes.' She sniffed again, in probably a very unalluring way, but Alex just smiled lovingly at her.

Goodness. She hadn't actually replied to him. 'I love you too,' she said, rushing the words out.

'Oh, thank God.' Alex was beginning to beam. 'I was starting to worry that you were crying tears of pity and that you just wanted to get away from me.'

'I *did* want to get away from you, but only because I found it too difficult being near you and yet so far from you.'

'I'm sorry. That was my fault. I was stupid.'

Emma shook her head. 'You weren't stupid. You're a widower. That's difficult.'

'I *was* stupid. But fortunately I came to my senses. I had actually worked out yesterday—before you left—that I wanted to tell you I love you and ask you to live properly with me as my wife. But in a further act of stupidity, to compound all the rest of it, I decided to wait until today to tell you. And then I discovered that you'd gone.' Alex stood up and shook his legs. 'Deeply unromantic, I know, but that floor is both hard and uneven.'

Emma laughed and sniffed again, and then Alex drew her into his arms. He held her against his beautifully solid chest for a long time, with his cheek resting against the top of her head. And then he moved a little, tipped her chin up with his finger and leaned his head down to hers.

Their kiss was different this time. There was the knowledge that it would be good, the knowledge that they both wanted it and that they loved each other. And there was also the knowledge that they could take things to their natural conclusion, and that that would be good too—truly wonderful, in fact.

It was gentle at first, their lips just brushing. Emma almost sighed into the kiss. She wrapped her arms round Alex's neck and he held her very tightly. And then their kiss deepened, their tongues exploring, their hands moving too. There was physical urgency, but it was also as though they both knew that they had time now, and that they should enjoy fully every stage of their lovemaking.

The kiss went on for a long time, the two of them moulded together in front of the window. And then Alex ran a hand up from Emma's waist until it came to rest on the underside of her breast. Even through her dress his touch caused her to shiver, both from what he was doing with his thumb, causing her nipple to tighten, and from the promise of more to come.

And then with both his hands he took her round the waist and lifted her. She found herself with her legs wrapped around his waist, pressed against the wall, with Alex lifting her skirts with one hand to reach between her legs.

'What would you like to do now?' he murmured into her neck.

'I don't have the words,' she gasped as he bit her very gently, while plunging a finger somewhere very moist deep inside her.

'Come home with me.'

'Yes,' she said, beginning to pant.

'But first—' he kissed her mouth again and deepened his touch, and Emma moaned against him '—I think we should take a room here, now, for the night. Just one room.'

'Anything,' Emma managed to say, judders running through her as he touched her deeper and deeper.

'I love you, my duchess.'

'I love you too.'

Epilogue

Venice, February 1821

'This is wonderful,' Emma breathed, peeking out of the window of their *palazzo* bedchamber at the carnival in St Mark's Square beneath them.

'You're wonderful,' Alex said, coming to stand behind her and putting his arms round her waist, and looking over her shoulder.

The square was full of puppet theatres and all sorts of performers, including acrobats, tightrope walkers and clowns.

She turned to face him and slid her arms around his neck. 'Thank you so much for arranging this tour.'

They had held a ceremony to repeat their wedding vows on the first anniversary of their London wedding, and Alex had wished to mark their anniversary every year from then on.

On the third anniversary of their wedding, he'd presented Emma with an intricately embroidered mask like those worn at the many masquerades held at the carnival in Venice, knowing that it was an aspect of the Grand Tour that she'd particularly wanted to see, and wanting to give her a clue to the fact that he was planning that they would go on a Grand Tour of their own. And now this year, on their fourth anniversary, here they were in Venice.

He knew that Emma also harboured a strong desire to travel to India, and he did wish to gratify that desire in due course, but it had seemed wise to venture 'only' to Europe for their first foray into travel abroad with, as it turned out, an extremely large entourage.

They were accompanied by their children—they now had twin daughters as well as the boys—and attendant nurses, footmen, grooms, chefs, and others, as well as the stray dog, the abandoned bear cub and the indigent juggler that they—Emma—had collected along the way. For someone who was normally so pragmatic and un-fussy, Emma did not travel particularly lightly.

'There's no need to thank me. Thank *you* for being my wife. I'm enjoying our tour.'

Suddenly looking serious, Emma said, 'I really hope you *are* enjoying it. I mean, you seem to be, but I know that you love our corner of Somerset and would happily stay there for evermore without venturing further afield.'

'No.' Alex shook his head. 'I do, of course, love Som-erset, and, yes, I am of course a reluctant traveller in an-ticipation of any journey.'

Reluctant was an understatement when it came to his crossing the English Channel. The only person on their boat who was a worse traveller than him in a storm at sea had been Emma. While the rest of their party had been perfectly happy on the boat, the two of them had spent the entire crossing green at best and hideously ill at worst, and had been united in an immediate decision to make the rest of their trip over land only.

'But from the moment the ground stopped rocking beneath us after we disembarked the boat—' it had taken until some time after they'd arrived at Emma's mother's very bohemian but quite delightful villa in Paris for them both to lose the sensation that they were on a rocking boat '—I've loved our journey. My first Grand Tour was good; this is wonderful.'

'What's different about it?' asked Emma, twinkling at him and pressing her body to his, then kissing along his jawline while she ran one hand down his back before bringing it to rest on his backside. 'And, yes, I am indeed fishing for compliments.'

Alex smiled at the promise in her actions and reached down and kissed her full on the mouth, and slid one hand into her hair and cupped her breast with the other. 'I think we could spare a few moments before we go to the masquerade.'

He picked her up and crossed the room with her to land her right in the middle of their canopied bed. He lowered himself over her and began to rain kisses on her eyelids, her nose, her mouth, and down her neck, while she smiled and wriggled and pulled his shirt out of his pantaloons, and he applied four years' worth of expertise to undoing her stays as quickly as he could.

And then, as he traced his fingers around the underside of her breasts, smiling at the way she responded and then groaning as she reached for him inside his open breeches, he remembered that he had a serious point to make.

'What's different about this tour?' he said, still caressing her and smiling as he saw her eyes glaze a little. 'The opportunity to make love very regularly to my beautiful wife is, of course, one difference, but the greatest difference is the chance to share all the different spectacles and experiences with you and witness your enjoyment of them. With you as my companion, every journey that I take will always be better.'

Emma focused her eyes on him and smiled her beautiful smile. 'Thank you,' she said. 'And I, in my turn, know that I couldn't ask for a better companion to share this or any tour with. Nor a better husband to share my life with. I love you, Alex.'

'I love you too.'

He kissed her on the lips again. And then she gasped as, very deliberately, he began a slow but very enthusiastic demonstration of his physical love for her.

* * * * *

WHEN CINDERELLA
MET THE DUKE

To William

Chapter One

Miss Anna Blake

London,
November 1817

'I am really not certain that this is a good idea,' Miss Anna Blake said, surveying herself in the looking glass in front of her. She *wanted* it to be a good idea, because she didn't know whether she'd ever again have the opportunity to wear a dress as wonderful as this or be able to go to another Society ball, but…

'Nonsense. You deserve to have one last evening of enjoyment.' Anna's godmother, Lady Derwent, tweaked the gauze overdress of Anna's ball gown into place and gave the tiniest of ladylike sniffs before wiping very delicately under her eyes with her beringed fingers. 'I declare, you look like something out of a fairy tale, my dear: so beautiful. Your mother would have been so proud.'

'Thank you, but…' Anna began again. She was quite

sure that her mother would *not* have recommended quite such an audacious deception. She had practised a deception of her own, when she'd eloped with Anna's father, and had then had to spend Anna's entire childhood attempting—with little success—to repair the damage done by the elopement. She had therefore been particularly desirous of Anna's living as respectably as possible. The plan for this evening was *not* respectable.

'You're being far too cautious,' Anna's best friend, Lady Maria Swanley, told her. 'If anyone should ever find out—which they won't—it will be *I* whom they accuse of wrongdoing.'

'Hmm,' said Anna.

Nearly ten years of close friendship with Lady Maria, since they had entered Bath's strictest seminary together, had taught her that Maria's plots gave rise to much enjoyment but usually ended badly, for Anna, at least.

As the daughter of a rich earl, Lady Maria was usually protected from reprimand. Anna, by contrast, was the daughter of a groom. She was also the granddaughter of an earl, and sponsored by Lady Derwent, one of Society's most redoubtable matrons and a great friend of her late mother's, but in the eyes of Miss Courthope, the seminary headmistress, she was her father's daughter and someone who could be punished much more thoroughly than could Maria, so whenever Anna had engaged in any mischief—usually with Maria—she had afterwards felt the full force of Miss Courthope's ire.

That was one thing, and Anna had considered Miss Courthope's punishments a small price to pay for how much she'd enjoyed misbehaving, but hoodwinking most of the *ton* was another. Surely that could give rise to any number of consequences considerably greater than having to write out one's catechism three times or pen a letter of apology to the dance master.

'What if Lady Puntney finds out? What if I oversleep tomorrow?' Anna was starting work as a governess for the Puntney family in the morning. 'And what if your parents find out?' *How* had she allowed herself to be talked into this? Well, she knew how: both Lady Maria and Lady Derwent could be extremely persuasive and, if she was honest, Anna had been very happy to allow herself to be persuaded, and it was only now that the deception was almost under way that she was beginning to acknowledge her doubts.

'If my parents find out, it is likely that they will also have found out about my engagement to my darling Clarence, and they will be interested only in that,' Maria said.

Anna nodded; that much was true. Lady Maria's beloved Clarence was a curate of very uncertain means, and her parents had their sights set on the Duke of Amscott, no less, as their only daughter's future husband.

Anna was not convinced that her friend was making a sensible choice; Clarence might seem perfect now to Maria, but what if things became difficult in due course? He was of course a man of the cloth, so would—one would hope—hold himself to higher standards than did other men, but if he was anything like Anna's father and grandfather, his love would not endure in the face of life's obstacles.

When Anna's mother had fallen in love at the age of eighteen with one of her father's grooms, and then become with child and eloped with him, her father—

Anna's grandfather—had disowned her and refused ever to see her again. He had died a few years later. And after the money raised from the sale of Anna's mother's jewels ran out, Anna's father had left to make a new life for himself in America, with no apparent further thought for his wife and daughter. When Anna had lost her mother, she had written to her father, and had received his— very short and not particularly heartfelt—reply over six months later. She knew that he had written it himself— her mother had taught him to read and write in the early days of their marriage and she recognised his handwriting—so had to assume that it did express his own sentiments. He had not suggested that she join him in Canada or that he attempt to support her in any way whatsoever.

Anna had been rescued from penury by the women in her life—her mother's maid and then Lady Derwent— and she did not believe that men were to be relied upon. Lady Derwent had confirmed this belief; she had told Anna on more than one occasion that she was *extremely* happy to be a widow.

'And in the meantime,' Maria interrupted her thoughts, 'I *cannot* go to the ball.'

The Dowager Duchess of Amscott was holding the first grand ball of the Season this evening, and, according to Lady Derwent, everyone expected the duke to be there, searching for a wife. Lady Maria's birth, beauty and large dowry made her an obvious candidate for the position. When her parents had been called away and she had been entrusted to Lady Derwent to chaperone her this evening, Maria had suggested, most persuasively, as was her wont, that Anna attend in her place.

She had waxed lyrical about the dress that Anna

would wear, the people she would see, the dancing, the food, the enjoyment of participating in such an excellent but entirely harmless deception. Lady Derwent had immediately echoed her suggestions, and Anna had found herself agreeing most thoroughly with everything they said. Now, though…

'Lady Puntney will not find out,' Lady Derwent stated, with great certainty. 'Dressed as you are now, you look like one of Shakespeare's fairy queens. Lord Byron himself would write quite lyrically about you, I'm sure. When attired in the *garments*—' she scrunched her face disapprovingly '—you will wear as governess, you will still look beautiful, of course, but you will look quite different. I do not believe that anyone will make the connection. And we will leave at midnight so that you will not be too tired on the morrow.'

'The timing is quite serendipitous,' Maria mused. 'Had this ball not been my first, had I not been incarcerated in the country in mourning for so many years so that I know no one in London—' Maria's family had suffered a series of bereavements '—and had my parents not been forced to leave town and entrust me to the care of dear Lady Derwent—' Lady Maria's grandmother was ill and her mother had left post-haste, accompanied by her husband, to visit her in her hour of need '—this would not have been possible. And by the time my parents return, Clarence and I shall be formally affianced, and no one will make me attend any more balls as a rich-husband-seeking young lady. So it will all be perfect.'

She smiled at Anna.

'You look beautiful. That dress becomes you wonderfully. Perhaps you will find a beau of your own this evening, and marry rather than take up your position.'

Anna rolled her eyes at her friend. 'I shall be very happy as a governess.' She wasn't *entirely* convinced that that was true, but it would be better than relying on a man to protect her, only to be abandoned when he lost interest in her; and she was certainly very lucky to have obtained her position with the Puntneys.

'Harumph.' Lady Derwent did not approve of Anna's desire to be independent; she had asked her more than once to live with her as a companion, despite her obvious lack of need for one. 'Let us go. You will not wish to miss any part of the ball, Anna.'

'What if you change your mind in future, Maria?' Anna worried. 'How will you take your place in Society after I have attended this ball as you?'

'No one would ever dare to question me,' Lady Derwent said. 'Should you in the future change your mind, Maria, and decide that you do not after all wish to marry an impecunious curate with few prospects, and that you wish to take your place at balls as yourself, I shall inform anyone who questions me that their eyesight is perhaps failing them and that the Lady Maria they met at the Amscott ball was of course you, and no one will contradict me.'

Certainly, very few people, including Anna, chose to disagree very often with Lady Derwent.

Anna turned to look again at her image in the glass. She *loved* this dress. It would be such a shame not to show it off at the ball. She *loved* parties—the small number that she had been to. She *loved* dancing. And everyone who was anyone amongst London's glittering *haut ton* would be there, and she would *love* to see them all, and witness and take part in such an event.

She straightened her shoulders and beamed at the reflection of her two companions before turning back round.

'You are both right,' she said. She was going to take this wonderful opportunity and enjoy it to the full before starting her new, possibly quite dull life on the morrow.

'It will be so diverting to know that you are practising such a masquerade,' Maria said. 'A huge secret that no one else knows. And you will enjoy the dancing very much, I am sure.'

'Thank you, Maria,' Anna said.

'No, no.' Maria hugged her. '*I* must thank *you*. Just make sure you enjoy yourself.'

'I just want to check one final time that you are absolutely certain?' Anna asked again.

'We are certain.' Lady Derwent was already standing and moving towards the door. 'Nothing can possibly go wrong.'

Chapter Two

James, Duke of Amscott

'And that is all for now,' concluded the Dowager Duchess of Amscott, as she folded into neat squares the piece of paper upon which she had scribed her list of possible candidates for the hand of her son, James, Duke of Amscott, before leaving her escritoire to join him on the sofa opposite.

James raised an eyebrow. 'Are you intending to share the contents of your list with me?'

'Maybe. Maybe not.' She waved the piece of paper under his nose before whisking it away and tucking it into her reticule.

James laughed. The idea of getting married was not at all funny, but his mother could nearly always raise a smile from him. Which was impressive, given all that she had gone through in recent years, with the death first of her husband and then of James's two older brothers.

'On a serious note,' his mother said, 'I will of course discuss the list with you, but I feel that it might be best for you first to meet the various young ladies without any preconceptions. You are fortunate in having no need to marry for money and being able therefore to choose any young lady—of good birth, of course—for love.'

James looked down at his knees for a moment, to hide his eyes from her as a chill ran over him.

He did not want to marry for love.

He did not wish to love someone so deeply that he would be broken if anything happened to her, as his mother had been at the loss of her husband and two oldest sons, and as he and his sisters had also been.

Also, and even more importantly, he did not wish someone to love *him* deeply, because he wouldn't wish anyone else to be devastated if he died, and he veered between terror and resignation at the thought that it seemed extremely likely that he would die young; the doctors were not sure what had caused the early deaths of his father and brothers but their symptoms had all been similar, and it did not seem unlikely that their illnesses had been due to a family trait. It would be bad enough thinking of the pain that would cause his mother and sisters, but for him to choose to marry someone who loved him deeply only for the pain of loss to be inflicted on her too would be awful.

'James?'

'Yes, Mama. What an…excellent plan.' He could not tell her how he felt; he could not add to her sadness, especially when she was doing so well herself at pretending to be happy. He must maintain his own stiff upper lip, as she did.

And his emotions were confused. Because he *needed* to produce an heir. His current heir was a distant cousin residing in Canada, and James had no way of knowing whether the man would—in the event of James's death—look after James's mother and younger sisters in the way that he would wish. It would be infinitely preferable for a son of James's—infant or adult—to become the new duke.

And the existence of an heir—his son—would of course lessen his family's grief on James's death, in addition to securing their future. His wife would have a child or children to love, and his mother had already proved herself to be a most doting grandmother to his oldest sister's two young daughters.

He raised his eyes to his mother's and smiled as sincerely as he could.

'That is settled then.' She rose from the sofa. 'You will meet as many ladies as possible this evening, and should you develop a preference, you may undertake to improve your acquaintance of the young lady in question. If you do not have a preference, we will revert to my list.'

James rose too. 'Excellent.' *God.*

'We must hasten. The first of our guests will arrive soon.' She held her arm out imperiously.

They were hosting the first big ball of this year's London Season, and James's mother believed that the whole of Society would be scrabbling to attend. She was almost certainly right: wealthy dukes were always popular, irrespective of their personal attributes. They were even more popular when they were nearing thirty and unmarried.

He laughed at his mother's haughty gesture, and took her arm, wondering as he did so what chance there was that he would meet someone this evening with whom he could fall in love, should he allow himself to do so—he would not—or whether he would be happy to marry someone from the list.

He did need to marry.

And while he did not desire a love match, he did wish to choose his own bride rather than have one foisted upon him by his mother. He would like someone whose conversation he enjoyed, for example, although he probably wouldn't choose to live permanently with anyone quite as opinionated as his mother and sisters were...

As they entered the ballroom, his mother's voice pierced his thoughts. 'Amscott. I was telling you about my decorations.' She hadn't allowed him to see the themed room until now, eager, she said, to spring a surprise on him—or perhaps just to avert the strong possibility of his cavilling at her evident extraordinarily high expenditure. He had in fact been happy to indulge her, delighted to see her take an interest in something again; she had struggled with listlessness in the aftermath of their bereavements.

'I beg your pardon, Mama. I was lost in admiration of your design of the room.' It was certainly remarkable—and must indeed have cost a small fortune. The ballroom of Amscott House had been transformed into an exotic fruit orchard. There were so many orange and lemon trees—surely more than in the glasshouses of the rest of England combined—that the room had a definite citrusy scent. And were those...pineapple trees?

'I wished to make a splash, and I believe we shall do so. In addition, our ball will *smell* nicer than everyone else's.' His mother's air of complacence made him laugh again. 'So many hot bodies in the same room can often be quite unbearable.'

'Impressive forethought.'

'I must confess that I did not realise how very much scent the trees would give off,' his mother confided, 'but I am quite delighted now at how I shall be setting both a visual design *and* an olfactory trend.'

The first guests were announced before they had the opportunity to engage in further conversation, and James became fully occupied in greeting dandified men, bejewelled matrons, their eager-to-please debutante charges and the occasional actual friend of his.

'Lady Derwent and Lady Maria Swanley,' a footman announced, as a tall woman, her air almost as imperious as that of James's mother, swept into the room with a smaller and younger lady, who was dressed in a silvery, sparkly dress.

'Good evening.' Lady Derwent curtsied the tiniest amount in James's mother's direction, her demeanour as though she was conferring an enormous favour on the duchess, who responded with the smallest of smiles. James made a mental note to ask his mother on the morrow what argument she and Lady Derwent held; there was clearly some animosity between the two women, and his mother's stories were always amusing. 'Lady Maria is under my charge this evening; dear Lady Swanley has been called to Viscountess Massey's sickbed.'

'I am so sorry to hear that your grandmother is ill,' James's mother told Lady Maria.

'Thank you; we hope very much that she will make a full and speedy recovery.' Lady Maria's voice was musical, clear and warm in tone, so lovely to listen to that James instinctively looked more closely in her direction.

Her hair was a light brown, thick and glossy, her eyes green, her skin clear and her features regular, and her dress—cut low at the bosom and high at the waist—became her very well. She was certainly attractive, but, when his thoughts wandered vaguely to whether she would be on his mother's marriage candidate list, he decided that it was irrelevant; she was probably a very pleasant lady, but there were any number of pleasant, attractive young ladies here, and he could think of no reason that he would choose this lady over any other.

Indeed, how *would* he choose a bride given that his choice would not be directed by his falling in love? Perhaps he should ask his oldest two sisters which young ladies they got on with best.

'My son, the Duke of Amscott,' James's mother said, and Lady Maria turned in his direction with a smile.

And, good Lord, the smile was extraordinary. It displayed perfect, even teeth, it was wide, it was infectious, it showed one delightful dimple just to the left of her mouth, it was *beautiful*. James felt it through his entire body, almost uncomfortably so.

'Delighted to meet you.' His own mouth was broadening into a wide smile in response to Lady Maria's, almost of its own volition.

Lady Maria curtseyed and held out two fingers, smiling now as though she was almost on the brink of laughter, her eyes dancing. James had no idea what she was finding quite so funny, but he knew that he wanted to find out. He had the strangest feeling, in fact, that he wanted to find out everything about her, which was a ridiculous sensation to have, given that the entire sum of knowledge he had about her was that she was a small, pleasant-looking woman with a musical voice and the most beguiling smile and was accompanied by Lady Derwent.

He leaned forward a little and spoke into her ear, just for her, comfortable in the knowledge that the hubbub of voices around them would make it very difficult for anyone else to hear.

'Do you have a joke that you wish to share?' He accompanied his words with a smile, to ensure that Lady Maria would know that he was funning rather than reprimanding her in any way. He would not normally speak to a stranger, a debutante, in such a manner, but then debutantes did not usually look as though they held a big and amusing secret. And he couldn't remember the last time—if ever—that he'd had such a strong sense that he *would* get to know a particular person very well.

'No, Your Grace.' Her smile was no less mirthful than before as she continued, 'I am perhaps just overwhelmed by the occasion.' Her words did not ring true; she did not seem in the slightest bit overwhelmed.

She looked around the room before returning her regard to his. 'I adore these plants. They are quite remarkable. I have never seen a lemon or orange tree outside the covers of a book.'

'Remarkable indeed,' James agreed. 'I have it on the highest authority that the scent as well as the décor will make this one of the most successful balls of the Season.'

'I think your authority is right,' Lady Maria said very gravely. 'Every ball is judged by its scent. And it is particularly clever to use trees that will, I presume, no longer be bearing fruit as we enter the winter, so that no other host will be able to replicate this.'

'I had not thought of that. The design is my mother's; you and she are obviously both more astute than I.'

'Thank you; I am of course regularly complimented on my ballroom scent knowledge.'

She twinkled up at him as she spoke, and James laughed.

And then he found himself saying, 'May I have the pleasure of taking the first dance with you?'

As he finished the question, he realised the import of his words: asking a young lady whom he had never previously met, and who was presumably at her first ball, for the first dance could be taken as a mark of quite particular regard. Certainly, if he did not then wish to further their acquaintance, he would have to navigate things very carefully: on the one hand, he would have to ensure on his own account that he did not appear to single her out for any other special attention; but he would also, for her sake, have to make sure that he did not appear to slight her.

Somehow, though, he didn't mind; he again had the strangest sensation that he *had* to get to know Lady Maria better.

'I'm sure Lady Maria would be delighted.' Lady Derwent had clearly overheard his words and, as any good chaperone ought to do when a wealthy unmarried duke asked her charge to dance, was doing her best to ensure that his request was granted. In fact, if he wasn't mistaken, she had just given Lady Maria a small but quite forceful nudge.

To James's admiration, Lady Maria didn't acknowledge the nudge at all, not even glancing in Lady Derwent's direction before saying, 'I would indeed be delighted.'

'Amscott.' His mother's tone was sharp; she had clearly overheard his question and was less happy about it than Lady Derwent had been. 'You will remember my dear friend Countess Montague and her daughter Lady Helena Montague.'

As the introductions continued, James found his gaze following Lady Maria until she was swallowed up by the hordes of people swirling around her. Once he'd lost sight of her, he couldn't find her again, however hard he tried. And, he realised a few minutes later, when his mother remarked acerbically on yet another lapse in his attention, he was trying very hard to see her.

It would have been easier had she been less diminutive in stature, of course.

James had hitherto always thought he was more attracted to taller ladies, but he now realised that he'd been quite wrong.

Good God. At the age of twenty-nine years old, he was behaving like an infatuated moonling in his first Season. One beautiful smile had turned his mind.

He couldn't even remember what he'd been thinking about women and marriage only an hour ago. He was certain that he hadn't wanted to find any woman this attractive, but he wasn't quite sure why. Attraction and love were not the same thing, after all.

'Amscott.' His mother's sharpness had reached the pitch where it could cut a steak; he should concentrate harder on these introductions. She was a devoted mother and a generous-spirited woman, but she did not appreciate inattention.

* * *

Eventually, the introductions were completed and it was time for the first dance.

As he made his way across the room to where Lady Maria was standing with Lady Derwent, James was conscious of a genuine increase in his heart rate, which had him almost physically shaking his head at himself. After all, he didn't even know now whether he'd been imagining how attractive he'd found Lady Maria; perhaps when he saw her again he'd realise that he'd been quite mistaken.

And then, over other people's heads, he did catch sight of her. She was standing with some other debutantes, laughing at something another young lady had just said. Lady Maria then said something in her turn, and the whole little group joined in with the laughter—full, shoulder-shaking laughter, not just polite Society titters. He couldn't help smiling just watching them and realised that he would very much like to know what the joke was. And when he saw Lady Maria beam at the other ladies, he knew that he had not been mistaken in the slightest; she was remarkably attractive.

Perhaps half a minute later, he was standing in front of Lady Maria and Lady Derwent, with his heels snapped together, bowing his head to both ladies.

Lady Derwent was, unsurprisingly, wreathed in smiles. James didn't flatter himself that he personally was a hugely attractive catch on the marriage mart; that would presumably depend on a lady's particular taste. He did, though, believe that an unmarried duke in possession of a good fortune must always be attractive to the vast majority of young ladies and their chaperones, and it appeared that Lady Derwent was no exception.

Lady Maria was also smiling, but not quite so widely as when they'd met or when she'd been laughing with the other young ladies. He hoped she wasn't regretting agreeing to this dance. Perhaps she was one of those rare debutantes who had no wish to marry a duke.

Good God. In the past few minutes he must have thought about marriage at least five times. It was as though he had, like many men before him, lost his head to one pretty face. And good God again, he felt as though he didn't care and indeed would be more than happy to follow his instincts and court the young lady most assiduously.

As Lady Maria placed her fingertips lightly on his arm, he knew that he had to be imagining it, but it was as though this moment of their first touch was extremely significant, as though the contact was branding him in some way; he had the strangest sense that it would be the first of many such touches. Extraordinary; he was never this fanciful.

'You are recently arrived in London, I understand?' he asked her as they wove through the crowds of guests towards the dance floor.

'Yes,' she confirmed. 'I was previously in the country. I very much like London and over the past week or two have enjoyed prevailing upon my godmother to show me any number of places that I believe interested me a good deal more than they interested her.'

James laughed and then queried, 'You have been spending time with your godmother?'

'Yes. I… Yes, Lady Derwent, I mean. My mother was called away some time ago to be with my grandmother.'

'Oh, I see. I had understood your mother to have left town very recently.'

'I… No. Not particularly recently. Less recently than you might think. Do you reside in London all year round, Your Grace?'

Bizarrely, given that they really did not know each other, *Your Grace* sounded far too formal on Lady Maria's lips.

Suppressing a desire to ask her to call him James, and wishing that he could call her a simple Maria, he said, 'I have only recently inherited the dukedom. I imagine that I will spend the Season in London and the remainder of the year in the country.' He had the most insane urge to tell her that he was really quite flexible and, if his soon-to-be—he hoped—wife wished to spend all her time in London or all her time in the country, he would be quite amenable to either, as long as he could be at her side. He really did seem to have run quite mad. He didn't know Lady Maria. He didn't even know…well, anything at all about her.

And he did *not* wish to marry for love. Did he? No, he did not. *This* was clearly not love. He just had a very strong sense that she would be an excellent life companion, that was all.

He opened his mouth to ask any one of the many thousands of questions to which he'd like to have the answers—such as *Where would you like to live? How old are you?* and, quite possibly, *Would you like to marry me?*—just as she said, 'I'm so sorry to hear that. There can never be a good reason to inherit something.'

'No,' James agreed. 'My brother's death came as a devastating shock to all of us, but especially of course to my mother.' Good God. He never spoke about this, and here he was confiding in a complete stranger. Before he knew anything about her. Truly, something very odd had happened to him.

'I'm so deeply sorry. I can empathise. We have also suffered bereavement in my family. Like most families, I suppose.' Lady Maria paused and then, as though consciously changing the subject, looked around and said, 'I am enjoying this ball enormously.'

James smiled, grateful that she'd lightened the moment. 'So am I. I presume that this is your first?' He was clearly extraordinarily lucky to have met her immediately on her coming out. He was surprised though, now he thought about it: she looked a little older than he would have expected a debutante to be. In the most delightful way. On reflection, he would prefer his wife to be a little older than the youngest of debutantes. That way, their companionship, friendship—certainly not love—would be more balanced.

'Yes. I...' There was that hesitation again. Why did she seem to be choosing her words carefully? Did she have something to hide or was she just nervous at her first ball? He had so many questions about her; he *needed* to get to know her better. 'We were in mourning for a long period, which is why I haven't made my come-out until now.' Oh; perhaps the subject matter would explain her hesitation.

'Of course. I'm sorry.' He wanted to ask whom it was they had been mourning but didn't wish to upset her.

Neither of them had the opportunity to say any more

for the time being. The band had struck up and all involved in the first dance—a quadrille—were taking their places.

'I must apologise,' Lady Maria told him as they came together at the beginning of the dance. 'It is some time since I danced, and I might have forgotten some of the steps.'

'You look remarkably proficient to me,' James told her, wishing very much that this was a waltz so that he might stand close to Lady Maria and talk to her for the duration of the dance. 'It is I who must apologise in advance; there is every possibility that I will tread on your toes.'

Lady Maria shook her head. 'I am not exaggerating when I say that I will be forced to count my steps or I risk causing the entire ensemble to fail. Look.' And she began to mouth numbers, all the while looking straight ahead and smiling serenely, her eyes dancing.

James choked back laughter as they came together and then drew apart, before Lady Maria moved round gracefully, throwing a final 'one and two' at him over her shoulder as he went. James didn't know what Lady Derwent would say if she could hear her charge now, but he was sure that his mother would disapprove; she was a stickler for only the most proper of behaviour in public. James, by contrast, he now realised, had been waiting all his life for a lady who laughed irreverently through her first formal dance.

The nice thing about their dancing a quadrille was that he was able to give full attention to the other ladies he crossed briefly while having ample opportunity to observe Lady Maria's very much in-time and particularly graceful dancing.

She was, he could see, perfectly polite to the other gentlemen she encountered as they all moved around, but perhaps, he fancied—hoped—not quite so sparkling as she had been when talking to him.

Every so often, when he was glancing in her direction, she would look over at him too, and their eyes would catch. James couldn't remember a time when he had felt a greater sense of anticipation and enjoyment of the moments in a set when he would come together with his original partner.

When the dance finished, James said with great reluctance, 'I must escort you back to Lady Derwent.'

'Oh, thank you, but I am taken for the second dance.'

'Oh, yes, I should have assumed that you would be.' He should *not* be feeling mildly—strongly—irritated at the thought of someone else wishing to dance with her. He himself, after all, was about to dance with a different lady. And he barely knew Lady Maria.

'You should indeed have done; once it becomes known that the Duke of Amscott wishes to dance the opening dance with one, one becomes extremely popular with other young men.'

'I am certain that it is you with whom they wish to dance, and not just my partner.' James was quite sure that it wasn't just the social cachet of dancing with him that had attracted others; all she had to do was smile and surely she would have the world at her feet.

Lady Maria smiled at him. He *loved* her smile. 'It is very kind of you to say so.'

He returned the smile and then said, because he

couldn't help it, 'May I have the pleasure of dancing the waltz with you later?'

'I do have one dance left on my card,' she said, 'and I believe that it is a waltz,' and there was that dimple again.

Dancing twice with a lady at a ball was tantamount to stating a very serious intention towards her, especially when that ball was your own. James wondered very briefly what his mother and indeed the whole of the rest of the *ton* would think about the fact that he was making a statement of this magnitude at this very first ball of the Season. And then he realised that he did not care in the slightest. All he cared about, it seemed, was getting to know Lady Maria better.

'And perhaps I might take you into supper?' he suggested.

'That would be delightful,' she said, bestowing yet another stunning smile on him before being whisked away by a far-too-eager—in James's eyes—young viscount.

If his dance with Lady Maria had fairly flown by, the remainder of the dances until supper passed very slowly, other than when he was briefly partnered with Lady Maria during the movements within sets.

Each time that that happened, he felt the most ridiculous lifting of his heart. Truly, he didn't think he'd ever experienced such infatuation in his entire life. Every snatched touch of the hand, smile and couple of words exchanged felt like a gift from heaven. And every time they had to move on from each other, it felt as though he'd been deprived very suddenly.

* * *

Finally, supper was called.

James, wondering at himself, had been, as though under some kind of spell, waiting with increasing impatience for the end of the last set, knowing that supper would be coming. He'd also been unable to prevent himself through the entirety of the dance from keeping a close eye on Lady Maria's whereabouts. Truly, he was behaving like a love-struck youth.

He handed the young lady whom he had just partnered back to her mother and thanked her profusely for the dance, escaped before her mother could hint too forcefully that he might escort her into supper, and made his way over to where he'd last spied Lady Maria.

By the time he got to her, she was surrounded by several young sprigs together with several more mature gentlemen, two of whom were good friends of James's.

'Lady Maria.' James inserted himself between two of the men as he spoke.

'Your Grace.' She smiled at him and he realised that it had to have been at least half an hour since he'd last received a smile from her. He was already basking in the warmth of this latest one; each one felt as though it was a special gift just for him.

He held his arm out to her, internally raising his eyebrows at himself at the way in which his thoughts had suddenly become so poetic.

'Thank you.' She accepted the arm—and good God, he almost shivered at her touch—and smiled around the group of men, and then they began to process with all the other guests towards the supper room.

'I am looking forward to seeing how my mother will

have had the supper room decorated,' he told Lady Maria as they walked. 'I have not yet seen it; I don't know whether she will have continued her theme in there.' Well. It was fortunate that he was a duke; if this was all the conversation he could provide, he would have to hope that his title would attract Lady Maria.

'I'm sure it will be as striking and beautiful as the ballroom. I look forward to finding out whether it smells as wonderful.'

James was spared from having to search for any more words—truly this was the first time in his life that he'd ever been struck so near dumb—by their entry into the supper room.

And... Good Lord. His mother had certainly not held back.

James and Lady Maria both stood for a moment, staring.

It was Lady Maria who regained her powers of speech first. 'It's...most striking,' she said. 'And elegant.'

James nodded, still speechless. He wasn't sure that *elegant* was the right word for it.

'I like the green,' Lady Maria persisted. 'It's very... botanical. Like the ballroom.'

'It certainly is...apple-coloured,' James said.

'And the pink is quite like a fuchsia. Which is also botanical.'

'Indeed.'

The supper room was hung with lengths of bright pink-and-green-striped silk, and the colour theme continued to the tables, the plates, the *floor*. It was truly the stuff of intense migraines.

In addition, the stripes were so wide but so ubiquitous that certain people's clothing was almost camouflaged.

'I like it.' Lady Maria had clearly entirely recovered from the shock now, and spoke quite definitively. 'I foresee that this will set a fashion for stripes.'

'I sincerely hope that you are wrong. May I seat you at a stripy table and place a selection of food on a stripy plate for you?' James said.

'That would be wonderful. I shall of course view you as a failure if you do not manage to choose striped food for me. And I would expect you to match it to the plate.'

James laughed. 'Your word shall be my bidding.'

Once he'd seated her and was next to the buffet table, he realised that he had a dilemma: like the lovelorn juvenile he appeared to have become, he just wanted to rush straight back to Lady Maria, but he also wanted to impress her. Impress her with his food choices, though? Really? What was he becoming?

It was the first time in his life that he'd worked as fast as he could to match food to a plate but he did his best and soon he was back with Lady Maria. As he sat down, he was conscious of a lightening of his shoulders, a smile spreading across his face, really just a strong sense of *happiness*. Utterly ridiculous, really, because he didn't know her at all. By the end of this supper, he might have discovered that the two of them were extremely incompatible.

'I'm extremely impressed,' Lady Maria said. 'I had not thought you able to meet the challenge. I particularly like the way you have covered the food of the wrong colour with hams and asparagus to maintain the pink and green stripes without causing me to have too monotonous a meal.' The contrast between the seriousness of her tone and the laugh in her eyes was *adorable*.

As he grinned at her, and laughed, James was quite certain that he was not in fact going to find that they were incompatible.

As friends and companions, obviously. There would be no love involved.

Chapter Three

Anna

'I think you will find—' the duke leaned in as though he was about to impart extreme wisdom '—that the presentation of food in stripes to match a plate is one of the greatest challenges imaginable. Much greater, for example, than those undertaken by the dragon-slaying knights of yore.'

Anna laughed before inclining her head and saying with her best air of great seriousness, 'I think you're right. There is no ancient king who would not immediately reward such a knight with his daughter's hand.' She was enjoying herself immensely; she had never before in her life had this kind of conversation with an attractive man—other than the music master at her seminary in her last year of school, for which, when they were overheard by the Latin master, she had been roundly punished and the music master had not, which had not seemed very fair to her, but of course men and women were held to very different standards.

She was *very* glad that Maria and her godmother had persuaded her into attending this evening; she could be doing no harm to anyone and was having the most delightful time.

'If I were such a knight, I would be truly honoured to receive the hand of a maiden discerning enough to wish her food to be in stripes.' The duke looked directly into her eyes as he spoke, a half-smile playing about his lips. Anna felt her heart do a gigantic thump, and swallowed hard.

She and the duke were sitting close enough to each other that she could see the faint shadow where his beard growth was already restarting, the deep blue of his eyes, the thickness of his wavy dark hair. His shoulders were broad and she had the oddest feeling that if one allowed oneself to lay one's problems on those shoulders, one would be protected from the world. For a moment she felt a surge of real wistfulness when she thought of the fortunate young woman whom he would marry in due course.

Although, of course, he was probably just like all other men— kind and caring and dependable…until he wasn't.

At this moment, though, it was easy to imagine that he might be a rare, truly dependable man. She had had that impression of him from the very first moment she saw him; she'd been on the brink of laughter at the audacity of the deception she and her godmother were practising, and she'd felt so immediately comfortable with him that for one silly moment she'd almost confided in him.

They were still staring into each other's eyes, not speaking.

This would not do; she needed to look away, find some light words to cut across this…tension that she felt between them.

The duke was still gazing intently at her, and his smile was growing.

'I have so many questions for you,' he said.

'You do?' Anna's voice had emerged as a squeak.

'So many. I hope…' He paused for a moment, and his smile turned wry, almost as though he were laughing at himself. 'I hope that I may have the opportunity to get to know you well enough to ask them all.'

Anna swallowed again. She had no experience of meeting men in polite Society but she couldn't help feeling that—even though he knew nothing of her— the duke's flirting was in earnest. As though he was genuinely interested in getting to know her well.

Oh, of course: he was interested in getting to know *Lady Maria Swanley* well; as the daughter of an earl who was possessed of what Maria had confided was a truly enormous dowry, she would attract any number of suitors, including dukes, and that was exactly why Maria had not wished to attend this ball. She had *foreseen* this.

What Anna should probably do now was change the subject, converse on lighter matters, and certainly not flirt back. Except…

'*I* believe that I have a question for *you*,' she said, unable to resist the temptation. Although…what was her question? There were many things she would love to know about him, but all her questions would sound remarkably forward if she asked them now.

'I am all yours.' His smile was becoming ever more, well…intimate. As though it was just for her. 'Perhaps we could…*exchange*…questions.' The way he said it made Anna feel really quite warm, inside as well as out. It was almost as though he'd been about to say they could exchange…something else. 'A questions game, perhaps. She, or he, who can't think of another—sensible—question to ask on their turn, is the loser.'

'And what is the winner's reward?' she found herself asking.

'Perhaps that should be for the winner to decide?'

'I'm sure I will win.' Anna held his gaze and faux pursed her lips. She was quite sure that she shouldn't be conversing with the duke like this, but it was as though she was under some kind of compunction. Also, she never liked to turn down a challenge—which was, of course, partly why she was here in the first place; Maria had begun the whole charade by challenging Anna to take her place.

'I'm ready whenever you are. Ladies first.'

'Let me think.' Rational thought was quite difficult when she was sitting quite so close to the most intriguing and handsome man she'd ever met. 'If you were decorating a ballroom, how would you decorate it? Yourself. Not delegating to anyone else.'

Anna wasn't *very* pleased with her question, because it was a little dull, but it was better than nothing.

'Good question. In that it is one I have never before asked myself. I fear that my answer might disappoint you. I would aim for simplicity.'

Anna shook her head, mock sorrowfully. 'I am indeed disappointed. That is no answer.'

'You're right. I beg your pardon. I shall now apply myself to thinking of a better response. I do like the colour blue.'

'Better,' Anna approved. 'What kind of blue, though?'

'A mid blue. Similar to the sky on a summer's day, but a little darker.'

'That's a very nice colour. Stripes?'

'No stripes.' The duke looked into her eyes again and shook his own head. 'I must change my answer. I have just realised that my favourite colour is green. The green of your eyes.'

Anna chose to laugh. 'Now you are becoming ridiculous, Your Grace.'

'My name is James, and yes, I do fear that I am ridiculous. But at the same time…not.' His face was suddenly completely serious, and Anna was suddenly extremely breathless. 'Another colour that I now very much like,' he continued, 'is silver. The silver of your dress.' His gaze flickered lower, for the merest of seconds, to her chest, before returning to her face.

Anna came very close to repeating a very overcome *Oh!* before pulling herself together and saying, 'Would you have green and silver stripes?'

'I confess that I would not have stripes. I would instead decorate the entire ballroom in the green of your eyes and the entire supper room in silver spangles.'

'Would the green not feel a little monotonous?' Anna was *not* going to give in to the flutter in her stomach.

'Never. I feel it would be easy to look at the colour of your eyes every day for the rest of one's life.'

'If I had a fan, I would now rap you over the knuckles,' Anna told him, mock sternly. 'As you know, I was referring to the ballroom decorations. I feel, however, that we have exhausted this topic, and should move on.'

'Before I make further outrageous references to your beautiful eyes?'

'Exactly.'

'In that case, I believe that it's my turn for a question,' he said.

'I'm really not sure that I should grant it, considering how poor your response to my question was. I am, however, feeling generous.'

The duke's grin transformed his face from somewhat austere handsomeness into boyish cheekiness, and Anna was suddenly certain that she would remember this evening, this supper—and his grin—for the rest of her life.

'Thank you,' he said. 'So kind.'

She laughed.

'I have many, many questions,' he continued. 'It's difficult to choose. I will start with a small one. Of a different nature. What is your favourite food? Did I select well for you?'

'You did select well.' Anna had barely eaten a mouthful, she realised; she'd been too busy with their conversation. 'I like a lot of food; it's hard to choose a favourite.'

'No, no.' The duke shook his head. 'You are in danger of answering this question as badly as I answered yours.'

'Please accept my deepest apologies.'

'I will accept them *if* you answer the question properly.'

'That's very gracious of you, Your Grace.'

'James.'

Anna applied herself to deciding on her favourite food—asparagus and chicken—and then the duke (she really couldn't call him James) told her what his was—a most unimaginative steak, but he allowed that asparagus was delicious.

Eventually they decided that their question game had been a draw, and then their conversation—punctuated by mouthfuls of the most delectable food—continued in the same silly but utterly delightful vein until supper was ended.

Anna couldn't remember a time when she'd been more disappointed for a meal to finish. There was still, however, their waltz to look forward to. Although… she was beginning to be worried that for some strange reason the duke might like her for herself, rather than for Lady Maria's birth and connections, in which case would she be doing him a disservice to waltz with him? Maybe… But on the other hand, if he did enjoy her company, he would—perhaps she was flattering herself but he *might*—be sad not to see her again, and it probably wouldn't make much difference whether or not they shared another dance. Conversation, and getting to know each other a little, drew people together more than dancing, surely.

As he bowed deep over her hand when he released her to her partner for the next dance, a Mr Marsh, the duke said, 'I look forward to our waltz,' before raising his head and giving her that same intimate smile.

Anna was going to look forward with great anticipation to their dance.

As she walked towards the dance floor with Mr Marsh, she caught her godmother's eye. Lady Derwent was swivelling her eyes and jiggling her eyebrows in the most dramatic way.

'Would you mind if I spoke to my godmother for one moment before the dance?' she asked Mr Marsh.

'Certainly.'

'The duke is being most marked in his attentions,' Lady Derwent whispered as soon as Anna reached her side. 'There is every indication that he might wish to marry you.'

'Surely not.'

'Oh, I think so.'

'Well, I clearly can't marry him. I am about to become a governess.'

'Piffle. Your grandfather was the Earl of Broome, and Lady Puntney would certainly understand.'

'But I've lied to the duke. And I *am* ineligible. I mean, I'm sure it's moonshine anyway. But if it weren't, I wouldn't be able to.' And Anna had no interest in the institution of marriage; since men were not to be trusted to treat women well, she would probably be better off as a governess. At least she would have some independence and would not be relying on anyone other than her employer.

Lady Derwent wrinkled her brow and stared into the distance for a moment, and then said, 'I think on reflection that for the time being you are right. Now go and dance with Mr Marsh. He's delightful.'

'Thank you. Remember that we need to leave at midnight.' Anna could *not* be late tomorrow.

'Certainly. In the meantime, enjoy the rest of the evening.'

* * *

Mr Marsh was a very nice man, and Anna was determined to make the most of *every* dance this evening, not just the ones with the duke, because it was entirely possible that this was the only ball she would have the good fortune to attend in her entire life. But if she was honest, it was difficult not to be very aware of where the duke was at every moment—it was easy to see him because of his height—and also difficult not to fizz with anticipation ahead of her waltz with him.

She did enjoy dancing and some very nice conversation with Mr Marsh, and she was almost sorry to leave him at the end of the dance.

Except she wasn't really, because it was time for her second dance with the duke.

She had learnt the waltz during her seminary days, and earlier that day Lady Derwent had mangled one on the pianoforte while Lady Maria took the role of gentleman and led Anna round Lady Derwent's drawing room in a practice waltz. The practice had not gone well, due to Lady Maria's constantly forgetting that she was supposed to lead, but Anna was confident that she could remember the rudiments of the dance sufficiently accurately to acquit herself adequately this evening. Earlier, she and Lady Derwent had agreed out loud, so that others might hear, that she might waltz. She was quite sure that she was ready for the dance.

She had not, though, taken into account the way her heart would thud so very hard in her chest and that her anticipation of the duke's touch would cause her mind to falter.

'I've been looking forward to this dance,' the duke murmured as he took her in his arms.

Anna didn't trust her voice to come out sounding normal or indeed her mind to produce any sensible-sounding words, so she smiled and said nothing. How had she been naïve enough to think that a waltz would draw two people together less than conversation might?

Her senses were quite flooded by the duke, and in every way; he even *smelled* good. The only way she could describe his scent was just, well, *masculine*. A delightful kind of masculine. He *felt* good; his height and the width of his shoulders and the latent strength evident in his arms as he held her gave the impression of security and, again, extreme masculinity. Just *hardness*. And, of course, when she turned her face up to his, he *looked* good. His strong features and jawline, the way he looked harshly handsome in repose but delightfully cheekily handsome when he smiled... And the way his body looked in his perfectly fitting evening clothes.

The whole was just...magnificent. And, in this moment, she felt like the luckiest woman in the world. And, also, one of the least lucky, because nothing could ever come of her meeting the duke; this was for one evening only. She would remember it, however—perhaps be almost spoilt by it—for evermore.

Since it *was* for only one evening, she should *not* allow herself to feel maudlin; she should instead enjoy every last minute of this dance, and indeed the rest of the evening.

So she directed a huge smile in the duke's direction and sank into his hold. Her hand fitted perfectly inside his much larger one, and the way he was holding it made her almost shudder with delight. Although not as much as did the way his other hand rested lightly on her waist, and the way when they turned she sensed the hardness in his thighs and his chest. The way their bodies touched and moved together through the dance felt almost scandalous in its intimacy.

And then, as the duke led her through a turn, she looked up at his face, and if she'd already thought that this experience was intoxicating, well, she'd been wrong. What was truly intoxicating was the way he was looking at her now, as though they were the only two people in the world, as though with the half-smile on his lips he was making her some kind of promise, as though he saw deep inside her and very much admired what he saw.

Anna knew that she was being fanciful; from one smile one could hardly tell what a man was thinking. Perhaps he was just thinking that he liked the—really quite lovely—flowers that Lady Derwent had procured for her to wear in her hair, or perhaps he adored the waltz and smiled like that at everyone with whom he danced.

And then she stopped bothering to think, because it was far too much effort and definitely served no good purpose, and just gave herself up to enjoying the dance.

Some time later—she had no idea how long—she, or the duke, it was hard to tell, became aware of being jostled by others. She looked round and saw that the dance had come to an end. She was still held in the duke's strong arms, and he showed no sign of letting go of her yet, for which she could only be deeply grateful.

It defied belief, but somehow, over the course of this

short evening, it felt almost as though he had become very important to her, even though she barely knew him.

'That was…wonderful,' he said, still not releasing her.

'It was. I must thank you, very much.' She had a sudden mad wish to tell him the truth about herself, but, no, she couldn't; the secret was only half hers to impart, and, in addition, if he did choose to tell anyone else, or anyone overheard them, it could give rise to the most dreadful consequences.

'Would you like to take a turn outside on the balcony?' he asked, *still* not relaxing his hold on her. She in her turn, she realised, was still clinging onto him.

'I believe that I am taken for the next dance.'

'It is not for a few moments and, if you were to feel faint, I am sure the gentleman in question would release you from your commitment?'

'I *do* feel somewhat faint,' Anna agreed. It wasn't even entirely a lie; surely any lady would be feeling somewhat wobbly after being held quite so intimately for quite so long by a man like the duke.

'Then you must immediately get some fresh air.'

They were interrupted by an elderly man, who was powdered and painted in the way of the previous century. 'I believe that the next dance with Lady Maria is mine.'

The duke and Anna both moved a little way away from each other and dropped their arms. It was as though they had been in their own little universe and someone else had entered.

'Sir Richard. I'm afraid that you will have to excuse Lady Maria,' the duke told him, his demeanour suddenly quite haughty and even a little intimidating. 'She feels ill and is in need of fresh air.'

'I would be very happy to escort the lady myself to seek fresher air.'

'That is very kind, but I will perhaps return myself to my godmother,' Anna said. However much her mother had come from this world and however much at all levels of society men had rights that women did not, she still could not stand and listen to two men discussing what she was going to do next without attempting to interject.

'Certainly,' the duke said very promptly. 'I will escort you over to her.' He nodded to Sir Richard, whose face appeared to be purpling beneath his paint, and then somehow manoeuvred himself and Anna so that they were walking away from him.

'Would you like to return to Lady Derwent now or do you perhaps feel that you might be better served by breathing some fresher air first?'

Anna was quite sure that she ought just to return to her godmother, because would it not be quite scandalous for her to walk outside with the duke? But no one knew who she was, and she wouldn't see any of these people again at an occasion like this. No one would connect her with Lady Maria after this because they looked so different, and, anyway, Lady Maria would be getting married. And Anna's future employer—should they see her—which she did not think likely—would never recognise her in governess garb after seeing her dressed like this. And she so *very* much wanted to steal just a few more moments with the duke.

'Upon reflection,' she told him, 'I do believe that fresh air would serve me very well at this moment.'

As the duke made a way for them through the crowd, Anna allowed herself for this one moment to feel special, to relish these few minutes where he was effectively hers. The lady for whose hand he offered would be very lucky.

She thought for a moment of Maria. How could she possibly wish to marry Clarence, her curate, when she could presumably have had the duke at her feet? It would be remarkably easy to fall in love with the duke.

But of course Maria had already fallen in love, and Anna had to admire her bravery; very few young ladies would have the courage to choose to marry someone in Clarence's straitened circumstances. Although Anna's own mother had of course been much braver than that: she had married her father's second groom. Anna hoped Maria was making the right decision; in the case of her parents, their difference in stations and the change in her mother's circumstances upon her elopement had put a strain upon her parents' relationship until eventually her father had left.

'You look as though you're thinking about something very serious,' the duke said as they stepped out of the long glass doors leading to a terrace along the back of the house. 'Please don't feel that you have to walk out here with me if you do not wish to; I would be more than happy to return you immediately to Lady Derwent.'

'Oh, no, I am very happy. That is…if you would still like to walk?'

'Very happy indeed,' he murmured, which made Anna smile.

As they moved along the terrace, he said, 'We are fortunate in having a particularly nice rose garden. Down those steps.' He pointed ahead. 'Would you like to take a walk around it? The moonlight and clear skies allow us to see quite well tonight.'

'I should very much like to, thank you.'

They continued towards the steps, Anna holding the duke's arm, and he said, 'I realise now that I was dreadfully short-sighted in not asking you what your favourite flowers were when we were asking questions of each other.'

'Fortunately, roses are some of my favourites.'

'Mine too,' he said. 'What a happy coincidence.'

Anna laughed; it was as though her senses were so heightened at this moment that the tiniest joke must seem hilarious.

'Take care on the steps,' the duke instructed. 'They are quite uneven and guests have been known to fall on them even in broad daylight. Allow me to hold your arm a little more tightly.'

Anna was more than happy to have her arm held more tightly. In fact, she couldn't think of anything she'd like more right now than to be held tightly by the duke.

'Thank you,' she said, a little breathlessly.

It was most enjoyable descending the steps clamped hard against his side. Anna couldn't believe that it was necessary for him to hold her steady with quite so much determination, but she certainly wasn't going to quibble. She had determined to enjoy this evening, and proximity to him could only enhance her enjoyment.

The steps safely negotiated, the duke drew her left. In the hazy light, Anna made out an archway into a walled garden, and then a profusion of rose bushes, laid out in a very regular fashion.

'These are indeed beautiful,' she said. 'I very much

like seeing a gardener's work: the love and care put into the planting and nurturing of the plants.'

'I agree, although in truth our head gardener, Alliss, whilst very talented, is a very grumpy individual who would be most put out if anyone suspected him of putting love into his work.'

Anna laughed. 'I refuse to believe that no love has gone into this planting. Look at them. They're wonderful. Quite beautiful.'

'Mmm.' The duke was not looking at the roses; he was looking at her. 'You are also very beautiful,' he told her, his voice completely serious. 'Your smile is… perfection.'

Anna felt his words to the very core of her body, and swallowed, suddenly suffused with emotion. While she had been educated as though she would one day take her place in Society and she was now two-and-twenty years old, quite old enough to know the ways of the world, she had no idea to what extent men spoke to women like this just for fun. Lady Maria was a young lady of quality, though, and chaperoned by Lady Derwent, and the duke was under his own roof. It seemed quite unlikely that he would attempt to take advantage of her; it seemed possible therefore that he really might mean his words. For the moment, at least.

Perhaps she should tell him now who she really was; being here under false pretences was beginning to feel terrible. But no, she'd already been over this in her mind, and she couldn't. It was not Anna's secret to share; she would be betraying Maria.

'Would you care to sit down?' the duke asked.

'There's a bench over there in the corner, with a lovely view of some of the better rose bushes.'

'That sounds delightful,' Anna said primly. She would tell him *something* to ensure that he was not led into believing she could be courted. And she would enjoy his conversation. And then she would leave.

She gasped as she sat down; the stone was very cold against her skin through her thin dress.

'I'm so sorry,' the duke said immediately. 'I should have been more considerate. Allow me to warm you with my jacket.'

'Oh, no, I… *Oh!*'

The duke had immediately divested himself of his jacket and placed it around her shoulders, and it was the most wonderful sensation being enveloped in his clothing, his scent again and the warmth from where his body had just been touching it.

'May I…?' He lifted his arm as though to place it around Anna's shoulders. She was fairly sure that she should say no, but she couldn't quite remember why. It wasn't as though a gentleman placing his arm around one's shoulders was *kissing*, after all.

So she smiled at him, and he smiled back at her, and hugged her into him.

And this felt even more intimate than their waltz had, because now they really *were* alone, rather than just feeling as though they were.

She had no idea what might happen next, but she was aware that, even though she barely knew him, she did trust the duke. Which was ridiculous, of course, because all she really knew of men from first-hand experience was that they were not to be trusted.

'Where is your childhood home?' he asked. 'Is it similar to London or very different?'

'It is in Somerset, and very different from London.' Anna had grown up in Gloucestershire, but Lady Maria's family home was quite close to Bath. Anna knew it reasonably well, having been invited to stay with her best friend on three occasions.

'Oh, yes, you mentioned that you had been enjoying visiting the sights of London. What do you have planned for tomorrow?'

'Tomorrow, I... I think...' Anna suddenly had a large lump in her throat at the mention of the next day. Tomorrow she would be leaving behind any pretence that this life could possibly be for her, and moving into the Puntneys' home before beginning her employment in earnest the following day.

'I ask...' The duke shifted a little on the bench so that, while still keeping his arm around Anna's shoulders, he was now also facing her. 'I ask because I should very much like to call on you tomorrow.'

'Oh!' *Oh.* Oh, no. This wasn't the way Anna had foreseen the deception going wrong, but it definitely *was* wrong.

The duke was looking—gazing—at her in the most *exciting* way and all she could do was swallow.

'I would like to take you for a drive in Hyde Park.' He lifted the hand that was not around Anna's shoulders, and very gently traced the curve of her cheek with one finger, which caused Anna's breath to hitch. 'I would also like to take you for a drive in Richmond Park.' He moved a little closer. Anna could hardly remember how to breathe. 'And I would like to show you around my estates.' He moved even closer. 'Further, I would like to assist your godmother in showing you as many of the sights of London that you would like to see.'

He drew her a little closer to him with his arm, and moved his free hand so that it was in Anna's curls, cupping the back of her neck.

'I would like—' the duke's voice was low and husky now, and every word he spoke sent a shiver through Anna '—to do so many things with you. I know that we've only just met but I feel…' He paused and then continued, 'I'm sorry. That's far too much. To begin with.' He tugged her hair very slightly, very gently, so that her head was angled exactly beneath his. And then, very, very slowly, he leaned towards her and brushed her lips with his. 'I would very much like to call on you tomorrow.'

'I would like that too, but…' Anna barely knew what she was saying. She was very aware that she had to tell him something *now* so that he wouldn't be holding any misconceptions, but she was even more aware of how he was holding her and where his lips had just touched hers.

'That.' The duke brushed her lips again with his, for a little longer this time. Anna's heart was beating *so* hard. 'Is.' He dropped another kiss on her lips and Anna wondered through the mists of feeling whether she might explode with…something. 'Wonderful.'

And then he kissed her for longer. And then he parted her lips with his tongue, and Anna felt it throughout her entire body. And then she found herself kissing him back, and it was truly, truly the most delicious thing she'd ever done in her entire life.

Anna had no idea how long they kissed for. She was

dimly aware of being held tightly by the duke, one of his arms now sliding around her waist, of winding her own arms around his neck and then plunging her hands into his hair.

When they eventually stopped the kiss, the duke took a deep breath and then just held her very tightly, his cheek against her hair. Being in his arms felt like the most natural place in the world to be, as though she *should* be there. Which was odd, because in reality she hardly knew him, and she was here with him under extreme false pretences.

As she thought that, she snuggled even more closely against him, wanting this moment to go on for ever.

And then, to her great disappointment, the duke planted a kiss on her forehead and drew back, easing his hold on her.

'We should be careful,' he said, his voice ragged. 'I could… I could… We could… We must not do things that a young lady should not do outside marriage. And to that end…' He moved a little further away and took his arm away from her.

'I would like to call on you tomorrow,' he said firmly. 'Much as I would like to stay out here, I think we should go back inside now. I do not trust myself to avoid temptation.'

Anna was going to have to tell him. As soon as possible.

She needed to find the words.

'I should give your jacket back to you,' she said first.

'When we are closer to the house. Otherwise, you will catch cold.'

'Thank you.'

They stood up and began to retrace their steps towards the building.

'I have enjoyed this evening very greatly,' the duke said as they walked.

'So have I. Thank you. It has been one of the most enjoyable of my life.' Anna knew that she would treasure the memory; she also knew that she would find it hard not to wish that he really could have called on her tomorrow.

When he pressed her hand on his arm and she smiled up at him in the moonlight, she suddenly felt quite tearful at the tender look on his face.

They were nearly at the terrace now.

'I must return your jacket to you,' she told him.

As he helped her out of it, his hands lingered for just a little longer than necessary on her bare arms, and she shivered through the entire length of her body in response.

'Thank you.' Honestly, her voice sounded quite tremulous.

She now felt very cold. Not just physically, but emotionally. As though the most wonderful interlude in her life had finished and it would take her a long time to feel warm again.

They trod up the steps and along the path together, Anna keeping her eyes fixed straight ahead because she couldn't bear to look at the duke.

And then, just before they stepped back inside the ballroom, she moved away from him and said, 'I'm so sorry, but I think I return to the country soon and will not be able to see you again.'

She looked up at him for a second and saw him just staring, and slightly frowning.

He reached a hand out to her and, ridiculously, because in reality she'd only known him for a few short hours, she felt as though her heart might break.

'Goodbye,' she said. 'Thank you so very much for a truly wonderful evening. Quite the best evening of my life. I have enjoyed it so very much.'

And then she walked away as fast as she could.

Chapter Four

James

James awoke slowly the next morning, from a dream where he'd been chasing something—maybe a butterfly—that he couldn't quite catch. He lay blinking for a few moments, conscious of a strong sense of dissatisfaction, waiting for clarity of thought to return, and then suddenly he remembered. Last night. Lady Maria. The strong sense of connection they'd shared, or he'd thought they'd shared. And then…her disappearance.

He pushed back his covers and swung his legs out of bed; he felt as though he had a lot to do.

Although, he realised, as he shook his head to clear it fully, it was far too early to pay a call on anyone. And he wasn't entirely sure that Lady Maria would *like* him to call on her. He couldn't decide which was the greater indicator: her sudden flight or the fact that she'd told him that yesterday evening had been wonderful, the best of her life.

He called for water and soap, still shaking his head

a little, wondering what exactly had happened to him yesterday evening.

Before the ball, if he'd been asked, he'd have said that he expected that at some point he would come to a sensible, measured decision regarding the choice of young lady to whom he would offer his hand in marriage. He had not had any real idea about how he might make that decision but he did know that he hadn't expected to know for certain after one evening—perhaps one minute—which lady he would choose.

He had also not expected that if he *did* meet someone with whom he could imagine spending his life, someone with whom he could enjoy companionship and friendship, he would be unlucky enough for the young lady to tell him that she would be leaving for the country and unable to see him again.

Had she meant it? He just didn't know.

He washed and dressed hurriedly—although he did take the time to ensure that his cravat fell well, in the hope that he would be able to speak to Lady Maria later—still with the strong sense that he was in a rush to take some kind of action, and then descended to the breakfast parlour.

As he sat to eat steak—which reminded him of eating supper with Lady Maria—he tried to marshal his thoughts.

The contrast between her telling him she was leaving for the country and that she wouldn't be able to see him again and the way she'd melted into the crowd of guests so quickly that he hadn't been able to follow her, and the fact that she'd told him with seeming great sincerity how very much she'd enjoyed the evening, was very confusing.

Perhaps she hadn't really meant that she wouldn't be able to see him again; perhaps she had just meant that when she left for the country she would be residing far from London and didn't expect to see him again *easily*. Or soon.

Perhaps she'd been as overwhelmed as he by the connection and tension there had been between them and had panicked a little. Perhaps she had thought he was merely trifling with her. She was certainly not experienced with men; he had had the strongest sense when he kissed her that it was the first time she had kissed anyone or been kissed like that.

He took a large swig of ale and frowned a little as he considered how he would plan his day.

It wasn't difficult, actually.

He *knew* that he wanted to marry Lady Maria. He needed to get married. He hadn't wanted to get married. He didn't wish to fall in love and he didn't wish anyone to fall in love with him. But they weren't in love. How could they be when they barely knew each other? They had merely experienced an intense connection of the sort that he could easily imagine would lead to an excellent understanding and partnership between them. And the intimate side of marriage would certainly be no hardship with Lady Maria. She would make the ideal bride for him.

And therefore he would like to propose to her today.

She would surely not be leaving for the country as soon as this morning, unless she had had word that her grandmother had taken a turn for the worse.

So he would pay a call on her as early as he reasonably could and hope very much that the reason that she had effectively run away from him last night was merely that she had felt overwhelmed by what had happened and had not understood that his intentions were serious and entirely honourable, and that she would accept his proposal.

And between now and then he should really do his best to do something better with his day than just kick his heels in impatience.

He achieved very little other than a ludicrous amount of pacing before the hour at which he might call on Lady Maria finally arrived.

He had sent a footman to enquire about where she was residing, given that her mother had left town, and had been told that she was staying in her own home, accompanied by two very elderly great-aunts. Their age would presumably explain why she had been accompanied last night by Lady Derwent.

Standing on the doorstep of the Grosvenor Square house, he found his hands going to his cravat to check it more than once, and realised that he was squaring his shoulders and taking deeper breaths than he might usually do.

The door was opened by a particularly stately butler, who showed him into a conservatively decorated parlour to the left of the hall.

James sat and then stood and then sat and then stood again as he waited.

And then, finally, the door opened and the butler announced Lady Maria and her aunt, Lady Sephranella.

The first lady to enter the room was aged and walked slowly with a stick. James greeted her politely, looking eagerly beyond her to where Lady Maria would appear.

The young lady who followed her into the room was not, however, Lady Maria.

He turned to Lady Sephranella, not wishing to be rude to whomever this young lady might be. Perhaps a cousin of Lady Maria's.

'I wondered whether I might be able to see Lady Maria,' he said.

'I am Lady Maria,' the younger lady said.

James frowned. 'I'm afraid I don't understand,' he said. This young lady was tall and blond-haired and blue-eyed, whereas the Lady Maria that he had met was smaller, brown-haired and green-eyed. This lady was beautiful, but his Lady Maria was *really* beautiful. Especially when she smiled. 'I wondered whether I might be able to see Lady Maria Swanley.'

'I am Lady Maria Swanley.' She spoke very slowly, as if to someone who did not have strong comprehension.

James shook his head.

'I met Lady Maria last night,' he said. 'Lady Maria Swanley.'

'Really?' The lady in front of him shook her own head. 'I'm so sorry but I don't entirely remember. It was of course a great crush—so wonderful that the whole world wished to attend your mama's ball—so one met a great many people. It is difficult to remember to whom one spoke.'

James frowned at her. She looked absolutely nothing like the actual Lady Maria. The only thing this lady and *his* Lady Maria had in common, he realised, was that this one's eyes seemed to be dancing with merriment, as his Lady Maria's had last night when he met her.

He… What? Could they… What?

Could they have played some kind of trick on him, on the *ton*? Surely not? *Why*? There had to be some other explanation. This Lady Maria really did look, however, as though she was on the brink of laughter.

'I am the Duke of Amscott,' he said.

'Yes,' agreed the lady.

'Last night, my mother held a ball.'

'Yes.'

'At the ball, I met and danced twice with Lady Maria Swanley.'

'I am Lady Maria Swanley.'

'I do not, however—' James was starting to find it difficult to get his words out without shouting '—recall having met you before.'

The lady cast her eyes down. 'I must confess that I would be a little hurt by your words, Your Grace, were it not for the fact that I do not easily recall you either.'

'Are you indeed Lady Maria Swanley?' James asked baldly, ignoring her last sentence.

'Yes, of course I am.' The lady's smile was so bland as to be suspicious.

'Are you confused, Your Grace?' Lady Sephranella quavered from the corner of the room. 'This is my great-niece, the granddaughter of my sister. This is Lady Maria Swanley. Have you come to the wrong house, sir?'

Could it be possible that the elderly lady and the butler were both colluding in a plot to pretend that this lady was Lady Maria? Why on earth would they do that? They *couldn't* be.

He took another long look at the lady who called her-self Lady Maria. She was still smiling blandly at him and her eyes were still dancing. She looked ridiculously mischievous.

'I have not come to the wrong house but I will bid you good afternoon.' Clearly, he needed to go and see Lady Derwent.

Twenty minutes later, he was waiting in a grand draw-ing room in Lady Derwent's Berkeley Square mansion, which, coincidentally, was directly opposite his own, on the other side of the gardens in the middle of the square.

'Your Grace.' Lady Derwent swept into the room in a rustle of stiff silk.

'My Lady.'

Greetings dispensed with, James came straight to the point. 'I would very much like to pay a call on Lady Maria Swanley today.'

'I believe that Lady Maria resides in Grosvenor Square.'

'She is not here?'

Lady Derwent raised her eyebrows. 'No?'

James had rarely in his life spent so much time in one afternoon wishing to grind his teeth. 'Yesterday evening, at my mother's ball, you introduced your goddaughter, Lady Maria Swanley, to me.'

'That is correct.' Lady Derwent moved to a chair near the fireplace and said, 'Please sit down.'

'Thank you. I enjoyed meeting Lady Maria.'

'We enjoyed attending the ball; thank you so much. I particularly liked the decorations. I believe that your mama will have created a fashion.'

'Thank you. Indeed.' James did not wish to discuss ballroom furnishings. 'I am a little confused. I have just been to call on Lady Maria at her house.'

'How very pleasant.'

'The Lady Maria that I met at her house was not the Lady Maria that I met last night.'

'Did you visit the correct Lady Maria? Maria is quite a common name.'

James had to work hard not to grind his teeth. 'Yes. I understand from you that the lady I met last night was Lady Maria Swanley. And the lady I visited today was Lady Maria Swanley. They were not, however, the same person.'

Lady Derwent inclined her head to one side and frowned slightly. 'I myself am also now confused. How could that be? I was not aware that there were two Lady Maria Swanleys.'

'I am sure there are not.'

'Then I do not understand what you mean.'

'Last night—' James was surprised that he was not now yelling '—I met a Lady Maria Swanley, whom you introduced as your goddaughter. I danced twice with her, I ate supper with her, I conversed with her.' He had *kissed* her.

Lady Derwent nodded. 'Yes.'

'And this afternoon I went to call on Lady Maria Swanley, at her house. A young lady came into the room where I was waiting. The butler and a Lady Sephranella, described to me as Lady Maria's great-aunt, referred to the young lady as Lady Maria Swanley. She referred to herself as Lady Maria Swanley. She said that she had been at the ball and thought that she had probably met me but did not remember me. I did not remember her at all because I have never met her before because she was not *my* Lady Maria Swanley.'

'*Your* Lady Maria Swanley?'

'I had—' James was aware that he had lost all dignity and he did not care '—that is to say, I formed quite an attachment to Lady Maria over the course of yesterday evening. I wished to call on her today to further our acquaintance.'

'I see.' Lady Derwent looked thoughtful.

'Forgive me if I appear rude.' James did not care at all if he appeared rude right now. 'I wonder if you could explain what has happened. Where is the Lady Maria I met last night and what relation does she have to the Lady Maria I met this afternoon?'

Lady Derwent placed her hands together, palm to palm, and touched them to her chin for a moment, before relaxing her fingers so that they clasped each other and laying her hands in her lap.

Speaking slowly, as though choosing her words carefully, she said, 'I believe that you met Lady Maria Swanley this afternoon.'

'Who was the lady I met yesterday evening then?'

Lady Derwent paused for a moment and then said, 'Lady Maria Swanley.' She turned and rang the bell next to her. 'Would you like to take tea?'

James looked at her for a long moment and then said, 'Thank you; I am afraid that I have urgent business to attend to and must leave.'

Lady Derwent nodded. 'Do visit again.'

'I should be delighted.' James just wanted to swear.

* * *

Marching away from Lady Derwent's house, James had the strangest sensation that his head was going to explode. Someone—everyone—had to be lying to him, because clearly at least one of the two purported Lady Marias was not the real one. But *why* were they lying?

Something was nagging at the edge of his mind. As his thoughts began to crystallise, he stopped dead in the middle of the pavement, and a little boy out with his nurse for a walk ran right into him.

'I do apologise,' James said, his mind working hard.

Both so-called Lady Marias had seemed mirthful on his first meeting with them. It was easy to imagine that the mirth might have related to a secret. And that that secret might be the impersonation by one of the ladies of the other.

The first Lady Maria had *known* that she was going to be meeting people that evening, in the guise of Lady Maria. The second Lady Maria had not known until he arrived that James would call on her today. Had the first Lady Maria been the real one, she would not have been mirthful about the masquerade that neither she nor the second Lady Maria could know might arise, as neither would have known at that point that he would make to-day's call.

Of course, the mirth might have been for a different reason.

But logic suggested that if one of the two ladies was impersonating Lady Maria, and they both knew about it, which they must do, and that was what had caused both ladies' mirth, it was the second lady who was the real one, and last night's Lady Maria who was the fake.

He turned round. He was going back to see Lady Derwent again.

'What a delightful surprise,' said Lady Derwent five minutes later, indicating that James should take a chair near to hers. 'I had not thought to see you again so soon, Your Grace.'

'No, indeed; this is very soon,' agreed James, sitting as directed. 'I will not take up too much of your time. I have merely come to say that I believe that the lady I met yesterday evening under the guise of Lady Maria Swanley was not in fact Lady Maria. I must apologise for any implied rudeness—' he bowed '—but it seems to me that you were aware of the deception.'

Lady Derwent studied him for a long moment, and then said, in much milder tones than she usually used, 'That would of course be an astonishing deception. Quite unbelievable, in fact; ladies such as I do not practise such deceptions.'

She was clearly lying.

James leaned forward. 'Who was the lady I met last night?'

Lady Derwent shook her head, a little sorrowfully, and said, 'Lady Maria Swanley.'

James tried not to roll his eyes and failed. 'I should be very grateful if you would pass on a message to the lady I met last night.'

'What kind of message would you like to pass on to… Lady Maria?'

'I…' James could not just blurt out a marriage proposal by proxy. 'I... I would very much like the opportunity to see again the lady that I met last night.'

'That is not a particularly interesting sentiment.' Lady Derwent sounded a little disappointed. 'Perhaps a stronger message would have a greater effect.'

James narrowed his eyes. Was she *encouraging* him to make serious advances? How very peculiar. Had she somehow orchestrated his meeting with last night's Lady Maria so that he would propose to her? No. That was preposterous. She could not possibly have known that he would be captivated by one smile, and she was hardly making it easy for him to see her now.

'If I am able to see her again, I am sure that I will have a stronger message for her,' he said.

Lady Derwent inclined her head graciously. 'I will bear that in mind.'

Three days later, James was taking tea with his mother and sisters, his mood still fairly bleak.

He realised now that it was a good thing that the young lady he had met had disappeared; he had to admit that some would describe the level of infatuation he had experienced as close to having fallen head over heels in love on first sight, and he did not wish to fall in love. He was beginning to come to terms with the loss of his father and brothers, and he did not wish to experience further loss. Women died in childbirth all the time, for example. And if the lady reciprocated his feelings and he did die young like his brothers, that would be terrible for her.

So, yes, with hindsight, he was inclined—when reflecting rationally—to think he'd had a lucky escape.

He could have been in danger of falling in love, and love was a dangerous emotion. Really, it was a good thing that he was unable to get to know the lady any better or propose marriage to her. He was quite convinced of it.

It was more difficult, however, to convince himself that he was feeling particularly happy or that life was particularly enjoyable. Stupidly, given that he did not know the lady at all—hell, he didn't even know her real *name*—he felt that he missed her. In addition, there was clearly an unsolved mystery surrounding her identity that he would have liked to have solved. And he didn't *think* she could be in any kind of trouble, given that she had been under Lady Derwent's protection, but he wasn't *certain* that all was well with her.

He had considered paying a detective to look for her, but rationally felt that he should not. He could not *force* her to tell him who she was.

'Ouch.'

His mother had just rapped him across the knuckles.

'James,' she tutted. 'You have been paying very little heed to us this afternoon. You appear to be wrapped up in thoughts of your own.'

'My apologies, Mama. I am a little tired.'

'You should get more sleep. We were discussing which young ladies you are considering getting to know better with marriage in mind.'

James suddenly felt very tired. 'I am not sure that I wish to marry soon.'

His mother frowned. 'I thought we had already discussed this.'

James sighed. In truth, they *had* discussed it, and he did have to produce an heir while he was still in good health. He'd been over this in his mind countless times now. He absolutely did not wish to marry someone with whom he was in love or who loved him. It was for the best that Lady Maria—or whoever she had been—had disappeared. As long as she was in good health, happy and safe. *No.* He was not going to start worrying about this again.

He took a deep breath and turned to his mother. 'Whom do you suggest I meet?'

Two days later, James and his mother called on a very pleasant young lady, a Lady Catherine Rainsford, a marchioness's daughter with a large dowry, a pretty face and easy but not overwhelming conversation.

On their return home, his mother pulled her gloves off and handed them to their butler.

'Lady Catherine is a delightful young lady.' She walked into the smaller of the two saloons leading right off the hall, her demeanour very much indicating that she expected James to follow. 'Do you think that you might like to marry her?'

'I...' James really had no idea whom he might like to marry. Well, he had an idea whom he would *like* to marry, but not whom he *would* marry. 'She does seem very pleasant.' He could certainly imagine being friends with her. 'And quite attractive.' He *supposed* he could imagine making love to her.

It was probably *good* that he didn't feel terribly excited by that. As he had told himself many times before, he did not want to be in love with his wife, and he didn't think he would fall in love with Lady Catherine. And she really would be very suitable. She was well-formed. Not too tall, not too small. She had a nice face and nice hair. She seemed reasonably intelligent but not a bluestocking. He presumed that she would be a good mother for his children.

Really, he couldn't imagine a better wife.

Except, well, he *could*...

This was ridiculous.

What had his mother asked? Whether he might like to marry her.

'Perhaps I might,' he said.

'James.' His mother's hand went to her mouth, and then she reached up and hugged him before releasing him and patting her hair in the mirror. 'Darling, I'm quite excited.'

'So am I,' he told her untruthfully.

'When will you propose to her?'

'Soon. I think. Although, I am not certain.'

'Oh.' His mother plumped herself down on a chair as though all the stuffing had suddenly gone out of her. 'I do think you should marry soon, my dear.'

James nodded. 'I know. I will.' He looked at his mother. He loved her and his sisters very much. He did need to ensure that their future was secure, and for that he did need at least one son. 'Soon. I just need a little time to get used to the idea.'

'Darling, if you don't feel comfortable marrying, please don't let me push you into it.'

James raised his eyebrows wryly. 'Really?'

'Yes. I'm aware that I have indeed been trying to persuade you into it, but I believe that you would be happy, should you find a young woman with whom you were compatible. I would be delighted for you if you came to love her as deeply as I loved your father.' She and James's father had had an arranged marriage that had turned out to be a very happy one. 'I thought... I wondered whether you were singling out Lady Maria Swanley at our ball, but you haven't mentioned her since then.' She had mentioned Lady Maria obliquely once or twice since the ball but this was the first time she had mentioned her explicitly.

'Yes. No. I haven't, no. She...left London.'

'Oh, I know why.' James's sister Charlotte had come into the room and caught the latest part of their conversation. 'Have you not heard the latest *on-dit*? Lady Maria has become engaged to a penniless curate, although he is of very good birth, I believe. Her mama is very unhappy about it, but I have it from dearest Eliza Featherley that because Lady Maria is now twenty-one she is old enough to make her own decision and intends to marry and retire to the country with him. He has a living in Hampshire.'

'Really!' their mother said.

Really, James thought. If this had been going on for some time, perhaps that was why Lady Maria had practised her deception. Perhaps she had sent a friend to the ball in her place because she did not wish to participate in the Season's marriage mart when she was already promised to her fiancé. But why would Lady Derwent have colluded in that?

'What is it about Lady Derwent that you don't like?' he asked his mother.

'We know each other well but we've never really been good friends. We came out in the same year and she nearly ran away with your dear father, before he saw sense and married me. She's always been quite wild. Even now. She acts the grand Society matron on one hand but on the other does not have a great regard for convention.'

'Very interesting.' Very interesting indeed.

They attended a musical soirée together that evening, because James's mother had ascertained that Lady Catherine would be there.

Shortly after they arrived, James looked round to discover Lady Derwent at his elbow. It seemed very much as though she was there by design. Perhaps she had more to say about Lady Maria.

'I wondered if you might be able to procure some lemonade for me,' she said.

When he had the drink, he found her sitting in a corner, waiting for him.

'Thank you.' She took the glass from him and patted the empty chair next to her. 'Do sit and keep me company for a moment.'

'Of course.'

James was barely seated before she said, 'I believe that you would find it of interest to walk near the cows' pasture in the north-west part of Hyde Park in the morning. At perhaps eleven o'clock.'

James raised his eyebrows. Presumably this had something to do with the fake Lady Maria.

'Indeed?' he asked.

'I am thinking about our last conversation,' she pursued. 'I would recommend that you take a walk there before coming to any important decisions.'

'For a particular purpose?' he asked.

'Eleven o'clock,' she repeated, as though he had not spoken.

'I will bear that in mind,' he said, blinking.

'Are you a musical devotee?' she asked.

'Erm, no.'

'Never mind.' She smiled at him and then launched into a description of the renowned soprano who was going to be singing to them shortly.

James nodded and said very little—he had no opinions to offer on the soprano in question—until eventually Lady Derwent said, 'You must go and find your mother. Don't forget. Eleven o'clock. Tomorrow.'

As James bent his head over her hand, he had no idea whether he would take himself to Hyde Park on the morrow or not.

He still wasn't entirely sure whether he would go to Hyde Park the next day, he told himself, as he endured a lengthy monologue from Lady Catherine on the subject of music, wondering the whole time whether he really would like to be married to her, and unable to stop thinking about Lady Maria—*his* Lady Maria—and wondering whether her presence would have made this evening more enjoyable (he was quite sure that it would).

He would not yet propose marriage to Lady Catherine. He needed to think a little more about it.

He was always going to have come to Hyde Park, he reflected fourteen hours later, as he walked his horse, Star, down the path that led to the spot that Lady Derwent had described to him the previous evening. Of course he was. As he'd listened to a succession of warbling sopranos and growling tenors, he'd reflected on the conversations that he'd had with her and had concluded that of course her suggestion—command—had something to do with his Lady Maria.

And if Lady Derwent was trying to arrange a meeting between him and the fake Lady Maria he couldn't resist attending.

When he came upon the clearing that Lady Derwent had mentioned, he found that there was no one there. His pocket watch told him that it was still five minutes before eleven.

The next few minutes passed unutterably slowly as he walked Star round, just waiting to see what would happen.

When he did eventually hear people approaching, he turned quickly, only to see that it was not Lady Maria.

Rather, the little group that was approaching comprised three children, a nursemaid and a grey-clad lady who was presumably a governess.

James's gaze rested on the group very briefly, before he resumed looking around to see if other people—in particular a small lady with a beautiful smile—might be approaching. And then, he could not say why, he found his eyes being drawn back to the little group, and in particular to the lady in grey. There was something about her...

He looked hard at her and, as he stared, her head turned in his direction, and she gave a noticeable start.

He hadn't been able to make out her features fully, due to the bonnet she was wearing and the fact that on glimpsing him she had then turned away, and yet he had the strongest feeling...

Was she...?

He dismounted, looped Star's reins around a tree and strode over to the group.

'Good morning,' he said, directing his words at the grey-clad woman. His accosting the group was of course somewhat irregular, but he felt a strong compulsion to confirm his suspicions.

'Good morning.' She kept her head lowered so that it was difficult to see her face, but her voice was recognisable, and so was her posture. Good God.

'Lady Maria!' he exclaimed.

She froze and then, after a long moment, looked up at him.

If he wasn't mistaken, her eyes were filling. Surprisingly, given that surely *she* had wronged *him*, he found himself feeling guilty.

'I'm afraid that you are mistaken,' she told him, shaking her head. There was no trace of her smile. 'Good morning. We must be on our way.'

'No,' he blurted out. He felt as though he *needed* to find out more about her. And Lady Derwent had clearly meant him to find this lady, whoever she really was. As though in some way they were *intended* to meet again.

The lady tilted her head very slightly to one side and said, 'No?' Her tone was significantly frostier than he had assumed her capable of.

Which was arguably quite ridiculous given that *she* had lied to *him*.

'I should be very grateful if you would afford me a few moments of your time,' he said.

'I…' She took a deep breath and then glanced over her shoulder at the nurse and children behind her. 'I am unfortunately busy.'

'Please?' Apparently he was begging. Which, again, felt quite ridiculous. 'Just a minute or two?'

She looked into his face for quite a long time before pressing her lips together and saying, 'One moment.' She turned to the maid and said, 'Elsie, I should be grateful if you would take the children for a short walk along the path over there. Children, please could you look at the different leaves on the trees and try to ascertain what type of tree they are?'

James waited a few moments so that the remainder of her party would be out of earshot, and then said in a low voice, so that they would not hear, 'I would appreciate an explanation. I take it that you masqueraded as Lady Maria at the ball.'

'Yes, I did. I am sorry if I offended you in any way.' She gave a small nod, as though to end the conversation, and took a step or two away from him.

'I don't think this is the end of the conversation,' James stated. How could she possibly think that it was acceptable to practise such an outrageous deception—in his house—and admit to it but behave as though that would be the end of it? At the very least, surely, she should tell him why. And apologise. And…

Well, he didn't know what else. He couldn't really work out how he felt about her any more.

Good God, he'd been on the brink of *proposing* to her. And she was… Well, he had no idea who she was. She was a governess. Who'd been pretending to be Lady Maria Swanley. The whole thing was preposterous.

Perhaps the personality she had presented to him had also been fake. He wasn't sure whether that thought made him feel angry or sad or… Maybe confused. And, yes, definitely angry.

'I would suggest that you owe me an explanation,' he told her.

'I…' She stopped and turned back to face him fully, before saying, 'Yes. The explanation is not entirely mine to give, however. Lady Maria and I are very close friends. Lady Derwent is my godmother. Lady Maria did not wish to attend the ball for reasons of her own, which I cannot disclose, and she asked me to go in her place. Lady Derwent persuaded me that it would be a good idea to enjoy one ball before I began my employment here. I beg of you not to tell my employer that I undertook the masquerade.'

'Your employer?'

'I am a governess.'

Of course. That explained the grey dress. And the children. It did not explain how Lady Derwent was her godmother and Lady Maria her good friend.

'I will not tell your employer.' He was still very angry but he had no taste for vindictiveness. 'I would ask, however: did none of you think of the consequences of your action? I cannot understand how any of you would think that it was an acceptable thing to do. It was rude, it was ridiculous, it was preposterous, it was *stupid*.'

'I'm sorry, I…' she began. And then she stopped and pressed her lips together and tilted her head slightly. 'I do understand that Society might not look kindly on such a masquerade. However, I am sure that it is rare for two people to meet and make a strong connection on such an occasion. Had I just danced and talked to a succession of different people that evening, and then disappeared, no one would have been any the wiser. Whilst I would have had one very enjoyable evening. I believe that your disapprobation is perhaps due to the fact that you and I spent a long time talking and that you feel that I misled you.'

James shook his head, not wishing to acknowledge that he had a personal reason for his anger. 'I cannot think it acceptable that you practised such a deception.'

'I would suggest—' her voice had turned to ice and somehow he liked her all the more for it '—that, as Duke of Amscott, it is perhaps difficult for you to understand the realities of life for women or less privileged men. Lady Maria had a very good reason for not wishing to attend the ball, and, had she not gone at all, people would have asked questions. Because she is a woman. I did not wish to become a governess, but I have no alternative. I do enjoy parties; that was the only ball I will ever have had the opportunity to attend as a guest. Because I am poor. When you have experienced being either a woman or poverty-stricken or both, I shall accept your criticism.'

James frowned. 'I do of course have the advantages of birth, wealth and sex, and I am sorry that you have had no alternative but to accept a role that you do not want.' They should not have practised their deception, however. Although…her words about being poor and having no further opportunity to attend a ball were very sad. She had seemed to enjoy the dancing very much.

He still didn't know who she was, other than Lady Derwent's goddaughter, or how she came to be in this position.

'You are a lady,' he stated.

She inclined her head.

'May I ask your name and why you came to be a governess?'

'I am sorry but I can see no reason to prolong our acquaintance. I wish you very well, and I apologise for any distress I caused you with the deception.' She gave him a quick smile—a small one, not one of her wide, joyful, wonderful ones—and then turned and hurried in the direction of the maid and her charges, calling to them as she went, so that if James attempted to speak to her again he would cause a scene.

He couldn't do that to her, of course, so he just stood, impotent, hands on hips, watching her walk away from him, wondering what he would do next.

He had the strangest sense that if his life were a play, everything up to the evening he'd met her had been the first act.

And now he'd entered a different stage of life, one in which this lady—whose name he still did not know— might, perhaps, feature heavily.

She couldn't, though. She had deceived him and she was a governess.

He should probably stop being so fanciful and put her out of his mind.

The nameless lady—*she*—was now surrounded by her charges, whose smiles and laughs, their faces up-turned to hers, suggested that they were very fond of her.

The little group disappeared around a corner, and James felt, well, bereft.

Maybe he should go after her after all. Find out her name and direction, request further conversation with her.

He took a couple of steps in the direction of the path they had taken, before checking himself. He should not cause the lady any difficulties with her employer unless he was going to propose marriage to her.

This morning, he had been certain that he would propose to her.

Now, however, he really wasn't sure. Well, of course he wasn't. All he knew about her was that she was a governess who had pretended to be Lady Maria Swanley and had spent an evening dancing and conversing with him.

He was definitely not going to propose to her.

He had had a lucky escape.

Chapter Five

Anna

Anna felt as though her legs would barely hold her up as she shepherded the children and Elsie around the corner.

What a horrible coincidence that the duke had come upon them like that. She came here every morning with the girls and rarely saw persons of quality out exercising. It was the wrong time of day for them—too late for gentlemen's morning gallops, and several hours earlier than the fashionable hour for the *ton* to be seen driving in the park—and it was also not the fashionable part of the park.

It had been extremely unlucky.

And extremely…upsetting.

She had spent a lot of time since the ball thinking about the duke and their evening together. When she'd told him that it had been the best evening of her life, she had not been exaggerating. It had been truly wonderful. Their dancing and their kiss had been truly perfect. But the thing that had been the best of all had been their conversation. She had felt as though they had had a genuine connection. And then, afterwards, she had wondered whether she had imagined it; she had thought that the duke probably met and forged connections with women all the time.

And then she had discovered from Lady Maria and her godmother that he had been to call on her the day after the ball. Her godmother had told her that he had at the very least wished to pursue his acquaintance with her, given his tenacity in asking about her.

It was hard not to wonder whether he might even have proposed to her.

And whether she would have liked to have accepted such a proposal.

She wasn't sure.

He had occupied much of her thoughts and dreams since she'd met him. She had replayed various parts of the evening they'd spent together over and over in her mind.

But men were not to be trusted.

Her mother had brought her up as a lady. When Anna's father had left, they had moved to a well-appointed, medium-sized house in a Cotswold village, living as a respectable widow and her daughter. They had socialised with the local gentry and had attended assemblies in Cheltenham. Anna had had every expectation of continuing to live in such a way. And then her mother had become ill and Anna had spent a lot of money—all their money—on doctors. And then, after her mother had died, she had discovered that she was entirely penniless. Lady Derwent had taken her in and had asked her, many times, to live with her as a companion, as the daughter she had never had. But Anna could not bear to take charity, and had decided that she must earn her living.

And here she was.

Of course the duke would never propose to her now.

And that was probably—certainly—for the best. Because she would never wish to be trapped in an unhappy marriage, and she knew that men's affection and love for their wives—and daughters—could fade.

Although she would have liked to have had children. But she must not dwell on these things.

She should be grateful for her employment and her friends and not think about the duke or about her life before her mother had become ill.

The way to avoid thinking about things was to keep her mind occupied in other ways. It was reasonably easy during the day, because looking after children made one very busy; it was the evenings that were more difficult.

Her employers, Sir Laurence and Lady Puntney, were very kind people.

Lady Puntney had told Anna that she did not wish her to be worked to the bone and that she must have early afternoons, evenings and regular days off, and enjoy excursions with any friends she might have.

Which was very kind, but it did mean that Anna had a good deal of spare time.

Sir Laurence had generously told her that she might read any of the books in his extensive library, and she had been doing her best to distract herself with literature. Unfortunately, his tastes, or those of his forebears who had stocked the library, tended towards the stuffier sort of fiction, and what Anna needed right now was something like a modern romance to keep her fully engrossed. She was currently reading Virgil in the original Latin, and it was a struggle to maintain her concentration; she regularly found herself staring at the same page for what felt like hours on end.

She had also tried to occupy herself in writing letters to friends, in particular Lady Maria and Lady Derwent, but had found it difficult to write much. Her words had tended towards the melancholy, and she did not wish to be or sound melancholic.

And she had never been particularly gifted at needle-work.

'Anna.' Isabella, the youngest of her charges, was pulling at her arm. 'You weren't listening.'

'I'm so sorry, Isabella; I was momentarily distracted. You should nonetheless strive for greater politeness yourself. One should not pull on another's arm like that.'

That evening, when she had finished her work for the day and was about to go to the library to try to find herself a more enthralling work of fiction than Virgil, perhaps something written in English, at least, the Punt-neys' butler, Morcambe, handed her a note that had been delivered to her during the afternoon.

It was in a thick envelope and addressed in a deci-sive-looking script.

Something made her heart beat a little faster as she pulled it out, and as she read the signature, she began to feel almost faint with shock.

The note read:

Dear Miss Blake,
Would you be so kind as to accompany me for a
short drive or walk when you are next able?
Yours,
James, Duke of Amscott

How had he found out who she was?

Well, that was a silly question. She realised that she had been naïve to think that she could effectively remain hidden from him.

It would have been easy for him to establish her identity in any manner of ways. Dukes had all the means in the world to undertake detective work, or of course her godmother might have decided to tell him; she had certainly been vocal about her disappointment in Anna's choice to become a governess rather than accept her charity and had begged her to remember that she could always choose to live with her, and Anna was sure that she had been trying to make a match between her and the duke. No, her godmother had promised her that she would not betray her to him, and Anna did trust her. He must have found out some other way.

Her mind was wandering; she didn't need to speculate how he'd discovered her name and where she was staying. She needed to decide what she was going to do now.

She couldn't see him. It would be too difficult and there was no point. And people might see them and talk.

However...

He seemed very determined and very tenacious.

Perhaps it would be better in fact to meet him once in person and explain definitively that she would not be meeting him again.

Maybe she would not reply immediately but instead reflect on the matter for a while.

Half an hour later, she was still in the library, having completely failed to choose a new book because all she could do was think about whether or not she should meet the duke.

She *was* going to meet him, she suddenly decided, as she picked up and discarded a book containing the poems of John Dryden. Otherwise, she would constantly wonder whether she might see him again anyway. Every time she left the house she would be distracted, looking over her shoulder, wondering whether he might be around the next corner. That would not be an enjoyable way to live; it would be better to meet him once and be done with it.

She sent off a note suggesting that they meet in three days' time—sooner than that seemed *very* soon—she felt as though she needed to prepare herself in some way—but longer than that would just be a *lot* of probably disagreeable anticipation—and within the hour received an affirmative response in his decisive script.

And so now she just had to wait and wonder. For three whole days. She should in fact have suggested tomorrow.

The day of their meeting dawned fine and fair. They had agreed to meet at two o'clock in the afternoon, a time at which the children were regularly looked after by their nursemaids while they played for half an hour after their luncheon.

Anna had already taken a small number of solitary walks in the early afternoon to visit shops to purchase necessaries and on one occasion to take a walk with Lady Maria, who had told her all about the duke's visit to her. Anna had not enjoyed hearing about his evident bewilderment, anger and perhaps misery when he'd realised that he'd been deceived, but had been powerless to stop herself asking for every detail of Lady Maria's conversation with him.

Despite her busyness with the children, the morning and luncheon passed very slowly until eventually it was time for Anna to ready herself for her walk with the duke.

Regarding herself in the looking glass, she reflected that she looked very different from how she had at the ball. Her hair was dressed in a plain manner now, pulled close against her head and fastened into a knot at the nape of her neck, and her dress was equally plain: a brown serge morning dress, which paid no particular note to the fashions of the moment.

Anna sighed, and then chastised herself mentally. She had known that this was her lot and she was extremely lucky to have found herself employment with such a pleasant family; and she had had the good fortune to enjoy that one week in London with Lady Derwent and the experience of attending the ball. There were many people in significantly worse situations than she, and she must not complain.

Five minutes later, she let herself out of the front door of the house and trod down the four wide steps leading to the pavement, before turning left towards the corner where she'd agreed that she would meet the duke.

He was already waiting for her.

He had taken her breath away when he was dressed in pristine evening dress, and he took her breath away again now clothed in plain but exquisitely tailored morning dress.

'Miss… Blake,' he said as she drew near to him.

'Your Grace.' She could hardly hear her own voice over the immense thudding in her ears from her racing heart, and all of a sudden her legs felt quite weak.

This was silly. She was just…

She was just going to go for a walk with the only man whom she had ever kissed, a man who was devastatingly attractive and to whom she had lied. Of *course* her heart was beating fast.

'Shall we walk?' He held his arm out to her and, after a little hesitation—it seemed odd for a governess to walk holding a duke's arm—she took it. 'This way?'

They turned left from Bruton Street, where the Puntneys lived, into Berkeley Square, and began to stroll along the side of the square.

A silence, which Anna did not like, began to stretch between them.

'It is a beautiful day for the time of year,' she ventured.

'Yes, we are lucky.'

They relapsed into silence for another minute or so, until the duke said, 'Could I ask… That is to say: I am aware that this is of course none of my business, but are you happy; is your employment palatable to you?'

'Certainly I am happy, thank you,' Anna said robustly. It *was* none of his business, but she had already treated him shabbily in deceiving him at the ball; she could not be rude to him now as well.

And she was *not* going to give in to the thoughts that intruded too often that the life of a governess could become very sad; she would of course have the opportunity to become involved in and shape the lives of her charges but she would be entirely at the mercy of her employers as to how long she remained with them and whether she was able to continue her acquaintance with the children when she no longer worked for the family. And as a governess she was now in a strange position, neither servant nor member of the family.

No. She should not allow herself even to think these things. She was very fortunate in her employers; they were very generous and paid her a salary of eighty pounds per year, where many governesses in their first role with a good London family might expect no more than forty pounds, and if she was careful she should be able to save most of it. And she had very good friends in Lady Derwent and Lady Maria. Indeed, Lady Maria had recently informed her that she would be appointing her godmother to her first child.

So Anna would certainly not end up in the poorhouse and she would have friends to correspond with and she was much more fortunate than many.

And she would of course become used to her new situation very soon.

'I am glad that you are happy,' he said.

'Why, thank you,' Anna said, allowing herself to sound a little acerbic. She did not require his pity.

'I apologise. Perhaps that sounded a little patronising.'

Anna *really* didn't want to be rude, whatever the provocation, and she also still, obviously, felt guilty about her masquerade at the ball, so she didn't exactly agree with him; she just murmured something that he might interpret how he liked.

He laughed. 'You're right. It did sound patronising and you are too polite to say so. What I meant was… well, yes, I would like to think that you're happy and, yes, I think I should perhaps say nothing else on the subject.' He paused, while Anna tried to hide a smile because it was really quite endearing how much he was tying himself into knots, and then he continued, 'This is another thing that is difficult to say without sounding patronising or odd but I would like to let you know that I have not asked any further questions about you other than your name and direction. I did not wish to intrude.'

'May I ask which of my friends furnished you with those details?' She could not help feeling that, if one were prone to melodrama, one might describe it as a betrayal.

'I did not ask your friends and I do not think they would have told me. I mentioned it to my man of business. He has his ways. I apologise; I should have told you that immediately so that you would not feel let down by Lady Derwent or Lady Maria.'

'Thank you!' She smiled at him; whatever else, he was very thoughtful.

There was a brief pause again, and then the duke said, 'This way perhaps?' when they came to the corner of the square, and they continued straight ahead, in the direction of Hyde Park.

'The trees are turning very autumnal,' Anna said.

'Indeed they are. The leaves are most attractive at this time of year.'

'Yes indeed.'

Anna suddenly realised that she did not wish to feel any regrets after this walk. There could be no friendship between a governess and a duke, and, even if there *could* be, it was quite possible that if the duke ever found out that her father had been a groom he would cease any acquaintance with her, so there was no point in their seeing each other again. If there was anything she would like to say to him she should say it now.

'I would like to apologise for having deceived you,' she said. She had partially apologised when they'd met in the park, but not entirely, because at the time she'd been quite angry with him. She *should* apologise, though. 'I would like to explain in more detail how it came about, if I may.'

'I should be very interested to hear in full.'

'Lady Maria and I went to the same seminary in Bath. She is my dearest friend. She is a few months younger than me. I am now two-and-twenty years old. She did not come out when she was younger because very sadly her family suffered a series of bereavements. Her parents wished her to make her come-out this year. But she, for reasons that are not mine to divulge, did not wish to do so. When her parents left town to visit Maria's grandmother, Maria's mother asked my godmother, Lady Derwent, to chaperone Maria to the various balls she was to attend. She came to take tea with Lady Derwent and me, and told us how she felt.

'It was my godmother who suggested the deception, thinking that it would be nice for me to go to a ball and that there could be no harm in it. Lady Maria thought it an excellent idea and I, despite seeing the obvious problems that might arise, such as did in fact arise, allowed myself to be carried along with the plan because I had never been to a ball in London and desired to go to one. My godmother provided me with my dress and escorted me there. I do realise that we should not have entered into the deception and I apologise for having got a little angry with you in the park.'

'No; I must apologise for my initial lack of understanding. And my own anger. And you are right that had you and I not met and…and spent time together… it might have been possible for the deception to go unnoticed, had Lady Maria not been home to callers the next day and then retired to the country.'

'That is exactly what my godmother said when she was persuading me into joining in her plan.'

'Clearly it is a case of great minds thinking alike.'

Anna laughed. 'Perhaps.'

She was very pleased to have had the opportunity to say all that she'd just said, she realised.

Clearly, frankness was a good thing.

'Why did you wish to meet me for this walk?' she asked.

'I…' The duke paused for a while, and then said, 'That is a good question. I don't really know. I think I just wanted to confirm to myself that you were happy. And find out—perhaps entirely out of curiosity, which is of course quite reprehensible—why you indulged in your masquerade. And perhaps I had some residual anger about it, which is now dissipated, because I accept that you could not have predicted how the evening would progress.'

'I see.' She did not entirely see, but of course a duke had a different life from that of most people. He probably wasn't used to not finding out the answer whenever he felt curious about something. It would be like a normal person having an itch that they couldn't reach.

'May I ask why you consented to come for the walk?'

'You may.' There could be no harm in her being honest. 'I think that had I not met you today I would have wondered if I *should* have met you, and what you wished to say to me, and I do not find it particularly comfortable constantly wondering about something.' And *that* would have been an itch that continued to irritate.

'I see. You know, I think I have just worked out why I asked if we could meet.' He paused for a moment as they entered the gates of the park. 'I feel that it is possible that even by the end of my sentence I will regret saying this to you, but I think that I wished to see you again because I...missed you.'

'Oh!' Anna felt her heart give the most enormous lurch.

'Yes, *oh*. I think I was right in predicting that I would regret my words. May I change the subject and draw your attention to that particularly assiduous woodpecker there?'

'Certainly you may. I have always liked the green of a woodpecker's beak.'

'Green is a delightful colour.' A laugh entered the duke's voice as he continued, 'I believe that I have already mentioned that I very much like the green of your eyes.'

'It is very kind in you to say so, and also something that a duke should not be saying to a governess,' said Anna repressively. She really did not wish him to flirt with her now. When she had been playing the role of Lady Maria, that had been one thing, but now, well, now she needed to maintain her reputation and she did not wish to be beguiled into thinking in *that* kind of way about the duke.

'I must apologise,' said the duke instantly. 'You are quite right.'

Anna did not wish any further awkward silences to arise between them. It was clear that this should be their last meeting, and from his immediate agreement with her words it was obvious that he agreed. She knew how much she could enjoy his company, and she might as well make the most of it now, for these last few minutes.

'We could perhaps take a turn around this small pond,' she said, 'and then I will need to return. I will be instructing my charges on geography this afternoon.'

'Indeed? Which geography will you be teaching them today?'

'I found an atlas with a particular emphasis on the British Isles in my employer's library, and whilst, being girls, they might not have the opportunity to travel further afield than England, I hope that they might be able when older to travel to other parts of this country, so I plan to instruct them most carefully in the geography of England.'

'I agree that a knowledge of geography is a very important part of a good education. Have you travelled yourself?' asked the duke.

'I know Gloucestershire well, as I grew up there, as well as Bath and Somerset, where my seminary was and where Lady Maria's family home is. I have never, however, travelled to the north of England. I believe the Lake District amongst other areas to include wonderful scenery that I should like to have the opportunity to visit one day, but of course I don't know whether that will happen. It is something to aspire to for the future. Have you travelled, Your Grace?'

'Yes, I was fortunate enough to do a Grand Tour when I was younger, and have also had the good fortune to travel within England.' He stopped, and then said, 'I am aware that I have been very lucky to have the opportunity to travel; I'm not sure that I recognised that sufficiently at the time.'

'I hope you don't feel that you must almost apologise to me for your fortune in that regard,' Anna told him. 'It is not your fault that you were born to the life you lead, any more than it is a chimney sweep's fault that he was not.'

'That is true, but it is difficult at times not to feel the weight of good fortune.'

'That is of course to your credit, but, rather than apologise to me, tell me some of your most interesting stories. I love to hear first-person accounts of such travels rather than reading about them in fusty books.'

'Well now, that is quite a challenge. I feel beholden to tell you some stories that are either genuinely amusing or genuinely interesting or genuinely not common knowledge.'

'Yes, indeed.' Anna found herself twinkling up at him as they walked slowly along beside the pond. 'I shall certainly be judging you most severely on the quality of your anecdotes.'

'How many anecdotes would you like?'

'Hmm.' Anna pretended to consider. 'Since you have raised the categories yourself, I should like one amusing, one interesting and one not common knowledge.'

The duke nodded very seriously. 'I accept your challenge. Let me prepare for it first.' He squared his shoulders and then rolled them, which made Anna giggle.

And then he told her some truly *excellent* stories, which took them most of the way back to the Puntneys' house and made Anna wish greatly that she could walk with him again.

When she had finished laughing at the conclusion to a story about how he had mistakenly stumbled into a literary salon, when under the impression—due to his imperfect grasp of the Italian language—that he would be attending a masquerade and was therefore dressed as a monk, they were at the end of the Puntneys' road.

'You have succeeded very well in the challenge,' she told the duke, trying very hard not to feel low at the thought that she might well never see him again. 'I am most impressed.'

'I feel a little guilty that I have monopolised the conversation since we were at the pond.'

'Not at all; I very much encouraged you to tell me your stories and I very much enjoyed them. For example, I have never had another first-hand account of someone meeting an elephant and do not think I shall do so again.'

'In that case I shall say that I am pleased to be of service.' The duke stopped walking, and Anna did too, because she was still holding his arm, very much as though their arms belonged perfectly together, which was clearly a silly thing to be thinking. 'I am not pleased, however, that you have not had the opportunity to tell me any of *your* stories; I should very much enjoy hearing anything you might say, getting to know you better.'

His words made Anna feel both very warm inside and very sad that there would be no opportunity for them to talk further. She took her arm away from his because there was no need to hold it when they weren't actually walking, and she was a little worried that she might start to cling on to him if she didn't move away a little.

'It is very kind of you to say so,' she said in as hearty a voice as she could muster, to avoid any of the emotion she felt surfacing, 'but I am sure that I have nothing of interest to say.'

'Firstly—' the duke turned a little so that they were facing each other under the tree beneath which they were standing '—everything you say must be of interest to me, and secondly I cannot believe that you do not have interesting stories. Looking after young children must give rise to many anecdotes. Who is the naughtiest of them?'

'Lydia, the youngest, is particularly naughty,' Anna owned, 'but in the most adorable way. It is in no way a character defect—' she was already extremely fond of all the girls '—but merely liveliness. But it does give rise to some quite extraordinary situations at times.' And then, as they continued to stand there under the tree, she found herself telling him about the slugs that Lydia had smuggled into her mother's bedchamber and the ensuing screams when they had been discovered by Lady Puntney and her maid.

'Oh, my goodness,' she suddenly said across the duke's laughter, which was truly the most attractive laugh—deep and rumbly—that she'd ever heard; she was sure that one could listen to it every day and not get bored. Clouds had crossed the sun and caused the sky to grow much darker. 'Do you know what time it is? I must hasten back.'

'Of course,' the duke said immediately. 'I must apologise for keeping you.'

He held out his arm to her and she took it wordlessly

and they began to walk along the road towards the house at a very fast pace.

'I very much enjoyed the walk; thank you,' the duke said when they reached the house. 'May I have the pleasure of walking with you again?'

'Oh, no, I'm not sure…' Anna was suddenly a little breathless. 'I thought… I'm not sure that we should make a habit of this. I don't think that it is usual for a duke and a governess to walk together.'

'Perhaps just one more walk, so that we might finish our conversation?'

'Is it indeed unfinished, though?'

'I believe that it is.' Anna knew that she had to be firm, even though it felt so—stupidly—deeply sad to say goodbye now. It could not benefit either of them to spend more time together. And, even if she were someone whom a duke might marry, would she want to place all her dependence on one man with whom she had already, she had to admit, felt such passion? Knowing the way her grandfather and father were capable of treating women, could she trust any man? If ever she were to have the occasion to marry, would it not be better—safer—for her husband to be someone whom she liked but did not feel great passion for?

'Perhaps one more walk? In due course? If you like?'

'I don't know.' She was very tempted but really she shouldn't. She looked up at the house; she didn't want anyone to see her with the duke. 'I must go inside now; goodbye.'

'Of course.' He immediately let go of her arm, which instantly made her feel a little bereft. Truly, she was ridiculous. 'Goodbye. I hope to see you again.'

'Goodbye.' Anna decided not to reply to his last few words; she didn't trust herself not to be weak and say perhaps they might meet again.

She purposely didn't look back at him as she went through the door, and then, as she closed it behind herself, regretted not having allowed herself one more look at him.

It would definitely be for the best not to see him again.

Chapter Six

James

James was disappointed that Miss Blake didn't turn for one last goodbye as she entered the house, and then he was disappointed in himself for being such a fool.

Bruton Street, where she now lived, gave directly onto Berkeley Square; it was astonishing to think that the entire time he had been wondering about her whereabouts she had been living so close by. As he walked the short distance in the direction of his home, he found himself scuffing at leaves with his foot, dissatisfied with…well, life. And himself.

Was Miss Blake right, that dukes and governesses should not go for walks? Would he be compromising her? He wouldn't be compromising her in terms of her eligibility for marriage in that he didn't know of a single bachelor of his acquaintance who would look amongst the ranks of governesses for a wife. Would he, though, be compromising her in the eyes of her employers? Would she be in danger of losing her job if she were seen with him regularly?

Maybe. If so, he should of course not see her again. Perhaps, though, it would not matter.

He did not, he realised as he kicked a particularly large pile of leaves, have any idea what Society's rules were for governesses, beyond being aware that they occupied quite a unique space in the social hierarchy. They were ladies, and certainly not servants. But they were working for a living and could not therefore be regarded as part of Society.

Why did he care? Why was he interested? Did he really wish to see her again? Was he still tempted to propose marriage to her?

Did dukes marry governesses? Could *he* marry a governess?

What was her birth? It must be respectable, presumably. Lady Derwent was her godmother and she had been educated at the same Bath seminary as Lady Maria.

Why was she a governess?

And had he not decided last week that he had had a lucky escape because he didn't *want* to fall in love with the lady who would become his bride, and hadn't it occurred to him that he could be in danger of falling in love with her?

So would it perhaps be better if he did not pursue their acquaintance any further?

He rounded the corner of the square. More leaves. He gave those a kick too.

Maybe he would ask her if she would like to take just one more walk.

Not immediately, though. It would be poor behaviour to make her feel under any kind of obligation or pressure to meet him again.

* * *

When he walked into the main drawing room in his house, very ready to bury himself in the newspapers for some time, to give himself some respite from thinking too much about Miss Blake, he found his mother and two of his sisters in the room.

'James.' His mother beckoned him over to her. 'We should decide on the date of your wedding.'

'We should? But I have not yet decided on a bride. And I have not yet ascertained whether any young lady would consent to marry me.' He didn't sit down because he clearly wasn't going to want this conversation to continue for any length of time; he would much rather go to his study to look through some papers there.

His mother frowned and indicated very forcefully with her eyes and raised brow that he should sit beside her.

'I thought we had agreed that you were on the point of proposing,' she said.

'It is a very big decision. I need time to feel certain that I am making the right one.'

'I do understand that.' His mother's tone had softened. 'But equally I do feel that time is perhaps of the essence.'

From his side, James could understand his mother's impatience. She had lost her husband and two oldest sons in the space of only two years and was obviously still grieving, and much more anxious generally than she might have been before, and she had her five youngest daughters to think about. The oldest of his sisters was four-and-twenty and had been married for four years and had two daughters of her own now. His next oldest sister was only seventeen and not coming out until next year—his mother, while eager to know that her children were provided for, did not approve of marriage for young ladies before the age of eighteen. And his four youngest sisters were two sets of twins of fourteen and twelve.

That was a lot of people to ensure security for.

'Yes,' he said. She was right. Time was of the essence. He did need a son as soon as possible. What if the same illness that had struck his father and brothers struck him?

He wished he'd never met Miss Blake. She was confusing him too much. He needed to be able to think clearly.

Three days later, James had boxed hard at Gentleman Jackson's Boxing Saloon, he had ridden hard, he had boxed again—Gentleman Jackson had asked him if it was anger that was causing him to spar so well and James had just boxed even harder—he had played cards with friends and drunk far too much the evening before last, and he had attended two balls and the opera once, and he was still struggling not to think about Miss Blake. But he was now, with his mother, standing outside a house on Clarges Street, about to pay a call on Lady Catherine Rainsford, who remained his mother's preferred candidate for his hand.

'Perhaps after today you will feel inspired to make an offer,' his mother said to him just as the door was opened by the Rainsford family's butler.

'Perhaps,' said James unenthusiastically.

Within fifteen minutes, as he and Lady Catherine sat and smiled at each other and occasionally produced a few insipid words before smiling some more, he knew that he couldn't do it. So many little snippets of sentences or references reminded him of Miss Blake, or made him wonder what her views on them might be, or caused him to imagine her laughing when he responded with sarcasm or wonder what joke she might make. It was as though he was under a spell, and he could not in good conscience propose to one woman while temporarily in thrall to another.

He intended to be an unfashionably faithful husband, as his own father had been, and, while he did not want to fall in love, he did not want to be thinking about another woman throughout his marriage.

What he should probably do was see Miss Blake again, if she were willing, and have a long conversation with her, get to know her better, and see if that put paid to this inconvenient hankering after her company that he was currently feeling. It felt like an infatuation; he needed to cure himself of it before committing to marriage with someone else. And everyone knew that familiarity bred contempt; if he spent more time with Miss Blake, he would no doubt cease to be so curious about her.

Three hours later he was waiting with bated breath for a response to the note he had dashed off asking Miss Blake if she would care to accompany him to Gunter's Tea Shop to sample their ices. Four hours later he was still waiting. And by the time he left the house for a dinner with close friends at White's, he still felt on tenterhooks even though it was clear that he was not going to receive a reply this evening—or, perhaps, at all.

There was still no reply by the time he took luncheon the next day.

And then, late in the afternoon, he received a note addressed in Miss Blake's hand. Even her handwriting appealed to him, he realised, as he tore open the envelope. It was well-formed, easily legible, very attractive to look at… Reminiscent of the lady herself in many ways.

If her handwriting appealed to him, the content of her note did not.

Your Grace,
I regret exceedingly that I am unable to meet you
again.
Yours sincerely,
Anna Blake

And that was obviously that. Clearly, he could not beg her, or make her feel uncomfortable, by asking again. He could, of course, hover regularly in Bruton Street or go to Hyde Park when she would presumably be walking with her charges, but that would be shocking behaviour when she had told him so definitively that she did not wish to see him again. That really was very much that.

And everything suddenly felt very flat.

He didn't particularly want to do anything now, but he was not going to allow himself to sink into any kind of misery just because a young lady—a governess— had told him that she did not wish to accompany him to a tea shop.

He had managed to keep his own spirits and those of his mother and sisters reasonably steady through the terrible loss of his father and brothers, so he was certainly not going to succumb to despondency over Miss Blake.

She was just a lady with whom he had enjoyed a very pleasurable evening and a nice walk.

And now he was going to go into the library and look through the post that he had received earlier in the day and had not opened because he had been waiting for Miss Blake's note.

The usual invitations and various other missives he had received caused him to sigh with boredom, but he continued. Soon, this feeling would pass and he would carry on with his life perfectly happily, and by the end of the Season he would, he trusted, have come to an agreement with a pleasant and suitable young lady.

He was almost yawning as he pulled out yet another note, written in an ornate script. He'd begun to make little bets to himself as to what each invitation would be. This one he would wager would be a dowager's musical soirée.

It was in fact an invitation to call with Lady Derwent in two days' time.

He re-read it. Yes, it was indeed addressed to him rather than to his mother.

Well.

It seemed very likely that the invitation was related to his acquaintance with Miss Blake. And therefore of course he was going to go.

When he arrived very punctually—at the somewhat surprising time of half past two—to see Lady Derwent, her butler showed him immediately towards the same saloon in which he had been on his previous visit.

As he approached the room, he heard more than one female voice from within. And…if he wasn't mistaken, one of them was Miss Blake's. Or was that just wishful thinking? He had thought he'd caught a glimpse of her more than once in the park and in the street and had whipped his head round each time only to discover that he'd been wrong; this was probably just the same.

The butler opened the door for him and announced his name.

And if James wasn't mistaken, there was an audible gasp from within.

And, yes, as the door opened wider, he saw Miss Blake, sitting directly opposite, her beautiful mouth formed into an O shape and her eyes wide.

She remained like that for a long moment, before recovering her composure and casting her eyes down, whilst murmuring, 'Good afternoon, Your Grace.'

'You are early,' Lady Derwent admonished him. 'I had not expected you for another hour.'

James looked at the clock on the mantelpiece and frowned. He could not directly contradict her but he *knew* that he was exactly on time.

And then he looked at her more closely. He couldn't say exactly in what way, but he could swear that she looked almost sly at this moment. As though she were plotting something.

Had she planned this on purpose? Invited him at the same time as Miss Blake so that they would meet each other again?

He looked back to Miss Blake. She was now sitting with her hands folded in her lap, her eyes downcast but otherwise looking entirely composed.

'I do apologise,' he said to Lady Derwent. 'I must have misread your writing.'

'Or perhaps misremembered,' she said. 'Well, no matter. Now that you are here, you must take tea with us. I shall ring for Buxton.'

'I must take my leave,' Miss Blake said.

'Nonsense,' Lady Derwent told her. 'You have only just arrived, and I still need to hear your news and tell you mine. The duke will not mind. None of us need to pretend that you have not already met.'

'No, indeed,' agreed James. 'I think we are all aware that we met at the ball.'

A tiny gasp came from Miss Blake's direction.

James was tempted to ask her if she was quite all right but decided that it would be better to ignore the sound.

'Your news, Anna,' Lady Derwent said. 'You were telling me about your excursion to the British Museum. I am sure His Grace would be interested to hear about it.'

'I am afraid that I have little of interest to tell,' Miss Blake—Anna—said. 'As we were on the point of looking at the Rosetta Stone, Lydia declared herself quite ill, and we had to leave very quickly.'

'Was she genuinely ill or just not very interested in historical artefacts?' James asked.

'The latter, I fear. I considered reprimanding her and then decided that a far better punishment would be to take her very seriously and insist that she keep to her room for the remainder of the day and take just some chicken broth. She was extremely bored and recovered remarkably quickly.'

'You are clearly an excellent governess,' Lady Derwent said approvingly, while James smiled. 'I should not like to think of your allowing the girls to be naughty.'

James raised one eyebrow very slightly at Lady Derwent. Surely this was the pot calling a kettle black; pretending to be ill to avoid being bored at a museum could not compare with instigating an impersonation of a ball guest.

'I know what you are thinking.' Lady Derwent leaned forward and rapped him over the knuckles, which James saw out of the corner of his eye caused Miss Blake's eyes to dance. 'Irrespective of what they might do in later life, it is important for children to be taught to behave properly.'

'Indeed it is,' Miss Blake agreed. 'And I am doing my best to instil discipline into them. It is hard sometimes, because one is tempted to laugh.'

'Did you have a governess, my lady?' James asked Lady Derwent very blandly.

'I did, and she failed utterly to indoctrinate me with discipline, but that is not to say that other children should not be taught better than I.'

Miss Blake laughed. James adored her laugh. It was light but full, and, if you caused that laugh you felt very proud of yourself, and if you did not know the reason for her mirth you immediately wished to find out the reason for it.

And now he was laughing at himself for thinking far too much about *her* laugh.

'Were you educated at home or at school, Your Grace?' Miss Blake's question was the first of a personal nature that she had asked him; he had had the impression that she did not wish to discuss either his life history or her own. Perhaps she felt on safer ground with Lady Derwent present.

'I began with nurses at home in the country, and then had a succession of tutors—some did not stay long because my two older brothers and I were close in age and not well disciplined, and then I went to Eton, followed by Oxford.' He looked at Miss Blake. He would very much like to know more about her background. 'I understand that you were educated in Bath, at the same establishment as Lady Maria?'

'Yes, I was, and we both enjoyed it there most of the time.'

'Were you both angelic students?' he asked.

'Not always,' Miss Blake admitted. 'But I flatter myself that my experience of breaking the rules a little will make me a wiser governess.'

'I think you're right,' James agreed. 'In fact, one might say that you were particularly prescient in undertaking any naughtiness. You were merely exploring all options for the future.'

'Exactly.'

'Did you ever swap identities with someone?' he asked.

'I must reprimand you, Your Grace, for such a particularly indelicate question.' Miss Blake tsked. 'We do not refer to specific past misdemeanours.'

James laughed out loud. 'Apparently I must apologise.' He realised that at some point he had clearly entirely forgiven Miss Blake for her deception at the ball.

'Indeed you must,' Miss Blake told him.

'Were you instructed at home before you entered the seminary?' he asked, still very interested to hear all about her early life.

'Her mother, my dear friend, instructed her,' Lady Derwent said. 'Your Grace, are you a devotee of poetry? Before you came, we were discussing Lord Byron's *The Bride of Abydos*.' It was very much as though she was changing the subject. Did she not wish him to discuss Miss Blake's childhood with her?

'I must own that I do not regularly read verse,' he said, and the conversation continued from there, through literature—with minimal contribution from James—and a discussion of the library of Miss Blake's employer and James's own library.

'Sir Laurence's library is remarkably well-stocked,' Miss Blake concluded.

'Does he have copies of the romances you like so much?' asked Lady Derwent.

'Sir Laurence does not share my taste in that regard, for which one can only admire him.'

'I, however, *do* share your taste.' James could not believe his luck. This would give him a very good excuse to see Miss Blake again. 'That is to say, my mother does, and she would very much like to lend her books to you, I know.'

He would have to remember to purchase the necessary books. He could enquire of his married sister perhaps which would be the best ones to buy. Or perhaps he would just buy all such books stocked in London so that there could be no possibility of his disappointing Miss Blake.

'Oh, no, I couldn't possibly.' Miss Blake shook her head firmly.

'Nonsense.' Lady Derwent sounded even firmer. 'I think it a marvellous idea. You are working very hard, my dear, and you will be a better governess to your charges if you enjoy your reading when you are resting. His Grace will, I am sure, bring the books to you when you next have a spare moment. Perhaps tomorrow? Or the day after tomorrow?'

'Thank you.' Miss Blake spoke a little faintly—Lady Derwent was indeed very forceful—and James would almost have felt sorry for her if he had not been so pleased that he would have such a good opportunity to see her again. 'That is extremely kind. Perhaps if you…you could perhaps send a footman with them?'

'I am sure His Grace will be very happy to deliver them to you himself. In fact…' Lady Derwent looked thoughtful.

James had the strongest sense that he and Miss Blake were pawns in some game that Lady Derwent was playing. Did he mind? He wasn't sure. It would of course depend on whether the aim of her game aligned with his own. At this point he wasn't entirely sure of his own aims. He did want to see Miss Blake alone again, for the purposes of curing himself of this ridiculous infatuation. And then he would like to marry someone with whom he would not be desperately in love. It did not seem particularly likely that that was what Lady Derwent was planning.

'I'm afraid I must leave now.' Miss Blake gathered her gloves and reticule and rose to her feet before her godmother could continue down whatever line of thought she had begun. 'Thank you so much; I have very much enjoyed our tea.'

Lady Derwent rose too. 'I would usually suggest that His Grace escort you home, but as he is so recently arrived I should like to talk to him for a few moments. One of my footmen will walk with you.'

James also rose, in order to bid Miss Blake goodbye. As he took her hand in his and looked down into her beautiful green eyes, he found it an effort not to press her fingers far more tightly than a mere goodbye warranted.

'I will look out for those books for you on my return home,' he told her.

'Thank you; that is very kind.'

And then she was gone and the door was closed behind her, and Lady Derwent was gesturing him to be seated.

'Now.' She leaned forward and tapped him on the knee. 'I believe that my goddaughter's reluctance to prolong her acquaintance with you comes from a belief that a governess cannot have a friendship with a duke. Of course, one would imagine that it might be quite irregular. But it would not be irregular for a duke to propose to a governess who was a gentlewoman of good family. It *would* of course be irregular for a duke to pursue a friendship with a lady whom he did not wish to marry.'

'Yes.' He would have liked to have asked what Miss Blake's birth was, but did not, he realised, have quite the same knack for outrageous frankness that Lady Derwent had.

'I expect my goddaughter to be treated well, as you would treat any other gently born lady,' Lady Derwent said.

'I would never wish to do her any harm,' James told her.

'Then I imagine that you will make up your mind one way or the other as to what you want as soon as possible. In the meantime, I shall be holding a literary salon on Friday. Given your interest in modern literature, you will be pleased to attend.'

'Thank you.' Good God. James very much hoped that Miss Blake would also be made to attend, otherwise it would almost certainly be a torturous experience. *Could* governesses venture out in the evenings? Did they? He really did not know. He would just have to hope.

'And now, I find myself a little fatigued,' Lady Derwent told him. 'I look forward to seeing you on Friday.'

James laughed. It didn't surprise him that his mother and Lady Derwent did not like each other. They were so similar that they could be nothing but bosom friends or sworn enemies.

The next afternoon, at two o'clock, after a very busy morning visiting first his astonished sister—she had not seen him before luncheon for several years—to ask about the latest popular novels, and then Hatchard's bookshop on Piccadilly, James was outside the Puntneys' mansion, looking forward to seeing Miss Blake.

As he lifted the knocker, though, he suddenly realised that he couldn't do this. She had been cajoled, effectively, into seeing him, by her godmother and by him.

If she did not wish to see him then he should certainly not force her to do so.

It was pure selfishness in him to wish to see her, spend time with her, in order to cure himself of the infatuation he currently felt. He had felt that there was a mutual attraction between them. What if she had felt it too, and what if she were disappointed if he asked her to accompany him for a walk and then did not wish to see her again?

He should not do that.

So when the Puntneys' butler opened the door to him, he asked him if he would be able to present the books to Miss Blake with his compliments on behalf of Lady Derwent, before handing the pile to him and leaving.

He would just have to hope that time would help him forget his ridiculous infatuation.

Chapter Seven

Anna

Anna had been—pathetically, she knew—unable to help herself peeking out of the window at the street below to see whether the duke would indeed come to see her with the books.

She had known that she would be very grateful to have them, if he did come.

She hadn't been sure whether or not she would be grateful to see the duke himself, though.

If she was honest, she *loved* his company, but it could be of no benefit to her to see him again, and so she would prefer to put an immediate end to their acquaintance.

And yet…when she'd seen him round the corner into the street and walk along with what looked like four books under his arm, her heart had given the most tremendous lurch.

When he disappeared out of sight after going up the steps from the pavement to the front door, she couldn't help going over to the looking glass above the mantelpiece to pat her hair into place, and then allowing herself to give her cheeks just the tiniest of pinches to bring a little colour to them. She smiled at her reflection and almost danced to the door to begin to descend the stairs from her attic floor in anticipation of being told that she had a caller.

She was in the hall before a footman had reached her and…

Oh.

There was a pile of books on the marble-topped chiffonier to her left, with a card on top of the pile, and no sign of the duke.

She felt her smile drop and her hand go to her throat. She'd been so silly. *So* silly.

The duke had obviously *not* been intending to see her or as interested in her company as she was in his. He had obviously just been *made* by her godmother to provide the books and had been too polite to demur. So he had clearly dutifully collected some together and had brought them and…gone away again.

And that was *perfect*, she thought, as she looked at his card. *Perfect*. Exactly what she would have chosen, in fact. Definitely.

Three days later, at eight o'clock in the evening, she alit from Lady Puntney's carriage outside her godmother's house. Truly, Lady Puntney was the most wonderful employer; she had told Anna that she positively *insisted* that she attend Lady Derwent's literary salon because it could only benefit the girls if their governess discussed literature with people who knew the great Lord Byron well. She had also whispered to Anna, in a joking fashion, poking fun at herself—because, as she had already owned, she was hoping to climb as high in Society as possible, in as nice a way as possible—that if Anna wished to introduce her to such an illustrious personage as Lady Derwent, that would be wonderful.

Truly, there was no need to hanker after the friendship of the duke. Anna was most lucky in both her employer and her godmother, not to mention her wonderful best friend, Lady Maria, who would be here this evening.

Lady Derwent had told Anna that the evening would comprise a select group of ladies meeting to discuss the most recent work of Jane Austen, *Emma*.

Most fortuitously, *Emma* was one of the books that the duke had delivered to Anna on Tuesday, and from the first page she had loved it. She had read late into the night, until her candle burnt out, for the three nights since she had received it, unable to put it down. She had finished it that afternoon, while her charges rested with their nurses, in lieu of taking her usual afternoon walk around the garden square. Forgoing her daily exercise was in direct contradiction of her own strict tenets on how a lady should live, but it had been worth it because she had very much enjoyed the ending of the story and would now be in a position to discuss it with the other ladies.

Lady Maria greeted her at the door to the salon with her arms held out, and Anna embraced her gladly. Her godmother then hurried over.

'Anna, dearest.' She pulled her properly into the room, and said, 'Allow me to introduce you to our fellow devotees of literature.'

As Anna was introduced to a series of ladies, she was

extremely grateful for the dresses with which her god-mother had presented her before she took up her govern-ess role; the one she was wearing now was a delightful primrose yellow muslin, which she knew was of the lat-est mode and hoped became her quite well. Everyone here was smartly attired and she would not have enjoyed wearing one of her brown or dark blue day dresses.

'I'm delighted to...' She suddenly gave the most tre-mendous start in the middle of greeting a very well-dressed lady of perhaps forty years old whom Lady Derwent had introduced as a Mrs Travers; she had per-ceived out of the corner of her eye, at the far end of the room, a group of three men.

Two of them were dressed rather unusually, the way one might imagine poets to dress, with loose jackets and spotted cravats. And the other...

The other was a tall and broad gentleman with thick dark hair and very neatly fitting and not at all poetic-looking clothing, and an expression of slight horror on his face, which made Anna's lips twitch, even as she felt her stomach churn.

She forced her attention back to the ladies to whom she was being introduced, and flattered herself that she managed to produce quite acceptable smiles and greet-ings, despite the whirring of thoughts inside her head.

And then her godmother took her over to the men.

She introduced Anna to both the spotted cravat wear-ers, while Anna tried very hard to focus on the introduc-tions and produce a few polite words, while her mind whirred and her eyes seemed to want to swivel in the direction of the third gentleman.

And then Lady Derwent said, 'And, of course, you

are acquainted with His Grace,' and Anna was able to look directly at him without appearing rude.

Anna and the duke said, 'Indeed,' at the same time. He inclined his head slightly, his expression unmoving, and she gave him a small smile.

'Thank you so much for the books.' Anna had of course written a note thanking the duke—a note that had taken her far more time than it should have done to compose—but obviously must thank him properly now.

'It was my great pleasure. I hope that you will enjoy them.'

'I have already finished reading *Emma* and enjoyed it exceedingly; I am sure that I will enjoy the others too, and am very grateful for the opportunity to read them. I must confess that I was so engrossed in the story that I read late into the night three evenings running and was only stopped by my candle burning right down; I am very eager to start the next one but will wait a little, both to enjoy the anticipation of it and to recover from the lack of sleep that I experienced this week.'

The duke laughed, and said, 'I'm very pleased to hear how much you enjoyed it and will be equally pleased to lend you more books from my mother's collection when you have finished those. Which do you intend to read next?'

Anna's reply—Fanny Burney's *Evelina*—was interrupted by Lady Derwent clapping and addressing the assembled company.

'We are now going to discuss Jane Austen's *Emma*. For those who have not read it but intend to do so, those of us who *have* read it will take great care to avoid telling you what happens at the end. Let us arrange ourselves so that we can converse more easily as a group.'

Within a small number of minutes, with a firm and slightly terrifying authority that Anna imagined many army generals could only dream of attaining, Lady Derwent had directed the assembled company to sit in a semicircle.

Somehow—Anna was sure that it was by design but had not been able to pinpoint how she had actually managed it—Lady Derwent contrived to seat the duke on the left-hand end of the half-circle, with Anna immediately to his right, so that if he wished to enjoy any quiet conversation it could only be with her.

Truly, her godmother was incorrigible in her apparent quest to throw Anna together with him.

And truly, Anna's heart should not be lifting in the way that it was at the prospect of more time talking to him. Allowing herself to enjoy his company could only lead to despondency in the future. Clearly nothing could come of an acquaintance between them; dukes did not marry the daughters of scandal, and indeed that was a good thing: Anna should keep on reminding herself that she had seen the misery caused by her parents' incompatibility—both in rank and in temperament—and did not wish to participate in such a union herself. Husbands in general were rarely to be relied upon.

Having finished her directions, Lady Derwent seated herself in a large chair that had been placed facing the middle of the semicircle, and some distance back so that she was able to see everyone without having to turn her head too much.

'With whom should we commence?' She looked in the

duke's direction, very much as though she had always intended to ask him first. 'Amscott, as one of the few gentlemen here, should you like to give us your thoughts on the main themes of the book?'

'I…am…still reading it and so would not like to say too much now in case my views change when I reach the end of the book. Which I am very much enjoying.'

'What did you think of Emma herself at the beginning? And of Mr Knightley of course?' asked Anna, unable to help herself poking a little fun at him. It was extremely obvious that he had not read any of the book at all.

'I thought Miss Austen's execution of the entire book was masterful. I like her use of literary devices and the setting in which she places the story and her characters. I should be very interested to hear your views on her writing, not to mention her characterisation. Of Emma and Mr Knightley in particular,' the duke replied. Quite masterfully, in fact. He really did give the impression of almost knowing what he was talking about.

'One last question,' Anna said, really unable to resist. 'What did you think of the relationship between Jane Fairfax and Frank Churchill?'

The duke narrowed his eyes at her for a moment, which made her lips twitch further, before smiling blandly and saying, 'I very much enjoyed reading about their relationship. I thought that it was written very well. I should very much like to hear your thoughts now, though. I fear that I have been monopolising the conversation for too long.'

'I would be very happy to—perhaps—bore you with

my many thoughts, as I quite devoured the book, but have one final question for you,' she said.

The duke nodded and murmured, 'Of course you do.'

'Who was your favourite character, and why?'

The duke shook his head. 'No,' he stated. 'I enjoyed the book so much that I cannot choose. I do not mean to imply that I found each character equally worthy of my liking or equally flawed, but they were so well drawn by the author that I cannot choose one above the other.' His head was turned in the direction of Lady Derwent, but he shot a triumphant glance in Anna's direction as he finished speaking, which caused her to have to swallow a giggle.

'Most illuminating,' Lady Derwent said. 'Anna, do you agree with the duke's thoughts?'

Looking straight back at her godmother, trying hard not to be very conscious of the duke's eyes on her, Anna said, 'They were certainly very comprehensive. More specifically...'

She had a lot to say, having read the book so very recently and having enjoyed it so very much, and soon was so engrossed in conversation with others who had genuinely read it that she almost at times forgot how close to the duke she was sitting and how if she moved a little to her left their shoulders and thighs might almost brush against each other.

It was wonderful. She hadn't previously experienced discussing literature with others in this way; her parents had not been readers, and Lady Maria and her other friends at the seminary had been reluctant scholars at best—although it did seem this evening as though Lady Maria had read at least some of *Emma*. Perhaps the problem had been the dry nature of their reading material at the seminary.

The discussion—with nods and murmured agreement from the duke—continued for a gratifyingly long time, with, amongst other things, different opinions offered as to Miss Austen's motivation behind her writing, the reasons that the writing was so particularly effective, and discussion as to whether any of her characters might be based on people whom Miss Austen knew, and whether any of the present company might have met any of those people.

As the conversation eventually descended into general gossip, Anna found herself turning to the duke—it would have been rude of her not to have done so as he would have had no one else with whom to converse— and being unable to resist the temptation to say, 'You must be pleased not to be dressed as a monk this evening.'

He cracked a laugh. 'I am delighted not to be dressed as a monk and even more delighted that my telling you that story clearly made an impression.'

'I must confess I would have enjoyed seeing you in religious garb this evening.' She smiled at him and added sarcastically, 'You look as though you are *very* pleased to be here.'

'As you will have noticed, I am extremely devoted to all forms of literature and very much in my element here,' he said, rolling his eyes just a little, which made Anna laugh.

'I do hope that hearing our thoughts will not have ruined the end of the book for you, Your Grace,' she said with faux sincerity. 'I understood you to say that you had read most of it already, and certainly your expressed thoughts indicated a wide knowledge of the book.'

'What I was most proud of in the expression of my thoughts,' he replied, 'was that they were so very applicable to almost any well-written work of fiction. And of course one's views on any book one has read are subjective, and so I could not be called wrong.'

Anna laughed. 'Very cunning; I am not surprised that you feel proud. Are there any books that you have read recently that you would like to discuss in more specific detail?'

The duke narrowed his eyes at her. 'Without wishing to be impolite in any way, I cannot answer that question until I understand the possible consequences. Would I be required to discuss the book more widely, and is there a risk that I would have to do so today?'

'My godmother wrote to me yesterday to ask if there was a particular book that I should like to discuss at this salon, and I understood from her that our conversation would be confined to the works of Jane Austen, but I'm sure that if you wished to hold forth about another author we should all be most eager to hear what you had to say. I would be very happy to suggest that to my godmother.'

'I cannot believe you would treat me so shabbily after I sent you the book that you have just enjoyed so much.'

'You are quite right.' Anna gave him a fake contrite smile. 'I am very grateful and must no longer torment you.'

'Indeed you must not.' His smile, coupled with the way he was gazing into her eyes as though the rest of the company did not exist, was suddenly making her feel quite breathless.

'If I give you my assurance that I will not mention your answer to anyone else,' Anna said, trying hard not to be too overcome at his proximity, the intimacy of his lowered and beautifully deep and raspy voice and the squareness of his jaw, 'would you tell me your favourite author?'

The duke leaned another inch or so closer to her. 'If it is to remain our secret—' the increased raspiness of his voice caused Anna's skin to raise in goose bumps '—I am prepared to confide in you.'

'I shall be honoured,' she said, still breathless, 'to be the holder of your confidence.'

The duke's eyes dropped from her eyes to her mouth for a moment, and Anna swallowed.

'That is…good to hear,' he said.

Anna found herself moistening her lips with her tongue.

'So…my secret.' He was looking at her lips again, and Anna felt as though they were the only two people in the world.

'Mmm?' she breathed.

'You must remember that you have promised not to tell another soul.'

'I shall remain faithful to that promise.' She could not have told why this conversation felt so extremely daring.

'So your question was…? I just want to make sure I answer it quite correctly.' The duke turned a little further in her direction, his eyes not moving from her face, and the sides of their knees brushed.

'Oh,' Anna squeaked.

A small smile played about the duke's lips and Anna smiled back.

They were just *looking* now, gazing at each other, as though they were quite alone.

Which they were not, she suddenly remembered.

'The question,' she said, as firmly as she could.

'Ah yes, your question. *Any* question, Miss Blake, and I will answer it as long as my response remains secret.'

Anna took a deep breath. Her stomach seemed to have turned completely liquid. A very warm liquid.

What had they been talking about? What *was* her question? Oh, yes.

'Who,' she breathed, 'is your favourite author?'

'My favourite author,' the duke said very slowly, and Anna could not help watching his beautifully firm mouth as he formed the words, 'is—' he leaned even closer to her and their knees brushed even more '—Jethro Tull.'

'Jethro Tull?' Her voice had gone squeaky again.

'The only author I have read recently.'

'I am not—' she was almost forgetting what they were talking about, because the way he was gazing at her was so—well—*exciting* '—familiar with Mr Tull's works.'

'He wrote about agricultural machinery and farming methods in the last century. I have just been dipping into his work *Horse-hoeing Husbandry*.'

'Oh. How…fascinating.'

'Extremely fascinating.' The duke's lips quirked up and Anna couldn't find any more words, because it didn't feel as though it was just Mr Tull whom the duke found fascinating.

And then they just sat and smiled at each other, and Anna felt as though her heart might beat right out of her chest.

She loved the tiny lines at the corners of the duke's

eyes when they creased as his smile grew, as it was doing now, and she loved the sheer breadth of his shoulders and the way she could see his muscles move under his tight-fitting jacket. And she loved just *being* with him.

He was looking at her lips again and she wondered whether she might explode. She really did need to re-start some sensible conversation.

'How often do you read Jethro Tull? And how many books did he write?' she asked, trying not to sigh at the sheer deliciousness of this conversation.

'I am not sure exactly how many books he wrote and I am not an avid reader but I do on occasion enjoy reading—' the duke's voice dropped a little '—when I am in bed, before I go to sleep.' His throat worked as she stared at him, unable to stop herself imagining him in, well, *bed*. The way he was swallowing indicated that perhaps he was having similar thoughts. Perhaps in relation to her.

'In bed,' she repeated, and then gasped. What was she *saying*? Respectable governesses did not talk about *beds* with unmarried men. Especially not in a literary salon in the company of others.

She took a very deep breath and said, 'I must try Mr Tull's works myself,' with as much briskness as she could muster.

'I would be very happy to lend them to you any time you should like to read them.' The duke's tone was very serious, but his eyes were very playful, and the combination was irresistible.

'I should not like to deprive you of your own reading matter,' Anna replied, only just capable of forming a rational sentence.

'My feeling…'

To Anna's huge disappointment, the duke was interrupted by Lady Derwent clapping her hands. 'I think it's time that we all took some refreshment.'

She had groups of small tables surrounded by chairs at the other end of the salon, and they all dutifully followed her over to them.

'I would like to sit with my goddaughter and of course the duke,' she announced. 'I make no pretence that I don't enjoy the company of a handsome young man.'

And before Anna had time to think about whether she was pleased or not to be seated at the same table as the duke and her godmother, she'd been marched by Lady Derwent over to her table.

'I must say, Amscott—' Lady Derwent took a dainty bite of a small crab tart '—your blathering about the book was admirable. One might almost have imagined that you had read it.'

The duke leaned back in his chair, his broad shoulders far too wide for its back, and grinned. 'I was not aware until four days ago that you were summoning me to this salon. Had I had longer, I would of course have been delighted to have read the entire book.'

'In that case—' Lady Derwent smiled triumphantly '—I shall tell you now what book we intend to discuss next time.'

Anna felt herself smiling inside at the thought that there would be a *next time*, even as she realised that it would be very dangerous to allow herself to become too attached to such occasions.

Perhaps, though, perhaps she might have an interesting and full life if she could continue to attend select events like this with her godmother. And perhaps one day she might meet a man whom she could hope to marry who might make her feel the way the duke made her feel. Actually, why had she just thought that? Hadn't she decided that if she could avoid it she would not like to be married? Or if she did marry should her husband not be someone who did *not* make her feel the way the duke did?

'Next time?' queried the duke, and Anna immediately felt her spirits sink a little. Which was very silly; this salon would have been hugely enjoyable even without the Duke's presence, she was sure.

'Next time,' her godmother said firmly.

The duke laughed. 'I will of course be more than happy to attend—' he glanced for the merest of seconds in Anna's direction, which made her smile '—any number of book discussions.'

'Do you undertake to produce an equally profound analysis of any book, Your Grace?' Anna asked with her most demure air.

'Certainly,' he said.

And then he nudged her foot very gently under the table with his own foot, while continuing to hold a particularly bland expression on his face, which made her gasp considerably less gently.

'Are you quite well, Anna?' her godmother asked.

'Very well, thank you.' Which was true as long as her heart didn't jump right out of her body with all the thudding it was doing as she wondered what the duke might do next.

The three of them then conversed amicably on a number of unexceptional topics, and the duke behaved equally unexceptionably throughout. Which was really quite disappointing.

When in due course some of the guests began to take their leave, Anna stood up too, with some reluctance.

'Thank you so much for the evening,' she said to her godmother. 'I have enjoyed it exceedingly.'

'You will go home in one of my carriages,' Lady Derwent instructed. 'The duke will escort you outside.'

'Of course.' The duke stood up very promptly and held his arm out to Anna, and to her shame she felt herself almost wriggling with internal delight to have another opportunity to touch him, even in a completely innocent way.

As they descended the steps outside the front door, he leaned down so that no one around might hear, and said, 'We were interrupted in the middle of a conversation earlier. Perhaps we should resume it. Would you care after all to visit Gunter's with me? I believe the ices there are the best in London.'

Anna knew that she'd thought about this and decided that it was not a good idea to see the duke alone—or at all—again, but right now she couldn't remember why she'd thought so, and it also seemed that there could be little point in not accompanying him there if she was, for example, going to see him again at another literary evening.

So she said, 'Oh, well if they are the best in *London*, perhaps I cannot refuse.'

'Excellent.' His smile melted Anna's insides. 'I shall look forward to it. I will write to you tomorrow to arrange the time.'

As he handed her into the carriage, the duke pressed

her hand just a little more than was necessary, in the most delicious way, almost as though he were promising something, and held her gaze for far longer than necessary as he smiled at her.

Anna smiled back at him, wordlessly, and knew that she would look forward to their visit to Gunter's far more than she ought.

Chapter Eight

James

James had made hay while the sun shone and had written to Anna immediately on waking the next day to arrange to visit the ice cream parlour.

The response had taken far too long for his liking; it had not arrived until the afternoon. It was an excellent response, though: Anna had agreed to go to Gunter's with him the next day.

He drew up on Bruton Street in his curricle at the time they had agreed, feeling far more excited than any grown man should at the prospect of going to a tea shop and eating ices.

He needed to remind himself that the reason for spending a little more time with her was to confirm that they would not in fact be compatible as life partners. He just needed to cure himself of his ridiculous infatuation.

As he lifted the knocker on the Puntneys' front door, he reflected that he could no longer think of Anna as Miss Blake after hearing Lady Derwent address her by her Christian name. The name Anna was perfect for her: classic, poised, elegant, lovely-sounding and with a little cheekiness to it. Good God. It seemed as though the literary evening might have had an effect on him; he had become quite poetic.

The Puntneys' butler asked him to wait in the hall for a moment and rang a bell. Shortly afterwards, he heard steps and Anna came into sight around the bend in the staircase.

She smiled when she saw him and James smiled too and all of a sudden it was as though his day had brightened. And there was that damned poeticism again.

'Good afternoon,' he said, more interesting speech having deserted him for the time being while he got used to the very pleasant fact that he was with Anna again. 'You look very nice today. As always.'

She laughed. 'Thank you.'

She was wearing a dark green velvet pelisse over a dress of the same colour, with a cream beading. She looked delightful, and also expensively dressed. She couldn't possibly have the means to buy herself such clothes on a governess's salary, and indeed when he had seen her in the park she had been wearing a much less fashionable and intricately tailored gown. She had obviously fallen on hard times to have chosen to become a governess. How, he wondered, did she afford her clothes? Perhaps they were from her previous life. Or a gift from someone, perhaps Lady Derwent.

He would like very much to know how it had happened that she had become a governess. He did not like to think of her being in need.

'It is a beautiful day,' he observed, as they descended the steps outside the house.

'It is indeed,' Anna agreed. 'I had feared that it would continue to rain but the clouds seem to have entirely disappeared now.'

'Were you able to take your charges out this morning for their walk between rain showers?'

'We did manage a short one and I think that their nurse will take them into the garden for an hour now.'

'Let me help you up into the curricle. I have a blanket for you to wrap around your legs to keep you warm.' It was very pleasant taking her weight on his arm for a moment as he handed her up, and really quite disappointing that she had already arranged the blanket entirely successfully by herself before he was seated next to her and could offer to help with it.

'Thank you,' she said. 'I have not been in a curricle before; this is the most wonderful treat.'

'I am pleased that it is.' He took the reins and nudged his horses to start walking. 'Do you...' James very much wanted to ask her more about her background. Was he being curious for the sake of curiosity? No, he realised; he had begun to care about her and wanted to know whether she was genuinely happy. 'How did you come to be a governess?' Asking leading questions could only seem patronising; it was surely better to ask directly. Although...she might not wish to tell him. 'I'm sorry; please don't feel that you have to answer that question.'

'I am happy to answer it,' she said after a short pause. 'I think mine is not an unusual situation. My parents were sadly somewhat impecunious, and while my mother was alive we had enough money, but with her loss I also lost all financial means. I realised that I would have to earn some money, and was extremely fortunate to find this position with the help of Lady Derwent. She would have very happily paid me to be her companion, but she is not yet at the stage of life where she genuinely requires one, and I would prefer to maintain our relationship as it is, without receiving too much charity.'

'I'm so sorry about the loss of your parents. Was it recent?'

'Thank you. My father, he, that is to say, I… We…' She paused and then continued, 'We lost him some years ago. My mother more recently. I am very lucky in having such a wonderful godmother, however. I know that you have also experienced loss; it is deeply tragic but I believe those of us who have the good fortune still to be here must do our best to enjoy the life that we have, when we are ready, of course, after the first deep grief.'

'I agree.' He took the reins in one hand and covered her hand for a moment with his own. What he wanted to do, he realised with a shock, was hug her tightly against him to comfort her if he possibly could.

'Thank you. And that is why,' she said, a slight tremor in her voice indicating perhaps that she felt more emotion than she was owning to, 'we must enjoy every last morsel of our ices today.'

James laughed. 'I agree with that too.'

As they drove at a leisurely pace down the road and into Berkeley Square, where Gunter's was located, part of him just enjoyed being physically in her presence, part of him produced vague small talk to match hers, and part of him reflected on what she'd just said. He realised that she had answered his question about her background without answering it in the slightest. What was the story behind any lady of quality becoming a governess? Any such lady would have been brought up in the way Anna clearly had, and would then have fallen on hard times and decided that she needed to seek employment.

And while she had confided in him the information about the loss of her parents, of *course* she had lost them; she would presumably not otherwise have to work as a governess.

Her answer had in fact been very similar to his about Miss Austen's book: quite generic.

Of course, she had answered in that way because she didn't want to give him any further details, whereas the reason that he'd answered in that way had been that he hadn't read the book. He should respect her wish not to disclose more. And since he was only here to cure himself of the ridiculous infatuation he felt for her, there was no need for him to find out anything else about her background.

'On a different note,' he said, 'but continuing with the theme of making the most of life, I was so taken by your passion for *Emma* that I have started reading it myself. I don't think many amongst my friends have read it and presume that Miss Austen might have had a female audience in mind when she wrote it, but I must own that I am enjoying it and that I do, like you, very much like the way she writes, and her wit.'

'Well! I am very pleased to have been of service to you. And I have to admit that I am a little surprised. On Friday you did not have the air of a man who wished to engage closely with literature.' Anna glanced sideways up at him as she spoke, with a smile that held a cheeky edge, and James smiled back at her.

And then they had one of the moments that they'd been having where they just smiled—foolishly—at each other without speaking.

James had slowed the horses to a standstill outside the tea shop. Anna's face was tilted up towards his, and he had a feeling that if they were not in quite such a public space, he would not be able to help himself doing what he'd done at the ball, and leaning down and kissing her. *Damn*, he wished he could. Her lips were slightly parted, her cheeks were a little flushed, her sea-green eyes were framed by long eyelashes, her gaze was direct, and the whole made for, well, for extreme temptation.

They were, however, surrounded by other stationary carriages; it was common practice for people to drive up and be served as they waited.

'A waiter will come soon to take our order,' he told Anna, to distract himself from the lushness of her lips.

'I am very much looking forward to tasting the ices.' She frowned. 'How are you reading *Emma* having given your copy of it to me?' she asked.

Damn. He was an idiot. If he wasn't careful, he'd end up admitting that he'd bought all the books he'd 'lent' to her. He had in fact bought a second copy of *Emma*.

'My sister and mother both had copies of it. You can never have too many copies of a good book.' He was an excellent liar, it seemed. He wasn't sure whether he should be proud of that or not.

'Oh, I see. Thank you again for lending the books to me. I am of course able to give them back to you any time you desire.'

'I would be very happy for you to keep them for as long as you like. From what you have said, I believe you to be a much keener reader than any in my family other than perhaps one or two of my sisters, and I'm sure that every author would like his or her books to be read as widely as possible.'

'Thank you.' The smile she gave him would have been more than enough reward for something considerably greater than the procurement of a few books.

'My very great pleasure, I assure you,' he told her.

'Tell me about your sisters? It sounds as though you have several?'

'Well.' James was more than happy to talk about his family, whose company he liked very much. 'You must interrupt me immediately if I talk for too long. There is a lot to say: I have six sisters.'

'My goodness.'

'Indeed.'

He had her laughing with several anecdotes about his sisters, which he found immensely gratifying. He liked the sound of her laugh, and he liked to think that he had made her happy in some way, and everyone enjoyed laughing.

As he watched a waiter approach them, he finished another story about his two youngest sisters, and said, 'I have been speaking for far too long. Do you have any siblings?'

'No, I don't. I would have liked to, I believe. It must be wonderful to be surrounded by so much family. Oh, look at the different ices that people are eating.' She nodded at the occupants of some of the other carriages. 'I have no idea what flavour I'm going to choose.'

She clearly did not wish to talk about her family for long. Perhaps it was understandable given her recent losses. And of course he certainly should not lead the conversation in directions she did not wish to follow.

'There are certainly some quite remarkable flavours,' he said. And then he added, 'I have been here a few times before, always with my sisters,' because for some reason he did not wish her to think that he'd escorted any other young lady here in the way that he'd escorted her.

A few minutes later, as Anna perused the menu, he took the opportunity to watch her. Her face was beautifully expressive and the colour of her hair quite delightful. He could happily just look at her for a long time. Which, frankly, seemed a little odd, as though he'd lost his wits.

'My goodness,' Anna interrupted his thoughts, looking up from the menu. 'I know that you've been here before but I can't resist reading some of these flavours out loud; some of them seem quite remarkable. We may choose between maple, bergamot, pineapple, pistachio, jasmine, white coffee, chocolate, vanilla, elderflower, Parmesan, lavender, artichoke, and coriander.'

James could not recall a time when he had more enjoyed someone reading a list. He very much liked Anna's voice, and he very much liked the way she wrinkled her nose at him when she found something amusing.

'By what are you most tempted?' he asked.

'I can't quite decide. I should like to taste the ones that I think will be *nice*, obviously, but I should also like to taste the ones that I think will be *odd*. Just to see what they're like. So I fear that I am going to be most indecisive.'

'May I make a suggestion?'

'Of course.'

'Why don't you choose several ices—some odd and some nice—and taste them all?'

'I don't like to waste anything,' she said. 'One sees and hears of such poverty. It does not seem right to order food that one knows one cannot finish.'

James wondered what poverty she had experienced herself to have decided that she needed to work.

Her point was valid and he did not wish to waste food either, but he did want her to have a good time and to taste whatever she wanted.

'I have an idea,' he said, pleased with his own genius. 'Choose a small selection now and we will return soon and taste more of the flavours. I am very happy to return as many times as you like.'

'You are very kind,' she told him, smiling.

That *smile*. James was almost sighing just at the sight of it.

'I am not kind, I am quite selfish,' he told her. 'I very much enjoy your company and therefore I am heartily enjoying our visit. I would enjoy a second and indeed third or as many as you like.'

'I cannot trespass upon your kindness to that extent, but I am certainly looking forward to tasting the ices now.'

James was *definitely* going to want to persuade her to return, he thought, but he could pursue that later. Perhaps when she had tasted some of the ices and was feeling wistful about the ones she had not sampled.

'For the time being,' he said, 'I feel that you have a big decision to make. We can certainly manage four flavours between us; I am a very competent eater. Which will you choose?'

After much deliberation, during which James could not take his eyes off her as she read the menu, tilting her head to one side to think, she announced, 'I think I am quite decided. Parmesan. Obviously.'

'Obviously. You have to have a cheese one.'

'Yes indeed. Also artichoke, because I have to have a vegetable. Violet, because I have to have a flower. And pineapple and maple because I have to have one that I think I will actually like.'

'The perfect combination. Parmesan, artichoke, violet, pineapple and maple. I can't imagine a more delectable mouthful.'

'Your Grace.' She fixed him with a stern look. 'Are you trying to put me off? Because I must tell you that you are succeeding quite well and I might have to reconsider my choices.'

'Miss Blake.' He wished so much that he could call her Anna. This formality seemed ridiculous. 'Firstly, I should like it very much if you called me James.'

'Do you not think that is perhaps too familiar?'

He lowered his voice so that there could be no possibility of anyone else hearing and said, 'I do not wish to be indelicate, but I feel that when one has kissed someone, it cannot be thought improper to call them by their Christian name.'

'Oh!' Her squeak was one of the most adorable things he'd ever heard. 'Your Grace. *James.*'

'Yes?'

'You are quite outrageous.'

'I cannot apologise, unfortunately, because I enjoyed it very much.'

'I really do need one of my godmother's fans to give you a well-deserved rap.'

'My knuckles are very grateful that you do not have one. Although… I think you would look delightful peeking over the top of a fan.' He could not resist teasing her; the combination of her laugh and her pout was one of the most alluring things he'd ever seen.

'I feel that our conversation is going sadly awry. I believe that you had something else you wished to say to me?'

'Yes, I think I did.' James smiled at her. 'I think I've forgotten, though. You make me forget myself.'

Anna leaned towards him and very deliberately did a large and most unladylike roll of her eyes.

'Miss Blake. I am shocked.'

'So am I,' she said sunnily, which made James laugh, a lot.

Soon Anna joined in with the laughing, and it turned out that there was little he would rather do than laugh about absolutely nothing with this wonderful woman.

They eventually calmed down, and as they wiped their eyes, Anna still hiccupping slightly with giggles, it occurred to him that he really hadn't done very well at pushing this infatuation out of his mind.

He hadn't actually spent that much time with her yet, though. Maybe the way she ate her ices would give him pause for thought. Or maybe the way *he* ate ices would cause *her* to wish herself anywhere but here. Maybe by the end of this afternoon, they would both be heartily relieved never to see the other at close quarters again.

A waiter interrupted his thoughts to place their ices in front of them, so he was going to find out sooner rather than later whether ice-eating made any difference to his silly infatuation.

'I intend to be scientific about this,' said Anna, clearly not as distracted as he was. 'I think I'm going to start with the one I think I will like least and finish with the one I expect to like the most.'

James shook his head. 'Is that not very risky? What if the one you think you will like the least is in fact the one you like the most? It would be disappointing to begin well and finish badly.'

'That is very true.' Anna paused, her spoon mid-air. 'I need to think about this carefully.'

'But not too carefully in case the ices melt.'

'Very true. Perhaps I should take one mouthful of each in the order I expect to like them going from worst to best, and then re-evaluate the situation.'

'Very sensible,' James approved.

'However—' her spoon was still in the air '—I now realise that I am being very rude to you. Very self-centred. Which ones would *you* like to try first?'

'No, no, this is your treat and we agreed that I am just here to finish up whatever you do not wish to eat.'

'Are you sure, though? I feel that I am imposing on you.'

'You could never impose on me,' James said, very seriously, meaning it.

Anna looked at him for a long moment, her own face very serious all of a sudden, and then said, 'You are a very kind man.'

'Really, no,' he said. God. He was in fact only here

because he wished to clear his mind of the infatuation he felt for her. That was not kind at all.

'We must agree to differ and we must begin to eat or as you say they will melt.' She looked between them. 'I am of course going to try the artichoke one first, because I do not expect to like it as much as the others.'

'Of course.'

She placed her spoon in the artichoke ice and scooped a little out.

And so far, watching her take ice cream was not helping James's infatuation level at all. The way she held her spoon, the way she concentrated and then looked up at him with a little smile, were all quite delightful. Delicate but not *too* delicate.

And then she opened her beautiful mouth and put the spoon in and, oh, good God, the way she held the spoon in her mouth for a second; James was imagining her holding *other* things in her mouth. And the way she was tasting it, savouring it.

How had he managed to sit opposite her and eat an entire meal with her during the supper at the ball without exploding with desire?

As she finished the mouthful, Anna gave a little wriggle, which caused her chest to move far too alluringly for James's sanity, and said, 'I was mistaken.'

'You were?' James managed to ask.

'Yes. Artichoke ice cream is divine. You must try some immediately.'

'Certainly.' His voice sounded somewhat like a croak.

He put his own spoon into the ice and then put it into his mouth, incredibly conscious the entire time of Anna's eyes on his hands and mouth.

'That is wonderful.' He wasn't certain whether he was referring to the ice or to the way it felt having Anna's eyes following his every movement.

She swallowed and raised her eyes to his. 'Yes.'

Their eyes held for a long time, before Anna pulled hers away with what looked like an effort and said, 'We should try the next one.'

'We should.'

'Violet,' she said decisively.

And then she took a spoonful of it, and, even though he'd already seen her place a spoon in her mouth and suck gently, the sight of her doing it still caused his body to respond most uncomfortably. At this rate, he was going to be a gibbering wreck by the end of the afternoon.

Anna closed her eyes for a second and put her head to one side, looking as though she was focusing very much on the taste she was experiencing, and then opened her eyes and swallowed.

James took a deep breath and shook his head slightly to clear it.

'How was that one?' he asked, very impressed at how normal his voice sounded.

'Very nice but not as truly wonderful as artichoke. Which is the opposite of what you would expect.'

'That *is* interesting.' James plunged his own spoon into the ice, trying hard not to think crude thoughts about plunging other things into places, and tasted. 'You're right,' he said. And then for some reason he couldn't resist adding, 'It seems that we have *very* compatible taste in ices.'

'I think,' said Anna, placing her spoon very deliberately into the next ice, 'that that remains to be seen. For all we know, we might disagree enormously on the next ones.'

'That is a very fair point,' James acknowledged, as he watched her again before taking his own mouthful.

As they continued to taste the ices together, James's enjoyment of watching Anna only grew, if that were possible.

'The artichoke is still my favourite,' concluded Anna after their final tasting. 'Although the pineapple and maple is a close second.'

'I agree.' James would agree with absolutely anything she might say right now. 'And that proves that we are compatible when it comes to ices.'

'No, it proves we are compatible when it comes to *these four* ices.'

'In that case,' he said triumphantly—although he wasn't even sure that this what he wanted; he knew that at the beginning of the afternoon it hadn't been entirely—'we will have to come again and sample another four.'

'You might be right. Not definitely right, but probably. Now, I am afraid, with great regret, that I ought to return to the house.'

'Of course.' James was conscious of huge disappointment, which was at odds with what he'd intended from this afternoon. He thought. It was actually quite difficult to remember.

Maybe because his infatuation was, if he was honest with himself, growing. And maybe that was because, once Anna had told him the bald facts about her family, they'd just reverted to engaging in frivolous small talk. And so, really, he still knew hardly anything about her.

As he collected up his reins and encouraged his horses to move forward, he found himself asking, 'Do you drive?'

'No; I have never had the opportunity. I do love horses, though, and much admire this pair.'

'And of course the skill with which they are being driven.'

She laughed. 'Of *course* I admire your skill.'

James laughed too, and then found himself saying, 'I think we are fated to visit Gunter's again. We need to sample a lot more ices, as you rightly said, because we need to determine whether our ice cream tastes are indeed compatible, and I feel that you should have at least one opportunity to drive a carriage. We could combine the ice-eating with a driving lesson.'

And, good God, what had come over him? He *hated* being driven and under no circumstances—normally—would he acquiesce to a request to drive his horses, let alone *offer* such torture. He would worry about his horses and he would worry about his sanity. But now, when he thought about it, he didn't even think it would *be* torture.

Apparently he would do almost anything to spend time with Anna.

Chapter Nine

Anna

Anna did a gigantic swallow as she looked at the duke—James—holding his horse's reins and smiling at her. He was…he was…*sublime*.

His humour.

His kindness.

His strong, handsome features.

The evident strength in his arms, across his shoulders, ensured that she felt safe at all times in his presence. Well, not *entirely* safe; she was beginning to think that her *heart* might not be safe. But physically she knew he would protect her. She was *sure* he was a good driver.

She was also sure that she would be much better served to thank him for the ices and say goodbye and that she would perhaps see him another time, perhaps at another literary salon at her godmother's.

But…

'I should like that very much,' she heard herself saying.

'Why don't you take the reins now?' he suggested.

'Now?'

'Well.' He looked around at the relatively narrow road they were in. 'Not exactly now. But perhaps we could go somewhere less busy and you could begin your first lesson. I think the village of Kensington might be a good place to start.'

The sensible thing to say would of course be that she should go back now...except Lady Puntney had suggested that she take the entire afternoon to herself as she had admitted to having a headache yesterday—probably due to such a lack of sleep from reading late and then thinking about the duke—and Lady Puntney did not wish her to be ill. And so she *could* stay for just a little bit longer.

'I'd love to just for a few minutes,' she said. 'Thank you.'

'There is really no need to thank me,' he said as he manoeuvred them through what felt like an impossibly small gap and which at the hands of a less confidence-inducing driver would have caused Anna to close her eyes and cling tightly to the side of the carriage. 'Really, I'm being quite selfish; I'm sure I will enjoy teaching you.'

'In that case, I must ask you to thank me for agreeing to your suggestion.'

He smiled at her as though her very weak humour had amused him deeply, which made her smile in her turn.

They lapsed into silence, but it was a nice, comfortable one, unlike the one they'd had at the beginning of the walk they'd taken. It felt as though—even though Anna had been careful to keep their conversations quite frivolous—they had become friends.

Well, it wasn't *entirely* comfortable. Anna felt as

though her heart was bursting with…something, and she was most *un*comfortably aware that she very much wanted him to kiss her again.

When they went over a bump in the road and they were jiggled in their seats and their legs almost touched, it felt incredibly exciting and then very disappointing that they settled back into the same positions they'd been in before.

And as she watched his hands—so strong and yet light on the reins—she found herself wondering how it would feel to have them on her.

And when she looked at his profile as he concentrated on the road, and then caught his eye when he glanced briefly at her with a smile, well then her mind was filled with memories of their kiss.

'I think this is as good a place as any,' the duke said after a few moments.

'For what?' asked Anna, unable to collect her thoughts.

'For teaching you to drive?'

'Oh! Yes, of course.' She hoped he hadn't realised that her mind had been quite so far away from driving, focused at that moment on his thigh next to hers. She looked around. They were in a wide, quiet, tree-lined road, bordered by pretty houses. 'Is this Kensington?'

'Yes, it is.'

'It's very peaceful after the hustle and bustle of London. And yet really quite close.' Perhaps one day in ten or twenty years' time, when she had saved enough money from her salary, Anna might be able to purchase a small house in a place like this.

'Yes, it's very nice.' The duke smiled at her in such a way that Anna felt as though all he could see at this moment was her. It was quite intoxicating being regarded in such a way. And she feared that she might be returning his gaze with an identical one.

After a few beautifully long moments, he lifted one hand towards her, and then replaced it at his side and swallowed.

'Perhaps you should move a little more towards the middle of the seat,' he said.

Anna just stared at him, in mute question. Was he suggesting that they…

'So that we might begin the lesson,' he clarified.

Oh! Of course. Of *course* he hadn't been suggesting that they move closer so that they might kiss.

Anna nodded and slid sideways, as he did the same, until they were seated very close to each other.

Their upper arms were touching now, which was making Anna very warm inside. Apparently it wasn't making the duke's insides turn to mulch at all, though, because he was able to speak in a perfectly normal voice, saying, 'I'm going to give you the reins now and show you how to hold them. Perhaps…'

She looked up at him as he regarded her and then the horses as though he was trying to solve a particularly knotty problem.

'I must confess that I haven't ever tried to teach anyone to drive before,' he said. 'I feel that it would be prudent to make sure that I am able to stop the horses bolting if they get alarmed in any way or if you pull on their mouths, which I am *certain* you won't, but we should consider all eventualities.'

'Mmm.' Anna's heart was beginning to bang very loudly in her chest; at this rate it would be so loud that it might cause the horses to take fright. She had no space in her brain to think about holding the reins correctly because her entire being seemed to be taken up with drinking in the duke's proximity and wondering what would happen next.

'I wonder,' he said, 'whether the wisest thing might not be for us both to hold the reins, like this. If you agree.'

And he put his left arm around her so that she was encircled by his arms and held the reins in front of her. He was warm and hard and big and smelled wonderful, and Anna couldn't imagine that there could be a nicer place in the world to sit than right here, right now, within his hold.

'Is that all right?' he asked, his voice low, his breath whispering across her cheek.

'Mmm.' She really didn't have any words. She glanced over her shoulder at him and saw that he was smiling at her in such a fond manner that she almost had to close her eyes to recover from the…well, the sheer delight of it.

'So you should take the reins,' he said.

'The reins,' she repeated. All she could think about was the way her back was against his chest and just how big and hard it felt.

'Maybe we should hold them together.' His voice was low and husky and he could have said any words at all and they would have sounded delightful, exciting, fascinating…

'Mmm.'

He put both the reins in his right hand and then took her left in his—it fitted *beautifully* inside his larger hand—and transferred both reins to their left hands, and then took her right in his and transferred the right rein back.

'Look,' he said. 'You're driving.'

'Mmm.'

'You seem—' his mouth was even closer to her ear now, his breath almost tickling her '—to be unusually lacking in speech at the moment. Perhaps you are overcome by…the idea of your first driving lesson?'

Anna took a very deep breath, which caused her to be pressed more tightly against his chest, and found some words.

'That is exactly it,' she achieved. 'I am extremely overcome by…that.'

'I find you to be an excellent driver.' His voice had sunk extremely low.

'I'm not sure that I am actually driving. The horses are stationary.'

'That is a mere detail.'

'An important one, though?'

'You are demanding, Miss Blake.'

'In *every* way.' She had *no* idea where her words had come from but she had *loved* saying them. She didn't even really know what she meant by them but…

'In that case—' he tightened his arms around her a little '—perhaps you would like to move the horses on a little.'

'I think I would.'

'Go like this with the reins.' He took his hands away from hers for a moment—which she really did not like, and not just because it was a little terrifying thinking that she was the one in charge of the horses for that moment, but because she *liked* his hands on hers—and showed her what to do.

She moved the reins herself and the horses began to walk forward, in perfect harmony with each other.

'Oh, my goodness,' she said, entranced. 'They're beautiful. And I'm driving them.'

'Indeed.'

They continued to move forward in a straight line, Anna watching the proud backs and haunches of the horses and feeling the duke's embrace.

She was so deliciously happy with where she was that she almost didn't register that there was a bend coming up.

'We will need to turn,' the duke said, his mouth against her temple. 'The horses are extremely intelligent but it would nonetheless be wise to encourage them a little to follow the line of the road.'

'By pulling gently with the left rein?'

'Exactly,' the duke approved. 'You are indeed a natural driver.'

As they rounded the corner, Anna said, 'I see that it is in fact the horses who are natural drivers.'

'I did choose this pair for today knowing that they are reasonably placid, as they were going to be standing for some time while we ate,' he acknowledged, 'but I am quite certain that you would drive any horses very well with very little practice.'

They continued for a few minutes until they were beyond the village and then he said, 'Perhaps we should take this turning here.'

After a few more moments, they came to a clearing.

'I wonder whether we should stop for a moment to enjoy the scenery?' he suggested.

'I think that would be very nice.' Anna suspected that he was tempted to enjoy the scenery in the same way that they had enjoyed the rose garden at the ball. The sensible part of her mind was suggesting that it would not be a good idea to engage in any more flirting, or kissing… But the rest of her was, frankly, quite desperate to be kissed just one more time.

'We stop the horses like this,' the duke told her, helping her to apply just a little pressure with the reins.

They came to a halt under a large oak tree, still not entirely divested of its leaves despite the progression of autumn. The duke removed his arms from around Anna, leaped down and looped the reins around the tree's trunk, before returning to the seat in one lithe move.

And then he settled himself back where he had been sitting before.

'I wonder whether, without the horses and reins to distract us, we might find an even better position for you for driving,' he said, his voice very throaty. 'Like this, for example.'

He placed his hands on her waist and lifted her a little so that she was in a slightly different position against his chest.

'I think that might work particularly well.'

'Mmm.' Anna could hardly breathe. She *loved* his hands on her waist, large against her body.

'Did you enjoy that?' His mouth was almost touching her temple as he spoke.

'Enjoy…?' Enjoy his hands on her waist? Very much so, yes.

'Your first driving lesson.'

'Driving.' Of course that was what he had meant. 'Yes, thank you.'

'I enjoyed it too.' His voice was *so* deliciously throaty.

She turned a little to look up at him over her shoulder, wriggling a little against him as she did so, and smiled at him.

'Damn,' he said.

She raised her eyebrows, suddenly—even though she wasn't sure how—feeling in some way as though she was in control of this conversation. A conversation without words.

He gazed at her eyes, her mouth, her tongue as she moistened her lips.

And then she wriggled more against him and pouted a little at him.

'Damn,' he repeated.

And then, very slowly, but with very clear meaning, as though nothing could have altered his course, he leaned down and kissed her on the lips.

This kiss was different from the first one they had shared at the ball. It was not tentative, or a mere brushing of lips. It was immediately hard, and demanding, the duke's tongue entering her mouth immediately, *wanting*, wanting things from her, and causing her to want too.

She turned further towards him and reached her arms up around his neck, loving the way that the movement meant that their chests pressed against each other.

The duke groaned and then slid his right arm further around her waist.

His left hand was on her waist, his fingers on her ribs, and then it began to move up her body.

Anna took a sharp intake of breath as his hand moved to cup the underside of her breast, as all the while they continued to kiss. This felt so very, very daring, and so very, very perfect, and she just wanted him to touch her more, further…

She pushed her hands into his thick hair, almost as though she wanted to anchor him to her, as they continued to deepen their kiss. His hand was moving further now, on her breast, and *oh*. Even through the fabric of her dress, his touch felt wonderful.

And then he lifted her so that she was on his lap. He put his right hand into her hair, and tugged very gently, so that she leaned her head back a little, and then he began to kiss her very slowly along her jawline, as she sat encircled in his arms, her hands still in his hair, her body truly on fire.

With one hand he continued to caress the underside of her breasts and with the other he somehow undid the buttons of her pelisse until he had it open and was kissing her along her collarbone and then down and down, with what felt like great intent, towards the neckline of her dress.

And then, somehow—he had very clever hands— he had the neckline lower and had her breasts released from their constraints and he was kissing, caressing, nipping, and Anna was just *shuddering* with the sheer delight of it.

As he continued, she pushed her hands inside his shirt, wanting to feel his hard chest. She could feel corded muscle, and strength, and she could feel what he was doing to her, and it was utterly, utterly blissful.

As they continued to explore each other with their hands, she found herself kissing, almost biting his neck as he sucked and nipped on her, and it was one of the most wonderful things she had ever experienced.

And then…one of his hands moved to her leg, and he began to run his fingers along the length of her thigh, and even through the fabric of her dress his touch made her shiver even more, as his hand rose higher. She reached down to his thigh, marvelling at the solidity of it and the bunching of his muscles, and enjoying how as she moved her fingers higher up his thigh, his breathing became faster.

And then he moved his hand under her skirts, and now his hand was on her bare skin, tracing further and further up her leg to where she now felt liquid and… almost *desperate*.

He continued to kiss her neck, her breasts, her shoulders, tormenting and delighting, as his fingers circled closer and closer, ever higher on her thighs. She was clinging to him, one arm round his neck again now, holding his shoulders, the other on his hard thigh.

And then, finally, his fingers reached her most intimate parts, the shock of his first touch there causing her whole body to shudder.

'Your Grace,' she panted, as he began to move his fingers with what felt like real purpose. She could barely think but she knew that she wanted to feel him too.

He halted the movement of his fingers. 'I'm sorry; would you like to stop?'

'No, no, please, please carry on.'

He laughed and resumed his touch.

Anna couldn't think now, all she could do was feel, and judder and cling to him.

She reached for his breeches, feeling the hardness of him there, and worked to open them. When she had her hand on him, she felt—with great satisfaction—him judder too.

'Oh, my God, *Anna*. Call me James.'

'James,' she said on a long pant—maybe a little scream if she was honest—as his fingers began to move more and more and the pressure built.

As she spoke his name, she suddenly wondered *what* she was doing, and whether it could be dangerous for her.

'James. Stop,' she managed to say. 'Could I become with child like this?' She didn't *think* she could, but she *had* to be sure.

'Not if I do not enter you.'

His fingers and mouth had immediately stilled when she'd asked him to stop, and she didn't like it, and if it couldn't result in a baby, then she couldn't bear the thought of stopping *now*...

She didn't have the words to ask him to continue, though, so instead she just increased her hold on him and began to move her hand.

'Anna? Do you...?'

'Mmm, yes.'

'You are certain? Because maybe...' He ended on a groan as she moved her hand more.

'Extremely. Certain,' she said, moving very deliberately.

And then he moved his hand back and kissed her hard and deep on the mouth before beginning to kiss her breasts again, and then she was lost to the pressure and sensation that began to build, just on the perfect side of unbearable.

Release came for Anna, and, she realised, for James, at almost the same time.

And then they just half lay, half sat under the blanket on the carriage seat, their limbs entwined, both of them still shuddering.

Anna was the first to stir. The day had become quite gusty, it seemed from the leaves beginning to blow around them, and the breeze on her bare shoulders had made her very aware of her nakedness under the blanket. She wriggled away from him so that she could adjust her dress. *Big* adjustments were required; she was quite scandalously undressed. Well. The undress was clearly not as scandalous as what they'd just *done*. All the kissing and touching and... Her stomach was dipping just at the *thought* of it all.

'Would you like any help?' James's voice was still quite ragged, which Anna had to admit she *loved*.

'I think—' she smiled at him as she adjusted her dress across her chest '—that I might have had quite enough *help* from you today.'

He returned her smile and lifted both his hands to cup her face, and then he placed a lovely little kiss on her lips.

'I don't think I could ever have enough such *help* from you,' he said.

'James! I can't believe you just said that.'

'Really? I have a *lot* to say in response to that.' He kissed her on the lips again and then smoothed her hair back and helped her to pull her pelisse around her shoulders. 'Firstly, I love hearing my name on your lips like that.'

'Secondly,' he continued, 'you can't believe that I just made a slightly warm comment about what we just did? Because I *assure* you—' he kissed her again before tracing one finger down her chest between her breasts, which made her shiver quite delightfully '—that what we *did* was a lot more shocking than what we might say.'

His face became very serious, and then he continued, 'I must apologise if you feel uncomfortable in any way about what happened, but I assure that you cannot possibly become with child without...'

Anna shook her head. 'We had already kissed and that was quite scandalous enough already to ruin a young lady of quality such as Lady Maria. And no one knows we are here...' She knew that she should regret what they'd done, because of course it was truly shocking behaviour, and it couldn't happen again, because even an employer as kind-hearted and caring as Lady Puntney would really probably have no choice but to ask her to leave if she knew of such an indiscretion, but if she was never to be married, which seemed probable, she would at least have this memory. 'And so...' She smiled at him, to signal to him that she had no regrets, and then bit her lip, because his expression was *so* serious.

'I would never, ever want to hurt you in any way, Anna,' he said.

'I know that.' She realised that—insofar as a woman could trust a man, she did trust him very fully. Well, she trusted him fully to treat her well within the context that he had of her, which was that she was a lady who had fallen on hard times. Arguably they should not have kissed, but many people kissed, and more, before they were married, even Lady Maria and her *curate*, it seemed. She wasn't sure how he would treat her if he knew that she was the daughter of a groom. She was sure that he would still be kind to her, because she was certain that he was a very kind, honourable man, but she wasn't sure that he would wish to spend any more time with her. In her experience, even the nicest of men were bound by Society's code. 'Thank you.'

'I think I should take you back now.' He tucked the blanket around Anna and gathered the reins. 'Perhaps I will drive now, if you don't mind, for speed. We have been out for quite a long time and I should not wish Lady Puntney to comment.'

'No indeed, and yes, I will allow that your driving is a tiny bit faster than mine. For the time being. Until I have spent a few more minutes practising and have become an expert.' It felt important to try to turn the conversation entirely away from what they had just *done*.

James smiled obligingly and said, 'Of *course* you will be an expert with the reins with only a few more minutes' practice.'

They both laughed and then lapsed into silence as they began to drive back towards London.

Anna did not wish to be silent; she would not be able to avoid being alone with her remarkably confusing thoughts later on and did not wish to be free now to reflect too much on what had happened.

'It really is very autumnal now,' she observed.

'Indeed it is. I particularly like red leaves at this time of year.'

'Have you travelled to Scotland? I believe that the forests there are particularly fine?'

They passed the next few minutes in most enjoyable discussion about the different botanical and zoological features of Scotland and its islands. That is to say, at times Anna almost managed to stop incessantly replaying in her mind what she and James had *done*. Most of the time, though, if she was honest, she had only half her mind on the conversation.

Eventually, as the conversation slid somehow to the discussion of some rather scandalous *on-dits* that James had heard from his mother about some of the ladies who had been present at the literary salon evening, Anna managed to participate more fully in the conversation, and soon couldn't stop herself giggling hard at some of James's more outrageous stories.

They arrived too soon at Bruton Street, and Anna was conscious of a sense almost of loss that she would be leaving James's company so soon.

As he drew up, he said, 'I very much hope that you would like to return to Gunter's to taste more ices. We have a lot of them to experience. And also, of course, you might wish to undertake more...*practice.*' He accompanied his last word by a meaningful eyebrow raise and a *wink*, which made Anna gasp.

'James!'

'Anna! What did you think I meant? I was referring to driving. Obviously.'

'Obviously indeed,' she said, and he laughed. 'Thank you very much for a wonderful afternoon.'

'I was extremely pleased to be of service,' he said, with another eyebrow raise, causing Anna to gasp again.

'I am afraid,' she said, adopting her primmest manner, 'that I can no longer thank you *for the delicious ices* because you appear determined to make inappropriate references at every turn.'

'You are correct,' he said. 'I would like to apologise but I fear that I do not feel particularly sorry.'

Anna held her arm out as haughtily as she could. 'I feel that it is now time for me to go inside.'

'Your word is my command.'

It took a very long time for them to say goodbye to each other—without touching each other at all, because of course there might be many witnesses—until eventually Anna went inside the house.

She found it remarkably hard to concentrate on— well, *anything*—because her head was full of this afternoon with James, and, like a young miss with nothing else to think about than pretty dresses and ribbons, rather than the mature governess she was, wonder how long it might be until next she saw him.

Gratifyingly, she discovered within the space of less than two hours that James perhaps felt similarly, when she received a card in the handwriting she now recognised. The more she knew him, the more she liked his script.

She was all fingers as she fumbled to get the card out of its envelope, so keen was she to read its contents.

She found when she opened it that he had written in entirely formal language, with no reference to anything inappropriate. She was heartily relieved, because one never knew when something might fall into other hands, but also she was a little disappointed, she realised.

The import of what he had written did not disappoint, however; he wished to make an arrangement now to take her back to Gunter's to continue their ice-tasting experience. As soon as possible, he had suggested.

Anna knew that it would be very silly to repeat what they had done. She also knew that she couldn't think of anything she'd rather do.

Lady Puntney had been quite outspoken about how pleased she was for Anna to continue to see Ladies Derwent and Maria, and any other friend she might wish to meet. And it was quite unexceptionable for a lady to visit Gunter's alone with a male friend. And she would probably meet James again at her godmother's next literary soirée. It could do no harm to meet him on occasion. She was sure they wouldn't be silly enough to kiss again.

Before she could change her mind, because it really was quite tedious going back and forth with pros and cons in her mind, she dashed off an acceptance of his invitation. She would look forward to seeing him again, but just for the ices. Nothing else.

The next morning dawned grey, the clouds in the sky heavy with water. By the time breakfast was finished, the heavens had opened and Anna had to acknowledge that she would not be able to take the girls for their usual morning walk; they would get drenched if they left the house.

It was the first day since she'd begun her role as governess that they weren't able to go out at all in the morning, and it was—as she could have predicted—not particularly enjoyable; the girls steadily became less well-behaved than usual, and Anna began to feel as though the four walls of the house were closing around them.

Finally, at around half past three in the afternoon, the rain had cleared up and the sky was cloudless.

Anna, with Elsie's assistance, hurried the girls into their outer garments and boots and set off as quickly as possible, just in case the clouds were going to change their minds and return.

As she did every time she walked out of the house now, since the duke—James—had told her that he lived in Berkeley Square, which was adjacent to Bruton Street, she couldn't help wondering whether she might bump into him while she was out.

It was *impossible*, she was finding, not to think about him quite regularly when she was inside the house too.

And, as they walked into the park at this very different time of day from usual, it was impossible not to look into each of the carriages of the fashionable people that they passed, just in case she saw him…

He wasn't in any of them.

Until…there he was.

Anna almost gasped out loud at the sight of his now achingly familiar profile and broad shoulders.

Her lips began to form into a smile and then she suddenly realised that he was not alone in the carriage. He was accompanying two ladies.

One of them was his mother; Anna recognised her from the ball.

The other…was a very young and very beautiful lady, who Anna did not recognise.

Perhaps she was the duke's sister, Anna told herself.

Except…she did not resemble James or his mother at all.

And the expression of extreme politeness on James's face indicated that she was not a sibling. Anna had met enough people with siblings to be aware that they rarely behaved together as though they were only acquaintances.

James was driving with another young lady. And his mother.

Which surely could only mean one thing.

He was planning to marry the young lady.

'This way,' she told the girls and Elsie a little more sharply than she'd intended, shepherding them as quickly as she could down the first path she saw, desperate for James not to see her.

She was *so* humiliated, she thought as she sniffed back tears. And the lady should feel humiliated too, of course, because he had been doing *that* with Anna while about to become, or perhaps already, affianced to her.

Actually, she thought, staring hard at a tree trunk as though that might give her inspiration, he couldn't already be betrothed. If he were, he could hardly risk being seen at Gunter's with Anna.

Gunter's. Should she still go there again with him? She didn't know. Should she write him a vicious note saying she had seen him with someone else and both she and the other lady deserved better than that and she never wished to see him again? Although maybe she would like to say that in person. Or perhaps she should just ignore him when he arrived in Bruton Street. That would be petty, though, and she didn't want to be petty, however badly he might have behaved.

Maybe she would go with him to Gunter's, enjoy his conversation in a very dignified manner and then tell him at the end that she would not be seeing him again and that she wished him well. And perhaps she would mention that she had seen him with the other young lady. Perhaps that would be the most dignified approach, with the added benefit of telling him that she *knew*.

Yes, that was what she was going to do.

She still felt *very* low, though. Which was of course very, very silly, because she had known all along that dukes did not marry governesses. And she didn't even *want* to get married.

And, since it was silly, she was going to pull herself together and concentrate on the children.

She gave a huge sniff—rather a honking one, which caused the girls to stare at her and Elsie to ask if she was quite all right—and gave them all a big smile. The Duke of Amscott was *nothing* to her. A mere acquaintance. She was not going to let him affect her at *all*.

The next afternoon, she went shopping for paints with Lady Derwent, who had decided that she would like to produce some watercolours.

Anna decided on the way there that she would not mention *anything* about the duke.

And she stuck to her decision very well until, as they were standing deliberating in Ackermann's Emporium, she saw on the other side of the shop the young lady with whom the duke had been driving yesterday.

'Who is that?' she asked her godmother in a whisper.

'Lady Catherine Rainsford,' Lady Derwent told her, still concentrating on the picture frames between which she was choosing. And then she suddenly looked up at Anna, her eyes slightly narrowed. 'Why do you ask?'

'No reason,' Anna said airily.

'I have seen the Duke of Amscott with her a few times. I believe that his mother is perhaps promoting a match between them. I have not seen great enthusiasm from his side, however.'

'Oh, I see,' Anna murmured.

It did make more sense that spending time with Lady Catherine had not been entirely the duke's choice, but it underscored the fact that he and Anna really could not continue as friends or acquaintances or whatever they were any longer.

She would meet him one final time tomorrow. And she might as well enjoy that meeting as much as she could before she finally told him that they must no longer see each other.

Chapter Ten

James

Three days after he'd last been with Anna, five minutes before the time he'd agreed with her, James drove up Bruton Street, already smiling at the thought of seeing her again.

He'd missed her, more than it should be possible to miss someone whom you last saw less than half a week ago. He wanted to hear what she'd been doing and thinking, and he wanted to tell her countless small anecdotes about what he'd been doing, from the most mundane, like what he'd eaten, to the social events he had been to and the gossip, through to important things like decisions he was making about his estates. He would also like to ask her opinion on when his seventeen-year-old sister, Jane, should make her come-out.

She was fast becoming—had already become—someone with whom he felt that he wanted to share everything: of *course* the lovemaking, although that really ought not to happen again, but also, really, *everything* else.

He couldn't help feeling that that might not be a good thing, but he also couldn't help just wanting very much to see her.

She was ready when he arrived, dressed this time in a mid-blue, delightfully form-fitting pelisse and a jaunty-looking hat.

'Good afternoon. You are looking very well.' He took her hand and kissed her fingers.

'Thank you.' Her smile had the same effect on him that it had done each time since he had first seen it, at the ball, and he beamed at her in response.

Then he frowned. Her smile—while always beautiful—was in fact not quite so wide as usual, as though she felt some constraint.

'Are you quite all right?' he asked her.

'Yes, thank you. I…' She paused, and then looked him directly in the eye. 'Yes, I am, thank you.'

And then she walked with him to his curricle, and as he handed her up into it, she seemed completely herself again.

He realised, once he had her settled on the curricle seat with a blanket around her legs and had jumped up on his own side, that he had so many things to speak about with her that he didn't know where to begin.

He should be polite, of course, and ask in greater detail how she was.

'Very well, thank you,' she replied, 'although I am at grave risk of becoming very tired again thanks to *Evelina*, which I started two days ago and am enjoying almost as much as I enjoyed *Emma*.'

'I am very pleased that you are enjoying it, and shall read it myself when I have finished *Emma*. And I am also very pleased that you have immediately led the conversation in this direction, as I—genuinely—very much wished to enquire about your thoughts on the relationship between Emma and Mr Knightley.'

'Your Grace…'

'James?'

'James.' She twinkled at him as she spoke his name and he nearly dropped his reins. She was so very alluring. 'Am I to understand that the man who told me recently that he did not read fiction is not only reading it but *enjoying* it?'

'That is correct.' He couldn't remember the last time he had read a work of fiction, and he didn't think he'd *ever* read something quite so…*romantic*…but he was not ashamed to say that he was enjoying it greatly.

'I would like to take sole credit for your epiphany but must allow that there were many others present at the salon, so I must share it.'

'No, no, it is all you.' He smiled at her. 'I assure you that there was no other lady there who could inspire me to stay up far too late at night.'

She gasped and he said, 'Reading, I mean.'

Anna visibly swallowed and then laughed, and said, 'I am flattered, Your Grace.'

'So you should be. Every tutor I ever had, as well as my schoolmasters and dons, would be deeply impressed. And now tell me your thoughts on Emma and Mr Knightley before your head is turned by my compliments.'

'Well. How far along in the story are you? I do not wish to spoil the end for you.'

They did not stop talking about *Emma* until after they

arrived at Gunter's, when they had to break to place their order.

'I must tell you,' James said, 'that I take full credit for introducing you to these ices, in the same way that you have introduced me to Miss Austen's works, and as such I allowed myself to order a special ice for you, with a flavour combination that I hope you will like.'

'Oh, how exciting.'

'I feel that you should also choose another four to sample. In case you do not like the one that I chose. And you are certainly under no obligation to say that you like it.'

Anna laughed. 'I am sure I shall. Thank you!'

'I think that you should withhold your thanks until you have tasted it. Now, which others would you like?'

'I feel that it should be a joint decision.'

'No, no; you chose very well last time and I think we should maintain tradition.'

'In that case…'

She chose lemon, carrot, cinnamon and Gruyere cheese. When she had finished ordering, James said, 'And we would like a little artichoke ice cream as well, if possible.'

'You're very clever,' Anna said approvingly. 'We will need to compare the best of these against the artichoke so that we may find the best of all.'

'Exactly. And I am really not sure what I wish to happen: will we be sad if artichoke is removed from its position of superiority or will we be delighted to have found something even more delicious?'

Anna frowned and nodded with an air of great seriousness. 'You pose a very important philosophical question.'

James laughed and reflected yet again that he couldn't imagine a better way of spending an afternoon.

When the ices came, Anna said, 'I am quite agog to see what flavour you asked especially for.'

'Chicken and asparagus,' James said, as the waiter got them ready for them.

'Oh, those are my two favourite foods.'

'I remember from the ball. I think I remember everything you have said to me.'

'Oh!' The little squeak she gave made James smile a lot. 'Thank you!'

After a pause, she said, 'We must taste it first, at exactly the same time.'

They took their spoons, and…the taste was…odd.

'I like it excessively,' said Anna, in a most determined manner.

'I must own,' James said, 'that it is not my favourite.'

'I like it very much.' Anna took another spoonful.

'You really don't have to,' said James as she failed to hide a quite alarming wince.

'I really do like it very much—' she looked a little as though she was going to be sick '—and I am extremely grateful for the lovely gesture, but I think it would be remiss in me not to try the other flavours.'

In the end, they determined lemon to be as good a flavour as artichoke but no better, and Anna had admitted that while she was extremely grateful that he had remembered her favourite food, she would not choose to eat chicken ice cream again.

'I foresee that we will have to return here many times to determine the absolute best,' he said, as they prepared to leave. He looked over at her, smiling at him with laughter in her eyes, and wondered if it was possible that his heart had just actually turned over.

He had fully intended to drive her straight home after they had finished their ice creams, with no detour during which any lovemaking of any kind might occur. And of course, he should certainly not kiss her again, as he had no thought—well, he didn't know whether he did or not, but he probably didn't—of proposing to her. As he'd determined before, he did not wish to experience any further loss, and marrying someone he loved would of course endanger him in that way. So they ought to go straight home. But on the other side of the coin, it would be a shame for her to have no further driving practice.

'Would you like to take the reins for a short while?' he asked. 'When I have driven us somewhere a little less crowded again.'

'Oh, yes, thank you, I would.' She hesitated, and then said, 'There should be no need for us to stop along the way, though, I think.'

Which was of course ideal. It really was. Really.

Her driving was genuinely impressive and he allowed her to take the reins by herself for a while—she was a very fast learner—and James genuinely did not intend that they stop along the way…

But somehow, when she handed the reins back to him, and their hands brushed, and she smiled up at him in *that* way, he was unable to resist the temptation just to give her the tiniest of kisses, and she responded in a way that he had not entirely expected but did very much appreciate. And then it would have been, well, really quite impolite, had he not secured the reins so that he could kiss her for just a little longer, and then it seemed that neither of them wished to stop kissing. And more.

And this time it was even better than before, because this time, while they were still exploring each other, they also already knew a little about what the other liked. James realised that a man could happily spend a lifetime making Anna shudder and moan in just that way.

When they finally finished, and he was trying to help her tame her markedly dishevelled locks and adjust her clothing to an acceptable state, all he could do was smile.

'You are very, very beautiful,' he murmured in her ear as he smoothed her pelisse into place over her extremely well-formed breasts and she shivered again under his touch.

He was beginning to think that he might have fallen in love.

Did he *want* to be in love?

On the way back into London, he managed to lead quite naturally, he hoped, into a question he very much wanted to ask. 'Tell me more about your parents?' It felt odd that, though they now had a very strong connection and he knew so much about her tastes in ices, literature, travel ambitions and stripy food, he knew absolutely nothing about her background.

'They were… I'm not sure how to describe them. That is not a question that I've been asked very often. Or ever, perhaps. Since I…lost them, no one has asked.'

And she had not answered the question in the slightest. Would it be rude of him to ask again?

'I'd very much like to hear if you would like to tell

me.' He would not repeat the question if she brushed him off this time.

'My father was…hard to describe. I remember him laughing with his friends. My mother was very kind and enjoyed helping others.' And that was that. She sounded very final; she clearly did not wish to say any more.

James realised that he didn't wish to know just about their personalities. He also wanted to know *who* they were, how they had spent their lives. He wasn't sure whether he *ought* to want to know those things: did they really matter or was it enough that they were *kind*? If he hoped to make Anna his duchess, though—which, thinking rationally about what he *wanted* in a wife, he still wasn't sure he did, but supposing he did—the world, Society, would want to know those things about her parents.

Did he want to make her his duchess? He just did not know. The desire that he felt for her was one thing. He could manage that. The love for her that he felt building inside him, though: he was not sure whether he could cope with that. Because what if something happened to her, as it had to his father and brothers in such quick succession? He couldn't bear to lose her. And what if he did indeed die young, like his brothers, as his mother feared he would, and Anna loved him the way he loved her, and she was left bereft? It did not bear thinking about; he was almost shuddering at the horror of it.

'Tell me about your father and brothers?' Anna asked at that exact moment.

Was she a mind reader, or was that a natural question following his to her?

'My father was unfashionably and unashamedly most

attached to his family and very much enjoyed spending time with us. He enjoyed hunting and shooting and fencing, and took my brothers and me out with him as soon as we were out of leading strings. And my brothers were both, I suppose, very similar to me in personality and tastes.'

He had also, he realised, described *them* as opposed to their status in life, but Anna *knew* who they were. And he had mentioned his father's activities, whereas after what Anna had said he was none the wiser about her parents' tastes.

'They sound wonderful,' she said. 'I'm so sorry for your loss.'

'And I for yours.' He reached out to squeeze her hand and she squeezed his back.

He was probably reading too much into her choice of words. It was after all difficult talking about relatives one mourned. Perhaps she had said all she could bear to say at this point.

When they reached Bruton Street, he felt a strong urge to ask Anna now when they could meet again. It was beginning to feel to him as though the days on which he did not see her were empty.

He did not ask, however.

'Thank you again; I very much enjoyed the afternoon,' he told her. And then he watched her inside before driving off.

He needed to restrain himself until he had made sure of his own intentions. He did not want to hurt her and so if he did not have serious intentions he should probably stop seeing her. She would be utterly ruined if anyone saw what they had done.

And, good God, he had run quite mad. After what they had done, he owed it to her—irrespective of his thoughts on love within marriage—to marry her. Of course he did. He should propose to her very soon. He...

Now was not the time, though.

He needed a little more time to think.

He should perhaps pay a call to Lady Derwent.

The next afternoon he was seated in Lady Derwent's drawing room wishing that he had called at almost *any* other time, or agreed in advance a particular time to see her; she had been taking tea with three dowagers when he arrived and they were all *extremely* interested to see him.

'Amscott, how are your dear mothers and sisters?' Lady Forcet asked him.

Time dragged as the ladies drew from him very small details about his family's health and whereabouts and marital intentions.

'None,' he said shortly in reference to his five youngest sisters.

Eventually, after he had wasted a good half hour of his life in her drawing room, Lady Derwent took pity on him and said, 'Perhaps we might drive in the park together, Amscott. You may call for me at half past four tomorrow.'

Twenty-five hours later, James was finally able to speak to Lady Derwent alone.

'I had expected you to bring your curricle,' she said as he handed her up into the chaise he had brought, assuming that she would not want to ride in a curricle. 'I am not in my dotage yet, thank you.'

He laughed. 'I must apologise. I will bear that in mind for any future drives we take together.'

As they moved forward, he opened his mouth to ask her immediately about Anna, but was thwarted when she began to talk to him about the weather. She continued onto the latest gossip from Court, and then the weather again, and then some exclamations about how bare the trees seemed now. And then the weather again.

Finally, she began to describe—in stunning detail—the exhibition at the Royal Academy that she had been to earlier in the week. She began with descriptions of what every lady she had seen there had been wearing, while James began to wonder if he would be able to speak at *all* during the drive, or whether this would be a wasted afternoon from the perspective of finding out a little more about Anna.

And then Lady Derwent moved on to talking about some of the paintings, before saying, 'My goddaughter would certainly appreciate the exhibition. Perhaps you should take her.'

Finally!

'Perhaps I should,' James said. 'I do not, however, know whether Miss Blake is particularly interested in art.'

'I am sure she would enjoy it.'

'Has Miss Blake visited many art exhibitions before now?'

'One or two only, I imagine.' Lady Derwent smiled at him. 'I commend you for hiding your frustration so admirably during the first part of our drive.'

'I assure you that I have enjoyed your company during the entirety of this afternoon,' James said cautiously.

'Fiddlesticks. The only reason that you wanted to see me was to ask me about Miss Blake, was it not?'

'A little,' said James, trying not to wince, 'but I am also enjoying the drive and hearing your views on other topics.'

'Gammon.' Lady Derwent rolled her eyes so thoroughly that James was worried she might give herself a headache. 'Enquire of me whatever you like about my goddaughter, and I will answer you where I am able and deem it acceptable.'

Good God. James was suddenly almost nervous. He had been trying to ask such questions for some time, and now he had carte blanche to ask what he liked. What if he did not like the answers? Also, was this really acceptable? To ask questions about Miss Blake to which she might not like him to know the answers?

It was not acceptable, he realised. He would *like* to find out everything about her, but he could not in all conscience go behind her back like this. He could not ask Lady Derwent a question about Anna that he would not ask her directly.

He was quite sure, however, that Lady Derwent had only Anna's best interests at heart.

Perhaps his best course of action was honesty.

In moderation. He was not going to disclose what had happened between him and Anna on their ice-tasting afternoons.

'In truth,' he said, hoping that he was indeed about to speak the truth, because he wouldn't like to lie to Lady Derwent, 'I did intend to ask you some questions about Miss Blake, but on reflection I find that I should not ask you anything about her that I would not ask her to her face. And therefore I do not have anything to ask about her.'

'I see.' Lady Derwent observed him for an unnervingly long time through her lorgnette, for so long in fact that James found himself struggling to keep his focus on his horses and the road.

Eventually, she cleared her throat and said, 'May I ask your intentions towards my goddaughter?'

James gave an involuntary twitch and caused one of his horses to stop for a moment, and the carriage to lurch a little.

'I must apologise,' he said, when he had them back under control a few moments later. 'I cannot remember the last time I drove so badly.'

'Perhaps you also cannot remember the last time someone asked you if you intended to marry their goddaughter or not.'

This time James laughed rather than jobbing his horses' mouths, which was an improvement.

'That is true,' he said.

'And what is your answer?'

'I...' This was not good. He should really have thought of this when he decided to call on Lady Derwent.

'Yes?'

'I admire Miss Blake very much,' he said. 'She is a most...admirable young woman.'

'Do you intend to propose to her, though? Do you love her?'

'I...' Good God. What if Lady Derwent relayed the import of this conversation to Anna? And what would Anna's thoughts be at this moment in time? 'I am not certain and—without wishing to sound arrogant and assuming that anyone to whom I might propose marriage would accept—I would not wish to raise anyone's hopes of a proposal—which of course they might or might not choose to accept or be happy about—before I knew myself what I intended.'

He did intend to propose, he was certain of that now, but he did not wish his proposal to be via Lady Derwent as proxy.

'So you called on me with the intention of asking about Anna? And then thought better of it because you did not feel it fair to ask about something that you would not ask her directly.'

James nodded ruefully. 'That is correct,' he said. 'I cannot ask you anything that Miss Blake would not choose to tell me herself.'

'That is laudable. If a little dull.'

'Thank you?'

Lady Derwent ignored him and continued, 'I am going to give you one important piece of information. I am also going to give you a warning.'

'Indeed?'

'I will begin with the warning. Do not trifle with my goddaughter's heart. She is a wonderful young lady and I should not like to see her upset.'

'I would not like to upset her,' James said.

'That is good. I understand that you have been seen with other young ladies, including Lady Catherine Rainsford. For everyone's sake, you would be wise to make your choice sooner rather than later.'

'Yes.'

Lady Derwent was, he had to admit, correct; and it

was right and proper that she should attempt to protect her goddaughter.

'I would not like to upset Miss Blake,' he repeated.

Lady Derwent ignored him again. 'The information that I think you might like to have concerns Anna's birth.'

James did of course wish to learn such information, but, the more he thought about it, the more uneasy he felt about betraying Anna's trust—such as she might have—and speaking about her in her absence.

'I'm not sure…' he began.

'Nonsense.' Lady Derwent spoke over him before he could finish his objection. 'She is the granddaughter of an earl.'

And there he had it, or part of it. Her background.

He couldn't tell whether he had been expecting that or not. Part of him, he realised, had worried that she might be of low birth, which would make marriage between them more difficult. His mother was a stickler for tradition and good breeding, although he hoped that her wish for him to be happy would transcend any feeling that the woman he married might not be of exactly the family his mother would have chosen. He had also, however, been quite sure all along that Anna was a lady.

'A particularly august earl,' Lady Derwent continued. 'Of a very old family. Anna's grandfather was the late Earl of Broome. The ninth earl.'

James frowned. He knew, distantly, of the Earl of Broome. The new—tenth—earl was young, younger than him. Perhaps something had happened within the family of the sort that he and his mother worried might happen if he, James, died without issue. Perhaps the earldom had passed to a distant cousin who had not provided for Anna on the death of her mother. The cur. If the man were in front of him now, James would want to throttle him. How could he live with the knowledge that his cousin was now forced to work as a governess? Surely the man could make her an allowance of enough to live modestly without working?

Perhaps he would ask his mother about the earl. Perhaps not, on second thought, or not until he had made up his mind exactly when—and how—he would propose to Anna.

Because, yes, of *course* he was going to propose to her. He had to. He had compromised a young lady of quality and it was irrelevant whether or not anyone else knew. *He* knew. He had to do the right thing by her.

Good God. He was going to propose to Anna. As soon as he could.

And if she accepted, they would marry. They would be husband and wife.

And that would be…well, it would be a lot of things.

It would be terrifying, because, obviously, due to the fact that she was wonderful in every way, he would end up—if he wasn't already—deeply in love with her. His wife. And so, if anything happened to her, he would be heartbroken, bereft.

But it would also be exhilarating, life-affirming, perfect… Because being married to Anna would enable him to see her every day: talk to her, laugh with her, make love to her, just *be* with her.

He would be the luckiest man alive.

He realised suddenly that he had been staring ahead while he thought, completely ignoring Lady Derwent.

'I must apologise,' he said. 'My thoughts were elsewhere. Thank you for letting me know.'

'There is no need to apologise. I presume you were thinking of my goddaughter.'

James inclined his head.

'I must remind you.' Her tone had hardened significantly. 'I would expect to hear either a happy announcement in relation to you and Anna, or nothing at all. That is to say: you must not trifle with her affections. If you do not intend to marry her, I would expect you no longer to spend any time with her. Her work as a governess does not preclude her from marrying and I do not wish her reputation to be sullied by you.'

'Of course.' James had nothing further to add, because he was certainly not going to tell Lady Derwent before he asked Anna that he hoped very much that Anna would like to marry him.

He would have liked Anna to have told him herself about her background, but he understood that it must be very hurtful and humiliating effectively being rejected by one's own family, and perhaps it was something that she did not feel she could discuss with anyone. Hopefully, in time, she would feel that she was able to confide in him—hopefully her husband.

Now he just needed to plan his proposal.

The next morning, after much thought, he sent a note inviting Anna to the opera that evening. She had mentioned in passing that she had never been, and he had been sure that, while she was not a woman to evince any self-pity, he had caught a wistful note in her voice.

He had been careful in his planning not to organise an

evening that might compromise her; he had also invited Lady Derwent—and had received her acceptance before he penned his invitation to Anna—as well as his mother, his married sister and her husband, and two or three other friends, and had told Anna that he was doing so.

He had thought long and hard about the timing of the opera trip. Should it be before or after he proposed—assuming she accepted the proposal? He had decided that it would be more comfortable for Anna to enter into a betrothal with him if she already knew his mother and sister a little better. And from their side, if they got to know her, they could not fail to like her, and he would wish his family and his wife to get on well together.

He was sure that Lady Derwent would then happily allow him to escort Anna home himself while she travelled in her own carriage.

He waited on tenterhooks for Anna's reply and was heartily relieved when he received an acceptance of his invitation within three hours of issuing it. Now he just needed to wait for the evening to come.

Chapter Eleven

Anna

Anna had just arrived back from her morning walk with the girls when she received James's card. As she had looked at the envelope and recognised his handwriting, her heart had—annoyingly—quickened, and she had decided to put it to one side and open it later. She had resolved yesterday evening not to continue her outings with him, however much she might like ice creams. And his company. And what they'd done together in the carriage each time.

She had been very lucky that no one had seen them on the three occasions that they had kissed—and more— and she couldn't risk being caught in such a compromising situation.

In addition, she had, she realised, developed feelings for James that were much stronger than mere liking, and she did not wish to have her heart broken. He would clearly not contemplate marrying her, as evidenced by his dallying with her in this way; she was sure that dukes did not do such things with young ladies of quality. Clearly, therefore, he knew her to be inferior to him socially, and that was why he had behaved the way he had. Equally clear was that he would need to marry and produce at least one heir relatively soon.

She did not wish to be heartbroken when he married someone else—Lady Catherine Rainsford for example—and she did not wish there to be any possibility that he might attempt to set her up as his mistress. Everyone knew that even the nicest of men behaved quite awfully in this regard.

So she hoped very much that he would be happy with whomever he married and she was glad—honestly, she was—that it wouldn't be her. Being deeply in love with one's own husband was a recipe for deep unhappiness. Dukes frequently had affairs outside marriage. Everyone knew that. Even if they did not abandon their wives in the way that her father had left her mother.

It was for the best, then, no longer to see each other. She did not wish to be any more heartbroken than she had to be.

Before she had opened the note, she had spoken quite sternly to herself. She would not accept whatever invitation it might contain.

Except…oh!

He had invited her to the opera with her godmother—who had apparently already indicated to him that she would be attending—together with his own mother and sister, and several other people.

Perhaps he held her in higher esteem than she had thought. It could not be possible—surely—that he would introduce her to his mother and sister in such a small group if he had dishonourable intentions towards her. Even though she was a governess and he had driven in the park with Lady Catherine between his two outings with Anna?

Or did he just regard her as a friend whom he would like to introduce to other friends? *Could* a duke openly have a governess as a friend?

Did he perhaps have intimate relations with all sorts of women? Anna had pushed that thought out of her mind as fast as it had entered; it did not make her feel good.

Whatever James's intentions, it must be quite unexceptionable to visit the opera with her own godmother as guests of a duke and his wider family and friends, and she would very much like to have the opportunity to go. There could be no risk on such an occasion of them succumbing to any temptation to kiss, so it could surely do no harm.

Once she had decided that, she had asked Lady Puntney if she would be happy for her to go. Her employer had, as usual, been quite delighted at her governess's moving in such august circles, and had told her 'dearest Miss Blake' that she must of course attend, and must enjoy herself as much as she could during her evenings off, so there had been nothing preventing Anna from accepting the invitation.

'Good evening, my dear,' Lady Derwent greeted her when—as agreed by an exchange of notes during the afternoon—Anna entered her godmother's carriage later that day. 'That mantle is most becoming; I am so glad that we bought it.'

The mantle in question was powder blue and lined and trimmed with fur and sewn with gold thread, and worn over a pale green silk evening dress. Both garments had been among Lady Derwent's more extravagant gifts to Anna, and she adored them both.

'Thank you. I am very grateful to you; I like it exceedingly.' She returned her godmother's embrace and said, 'You are also looking particularly fine this evening.'

Lady Derwent adjusted her own mantle into place and then spread her heavily beringed hands in front of her and regarded them with a complacent air.

'Yes, I think I am,' she said, which made them both laugh.

Laughing with her reminded Anna of laughing with James.

And this was silly. Really, *anything* nice reminded her of him. She wondered… She didn't want to wonder. She should *not* wonder; even if he did for some strange reason perhaps wish to…well, she couldn't even think it, but if he did wish something honourable, she was sure he would change his mind if he knew about the scandal of her parents' elopement and the fact that her father had been a groom.

If it began to look as though his intentions really might be honourable, she would have to tell him about her parents, as soon as possible.

The fact that he was introducing her to his mother did indicate that…

No, she mustn't think it.

She must, however, decide whether, should such a

thing occur, she would disclose the truth about her parents or just say no with no explanation.

When they arrived at the Theatre Royal, where they were to watch the opera, James was waiting in the road to meet them.

As he handed Anna down from the carriage, he applied just a little more pressure to her hand than might be usual, and fixed her with a particular look which made her feel quite warm inside; the look seemed to signal that he was extremely pleased to see her. A small smile was playing about his lips as he looked at her, and his eyes were focused on hers, as though she was the only other person that existed in his world.

The way he was looking at her was actually making her feel quite breathless.

'I am particularly pleased to see you here this evening,' he told her.

Anna had no words other than, 'Thank you,' accompanied by a shiver of pleasure.

As they made their way to his box, the hordes in the opera house's foyer parted easily for them due to James's broad shoulders and natural air of command. Anna could not remember a time when she had felt more protected within a crowd. It was a sensation that anyone would surely revel in.

The box was entirely velvet and gilt and felt beautifully luxurious. Glancing up, Anna saw that the ceiling was also very intricately decorated, with blue panels, relieved by white and enriched by gold.

James's entire *life* was luxury. She wondered briefly how he would feel about her if he knew that after her mother's death before Lady Derwent had effectively rescued her she had been living in a very small and somewhat damp cottage with a friend of her mother's, a Miss Shepson, another gentlewoman who had fallen on hard times, and had been forced to take in sewing to try to earn a few pennies so that she had money enough to eat. Heating had been a luxury she could not often afford, so both ladies had enjoyed the summer months considerably more than the winter ones.

'Miss Blake, you have already met my mother, the dowager duchess. I am not sure you are acquainted with my sister Lady Mallow and her husband, Lord Mallow.'

'I am very pleased to meet you.' Lady Mallow patted the empty chair next to her. 'Come and sit next to me so that we may talk more easily. You must call me Sybilla.'

'Thank you. And you must call me Anna.'

She and Sybilla exchanged mutual smiles, and immediately began a very comfortable cose; it quickly felt as though they had known each other for quite some time.

Just before the opera—Mozart's *The Magic Flute*—began, James made his way to the seat next to Anna's, on the other side from Sybilla, and Anna could not help feeling that there could be no more enjoyable way to be seated. Other than alone with James in his carriage but that was quite inappropriate and should not—could not—happen again, and she should not even think about it.

'Are you too warm?' James asked her in an undertone. 'Your cheeks are a little red.'

'Oh, no! I just…' She wondered what he would say—or indeed *do*—if she told him that she had been blushing at her own scandalous thoughts, involving him… 'I am very well, thank you, and it is the perfect temperature in here. I am very much looking forward to the performance.'

'I am pleased to hear it. And I too am looking forward to it; I shall very much enjoy watching it with you.'

Sitting next to James in the near darkness, knowing that he was so close to her, almost able to touch him without moving far, knowing what he felt like and how it felt when he touched her but prevented from doing anything of that nature by the presence of his sister on her other side and the others in their group around them was quite overwhelming.

The performance was wonderful. Anna was transported to ancient Egypt and fully engrossed in the story. Knowing that she was sharing it with James made it an even more intense experience.

When the interval came, she realised that she was almost tearful from the beauty of the story and the singing. It was blissful to be able to discuss and exclaim over the performance with James and his sister, and to witness their funning with each other and the sibling bond they shared.

A few minutes into the interval, there was some movement around the box. Sybilla rose to go and speak to a cousin, and another lady seated herself in her place.

James had just started saying something, but was interrupted by the lady in Sybilla's seat leaning very rudely across Anna as though she were a piece of furniture rather than an actual person, and saying, 'I should love to hear your views on this particular production of *The Magic Flute*, Your Grace.'

Anna couldn't work out whether she was more annoyed by the rudeness or sad about the very strong reminder that James—the lofty Duke of Amscott—could not possibly contemplate, even if he wanted to, marrying a woman like Anna. If someone were this rude when they believed her to be of acceptable birth, then how much ruder or dismissive would they be if they knew about her parents?

She glanced up at James and saw that his eyes were suddenly like flints and his expression rigid.

'I believe that introductions have not been performed,' he said in chilly tones. 'Miss Blake, this is Mrs Chilcott, an acquaintance of my mother's. Mrs Chilcott, this is Miss Blake, a particular friend of my family's and goddaughter of Lady Derwent.'

Anna smiled at him and tried not to feel horrified about the fact that her presence had caused James to be in this position.

'Oh. Miss Blake. Yes. Forgive me… I'm not quite sure…' The lady raised one eyebrow in a very haughty fashion. Anna stared back at her, quite taken aback at her rudeness.

'Not sure about…?' James's voice was now so cold it could have frozen water. 'As I said, Miss Blake is Lady Derwent's goddaughter and is also known by my mother. I am surprised that you do not know her, but she is recently arrived in town, and perhaps you were not at my mother's ball, where you would have met her.'

'Of course I was at your mother's ball,' the lady trilled. 'You and I conversed for quite ten minutes.'

'Forgive me.' The Duke's voice was still as hard as

stone. 'It was a busy evening for me and I spoke to a great many people.'

Anna did her best to smile as the lady began to brush over her rudeness in the face of the Duke's evident distaste for it, but it was difficult. Quite aside from the fact that men were not to be trusted, _this_ was why she would never be able to marry someone of his standing in Society. When it became known that she was the product of her mother's scandalous elopement with one of Anna's grandfather's grooms, she would regularly be the subject of this kind of rudeness, and it would be very difficult for her husband. How long would it be until he tired of the difficulty?

'Indeed,' said James for about the fifth time in response to yet another opening sally from Mrs Chilcott.

Eventually, Mrs Chilcott rose and said, 'It has been most pleasant to converse.'

Anna smiled blandly and James inclined his head the merest fraction, and Mrs Chilcott turned and left in what could only be described as a flouncing manner.

'I'm so sorry,' James said. 'I abhor such rudeness.'

'No, no; it was my presence that caused it.'

'Well, it _was_ your presence, but it was not _you_. Many people envy a young lady who is singled out by an unmarried duke of marriageable age.'

Anna screwed her face up a little. 'I am not sure it is that; I think it is rather that she did not deem me a suitable person with whom to converse.'

'Nonsense. That could never be the case.' James's smile was so warm that Anna felt her eyes to be suddenly moist. 'Let us not waste any more time talking about someone neither of us knows; instead let me introduce you further to my mother.'

He drew Anna over to the duchess, who was conversing with Lady Derwent, and soon had all three of the ladies laughing with his observations on the evening, before asking Anna, 'What aspect of the opera have you enjoyed the most so far?'

'That is a very hard question to answer,' she said. 'It's all wonderful. The theatre itself, the way the set on the stage is designed, the costumes, the music, and of course the singing and acting. I would find it very difficult to choose a favourite. The whole combine to make it a truly intoxicating experience.'

The duchess nodded. 'I agree. Too many people come to the opera merely to see and be seen. We must not forget that we are very lucky to witness such wonderful art on the stage.'

'That is very true, Leonora,' said Lady Derwent, and the two matrons smiled at each other. From what Anna had heard, this was a remarkable achievement on the part of James.

The three ladies found themselves in strong agreement on a variety of topics, and Anna enjoyed their conversation so much that she was almost sorry when the second half of the opera began.

As they re-seated themselves in preparation to begin watching again, James said sotto voce to Anna, 'I'm so pleased that you and my mother have established such a rapport, and that you seem to have struck up an immediate friendship with Sybilla.'

A shiver ran all the way down Anna from the back of her neck almost to her toes. It was nice—she thought—

to know that it was unlikely he would do her the dishonour of wishing to set her up as his mistress; no one sane would introduce their paramour to their own mother. However, his clearly wishing that she and his mother become better acquainted did indicate that he might indeed be considering proposing to her.

If she were an entirely different woman, who could ever dare to entrust her heart and independence to a man, and if she were from an entirely different, scandal-free family, that might be—would be—wonderful.

But as it was it was quite awful. Rejecting him *would* be for the best because it would protect her from being tossed aside by him at some point in the future.

She would have to tell him about her parents. She *couldn't* just turn him down with no explanation. If she didn't have the opportunity to do so this evening, she would ask him for a short meeting as soon as possible.

She didn't want the opera to end. In itself, it was a wonderful spectacle, but the reason she wanted it to continue for ever was that she was quite sure that it would be the last time that she would have the opportunity to spend time with James like this. And that was deeply, deeply sad.

She didn't want to be sad. She should make the most of these last few moments, enjoy the way that when anything particularly dramatic happened he turned to her, enjoy the way their glances caught, enjoy being able to look at his handsomeness, enjoy the sensation that for now, this evening, he was *hers*.

And when he smiled at her—in that particular, just-for-her way that she *adored*—she should just drink it in, for one last time, rather than stupidly feeling her eyes fill with tears.

Eventually, too soon, the performance was over, and Anna didn't want to think about the imminent end to the evening, so instead she busied herself with chatter to the people around them.

And then everyone began to take their leave.

As she was about to thank James for a wonderful evening and say good-night—knowing that this was the last time she would see him before their friendship ended—he turned towards her godmother and spoke in a low voice to her.

Then he turned back to Anna and spoke quietly to her. 'Lady Derwent is happy for me to escort you home in my carriage; I have something most particular to ask you.'

Ohhhh, goodness.

Oh, dear.

Well. She couldn't say no to the suggestion without making a scene and drawing attention to them in a way that could do neither of them any good. And it would be the ideal opportunity for her to tell him about her parents.

So after a pause, she just said, 'Thank you.'

She would tell him everything as soon as they got into the carriage and thank him personally for the lovely times they had spent together, and then he would take her back to Bruton Street and that would be the end of things. She should not be devastated at the thought that she would not see him again; she should be grateful that she had experienced Gunter's and the opera and…all that *pleasure*…with him.

* * *

When they reached James's carriage, he held his hand out for her to take as she ascended the steps, and held on to hers for a little longer than necessary, looking into her eyes as he did so. He had his lips half pressed together, half smiling, as though he was full of happiness.

Which made Anna feel the exact opposite.

She purposely avoided his eye while she was seating herself on the forward-facing velvet-upholstered seat of the carriage, both because now that the end was so near, even just looking at him was painful, and because she didn't wish to lead him to think that she was hoping for or would accept a proposal.

She was tempted to sit right in the middle of the seat to imply that he should sit opposite her rather than next to her, and then moved towards the right-hand corner at the last minute, worried that he would still sit next to her and they would then be far too close to each other.

He closed the carriage door behind him and did indeed sit down on the same seat as her, angling his body towards hers.

She lifted her regard from the floor to him and nearly gasped at the expression on his face. It was so…well, adoring. He was just *looking*, as though his entire being was focused on her and only her, and it was so much she could barely breathe. If only she hadn't been born of scandal; if only she could trust that he wouldn't cast her aside, as her father had done to her mother. She had to tell him. And she would do so, as soon as they set off and she was certain that no one could hear their words.

And then, before the carriage had even shown any

signs of moving, James reached forward and took her hands in his, and said, 'Anna.'

'Oh,' said Anna. 'James.' No, that wasn't the right thing to say. He'd sounded as though he was speaking in a very romantic kind of way, and so did she. And she mustn't. 'James, I...'

'Anna, I have a very particular question to ask you and I'm not sure I can wait any longer.' He moved a little closer to her so that their knees were touching.

Even though she *knew* she was about to put an end to all of this, Anna's insides were turning to liquid just at his touch, which was just so silly.

She felt the carriage begin to move forward and wondered how long it would take to get back to Bruton Street. Not very long.

He leaned forward and kissed her lightly on the lips and she wanted *so much* to reach for him, pull him close to her, kiss him properly. But no. She must not and she needed to stop him before he said anything that he would clearly regret later.

She wriggled backwards a little, and said, 'James, no, I...' She had to tell him *now*.

'I'm sorry; you are of course right. We should not... yet.'

Before she could react further, he lowered himself to one knee, re-gathered her hands in his, turned them over and pressed his lips hard to each of her palms in turn, before saying, 'Anna, dearest Anna, will you marry me?'

Oh!

No.

No.

She was—for this one moment—the luckiest woman in the world.

But really, she felt like the *un*luckiest.

She had so much she needed to say, immediately, but all she could manage was, 'Oh, oh, *James.*'

He kissed her hands again, before turning them back over and drawing them close to his chest and saying, his voice hoarse all of a sudden, 'Is that... Might I hope that that is a yes?'

Oh, no. This was truly, truly awful.

Anna closed her eyes. For one long moment she wished that she could just accept. But at some point she would *have* to tell him about her parents. And men being what they were, he would no doubt pull out of the engagement at that point. Better for both of them for her to tell him now.

She took a deep, juddering breath before trying to pull her hands away.

'I'm so sorry.' Her words were little more than a whisper; it was as though her voice did not work properly any more. 'I cannot marry you.'

He froze for a moment, and then let go of her hands and bowed his head briefly before slowly rising and sitting down on the seat behind him, opposite Anna.

The space between them suddenly seemed huge.

'I'm so sorry,' he said in a horribly croaky voice, after an awful silence. 'I had perhaps misunderstood; I believed... That is to say... Of course. Might I... There is of course no obligation to reply but might I ask your reason?' His voice, his demeanour seemed horrifyingly diminished somehow.

Anna had never seen him like this before and it was

dreadful. Previously he'd always seemed so big and strong—he *was* big and strong—but big and strong in spirit as well as body. He'd always seemed in command of every situation, confident, powerful.

It was terrible to think that her words could have reduced him somehow, and she very much needed to explain to him that her reason did not relate to *him*, it related to *her*.

She couldn't believe that at any point she had imagined that she might refuse a proposal without giving him a reason. She could never in reality bear him to think that she might not love him. No one—pauper or duke—should be led to believe that they were unlovable.

'Of course I will tell you the reason,' she said, despising herself for the fact that her voice was wobbling.

She drew a deep breath.

'I am not someone you can marry,' she told him when she was certain that she had command of her voice. 'I am not an appropriate wife for a duke.' She felt a tear dribble down her cheek and wiped it away with her fingers. 'I want you to know that any woman—lady—would be very lucky to marry you. It is not that you are not an acceptable husband; it is entirely that I am not an acceptable wife.'

'Anna. No.' James rose from his bench and moved back to sit next to her. 'That is not true.' He put his arm round her and pulled her against him with one arm before with his other hand very gently wiping the tears that were now coursing freely down her face.

Anna gave a gigantic sniff and said, 'It is.'

'No.' He pulled her even closer and kissed her forehead. 'Never. You are funny, kind, interesting, clever, wonderful, and of course very beautiful. You have all the attributes that any man could ever desire in a wife.'

Anna sniffed even harder, but nothing could prevent her tears now. She couldn't imagine a more wonderful set of compliments. All given under false pretences, of course, because she was not who he thought she was.

James wiped her tears again with his fingers, and then, taking her chin in his hand, gently turned her face towards his and then lowered his mouth to hers.

Anna allowed herself to return his kiss for one long—blissful—moment, before drawing back a little and saying, 'No, you don't understand, I can't.'

'I'm sorry. Of course.' James kept his arm round her but didn't attempt to kiss her again.

'I need to tell you something.' She took another breath, wiped under her eyes again, and squared her shoulders within the circle of his arm. 'You are wonderful. I have enjoyed spending time with you so very much.'

'Thank you. And I you.'

'I do very much wish you to know that.' She had to tell him *now* but it was hard to get the words out.

'I have also enjoyed myself with you very greatly.' He smiled at her and it felt as though her heart might crack.

When he reached for her again, she allowed herself for one moment to be drawn into his arms, to feel one last time the strength of his arms around her, his body against hers. If only she could stay here for ever.

As she clung to him, her face buried against his chest, she heard him say, his voice sounding impossibly deep, 'Anna, I love you, so very, very much.'

'I love you too,' she whispered, and then she lifted

her face to his, even though she shouldn't, because she couldn't prevent herself.

It was inevitable that they would kiss. There was passion, fire, and on Anna's side huge regret and sadness at what she knew was coming.

They kissed urgently and hard, before their hands found each other's bodies and they began to fumble with clothing, fast, telling each other to be quick because the journey was not that long.

Soon they were both hot and panting and, *oh*, the incredible pleasure of the cleverness of James's fingers and tongue. Anna was almost tempted to *beg* him to do *everything* with her this time—one final time—but sanity—a tiny modicum at least—prevailed.

As they helped each other return their clothing to a semblance of modesty, laughing and kissing as they did so, James said again, 'I love you so much.' The happiness and laughter in his voice was heart-rending, because he was about to be told something he clearly wasn't going to want to hear.

And that thought brought Anna to her senses.

'James, we shouldn't have, *I* shouldn't have... I'm so sorry. I have to tell you.' As she spoke, she felt the carriage come to a halt. 'But I think we've arrived. I need to tell you now.'

'My coachman will not open the door; we have as long as we need.' He was still smiling at her, clearly unaware that she was about to burst the bubble of happiness he seemed to be wearing, clearly assuming that her earlier refusal had perhaps been maidenly confusion.

'I am just going to say it,' she told him. 'I have been trying to preface it with softer explanations, and that led to what just happened, which really should not have happened again.'

James's eyes had narrowed and his smile had dropped as she spoke.

'Yes?' he asked.

Anna looked away from him for a moment, and then back into his eyes.

'My father was my grandfather's second groom. My mother and he fell in love and they ran away together. It caused a great scandal, and my grandfather disowned my mother and they never saw each other again. We lived quietly in the country, in some penury.'

James shook his head, his brow furrowing, as though he couldn't immediately understand her words. 'I... I'm afraid...'

'I should have mentioned: it's even worse than that, if that were possible. I was born six months after my parents ran away together. The scandal was great. My grandfather disowned my mother. Some of her friends remained loyal to her, in particular my wonderful god-mother, Lady Derwent, but most did not. Things became even worse when I was about nine, when my father left us. He now lives in Canada. I wrote to him when my mother died, but he showed no interest. When I referred to our having lost him, I meant that he had abandoned us.' Anna looked hard at James. The duke. His face had become like a mask, with no emotion showing. 'As you can see,' she pursued, 'I am not someone the Duke of Amscott can marry.'

James was entirely silent. He had released her from his arms and was sitting, with his hands on his knees, just staring at the floor of the carriage.

Anna felt very, very cold, and quite mortified at the way her dress was still in some disarray. How could she have touched him, allowed him to touch her in that way only a few minutes ago? Now it just felt sordid, embarrassing.

This was exactly like she imagined her mother's experience had been, when she'd been rejected by her own father when she got pregnant, and then rejected by her own husband when times were hard.

She realised now that a tiny part of her had hoped that the duke might say that he did not care about her birth. But of course he cared, and was rejecting her. That was what men did.

When, after what felt a very long time, the duke raised his head, she saw that his eyes had gone unpleasantly hard.

'You lied to me,' he stated.

Anna felt herself stiffen. It mattered to her, she realised, what James thought of her probity. And it mattered, more broadly, how men treated women, and how more privileged people treated less privileged ones.

She was not going to be accused of something she had not done. Yes, her birth was undesirable, but no, she had not lied. 'No, I did not. Obviously I did go to your ball in the guise of Lady Maria, but when I did that I was not lying to *you*; it was, as you know, just a silly deception. And since then I have not lied to you at all. I have not at any point pretended to be anything other than an impecunious governess who has had the great good fortune to be sponsored by Lady Derwent but who otherwise cannot take any place in Society.'

James's lips had formed into a hard line. 'You must have known what I intended. And yet you said nothing.'

'I believe that that is unfair,' Anna said. 'I saw you driving in the park with Lady Catherine Rainsford earlier in the week. Why would I presume that you were intending to marry me?'

'I was driving with her because my mother arranged it. It was not my choice. And you and I had already been intimate by then.'

'I could not have known that it was your mother who had arranged your outing. And—' her voice was suddenly shaking with anger now, at the injustice of *his* anger '—if I should have assumed that our being *intimate* would cause you to propose to me, should not that proposal have come immediately?'

'You should have told me sooner,' he repeated.

She glared at him. It was suddenly like looking at a stranger.

A stranger with whom she had had really the best times of her life and who had just proposed marriage to her.

No, he had not in fact proposed marriage to *her*; he had proposed marriage to someone else, a woman he had thought suitable to be his bride. A woman of excellent birth who had sadly fallen on hard times but who had no scandal in her background.

There could be no point in continuing this dreadful conversation.

And, frankly, if he could be this unreasonable, she didn't even care any longer what he thought of her. Because this proved that her fears had been right, that men's affections were always conditional and easily lost.

'Goodbye,' she said. 'Thank you for—' she could not call it a nice evening; it had begun gloriously but ended terribly '—thank you.' It had, after all, been kind of him to invite her to the opera.

'Allow me to help you down,' James said stiffly. 'Excuse me.'

His arm brushed Anna's for a moment as he reached for the door handle, and she had to swallow a sob at how it was now extremely awkward for them to touch at all.

Once out of the carriage, he held his arm out for Anna to support her as she descended the steps. She placed two fingers very gingerly on his arm and released it as soon as she was sure that she wouldn't trip; touching him in any way felt very wrong now.

'Thank you again,' she said in her most formal tone.

'It was a pleasure,' he said, with great insincerity. 'Good night.'

Anna nodded and then began to walk up the steps towards the house, before suddenly freezing.

James—she must begin to think of him as *the duke* again, rather than in such familiar terms—had looked incredibly angry, and perhaps hurt, and seemed still to believe that she had purposely deceived him. What if he told someone else her secret and the Puntneys found out and she lost her job?

She turned back in his direction. 'Your Grace.'

He turned round instantly. 'Miss Blake?'

She very much did not wish to have to do this. But she *needed* her employment and must swallow her pride.

'I am a devoted governess and irrespective of my birth I do have the education and knowledge to instruct my charges,' she said. 'If I lose this position I will be destitute. I would be very grateful if you would undertake not to discuss this—or anything we *did*—with anyone.'

'Of course.' He was extremely tight-lipped. 'I should not dream of it.'

'Thank you.' She must get inside and up to her bed-chamber before she allowed herself to *sob* as she felt she was about to do. 'Good night, then.'

'Good night.'

And that was that.

Chapter Twelve

James

James had cried at the deaths of his father and his two brothers but other than that he couldn't remember the last time he had even had a tear in his eye.

Now, watching Anna—Miss Blake—walk up the steps, her slim back held very straight, he didn't just have a lump in his throat; he felt as though he could easily spend a considerable amount of time bawling his eyes out.

He had expected this evening to be one of the happiest of his life. Instead, this. A real grief.

Suddenly, he took two steps forward. He couldn't let her go inside without apologising. He had accused her of lying. She was right: she had not lied to him. He had *felt* in that moment that she had, but she hadn't. He had lashed out from the depths of his misery, and that was a terrible thing to have done.

'Anna.' His voice sounded low, urgent to his own ears.

She froze for a moment, and then turned round, very slowly.

'Yes?'

'I am so sorry,' he said, in a rush to get his words out, feeling as though she might turn and slip inside at any moment. 'I apologise for having accused you of lying to me. I know that you did not. I am aware that much of our…relationship…has been instigated by me, and that you would not have been aware of my intentions initially. And you did of course tell me the truth as soon as I made my intentions clear. I must apologise from my side for not having made them clear immediately, the first time we…did things that we should not have done. I am sorry for everything and I would like you to know that I have very much enjoyed all our time together.' He was babbling, he realised, trying to make the situation better.

'I love you,' he concluded.

'I love you too,' she said. 'I wish you very well. Goodbye.'

And then, while he stood there staring, aghast but his mind strangely frozen so that he could not work out what he should do or say next, she turned back round and continued her way up the steps.

When she closed the front door behind her, it felt as though a door was closing on an unlived chapter of the rest of his life that he hadn't known he wanted until he met her.

He stared at the door for a long time, before turning and telling his coachman in a flat voice that he would walk.

And then he set off down the road. Walking felt like an extraordinary effort, as though his limbs had become entirely leaden.

God. Only perhaps twenty minutes ago, he and Anna had kissed, touched each other intimately, the precursor, he had assumed, to what would be blissful full lovemaking when they were married. And now...now they were entirely separate, and there could be no reason for them to see each other again.

His mind felt as leaden as his limbs.

He couldn't go home yet. He turned left instead of right and began an aimless walk through the streets of Mayfair as he tried to make sense of how he felt.

He hadn't wanted to marry at all but he needed to do so in order to produce an heir to secure his mother and sisters' futures.

If he had to get married, he had been adamant that he hadn't wished to fall in love with his wife, because he hadn't wanted to put himself in a position where he might experience further loss.

The entire reason that he'd planned to marry now was to take care of his mother and sisters. His wife being known to be someone of such scandalous background could cause his own family to be embroiled in the scandal. What if that harmed his sisters' marriage prospects? What if *they* then ended up as governesses, or in undesirable marriages? What if one of them, for example, fell in love with an impecunious curate as Lady Maria had done? In that instance, if she was no longer under the protection of a powerful man, could it cause her problems if her sister-in-law were someone from a scandalous background? What if he married Anna and they had a son and then he, James, died young as his brothers had, when their son was still a minor? Would Society accept Anna as effectively a regent for a child duke?

Life was damned difficult for women and it was a huge responsibility having so many sisters to set on a happy path in life, not to mention his mother, who had borne so much grief with so much dignity.

He could not bear any of his sisters to have to become a governess.

He did not like the thought of Anna being a governess.

He also didn't like the thought of her being sad. She'd cried so much. She'd looked stricken.

He'd been awful to her. He'd accused her of lying. She hadn't lied. She hadn't even knowingly misled him. She couldn't have suspected until recently that he planned to ask her to marry him. If doing things together that would clearly compromise her had caused him to propose, why had he not done so immediately? How could she have known that he would suddenly realise that he should, and that in that moment he was happy to do so because he loved her?

At least he had apologised to her. But the fact remained that he had done things with her that one should not do with a lady of quality who was not one's wife. She *was* a lady of quality; her grandfather was an earl. She hadn't told him that. She had only told him that her father was a groom. She had not tried to protect herself in any way.

He'd been right about never wanting to fall in love: this hurt damnably.

So maybe this was for the best. As long as Anna wasn't too miserable.

Chapter Thirteen

Anna

Anna awoke the next morning lying on top of her bed still in her opera-visiting finery, her head feeling as though a metal clamp was squeezing it and her mouth as though she'd munched through the feathers in her eiderdown during her sleep.

As she blinked painfully dry eyes, she remembered that she'd walked blindly through the house and dissolved into tears the second she'd closed her bedchamber door behind her. Eventually, after much revisiting of painful conversations and misery in her head, she had gone to sleep there without changing out of her gown.

She had been very naïve, she realised. During the early hours of the night she had admitted to herself that she *had* actually hoped that James would propose to her *and* that he would somehow convince her that the scandal surrounding her parents did not matter. But of course it mattered, and of course James—the duke— could not ignore it. Her grandfather had abandoned her mother. Her father had not been the best of husbands to her mother. She knew that men expected women to adhere to higher standards than those to which they themselves adhered, and if they fell short—often through no fault of their own—they did not support them.

Really, she was lucky that things had come to a head now and that the farce of their friendship had ended.

It did hurt very much, though. As did her head.

She *really* did not want to look after young children this morning. She didn't really want to do anything. But if she *had* to do something, it would be much more akin to crawling behind a large rock and hiding there than plastering a smile on her face and attempting to instil discipline and knowledge into someone else's children, however generous a salary she was being paid to do it.

She was ready for breakfast—which Lady Puntney had kindly decreed from the beginning she should take with the family—only a little later than usual. Her looking glass had told her that her face was unusually pale and that the smile that she practised was sadly lacking in authenticity, but she hoped that no one would notice.

She managed to force down some toast and some tea, and discovered that the old adage that food and drink always made you feel better was absolute nonsense. She just felt now as though she was going to be sick. She wasn't sure whether her nausea was due to tiredness or misery or both, but it wasn't helping.

Two hours of instruction on arithmetic followed by some handwriting practice just increased the headache that accompanied her nausea, but it was very helpful to be occupied so that she did not have to be alone with her thoughts.

She and the children took their usual Hyde Park walk later in the morning, and as they reached the pond they liked to walk around, Anna realised that the fresh air was doing her some good; it was clearing her head a little, and looking at the trees and birds was an excellent reminder that life was bigger than just one man. She *would* be happy again, and she *would* make a good life for herself. She was lucky to have this employment, after all, and she was lucky to have Ladies Derwent and Maria as good friends.

By the time they arrived back at Bruton Street, Anna was still feeling deeply miserable, but she had pulled herself together sufficiently to enjoy the company of the children and to be sure that she really could recover from this; it would be a temporary misery.

As she was removing her brown wool pelisse, the one she wore when she was performing her governess role, Morcambe, the butler, said, 'Lady Puntney would like to speak to you in the library.'

Anna had been looking down as she unfastened buttons, but glanced up at his face in surprise, because the tone of his voice was odd, quite cold. She almost gasped out loud at the look on his face. He had always behaved very paternally towards her, and had always had a smile for her and often a word of advice, but now he was entirely unsmiling, and staring at her almost insolently.

A cold dread began to creep over her as she stared back at him. What had happened?

'Thank you,' she said, mortified to hear her own voice shake a little. She gave herself a little shake and then said, in a much stronger voice, thank goodness, 'I shall go to her directly.'

'See that you do,' Morcambe said, and Anna nearly gasped again at the rudeness.

A minute later, purposely having taken her time, to persuade herself that she could not be intimidated by Morcambe—but in reality really quite terrified by the change in his demeanour—she entered the library.

'Please close the door.' Lady Puntney was standing behind a writing table. When Anna had closed the door, she indicated a chair in front of the table, and said, 'Please sit down.'

Anna seated herself, feeling quite wild with fear now, as though her head might explode from inside.

Lady Puntney sat down too, and clasped her hands in front of her.

'I am sorry about this,' she began. And then she paused, for a very long time, while Anna swallowed hard.

Perhaps they no longer needed a governess. Although why then would Morcambe have been so insolent in his manner towards her? Surely he should have been more sympathetic?

'I have, as you know, been very pleased with your service.' Lady Puntney's voice faltered. 'The children have very much liked you and indeed I have too. However…' She paused again as Anna blinked to dispel sudden moistness in her eyes. Clearly, she was being asked to leave for some reason. She *needed* a job, though, and this one was better than any other she might hope to get.

'The problem is…' Lady Puntney cleared her throat. 'That is to say…' She unclasped her hands and pressed her fingertips together and then re-clasped them. 'I do not wish to be unfair.'

Then please keep me on, Anna screamed inside. Externally, she kept her face immobile and concentrated on not crying.

'Mrs Clarke told me this morning that she had overheard something last night of which she felt it her duty to inform me.'

Anna went very cold all over.

Lady Puntney pressed her lips together before continuing, 'She told me that you had had a conversation on the doorstep late last night with the Duke of Amscott that clearly indicated that you have had some form of intimacy with him.'

Oh, no, no, no. Mrs Clarke was the Puntneys' housekeeper. What exactly had she heard? What had they said after they left the privacy of the carriage? Oh, no. This had happened because she had implored the duke not to tell anyone about what had happened between them. How *stupid* of her. Or perhaps it was his apology that Mrs Clarke had heard. Whichever, Anna had been stupidly, *stupidly* rash spending any time with him whatsoever.

She shook her head, speechless.

'Are you able to tell me that this was a mistake?' Lady Puntney continued.

'I...' Anna wanted so much to lie. Would it hurt a living soul if she *did* lie? She didn't think it would. She *was* a good governess; she cared about the children and she felt that she was educating them well. She was *not* a debauched person. She would not influence them badly in any way. She didn't like lying, especially to someone who had treated her as well as Lady Puntney had. But could it hurt anyone if she denied it? She wouldn't want to get Mrs Clarke into trouble for having invented something that she had not in fact invented. What should she say? 'I…'

'Miss Blake! Your hesitation tells me everything I need to know. I had hoped to be told that Mrs Clarke was mistaken. I am distraught.' Lady Puntney was indeed twisting her hands most agitatedly and her eyes looked moist, but it was hard to imagine that she could be as distraught as was Anna.

Anna took a deep, juddering breath. She could not allow herself to dissolve in tears or indeed to say nothing; she had to find some words to explain her situation reasonably, if Lady Puntney would allow her. And then, obviously, she would almost certainly still ask her to leave, but at least she would hopefully not then think ill of her for ever.

'I met the duke at his mother's ball at the beginning of the Season,' she said.

Lady Puntney nodded, as though she wanted to hear more, and Anna realised that of course she wasn't going to refuse to listen to her; she would be agog to hear any gossip about the duke. Well, Anna was not going to give her any gossip, including about her masquerade as Lady Maria, but she would do her best to clear her own name. Just in case. She was not going to volunteer the details about her parents, because that could do her no good and was nobody else's business, and if she was lucky Mrs Clarke would not have overheard that.

If Mrs Clarke *had* heard that, Anna would have to obtain a post far from London if she were to continue as a governess. Most families wished for governesses at least as well-born as they were—just a lot more impecunious.

She should continue her story.

'At the ball, we danced twice and spoke for a while. Subsequently he asked me to go to Gunter's, as you know, and to the opera. And yesterday evening after the opera he escorted me home and we had—' she was almost choking on the words '—a small disagreement and are no longer friends.'

'Mrs Clarke gained the impression that you and the duke had, in her recital of what passed between you, "done" some things together.'

'We, no, that is…'

'I must tell you that she then felt herself obliged to question the staff and a number of them were suspicious, and disclosed that there have been strong whisperings about you and the duke. They had assumed that if you were…exchanging intimacies with him…you were perhaps secretly betrothed.'

Anna closed her eyes for a moment.

'I am afraid,' Lady Puntney said, 'that, even though you might be innocent of anything untoward, there will now be questions about you in people's minds, and that could extend to me and to my daughters. And I have to be prudent.'

'So,' asked Anna slowly, 'even if you knew things that people had said were just rumours, you would still feel that you had to act on them as though they were truth?'

Lady Puntney stared at her for a long time and then nodded. 'Yes, I think perhaps I would have to. For my family's sake. Such is the world in which we live. My status is not sufficiently high to withstand any kind of scandal.'

Anna nodded. Of course Lady Puntney had to think of her daughters' future, and they could not have a governess to whom was attached any scandal.

And, of course, the scandal was *true*. And Lady Puntney didn't even know about Anna's parents, or the extent of the scandal that *might* attach to Anna now.

She paused and then continued, 'Miss Blake— Anna—I very much like you. I do not know what has happened between you and the duke. I must confess— speaking very frankly—that I had hoped on your behalf that perhaps the duke's interest in you might lead to marriage. I believe that it is very wrong that any indiscretion between you means that you must lose your employment while he loses nothing.' She sniffed. 'I do wish that I did not have to let you go. But I am afraid that I have to think of my family and our reputation. Servants do talk. And others might have heard.'

Anna bowed her head. 'I understand.'

'Anna, I will do what I can. I will not tell anyone about this, and I will provide you with a reference so that you may find another position. Perhaps, though, it would be best for you to move to another part of the country so that rumours do not follow you via my servants. I do not like to think that they gossip widely, but one must be realistic about human nature.'

'Thank you,' Anna managed to say before her voice threatened to give way to tears. She did feel very grateful; with a reference from Lady Puntney, and perhaps more help from Lady Derwent, she should indeed be able to find a position in another part of the country. She also, however, felt deeply, deeply sad.

Lady Puntney pushed her chair back, stood, walked round the table and held her hands out to Anna. 'Come.' As Anna stood, she pulled her into an embrace.

Anna did not mean to cry—in fact she was very keen *not* to do so—but somehow she found herself weeping onto Lady Puntney's shoulder as the other woman held her.

Eventually, she pulled away, and saw that Lady Puntney's cheeks were also tear-stained.

'I shall miss you greatly,' Lady Puntney said. 'I am angry with the duke and with this situation. I can no longer employ you but please remember that you have a friend in me.'

'Thank you.' Anna was still sniffing a little. She did fully understand Lady Puntney's position. If one were fortunate enough to have a good reputation, one had to guard it fiercely, and Lady Puntney had her three young daughters to think about.

'I cannot bear to think of you cast out entirely,' Lady Puntney told her. 'I am sure I could find somewhere in the country for you to stay, a cottage for you to reside in perhaps. Perhaps you should stay in a hotel while I attempt to organise something for you.'

Anna shook her head. 'Truly, that is most kind, but I can't allow you to do that.'

'You will have to make me a promise. You must not allow yourself to become destitute.'

Anna swallowed as she nodded, all too aware that such a promise might be difficult to keep.

Chapter Fourteen

James

Two days later, James handed his horse's reins to his groom and strode into his house, almost knocking over his butler, Lumley, on his way in.

'Is everything all right, Your Grace?' Lumley asked.

'Yes, thank you,' James lied.

'You seemed to be in a hurry,' Lumley persisted.

It was excellent having household retainers whom one had known one's entire life. Usually. Sometimes, like now, it was not excellent; it was really quite annoying.

'No particular hurry,' James said, and hurried away. Truth be told, he'd been doing everything fast over the past couple of days. This morning, he'd been dressed before his valet had had a chance to get his hands on his wardrobe and he'd practically gobbled his breakfast. He'd galloped hell for leather down Rotten Row. And now he was going to read his correspondence fast before perhaps going and raining blows in Gentleman Jackson's Boxing Saloon.

It was as though he had a compulsion to do things fast and furiously, to try to prevent the thoughts and the misery and the worry that kept intruding.

It wasn't working; as he sat down at his desk, he was, yet again, thinking about Anna. He was angry, although not with her; it was the situation. And himself, of course; he was definitely angry with himself. He was missing her. And he was worried about her; he hoped that she wouldn't be too upset.

He was *really* missing her. He just wanted to see her, talk to her, kiss her—obviously.

God.

Correspondence rushed through, followed by furious sparring with Gentleman Jackson himself, the freneticism of which earnt him some puzzled questioning, and then a gobbled luncheon and some more high-speed work, he found himself sitting with his mother in her boudoir.

He'd been avoiding her for the past two days, sure that she would ask him about Anna, and very eager to avoid talking to her about the situation.

'I am just returned from a call to the Countess of Maltby,' she told him. She looked down at the sewing in her lap for a moment. 'She had much to say on many topics.'

James felt himself tense a little. He did not wish to discuss Anna at all. Thank heavens he had not at any point told his mother that she was the ninth Earl of Broome's granddaughter.

'She asked about you and Miss Blake,' his mother continued, still looking at her embroidery, meaning that he was unable to see the expression in her eyes, 'and I told her, of course, that Miss Blake is an acquaintance of yours and the goddaughter of Lady Derwent, and that I have no further information about her.'

James said nothing.

'I presume that others will also be asking about her. Your attentions to her were most pronounced at the opera, and I hear that you were seen with her more than once at Gunter's.'

This was why he'd been avoiding his mother.

James drew a deep breath. He should say something that would ensure that Miss Blake's reputation would be damaged no further; if there was gossip surrounding her, she might lose her position.

His attentions to her *had* been very pronounced. He should acknowledge that to his mother, and ensure that she believed that Miss Blake had turned him down. Which she had. Except… Had it, in fact, been the case that he had walked away from her once she had told him about her parents? Without trying hard enough to persuade her to accept his proposal?

No, that was something to think about later.

'I was indeed courting Miss Blake,' he said. 'Unfortunately, she does not wish to marry me.'

'What?' His mother dropped her embroidery and her head came straight up. 'Am I to understand that you proposed to her?'

'Yes.'

'You did not tell me of this.'

'I am a grown man, Mama. There are some things that one does not wish to discuss with one's parent or indeed with anyone.'

'You proposed to her and she refused you?'

'That is correct.'

'Why would any young lady in her right mind turn down a proposal from you? You are handsome, you are a wonderful man, and you are a *duke*.'

Because she was a very courteous and considerate young lady. And honest. She could have withheld the information about her parentage until he was too far embroiled in their betrothal to be able to withdraw, had he been so minded.

Why *had* he been so minded when he heard the information?

Oh, yes. The impact that the scandal might have on his mother and sisters.

Miss Blake, though. What if he had compromised her? Well, he had. It was just that no one knew. *He* knew, though.

'James?'

'Sorry, Mama.' He'd been asked why Anna would refuse him. 'I believe that she just did not wish to marry me. She thanked me for my very kind offer and told me that she was very grateful but believed that we should not suit.'

'How could the life of a duchess not suit a *governess*?'

'Perhaps she—' James swallowed '—perhaps Miss Blake wishes to marry for love, as I know you did.'

'Well.' His mother's eyes were practically flashing with anger. 'How could she not love *you*? She could not find a better man.'

'I believe that you are biased, Mama.' James knew that she was wrong. A better man than he would not have allowed things to develop the way they had with

Anna. And, having allowed that to happen, he would have worked out a way to do the right thing for her while avoiding scandal for his family.

'I am not wrong. The young lady is clearly addle-brained.'

'Mama!'

'I make no apology, James. If I cannot state my mind in front of my own son, before whom might I speak frankly?'

James nodded. Fair enough, he supposed.

'I will say that I hope that you are not too distraught. While I am not sure of what family Miss Blake is, she is clearly a lady, and if she would have made you happy, I would have been pleased to welcome her into our family. If she refused you, perhaps she has a reason and perhaps it is for the best. There are many other young ladies who would like to make your acquaintance.'

'Indeed.' James nodded unenthusiastically. Of course there were. He was a duke. Unfortunately for him, he couldn't imagine ever liking—loving—another young lady in the way that he did Anna. And while he had not wanted to marry for love, he also couldn't imagine spending time with another woman, making love to another woman.

'I see that your spirits are currently low.' His mother shook her head. 'I am sorry, James.'

'Thank you, Mama. For your concern. We do not need to speak of it, however.'

'I shall not mention it ever again,' his mother said, almost certainly inaccurately. 'Let me distract you by telling you about some of the other *on-dits* that the countess shared with me.'

'Mama, this is how unpleasant gossip spreads.'

'James. You are my son. Neither of us needs to re-peat any of this further, but one needs to be able to talk to *some*one.'

James immediately felt guilty. He knew how much she missed his father, and his brothers, and of course she needed to be able to talk to him.

And she was right; he needed to be distracted.

'Tell me everything,' he said.

'And *that*,' concluded his mother at least fifteen min-utes later, after she'd regaled him with a series of the most bewilderingly convoluted anecdotes he'd heard in some time, 'goes to show that Miss Blake is indeed an unusual young lady. And while she is of course not of a family of note—' she was entirely wrong there, with re-gard to both the Earl of Broome, and the scandal Anna's parents had caused '—she is very prettily behaved and quite beautiful. And if the Marquis of Blythe can marry an *actress*, you can marry a nonentity.'

'Firstly, Miss Blake does not wish to marry me. And secondly, will the marquis not be subject to approba-tion?' James asked.

'Some perhaps, but it will soon be forgotten if he ig-nores it. He is the Marquis of Blythe, James.'

James stared at his mother. Was she…right? If he were to marry Miss Blake—if she would have him, which he strongly doubted now—would Society effec-tively forgive him? And therefore might there be no neg-ative effect on his mother and sisters?

'There are so many instances of august men marrying women of inferior status,' his mother was continuing. 'If the lady in question is very lady*like*, her supposed unsuitability is easily forgotten as soon as the next little scandal comes along.'

'I had not thought you so pragmatic,' he said. 'When you were compiling a list of prospective brides for me, you were particularly interested in birth.'

'I was. But…' His mother paused and then placed her embroidery on the little side table next to her. 'Come and sit next to me.'

James rose and took his place on the sofa next to her with a level of enthusiasm not much greater than he would have felt had she been a hungry lion.

To his alarm, his mother took his hands in hers.

'I want you to be happy,' she said. 'I know that you did not expect ever to inherit the dukedom and that you now bear a great weight of responsibility that you did not expect.' She hesitated and then squeezed his hands. 'I…saw you with Miss Blake. She is perhaps not of the highest birth, but she is of course vouched for by Sopho-nora, Lady Derwent. While Sophonora is, as you know, not one of my closest friends, no one can say she is not of the highest *ton*. Anyway, when you were with Miss Blake, you looked…happy, carefree, playful…in *love*.'

James was almost physically squirming by the time she had finished. *Who* had to endure such a conversation with anyone, let alone their own mother? This was even worse than being fussed over by one's housekeeper or butler.

'Sadly,' he said, wondering how soon he could pull his hands out of his mother's clasp, 'as I mentioned, the lady does not wish to marry me.'

'That is a great shame and I think she's very silly and

I am quite angry with her.' His mother still wasn't letting go of his hands.

'No. There is no good reason to be angry with her.' He couldn't believe that he himself had felt anger with her for one second.

If Anna *would* have him, if he told her that he did not care about her birth, would he wish to marry her? He *should* do so, obviously, having compromised her, even if no one had seen them. But would he *wish* to? Given that loving someone deeply carried such a risk of terrible pain if you lost them?

He looked at his mother, who was still holding his hands, and felt a sudden almost overwhelming pang for her loss. And for his own.

'Since we have been speaking plainly,' he said, 'may I ask if you would do it again? Marry my father? Even though you have now lost him?'

His mother stared at him for a long moment, and then said, 'That is a silly question, because I have my children. But even without all of you, certainly I would. I am very lucky to have had the time with your father that I did, and I would have been lucky however long it might have been. I would not have changed anything. James... Are you concerned about loving someone and then losing them?'

'Well, I...' Suddenly he really wished that he could confide in her, talk to her, tell her everything about Anna. But he couldn't, because she had already borne great loss and she already had far too much to worry about. And she was clearly wondering whether the loss of his father and brothers had damaged him in some way. Perhaps it had, but she did not need to know that.

'No,' he said. 'No. The truth about my acquaintance with Miss Blake is that I liked her very tolerably and proposed marriage to her, but she felt that she did not wish to become a duchess with all that that entailed. And that she did not love me quite as she felt she would like to love a husband.' It was a little horrifying how easily the lies rolled off his tongue, but it was necessary, he felt, to protect his mother.

He suddenly felt as though he would like to go for a walk, to clear his head.

'Would you care to accompany me for a walk?' he asked her, out of politeness, because now he really wanted to be alone, to have the time to clarify his thoughts.

'I should have liked that very much, and would like to do so tomorrow, if you have the time, but today I have agreed to shop for a new muff with Sybilla, a most important task, you must recognise.' She twinkled at him and kissed his cheek.

He smiled back at her and stood up. 'I will take my leave of you now, then, and will perhaps see you for dinner later.'

He let himself out of the house shortly afterwards and began to walk aimlessly down the road, as though all his energy had been diverted to his thoughts.

It all suddenly seemed quite simple.

He was a duke. Anna's grandfather was an earl. Her parents had created a scandal. She was, however, indisputably a lady of quality, in her demeanour, her personality, everything. More importantly, she was kind and honourable. She was also very beautiful, and he loved being with her. He loved everything about her in fact.

And one of the advantages of being a duke was, as his mother had said, that his status would transcend a generation-old scandal. And his sisters would have large dowries, which, combined with their birth, should of course allow them to marry whomever they chose.

And, really, that had all been obvious, or should have been, all along.

Had he been using it as an excuse?

Because he had been scared of getting hurt?

He'd behaved appallingly. *Appallingly*.

He had compromised her, whether or not anyone else knew about it—he trusted they did not. He should have proposed to her irrespective of whether or not he *wished* to marry her.

But he *did* wish to marry her, he realised as he rounded another corner and nearly walked into a tree. He wanted to spend as much time with her as he could, make her happy, look after her. If that time was limited, then he would still be lucky to have had that time with her.

But, good God, what if *she* loved *him*—if that were possible after the way he'd behaved—and he died young like his father and brothers had?

According to his mother, being with James would still have been worth it for Anna.

And from a practical perspective, Anna would still, presumably, be much better off as a dowager duchess than as an impecunious governess.

His pace had picked up, he realised, and his steps were leading him in the direction of Bruton Street.

By the time he arrived there, not long afterwards, he was almost running, in a particularly undignified fashion.

Banging on the door knocker, he realised that he must be wearing a very foolish grin at the thought of seeing Anna again.

God, he hoped that he would be able to convince her that she should marry him. If, of course, she did wish to. Perhaps she didn't. Perhaps she didn't love him. Perhaps…

'Good afternoon. I am come to visit Miss Blake,' he said to the butler who had just opened the door.

'Miss Blake no longer works here.' The man's sneer was extraordinary.

James's natural inclination would usually be to give him a severe dressing-down, except now he was more concerned with what had happened to Anna and why the man was speaking in such a derogatory fashion.

'Is Lady Puntney at home?' he asked.

'I will enquire.' And, good God, there was that sneer again. James had rarely ever been spoken to like this and he did not appreciate it. And damn, if the man would speak to *him* like this, how had he spoken to Anna?

As he waited in a very luxuriously decorated drawing room, his level of anxiety about Anna climbed as he had time to wonder further what might have happened to her.

The butler's sneering indicated that she might well have left under some kind of cloud; James very much hoped that that had nothing to do with him but the more he thought about it…

'Good afternoon.' Lady Puntney's smile was pleasant; James was not surprised given what Anna had told him about what a generous employer she had been.

'Good afternoon.' James had no appetite for small talk. 'I came to call on Miss Blake but I understand that she has left your employment. I wondered if you would be able to reassure me that she has come to no ill, and to furnish me with her new direction.'

'I…' Lady Puntney looked over her shoulder, and then took the few steps necessary to reach the door and close it, before moving to a chair near the fireplace. 'Please sit down.'

James inclined his head and took the chair to the other side of the fireplace, and waited, with some impatience.

'I very much like Miss Blake,' Lady Puntney began. 'And I have worried about her since she left.'

'May I ask why she left?'

'She… Well. This is awkward, but I feel that for Miss Blake's sake I should speak plainly. My housekeeper overheard a conversation between the two of you, and one of our housemaids had seen some rather…warm… behaviour between you. I could not, for the sake of my daughters and our reputation as a family, keep Miss Blake on.'

Damn. *Damn*. James had caused Anna so much harm. He wished she had told him what had happened; she could obviously have contacted him. She would not have wished to put him to any trouble, though.

God. He *hated* to think of her enduring the misery of losing her position. And where was she now? What if she had been cast out by all her acquaintance for what was *their* indiscretion, his and hers, not just hers?

'Could I ask where she is now?'

'I'm afraid that I promised her that I would not tell you. I assure you, however, that I understand her to be well and safe for the time being. We have corresponded.'

Lady Puntney was unshakeable in her refusal to betray her promise to Miss Blake, and James left soon afterwards.

He went straight to Lady Derwent's mansion. If anyone knew where Anna was, it must surely be her.

Lady Derwent was not at home.

'Is Miss Blake residing here?' James asked.

'I have not seen her.' The butler *might* be lying. Or he might be telling the truth. He had the art of impassivity very well mastered.

'Do you know when Lady Derwent will return home?'

'I'm afraid not.'

'I will wait,' James said firmly, and sat himself down on an intricately carved oak chair in the hall, so that no one might enter the house without him seeing.

The chair was hard, the afternoon was long, and James did not enjoy his thoughts; he was very worried about Anna, he felt incredibly guilty, and he was essentially just desperate to see her. It didn't bear thinking about where she might be if she wasn't with her godmother. Except he did think about it.

When, eventually, Lady Derwent did return, James was extremely disappointed to see that she was alone; he had been hoping that Anna might perhaps be with her.

'Your Grace,' she said. 'Interesting.' She handed her gloves to her butler. 'Come into my saloon.'

'What a pleasure it is seeing you,' she said, unsmilingly, as she settled herself on a sofa. 'Please do sit down.'

'Thank you.' James eyed her. He suspected that he would fare a lot better with her if he made the effort to engage in some social niceties, however much he wished—frankly—to yell *Where is my Anna?* 'I hope that you are well?'

'Very well, I thank you. A little frustrated, I must admit.'

'Frustrated?' James felt as though he was at the beginning of an intricate chess game, to which he did not fully know the rules.

'Frustrated,' she confirmed, before lapsing into what he knew was an uncharacteristic silence, and which he felt was perhaps designed to induce him to speak.

He had nothing to lose, he decided, in indulging her, as long as he was cautious.

'I am sorry to hear of your frustration. I myself am also a little frustrated.'

Lady Derwent raised an eyebrow.

James decided to plunge straight in.

'I love your goddaughter, Miss Blake,' he stated. 'I understand from Lady Puntney that she terminated her employment because of our friendship. Most immediately, I am concerned about her, and hope that she is well and in a place of safety. I would also like very much to speak to her, to explain that I was stupid and how much I love her.'

Lady Derwent nodded, thoughtfully. 'I see.' She looked as though she was thinking very hard.

'I would, therefore, be very grateful if you were able to tell me where she is.'

'I am able,' she said, speaking slowly, 'to tell you that she is safe and well and that I have seen her. And that I will do my utmost to ensure that she remains safe and well.'

'Thank God,' James said.

'Yes.'

James looked at her, looking at him, as though she was sizing him up, and waited. He had already asked if she knew where Anna was, and he didn't think she was a lady who would appreciate repetition.

'I understand that you and my goddaughter visited Gunter's together twice, in addition to our evening at the opera. My observation was that you had seemed to have become quite close.'

'Yes. I love her,' James repeated.

'And?'

'And I would like to marry her.' He supposed that this was the equivalent of asking a young lady's father if he might be permitted to propose to his daughter. It was not very enjoyable; Lady Derwent's eagle eye was making him squirm as though he were a child, and there was something quite peculiar about declaring his love for Anna to someone other than her. Had he, in fact, told her properly how very much he loved her? He wasn't sure that he had.

He cleared his throat. 'And therefore I would very much welcome the opportunity to see her again. I wondered if you knew where she was.'

'My goddaughter was very distressed, although doing her best to hide it, when I saw her. She asked me to promise that I would not tell you whither she fled.'

James nodded. Damn.

'I cannot break my promise to her,' Lady Derwent said. 'She needs to be able to trust *someone*.' A low blow, but fair enough. James should have been thinking more clearly and should not have let things happen the way they had.

'I would like to be able to prove to her that she can trust me,' he said. 'Because, as I mentioned, I would like to marry her, because I love her and would like to do my best to make her happy.'

'Prettily spoken,' Lady Derwent finally approved. 'I would like you to be able to propose to her again, *properly*, but I cannot break my promise. Perhaps… Let me think.'

And then she sat and thought, while James fought very hard not to tap his fingers or his foot or just say—shout—*Yes, what?*

Eventually, she said, 'I will send you a note later.'

That was it? She was going to send him a note? What if she didn't send it?

He looked at her. Yes, this was, unfortunately, clearly the most she was going to give him.

'Thank you,' he said, managing not to grit his teeth too much, and rose to leave.

Lady Derwent's note arrived in Berkeley Square shortly after he did.

Pulling it out of its envelope with fingers that were suddenly all thumbs, he discovered that Lady Derwent had merely written:

I will be at Hatchard's bookshop at eleven o'clock tomorrow morning and should like to meet you there.

The frustration was immense. Maybe he should try to ask Lady Maria Swanley if she knew where her friend was now. He half turned back towards the front door, before checking himself. He should not cause any more gossip than had already arisen. He would have to wait, and hope that Lady Derwent had something more interesting to tell him on the morrow than she had today.

He was at Hatchard's the next morning ten minutes before the hour, wishing to make very sure that he did not miss Lady Derwent.

The last time he had visited this shop had been to purchase books for Anna.

Really, everywhere and everything reminded him of her.

Dear *God*, he missed her.

Her humour.

Her quick understanding.

Her smile.

The way she made him feel when he was with her… complete, happy, as though there was nowhere he'd rather be.

He hoped so very desperately that she was all right.

As he stood there, thinking and worrying about Anna, he realised that he was beginning to *see* her everywhere, imagine that she was in front of him.

At this rate he would be accosting complete strangers thinking that they were her.

For example, at this moment he could see a smallish woman making her way along the road towards him, and for some reason—probably the way she moved—she reminded him so strongly of Anna that he could almost believe that she *was* Anna.

So much so, in fact, that it was difficult not to stare at her.

Especially since, as she drew closer, he could see that her hair was of the same colour and...

And... He blinked hard. It *was* her.

It was Anna.

Walking down Piccadilly towards him.

Chapter Fifteen

Anna

Anna had not particularly wished to visit Hatchard's—
or anywhere else—this morning, but she was deeply beholden to her godmother, and it did do her good to leave
the house and take some walks, rather than moping inside, wondering what was to become of her, so she had
agreed to join her when she had suggested this excursion.

The proposed outing had been for them to visit the
shops together, but at the last moment Lady Derwent
had told Anna that she was a little fatigued and thought
that she would do well to rest this morning as she had
a busy day ahead of her, but that she most particularly
wanted to purchase Jane Austen's *Northanger Abbey*,
and she would be very grateful if Anna would go on
her behalf to buy it.

Anna had vaguely wondered that her godmother
wouldn't send a footman in her stead, but perhaps Lady
Derwent was trying to ensure that Anna was kept occupied. She was clearly right to do so, because it had

certainly not been making Anna happy sitting inside reflecting on the turn that her fortunes had taken and what might have been.

She would also, of course, be able to browse the bookshelves herself, which she would enjoy. Reading was always helpful in taking one away from one's own problems.

As long as one could concentrate and a large duke did not intrude too much into one's thoughts.

She looked along the road at the shop as she approached and...

Discovered that the duke was yet again intruding into her thoughts.

Because, being fanciful, she could easily imagine that the large man standing outside the building was him.

Oh...*was* she imagining it, or was it actually him?

It couldn't be.

But that height and those broad shoulders, topped by his handsome face and thick, dark hair.

It...*was* him.

It was definitely him.

He was his usual elegant self, attired in a plain but perfectly cut dark coat, *very* attractively fitting breeches—*why* was her stupid brain thinking about *that* at this moment?—and impressively shiny boots.

His expression and posture were not as usual, though. He was entirely still, almost frozen, his hands fixed to his stick, his eyes staring and his jaw a little dropped.

If she hadn't been so stunned, she might almost have laughed at the way in which he was the personification of astonishment; it seemed that he had expected to see her as little as she had expected to see him.

For a long moment, Anna felt very much as though she imagined a chicken might in the presence of an unexpected fox—panic-stricken and unable to think—before she gathered her wits and wondered whether she might be able to just keep on walking, into the shop, and pretend she had never seen him. Apart from the stomach churning and near-faintness she was feeling, of course, but if she could just sit down for a moment, she was sure she would recover quite quickly.

Or perhaps she would just turn about and go somewhere else for a while and return when she was sure he would have left.

But, 'Good morning,' he said, while she was still trying to work out what she should do.

Oh.

'Good morning.' Her voice sounded distinctly odd.

'Good morning,' he repeated, before shaking his head. 'Apparently my wits are addled; that is the second *good morning* I have offered you.' His rueful smile was *so* attractive.

Anna found her own lips curling into a little smile too, which was odd, because she was fairly sure that she was still angry with him. She would not show it, however; she would rather retain any scrap of dignity she might have.

'Well, thank you for those good mornings.' She pointed at the clouds above them. 'They are not particularly apt.' Conversing about the weather was always a good ploy when there were no other topics that one wished to discuss. A few more weather-related words and she would be able to go inside and try to forget that she had seen him.

'Oh, no, they are extremely apt. Seeing you makes this morning good.'

'Oh!' Really? He sounded as though he was flirting with her. Was that usual behaviour in this situation? Surely not.

She should go; she really did not want to talk to him. Well, if she was honest, she *did* wish to talk to him, but it could only lead to further misery.

'It was most enjoyable to see you but I'm afraid I am rather busy.' She began to move past him towards the shop entrance.

'I had expected to see Lady Derwent here,' he said, just as she drew level with him. 'She asked me to meet her here. Is she joining you?'

Anna slowed to a halt. 'I… Oh. No, she isn't. She is unfortunately a little tired this morning, so she asked me to come and purchase some books for her.' She frowned. 'When did she ask you to meet her here?'

'I received a note from her yesterday evening instructing me to meet her here at eleven o'clock this morning.' He looked at his watch. 'Exactly now, in fact.'

Anna frowned. 'She is not forgetful,' she said slowly.

'Indeed,' the duke agreed. 'She could not possibly have forgotten that she had arranged to meet me here…'

'…when she requested me to join her on an excursion here, and then at the very last moment said that she was too tired to come but urged me to leave immediately because it looked as though it was going to rain,' Anna finished.

She shook her head.

Her godmother had *promised* her that she would not

tell anyone—especially the duke—that she was staying with her.

She had not told him, it seemed. She had planned this meeting instead. Why, though? What purpose could it serve?

None. No purpose. And, for goodness' sake, now her eyes were filling yet again.

'I think we both know,' she said with an effort, 'that there can be no benefit in our conversing. I will bid you goodbye.' She stepped towards the shop door.

'Lady Derwent had good reason to decide to orchestrate our meeting,' the duke said.

Anna stopped again and turned to look at him.

'I visited her yesterday afternoon,' he continued. 'Do I understand that you are staying with her? She did not tell me that.'

'Yes, I am; I asked her to tell no one.'

He nodded. 'It seems that she wished us to meet but did not wish to betray your confidence.'

'Yes.' Anna knew that she shouldn't ask, but she couldn't help it: 'May I ask why you visited her?'

'Because I wanted to tell you…' The duke looked around. 'This is really not the place for it. Would you care to walk with me?'

Anna was so very tempted. But she had been tempted by him before now, and it had cost her dearly. Now, on the off chance that she still had any reputation left, she must guard it carefully, and could not be seen with any men, especially the duke.

'No, thank you.' She took another step towards the door. 'I am going to do the errand I came to do for my godmother and then I am going to leave.'

'You know, I think I also have a fancy to purchase some books.'

'That was really not what I intended,' Anna told him. A little weakly, because, if she was honest, she didn't entirely want him to leave.

'I think it might have been what your godmother intended.'

'My godmother is wonderful but she is not always right. As we have already ascertained.'

She was very frequently right, though.

The duke pushed the door open and smiled at her.

Anna rolled her eyes at him and then stepped inside. He had a look in his eye that told her that he was about to say something quite outrageous. He would not be *able* to be truly outrageous inside the shop, though; they would run the risk of being overheard, and, while she didn't think he was easily embarrassed on his own account, she did think that he was likely not to wish to embarrass *her*. So there couldn't *really* be any danger in talking to him. Just a little.

When she got inside, she realised that this place was quite heavenly. She would have to return, if she was able, another time, when she wouldn't be distracted by the duke's presence.

'Is this the first time you have been here?' he asked as she looked around. Gazing at the shelves and shelves of books was infinitely easier than looking at him and reflecting on the miserable fact that their lives would diverge again after this ridiculous meeting.

'Yes.'

'It is quite special, is it not? Even I—not, as you know, a great book-lover—can sense magic here.'

'Yes.'

'What books are you here to purchase?' the duke pursued.

'I have a list from my godmother and she suggested that I also buy one or two of my choice, which is of course very kind in her.'

'What books are you thinking of purchasing for yourself?'

'I don't know. I'm afraid that I will need to take some time choosing them. Probably in silence.' She didn't want to sound as though she was encouraging him to talk to her.

She took a few steps further into the shop.

The duke followed her.

Several pairs of eyes rose from books and shelves to look at them.

'I wonder whether you should leave me now,' she whispered. 'We have been remarked. I do not wish to be the subject of any further gossip.'

'Of course,' he replied, also whispering. 'And of course I do not wish to force my presence on you, and indeed should probably not have followed you in here, so, if you would like me to leave immediately, I will do so. But before I go could I possibly explain that I have something of great importance to say to you?'

'I think we have already discussed everything there is to say.' Sad but true.

He leaned closer to her and, still whispering, said into her ear, 'I love you.'

Anna froze.

'What?' she said, quite loudly.

'Shhh,' several voices said.

'I love you,' he whisper-repeated.

Anna ignored him and marched down an aisle between two sets of shelves. She was suddenly almost *throbbing* with annoyance. Why had he said that? Why was he torturing her like this? Why was he still following her?

'Please leave,' she hissed over her shoulder.

'Please marry me,' he whispered back.

Anna stopped stock still, and he bumped into her back, nearly sending her flying.

He caught her with a hand on each of her upper arms as she stumbled.

When she was steady, she turned round to face him, filled all of a sudden with heat—*furious* heat—from head to toe.

'We—' she prodded him in the chest with her finger '—have already discussed this. The answer, if you remember, was no.'

'You told me that the reason was that your parents had caused a scandal.'

'Shhh,' someone said.

'My apologies,' the duke said.

'I don't care about scandal,' he whispered. 'The only reason I cared about it was that I was worried about my sisters. But that is ridiculous. I love you more than words could ever say and, if you love me too, I would like to spend the rest of our days together doing my best to make you as happy as possible.'

'No,' Anna stated.

'No what?'

'No, I will not marry you.'

'You should marry him,' a woman said from the other side of the shelves.

'Hmmmph,' Anna told her.

'Would you like to go outside to discuss this better?' the duke whispered. 'I had not planned to propose here in such a manner.'

'I am so sorry that your proposal is ruined—' Anna hoped that her words sounded as insincere as they were '—but I'm afraid that I do not wish to go outside with you.'

'Oh, please *do* go,' the woman from the other side of the shelves begged.

James mouthed, 'Please?' at her.

'Well...'

'Only if you don't mind,' he suddenly said. 'I do not wish to pressure you into doing anything you do not wish to do.'

'Indeed,' replied Anna, even as the treacherous part of her brain reflected that however annoying and infuriating James might be, he could not help himself also being remarkably kind and chivalrous; it did not occur to a great number of men to allow women the courtesy of making decisions, big or small, about their own lives.

'Good day to you,' she told him, conscious of a great weight of misery descending as she uttered the words.

Her misery was reflected in his face, she saw, as he opened his mouth to reply.

She didn't hear what he had to say, because they were interrupted by a woman sweeping into the end of their aisle.

'Amscott!' she said.

'Lady Fortescue.' He bowed his head slightly.

'I am the lady with whom you were communicating through the shelves,' she said. She turned her gimlet gaze on Anna and said, 'I do not know who you are, and do not think that now is the time for introductions. I am come to say that I think that you really ought to hear him out, in a better location than here. Now that I see who it is who loves you and wishes to marry you, I have to tell you that you are quite mad if you do not accept him, although that is of course entirely your own business.'

A *shhh* came from behind the shelves opposite where Lady Fortescue had been.

'Quite.' She made a shooing motion with her hands. 'Off you go.'

'I should very much like the opportunity to have private conversation with you.' James was not moving, the shooing apparently having no effect on him. 'But I do understand if you wish not to.'

As a matter of principle, Anna did not wish to speak further to him. But, also, she very much did.

It would be silly to allow her principles to cause her to wonder for ever what he might have said.

And she had already been very miserable because of him; it could hardly make matters worse.

'Perhaps a very short conversation,' she said.

'Very sensible,' Lady Fortescue approved. 'Please go now and leave the rest of us in peace. I shall of course say nothing about this to anyone should it come to nothing. If it *does* come to something, I shall expect to be a guest of honour at your wedding.'

Despite everything, Anna felt her lips twitch a little. She wondered if her godmother and Lady Fortescue knew each other well. They would certainly be a match for each other in the forcefulness stakes.

'I will bear that in mind.' James indicated behind him with his eyes and Anna nodded. 'Good day, my lady.'

And then they traipsed out of the shop, regarded the entire way—Anna could feel her eyes boring into her back—by Lady Fortescue.

When they got outside, they discovered that it was raining.

'Oh, dear.' James looked down at her with a rueful smile. 'I must hope that the weather is not indicative of the outcome of our conversation. Let us find a hackney. If you would like?'

'I would prefer to walk.' Anna tried not to be conscious of the damp already working its way inside the neckline of her pelisse. 'Your reputation is already going to be quite ruined by Lady Fortescue having overheard our conversation. If we enter a carriage together it will be even worse. And I myself must be very careful.'

'I do not care about my own reputation but fully understand your point about your own. I apologise. Let us walk instead, if you would like?'

'Thank you.'

As they began to stroll up Piccadilly, James said, 'Your comment about my reputation leads me directly to one of the things I was going to mention to you. If you are happy to hear what I have to say?'

'I am not sure that *happy* is the word,' Anna said cautiously.

'But?'

'But if you wish to say something to me, please do.'

If she was honest, she was quite desperate to hear what he had to say.

It began to rain significantly harder.

'Should we perhaps stand over here?' James led her in the direction of some large trees. The rain was so hard that Anna could ascertain no more than that they had very broad trunks.

It was a little less wet under the trees, but by no means dry.

'A good thing about it being so rainy is that we are unlikely to be remarked by anyone at all.' Anna was damp all over now. This was the kind of weather that caused less robust persons to become quite ill; and she had a nasty feeling that it would take her several hours to feel completely dry again.

'That is very true. A good thing.' James cleared his throat. 'Thank you for agreeing to listen to what I have to say. I don't think now is the time for small talk. Both because of the rain and because, well, because of what has already passed between us.'

'I agree.' Anna slightly wanted to stamp her foot. 'So what is it that you wish to say?'

'You are right; I was in fact engaging in small talk.'

'As you still are...'

He laughed. 'Sorry. Yes. Right. Well.'

Anna finally lost the ability to be at all patient. 'Oh. My. Goodness,' she said.

'Yes. Of course. Well. I have one big message for you.'

'What is that message?' Anna asked.

'I love you and would be the happiest man alive if you would agree to marry me, and I have several smaller messages which combine to create that one. Are you happy for me to continue?'

'Yes I am and thank you for asking.' Really, she didn't feel at all thankful; she just wanted him to *get on with it*.

'I spend a lot of time with sycophants, who will listen to anything I say merely because I am a duke,' he surprised her by replying, 'and I have no desire to force my conversation on you. Although I *am* extremely pleased that you are happy to listen.'

Anna nodded, just about managing not to roll her eyes. Had anyone, ever, in the history of irritating conversations, been as slow to say whatever it was they had to say?

'So,' he said. 'I didn't know that I would see you this morning. I feel as though I should really have prepared a speech. As I did not, I must apologise if my train of thought is a little rambling.'

Anna could contain herself no longer. 'It is extremely rambling,' she told him.

James nodded and smiled ruefully. 'I'm sorry. I feel as though this is the most important conversation of my life and as though I must not get it wrong.'

Anna just raised her eyebrows.

He laughed, before looking serious again.

'Here I go, then,' he said. 'You referred to my reputation. As I mentioned just now, I am surrounded by sycophants. That is because of my rank and my wealth. And as mentioned by mother recently, if I marry someone whose parents acted in a scandalous fashion a generation ago, no one would dare to mention it to me, and it would not have any impact on my mother and sisters, about whose reputations I of course care deeply. It would also not have any impact on my wife because I would not permit that to happen.' He looked suddenly very haughty and very ducal.

'I'm not sure…' she began to reply.

'Not sure?'

'I don't know.' If it was genuinely the case that the scandal would not ruin him—or his family—should she, could she marry him?

She didn't know. He had walked away from her very fast after his proposal the night of the opera. Why hadn't he tried to convince her immediately that they should marry? Would he be just like her grandfather and her father and not remain steadfast in the face of difficulty, or when he perhaps grew bored with her?

He cut across her thoughts. 'I'm not sure that that was the first thing that I should have mentioned. In fact, on reflection, I know that of course it isn't. I wish I had prepared what I was going to say.' He drew a deep breath. 'What I should have told you just now—and what I should have told you when I asked you to marry me—is that I am scared.'

'Scared?' Anna frowned, confused.

As she looked up at him, she saw him swallow and press his lips together, and suddenly she just wanted to put her arms around him, pull him against her, and provide reassurance against whatever was worrying him. Of course, on the face of it she had a lot more to be scared about than he did—for all she knew she could easily end up in the workhouse after all—but huge privilege did not preclude someone from feeling fear, and he had of course lost several close relatives quite recently. Perhaps it was related to that.

'I have been scared about many things. My father died quite young and my brothers very young, as you know. I found the pain of losing them very hard, both on my own account and that of my mother and sisters. I do not wish to experience such pain again, and I also do not wish to be the cause of someone else experiencing such pain. It seems to me that loving someone is therefore dangerous.'

Anna nodded slowly.

'With regard to loving you, I now realise that living without you, missing you, worrying about you, will cause me huge pain. And so, selfishly, I would like to marry you. I am worried, though, that I will die young as my male relatives did, and leave you to experience pain. I believe, however, that what I have to offer you is—baldly speaking—more than just myself as a husband; if something *were* to happen to me, you would be the Dowager Duchess of Amscott and—if we were lucky—the mother of the next duke, and your future would be secure.'

'Is that your reason for proposing?' she asked. 'Pity? Charity? To secure my future now that you know that my employment was terminated?'

'No. *No.* Of course not.' He sounded almost impatient. 'I could settle a large sum of money on you. I could employ you myself. I could buy you a house. Anonymously so that no scandal would attach to the purchase. I could do any manner of things to secure your future. And if you do not wish to marry me I will of course accept that, and I will beg you to allow me to help you financially. But securing your future *would* be a happy side effect of your marrying me.'

'Oh.'

It was a lot to comprehend.

After a few moments of reflection, she said, 'I am scared too.'

James nodded, his eyes fixed on her face, but did not speak.

'I'm scared of losing someone, as you are, but I think perhaps we all are, and something I have learnt is that it is wise to take happiness wherever one finds it.'

'I agree that that is wise.' He had his hands clasped in front of him, so hard that the knuckles were whitening, and his gaze was very intent.

'However,' she continued, 'I am also scared of relinquishing my independence to any man. My grandfather disowned my mother. My father abandoned us both.'

James swallowed visibly and said, 'I can understand that. I can offer you every assurance that your heart and your security would be safe with me, but I don't know how to convince you of that. Maybe… I can't. I love you, though. I would never…' His voice sounded harsh, raw.

Anna just stared at him, mute.

'I…' He stopped, swallowed again, and then continued, 'I believe that my happiness is bound up in you. I would very much like to marry you. I love you. I love your smile. I love your laugh. I love the way you make *me* laugh so much. I love your kindness. I love the way you tilt your head to one side and press your lips together when you are particularly annoyed and clearly fighting with yourself not to give someone—me—a stern set-down.'

Anna laughed, and then sniffed.

'I love everything I know of you,' James continued,

'and I would count myself indescribably fortunate to have the opportunity to spend a lifetime learning as much about you as I may. I would never disown you or abandon you.'

Anna sniffed tears back, suddenly—she could not say why—sure that he was not like her grandfather or father.

Of *course* not all men were the same. Take the Puntneys. Sir Laurence was clearly a most devoted husband. And Lady Maria's parents were happily married. Perhaps Anna had just been unlucky with her grandfather and father.

Perhaps her luck had turned when she met the duke.

'Oh,' she said.

'I would like so very much to marry you. And love and protect you for ever. I have never been surer about anything in my life.'

Anna sniffed and smiled at the same time.

For the first time since they'd moved under the tree, James began to smile too.

He unclasped his hands and reached for hers, before pulling her gently so that they were standing quite close together.

Then he got down on one knee, on the very wet ground, in full view of anyone who might walk past, and said, 'Anna Blake. I love you more than I can describe. Would you do me the great honour of accepting my hand in marriage?'

His features—so harshly handsome in repose, so delightful when laughing, but always giving the impression of strength, were arranged now in what Anna could only think of as vulnerable hope. It was the most beautiful expression she'd ever seen anyone wear.

'I love your face,' she whispered.

James screwed his loveable face up a little and then raised his eyebrows.

'And I also love *you*,' she told him.

James was still kneeling, still holding her hands.

'I cannot imagine anything better than being able to spend every day at your side,' she said.

'And without wishing to sound too impatient…?'

'I would love to marry you.'

'Oh, my God. Thank you.' He kissed each of her hands in turn, before rising to his feet—a most delightful flexing of his thigh muscles visible through his breeches as he did so—and drawing her into his arms. 'I love you more than words can say.'

And then he kissed her extremely thoroughly and extremely scandalously right there on the pavement, under the trees, in the rain, and it was quite wonderful.

Epilogue

Anna

The Lake District,
Christmas 1827

Anna tilted her head to one side as she regarded herself in the floor-length looking glass in front of her.

James appeared behind her. 'You look beautiful, as always.' He slid his arms around her waist and kissed the top of her head.

Anna allowed herself a moment to enjoy the pleasurable shiver his touch always gave her, before putting her hands over his and saying, 'We must hurry.'

'Really?' He turned her in his arms so that she was facing him, put one finger under her chin so that her face was raised to his, and kissed her full on the lips.

And then he kissed her again, hungrily, as though he *needed* her, now, even though they had been together only last night and after their ball tonight would be able to fall into bed together again.

Anna *knew* that they should go down to greet their guests, but she couldn't help herself reaching her arms round James's neck, anchoring him to her as their kiss deepened.

Still kissing her, teasing her tongue with his, he suddenly lifted her and carried her the few paces to the bed in the middle of the room and sat down on it with her on his knees.

As his mouth traced kisses into the sensitive skin at the base of her neck, he murmured, 'I very much like this costume.' And then he did something very clever with his fingers, so that suddenly the bodice of it was loosened. With one hand he cupped her breast and with the other he lifted her skirts, and Anna found herself wriggling so that she could move against his hardness.

'I like your costume too,' she panted, as he lifted his pharaoh tunic.

'You make,' James said between groans, as he moved inside her a few minutes later, 'the most alluring Cleopatra.'

'Thank you,' Anna managed to say. 'Oh, *James*.'

Afterwards, he held her close in his arms, until they were both calm.

And then Anna sat up and said, 'James! Our guests are probably already here.'

James moved so that he was lying on his back, looking at her, his hands behind his head.

'If you aren't careful,' he said, 'there will be no possibility of my going downstairs for a *long* time. You look extremely debauched, my beautiful duchess.'

Anna looked down at herself, entirely naked, save for her Cleopatra robe around her waist.

'Honestly,' she tutted. 'We have *guests* downstairs. Many dozens of them.'

It was the tenth anniversary of their wedding and James had arranged for them to visit the Lake District with their children—a long-held desire of Anna's but one that she had been unable to fulfil until now due to regular pregnancies—and spend the Christmas period there in a house on one of his estates. They had invited a large number of house guests, including, naturally, Lady Derwent, Lady Maria and her husband, Clarence—now a vicar with a sizeable parish—and their three children, and the Puntneys, with whom they had become firm friends, and this evening were holding a Christmas ball.

'Lady Derwent will be more than happy to greet them in our absence.'

'That is true but we really should go.' Anna hopped off the bed before James could tempt her to engage in any further lovemaking, and began to re-dress herself.

'I am the luckiest man in the world,' James said, sitting up. 'I have the most wonderful wife a man could ever wish for and five perfect children.' They had four boys and a baby girl, all of whom they doted on most unfashionably.

'And I the luckiest woman.' Anna never referred to the fact out loud, because she did not wish to remind James of past tragedies, but he had now lived several years longer than both his brothers, and appeared in excellent health. And he was the best husband a woman could ever wish for, having proved time and time again to her by his actions and words that he was entirely trustworthy, a very different kind of man from her grandfather and father. Not to mention, of course, very good company and extremely handsome.

They shared one more lingering kiss on the lips before Anna pushed James firmly away, patted her hair back into place and declared herself ready to descend to their party.

As they made their way down the house's grand staircase, they were greeted by a clamour of voices and an almost bewildering array of brightly coloured costumes. They had chosen a masquerade as a nod to Anna's impersonation of Lady Maria on their first meeting at James's mother's ball.

Anna put her mask on and said, 'We should have hidden our costumes from each other to see if we could find each other.'

'There would have been no point. From the very first moment I met you, it was as though I recognised you, even though I did not know your real identity. I would know you anywhere, whatever your disguise.'

'And I you.'

They smiled at each other, before Lady Derwent and James's mother came towards them. The two ladies had buried their differences and were now—usually—on the best of terms.

Except…oh, dear.

Anna glanced at James and saw that he was as wide-eyed as she felt she must be.

'You…both…look magnificent,' he told the two ladies, the merest tremor of laughter in his voice.

'Thank you,' they replied in tandem, neither of them smiling.

Anna decided to address the situation directly.

'I think that you both look truly spectacular and that, since Queen Elizabeth is widely regarded as having been the best of queens, and you are both the best of ladies, it is only right that you should both be her this evening. One can never have too many Queen Elizabeths.'

'Were that true,' Lady Derwent said, 'it would be a very fortunate thing.' She indicated behind her to the room.

And, oh, dear, again. There were a *lot* of Queen Elizabeths.

'I flatter myself that I am wearing better jewels,' Lady Derwent whispered, far too loudly, to Anna.

'I flatter *my*self that I have a smaller waist,' James's mother told James, not bothering to whisper.

James laughed out loud while Anna took an arm of each of the other ladies and said, 'Let us go and seek some refreshment and then perhaps sit down for a moment before the dancing begins.'

They were joined shortly afterwards by Lady Maria. Who was also dressed as Queen Elizabeth.

None of the Queen Elizabeths looked remotely amused.

Anna clapped her hands loudly in panic. 'I think it is time for the dancing to begin.'

Three hours later, she had danced until her feet were sore, including, extremely unfashionably, *three times* with her own husband (he had speculated that no one would know because they were in costume, and Anna had pointed out that everyone would know because there was no other man in the room with the same thick head of hair—greying most attractively now—and broad shoulders), and eaten supper with the openly warring Queen Elizabeths, and she was now taking a little rest, when the most handsome pharaoh in the room approached her.

He bowed low. 'Cleopatra. Would you do me the honour of taking a walk outside with me?'

'I should be delighted.' Truly, she was incredibly blessed that just the sound of her husband's voice could still send a shiver through her after ten years together.

She was shivering in a different way within seconds of going through the doors at the end of the ballroom, onto the terrace that ran along the back of the house above lawns that led down to a lake and beyond that a wood, the whole illuminated now by the full moon in the most fairy-tale-like way.

'It's *freezing*,' she squeaked.

'Indeed it is.' James put his arm round her and hugged her into him. 'This is the only way I can think of to warm you given that I have no coat or jacket to give to you.'

'Mmm, that is nice, but it's still *very* cold.'

'It is indeed too cold to be outside without very warm outer garments,' he agreed. 'I wonder... Perhaps we could sneak around the outside of the house and enter by a side door and make our way up to our chamber without anyone noticing...'

'That is a very good idea,' Anna approved.

And ten minutes later, they tiptoed into their bedchamber, both of them almost snorting with the laughter they were trying to hold back.

And then, almost before the door was closed behind them, James had Anna in his arms.

'You know that I thought about marriage from the very first moment I met you,' he told her between kisses. 'And that I loved you infinitely almost immediately, and yet I love you more with every day that passes. How is that possible?'

'It is the same for me,' Anna told him, as he began to make her gasp with pleasure. 'Thank you for being my wonderful husband. I love you.'

'I love you too.'

And then they spent the night celebrating their first decade of marriage in the most delightful way.

* * * * *

COMING SOON!

We really hope you enjoyed reading this book.
If you're looking for more romance
be sure to head to the shops when
new books are available on

Thursday 27th
March

To see which titles are coming soon, please visit
millsandboon.co.uk/nextmonth

MILLS & BOON